THE BROKEN BOUNTY SERIES

Survive
FOR
ME

EMBER NICOLE

Survive for Me Copyright © 2023 by Ember Nicole

All rights reserved. No part of this book may be used or reproduced in any manner whatsoever without written permission except in the case of brief quotations in critical articles or reviews.

No part of this book may be used to create, feed, or refine artificial intelligence models, for any purpose, without written permission from the author.

This book is a work of fiction. Names, characters, businesses, organizations, places, events, and incidents are either the product of the author's imagination or are used fictitiously. Any resemblance to actual persons, living or dead, events, or locales is purely coincidental.

Cover Design: Angela Haddon

Interior Formatting: Unalive Promotions

Proofreading/Editing: Robyne Hunt

ISBN: 9798860438484

dedication

*Have you ever been in a position
where you had to love someone
while they walked right into Hell?
And then had to figure out how
to love them even harder to bring
them back from it?*

*This is for both of you.
The one who's lost, and
going through Hell.
And the one who's so tired, but
refuses to stop loving.*

trigger warning

If you thought *Break for Me* was rough, be aware that this one is worse.

Physically, emotionally, psychologically...all of it.

But not without reason.

Some people need to be broken apart to allow another person to help piece them back together into something stronger.

Don't worry. Jersey is not dead. He's just being rebuilt.

The enemies-to-lovers vibe is still here. The main characters still don't know how to behave like adults. They're rough with one another, even while intimate. It's all consensual, just angry.

A main character is confined and tortured for days, physically and psychologically, deprived of basic necessities, and the violence is described in detail.

Main characters experience anxiety and panic attacks as a result of PTSD. A main character struggles with alcoholism.

Murders happen over the course of this story. Several of them.

There are detailed memories of lost loved ones, issues with various forms of depression, and retellings of a main character's wartime experience. Everybody curses nonstop and there's a great deal of heartache all around, but nobody cheats and there's no third act breakup.

Look at the positives, right?

This book is meant for readers over 18 years of age…because it contains graphic violence, detailed sexual encounters, manipulative lunatics, possessive and slightly crazy men (yes, plural, more than one. You'll meet the new additions shortly if you continue ahead), and some pretty foul language. The relationships included here are not healthy or realistic in any sense.

P.S. Ashlie…now. Now is the time to take your anxiety meds, pretty girl.

CHAPTER ONE

jersey

I guess I'd call it fucking karma that I woke up in the trunk of a car. Even with a bullet still lodged somewhere in my left shoulder, they weren't taking any chances with me. I had handcuffs on my wrists *and* ankles. They went so far as to put a fucking bag over my head before slamming me in here. I had no way to know how long I'd been in here, where we were headed, or what was coming next. I remembered busting out of a fucking window in that abandoned house to try to catch up to Trista and Memphis. I remembered hearing the gunshot, but I definitely didn't remember feeling it. Somebody's big ass boot stomping down directly on my face was what landed me in this trunk with no recollection of it happening.

The whole thing was less than ideal. I could admit that much. There was always a chance that the plan to rescue Memphis would go terribly wrong. The girls got away though. I was confident of that much. There would've been no point in keeping me alive if they'd managed to catch all three of us. So, what actually happened was something between everything going according to plan, and the worst possible outcome of all three of us dying right there in the hills of Tennessee.

I squirmed and writhed until I at least got the bag off my head so I could breathe just a little easier, but all the movement left my whole body in pain that might as well have been electrifying. It wasn't my first time getting shot, but experience with such a thing didn't lessen its pain with each new reminder. I tried to shift to lessen the weight my body was putting into lying on my shoulder, but it only furthered the stings of electrical current that radiated from the bullet wound. Trista had been entirely convinced that her stepdad, my boss, wanted her back to torture her before he killed her for the things that she'd taken from him. It was probably safe to assume that I was about to meet that fate. The organization that I worked for would use every bit of me to their advantage to try to draw Trista back out into the open where they could find her, and now Memphis, too.

I was formally trained to withstand torture to some extent, but I was about to find myself face-to-face with a version of me that I really didn't recognize now. Where my mind went to be able to survive that kind of abuse turned me into something that really wasn't even human anymore. Knowing that ahead of time didn't usually offer any help in avoiding it though. Something about it was linked to a survival instinct, and it happened whether I was ready for it or not; whether I wanted to go down that route or not.

The only sliver of sanity that I held onto in this confined space was the knowledge that Triss and Memphis would stay together. Even if they ended up hating one another, they'd stay together. Wondering how they actually got along and what was happening in their interactions provided me with my sole form of entertainment for this trip to wherever we were headed. Did Memphis hate Trista for what was happening? Did she blame Triss for this predicament that we were all in? Or did she blame me? Trista had a temper the size of fucking Jupiter, with an attitude to match. But Memphis had never tolerated it when I got snappy with her, and she was the

Queen of Sass when it came to me. Imagining them driving each other bat shit crazy was enough to make me smile, despite my current situation. I didn't know if they'd get along beautifully because Trista was exactly like me, or if they'd despise one another for the very same reason. Either way, Memphis would cling to Triss because she could keep them safe, alive, hidden. Trista would take Memphis with her just because I'd told her to do it. And by now, they should be well on their way to Indiana.

CHAPTER TWO
trista

I finally worked up the nerve to give the little stuffed Tigger back to Memphis so she could tuck him safely into the glove box of Jersey's Challenger, where he belonged.

"We should keep moving," I said quietly, opening Jersey's wallet for a card to pay for gas.

"Where are we going?" Memphis asked.

We both watched a folded piece of paper fall into my lap from the wallet as I opened it. I was ready for a fresh burst of tears when I realized it was the photo of Memphis that I'd taken from her house so Jersey could keep it, but I noticed writing on the back of it when I picked it up this time.

"What is it?" Memphis asked.

"We still went to your house after they picked you up," I explained. "Jersey was worried that you might've had a family there, someone who might've gotten hurt and needed help. We picked up the stuff that you'd packed too. It's in the trunk. But I found this picture in your living room and took it for him to keep. He wrote on the back. I don't know what it means."

I handed the photo over to Memphis, with the words still in my mind.

Triss – just in case.

Beneath it, he'd written an address somewhere in Indiana. Memphis sighed, and wiped the back of her hand across her cheek.

"It's his dropout plan," she said. "He knew I never had an escape plan. And he knew the chances of all of us making it out of that place together were slim, so he's giving us his dropout plan. He's telling us where to go. It'll be safe there."

"Indiana?" I asked, while she put the address from the photo into the navigation system on Persephone's dash. "He picked *Indiana* for his dropout location? Why did I imagine him aiming for some tropical island with a beach where absolutely no other people lived?"

"He does kind of seem like a city slicker all the way to his core, doesn't he?" Memphis added. "It's hard to picture him settling down for the long haul in the middle of a bunch of cornfields."

"Hard to picture him *settling down*. Period."

My nose even scrunched up at the words. He was older than both of us by a long shot, but nothing about the man said *settling down* type in any sense of the words.

The two of us knowing absolutely nothing about one another made for a weird stint of silence in the six-hour drive between wherever we were and the house in Indiana where Jersey was sending us. We should've spent that time figuring out what we were supposed to do next. We could've spent that time actually getting to know one another if we were supposed to be staying together. We could've gone deeper into just talking about Jersey, since he was the thing we had in common. Instead, we both just stayed quiet.

I couldn't make my brain move beyond this man who hadn't even thought twice about sacrificing himself to get us out of that house. Or the fact that he'd just been a regular family man at one point in his life.

Trying to picture him in the role of suburban dad, playing with his daughter in the backyard while a bombshell of a wife came outside to tell them that it was dinnertime felt…impossible. He'd been so cold and ruthless. He didn't even seem to know how to behave when he was forced to just sit beside me in this car for long lengths of time. And I was supposed to accept that this man had been *married* to another human? A woman had agreed to marry him *and* birthed a child by him. Then it was just as difficult to try to get my head around the knowledge that the same woman had taken his parents, his daughter, and herself from him while he wasn't even in the country. I'd been through some shit, but that was a very different level of *some shit*. Nothing in me could fathom having to just move on after the loss of a small child.

"Do you know anything about his family?" I finally asked when I couldn't let go of the thoughts of his daughter.

Memphis sighed. "A little."

"Can you tell me about them?"

The look on her face said she wanted to, but her words didn't match it. "He doesn't even know that *I* know. I don't think I should be the one to tell you about them. If you guys are, you know, going to be a whole thing, he should probably get to decide what he wants you to know."

For as much as I wanted to admire the sense of loyalty that she felt to him, I also wanted to reach across her and open the door to kick her little ass right out onto the asphalt. It wasn't jealousy that she knew more about him than I did, but it was definitely in the neighborhood. The only thing I could cling to about it was that Jersey hadn't been the one to tell her about them either. She'd found out on her own.

"His daughter," I pressed anyway. "How old was she? Just that one. Tell me that, and I'll drop it."

"Four. She was only four."

The ache in my heart ripped open into a full-blown canyon.

"His wife was probably a supermodel, wasn't she?" I asked.

"You're not doing so well at the *dropping it* that you *just* promised."

"I'm sorry," I added quickly. "I just can't picture him with a family. Just some regular guy, doing daddy-daughter things, taking his wife out for a weekly date night to keep the spark alive, watching Disney movies, reading bedtime stories."

"I don't know how *regular* he really was," Memphis said and laughed. "He was still a Raider."

"He mentioned that. I definitely thought it was something he was just making up. The Marine thing was believable, but I've never heard of *Raiders*."

"I don't think many people have," she said. "Think Navy SEALs, but better. Or worse, I guess, depending on which end of them you're experiencing. I looked into them back when Jersey was first assigned to me. He was scary way before he was doing this job."

"He wasn't just a soldier?"

She laughed, and it made me terribly uncomfortable.

"No. He was not. They're expected to be able to just survive in what they call *spartan conditions* in small teams. Like drop these guys in any setting, any climate, anywhere in the world under duress, and expect them to just do what they're told and get the fuck back out."

"Like a bunch of mercenaries?" I asked.

"I don't think they'd take too kindly to that label," she laughed. "I think the preferred wording is that they prevent, deter, and respond to terrorism. They just happen to also receive training in *unconventional* warfare capabilities to make sure they're successful by any means necessary."

"So, we really might not have to do anything at all to get him back ourselves? Maybe if we just wait long enough, he'll do it all himself?"

CHAPTER THREE

jersey

I felt like an eighty-year-old man by the time they were dragging my body out of the trunk of that car. Every muscle ached; everything was sore. They hadn't even so much as opened the trunk since they'd put me in it, so I'd pissed myself. If I'd had a way to get my pants down, I would've shit everywhere in that trunk just to make sure they'd also have to clean that up. If anybody here thought denying me the most basic of human decency would break me that quickly, they were about to be in for a real treat. I'd play this game for as long as my mind could withstand it, and then something much worse would take over and finish it for me.

Just knowing that some creature form of myself would eventually take over when I needed it to, didn't take away the very real pain that was still deep in the tissue of my shoulder when they lugged me from the car and toward a giant building. They didn't waste much time in getting the bag back over my head, so I didn't get a clear look at where we were, but once they'd pulled me inside, the noise was almost deafening. It sounded like hundreds of voices all talking at the same time. There was a constant mechanical whirring of what sounded like heavy machinery.

Several sets of footsteps moved around us in all directions. More than one foreign language was being spoken throughout the space as we walked through it. The sound of a door closing behind us muffled the noise some, but definitely didn't drown it out completely.

Rather than offering me the kindness of a chair, someone kicked the backs of my knees to drop me straight to the ground. Apparently, my old man bones weren't already throwing a big enough tantrum after being cramped in that trunk for what felt like days.

"You smell like piss and B.O., Mr. Jersey," an oddly calm and smooth voice said from somewhere in front of me.

"You work up a sweat when you have to kill a house full of thugs," I said into the bag, and mistakenly tried to shrug my shoulders. Suddenly, I was thankful that the bag was still hiding the very noticeable wince all over my face from the movement. "I would've showered and made myself pretty for whatever this is, but your boys didn't seem particularly interested in letting me out of that trunk for any reason."

"Well, I think we can all agree that it was better safe than sorry. Getting the carpet cleaned in that trunk is something we have to have done pretty regularly anyway. I'm sure you can relate."

Somebody ripped the bag off my head in a less-than-gentle fashion, and the fluorescent lighting in the room nearly blinded me. When my eyes finally focused, everything about the suit-wearing man who stood before me was confusing. He was tall and thin, with hair that was somewhere between blonde and gray. The permanent wrinkles around his eyes made me think he was probably older than me, and the pale, dead green of his eyes made me think he'd probably even seen much worse than me.

"I'd like to know *why* you made the choice that you did about my daughter, Mr. Jersey."

I don't know what I was expecting the President of our organization to look like, but whatever I was prepared for, it was not this man. Nothing about him suggested that he ran the underworld of

Philadelphia, or that people across this country and several others feared him.

"Somebody used my face to try to knock the mud off their boots so I'm actually a little fuzzy myself about what happened," I said.

He smiled and something inside me was instantly aware that he'd earned every bit of fear he'd ever pulled out of the people around him. He didn't come to life at the thought of inflicting pain on someone else. He somehow actually looked — more like death. Like it wasn't exciting to prepare to drain the life from another human, but rather that it was just another mundane task in his day. He walked toward me and stopped when the tips of his shoes were directly in front of my knees. He took my chin between his thumb and his index finger to make sure I was looking right at him.

Shame I was too dehydrated to have to piss again. There would have been no better time.

"I'll get my answers eventually, Mr. Jersey."

"I think just Jersey is probably fine at this point," I interrupted. "Might as well skip the formalities, huh?"

"I can guarantee you, my boy, that everything you think you've known up to this point has been a lie. Whatever she's told you, whatever service or good you believe you've done, I'm sorry to tell you that it's all a lie."

"Fortunately for me, I've never really been the do-good kind of man, so you're not really shattering any of my world views with that little revelation."

"Try to hold onto that attitude, Mr. Jersey," he said and chuckled. "It might help you get through what's coming."

He shoved me back hard enough by my chin that I was a little convinced his goal had been to break my neck. Landing on my handcuffed hands on the concrete floor sent the currents of pain from that bullet hole through my entire body again. I laid there in absolute discomfort for an eternity, but I was not about to aid these assholes in anyway so when they tried to lift me off the floor, I was fucking deadweight and I just let them do it themselves. They put the bag on my head again, but this time someone was nice enough to tighten what felt like a drawstring around my neck to make it just that much more uncomfortable.

I didn't even bother trying to walk with them when they pulled me from the floor. We were about to be locked into whatever fucked up game this was until I was dead, so I was going to be a pain in the ass at every possible turn now. It didn't feel the greatest on my shoulder that they had to drag me along with them, but it was worth it to know that they struggled to maneuver all two hundred and fifty pounds of my limp weight. It felt even more awesome when they tossed me across the concrete floor of the next room. I laid right where I landed without bothering to try to move for a few seconds. Somebody stopped right beside me to pull the bag off my head again, then Nate crouched right beside me to get his face closer to mine.

"She is absolute poison. Anything and everything she touches seems to find a way to destruction. You'll see what I mean soon enough."

I couldn't help but wonder what it meant for my own sanity that someone referring to Trista as poison only brought up the image of her smile.

The fact that she tasted like ecstasy.

And injected nitro right into my veins.

My pretty, little poison.

She had absolutely come with a warning label, in the form of a contract for her return to the man who hunted her. The same contract that I'd outright broken when I decided to keep her for myself.

"Hurting you isn't something that I *want* to do," Nate said while he grabbed me by an arm to raise me until I was sitting. "But I'm more than willing to do what it takes to get what I want. Smile for your girls, Mr. Jersey. This may be the last time that they're able to recognize your face."

He pressed a gun against the side of my head, and the flash of a camera on somebody's phone nearly blinded me while I glared right at this sadistic shithead.

That creature inside me that I put so much effort into holding back wanted more than anything to make him eat those words; shove them down his throat as far as they'd go until he choked to death on them.

My girls.
Not his.
Nobody else's.
Mine.

CHAPTER FOUR
trista

I think it was safe to say that Memphis and I were both confused when I parked the car in front of a giant, white farmhouse quite literally in the middle of nothing but cornfields. It was gorgeous, as far as old farmhouses that were probably haunted went. This was a sprawling two-story monstrosity with a porch that looked like it wrapped all the way around the entire house, with every door and window opening trimmed in black. It was beautiful in the most simple way, and nothing about it looked like the extravagance that I would've expected out of Jersey.

"Are you sure you put the address in right?" I asked, looking over the top of the car at Memphis.

"It does feel — weird."

By the time I'd looked back toward the house, a very unpleasant looking man was coming around the side of the house, walking right toward us.

"Is that a shotgun?" Memphis whispered.

"Sorry, ladies. This is private property. Move along," he said, but didn't stop walking until he was right at the front bumper of the car. He was a good ten inches taller than me with unruly blonde hair and a short beard that was more red than it was anything else. And he absolutely had a shotgun laying across his shoulders like it was just any old baseball bat.

"Folks are friendly in Indiana, huh?" I said. "Who are you?"

"That's not how this works," he said and chuckled. "*Who are you?*"

He took the shotgun from his shoulders to swing it casually between the two of us, like it was an extension of his arm, and it was just a normal way to point at someone.

"Is that loaded?" Memphis asked, shifting from one foot to the other uncomfortably.

He laughed again. "Of course, it's loaded. It'd be useless if it weren't."

"Okay, listen. We're here because Jersey gave us the address for this house. Told us to come here," I spoke up quickly.

"Am I supposed to know who *Jersey* is?" He asked, with a side-eye that made me want to scream at him.

"Right," Memphis said quietly. "Um, Vance Anderson sent us here. This is his car. We've got his wallet. We assumed this was his house?"

Vance Anderson.

And I'd picked a shitty name like Kyle for him.

I wouldn't have guessed any part of his real name if he'd given me a million chances over the next twenty years.

"You've got his wallet, huh? Telling me his name isn't going to convince me that he invited you here just because you're carrying something that also has his name on it."

"Who the fuck is this guy?" I asked Memphis. She let out a long sigh but held her stare at this frustrating man.

"Okay then," she said. "His wife's name was Elizabeth. He called her Liz. Their daughter was Faith. He was a Marine back in the day. Scary guy. Seems to be happiest when he's frowning about something."

His body visibly stiffened at her words and his eyes darted back and forth between us for a few seconds.

"And where is he now if he sent you two here?" He asked.

"Seriously, who the fuck are you? Is this Jersey's house or not? He wouldn't tell us to go to somebody else's house. He wouldn't trust just anybody with his name. Does he even know that *you're* here?" I demanded.

He looked my entire body up and down before he laughed. "I keep an eye on the place. Keep it nice. Keep it safe. He lets me live in the guesthouse out back as long as I keep it ready for him to be here at a moment's notice."

"How do you know him?" I asked.

He turned his left forearm outward for us to be able to see a massive American flag tattoo that took up all the space below his elbow.

"Semper Fi," he said. "Come on. I'll show you around. Are we expecting him to show up anytime soon?"

I looked across the car at Memphis. She looked the same way that I assumed I did; ready to burst into sobs any second now.

"No," I choked out. "Not anytime soon."

"Are those bullet holes?" He asked, nodding toward the driver's side of Persephone when I closed the door.

"Uh, yeah. They are," I said. "Know anybody around here who does body work? I imagine he'd expect us to get that fixed."

He laughed again. "If that's really his car, he'll want it parked in the garage around back with the other. I'll call his car guy to come look at it."

I glanced at Memphis as we followed him up the steps to the front door of the house. "So, not to sound too much like an ass, but he's got a whole secret house complete with a groundskeeper. Apparently, a car guy who makes house calls. How much money do you guys make on jobs like me?"

The lack of an answer that came with her giggle made me feel like I could throw up right there all over those front steps.

CHAPTER FIVE
trista

"So, will you be staying now that we're here?" Memphis asked our new friend as he stepped aside to let us both through the front door.

"I'm not going anywhere until Van tells me to."

Van.

Still never would have guessed it.

"I'm Trista," I said. "This is Memphis."

He scoffed at her name. "Memphis? And you call him Jersey? He got mixed up in some weird shit once he got out."

"I feel like that's putting it mildly," I said. "What's your name?"

"Kyle."

Of course it fucking was.

Nothing in the world could've prevented the crazed laugh that burst out of me.

No wonder Jersey reacted like a lunatic when I gasped and moaned that fucking name just to mess with him.

"That's funny?" He asked.

"It is. It really is," I said quickly. "Lead the way, Mr. Groundskeeper."

Because no fucking way could I ever call him his actual name now.

He glared at me for a good few seconds before he turned to take us through the house.

"I never imagined he'd be bringing girls here," Kyle said while he walked. "He's got his own stash of clothes and personal shit in his room, but he never told me to keep anything for women."

"So, we need to get our own tampons. I hear you," Memphis concluded with a giggle. He didn't turn around or even pause, but just the word brought a bright red flush up the back of Kyle's neck while he continued on his way. He pointed out different areas of the mostly open concept house as we walked by them. A massive, perfectly white kitchen with black countertops everywhere, a living room with a huge fireplace and the biggest TV I'd ever seen in my life mounted across the room from a sectional, a bathroom, a pantry, all these things that felt entirely too domestic, too calm and too ordinary, to be meant for Jersey. He stopped outside a closed door.

"This one is his room," he said and pushed the door open. Memphis and I both froze right where we were in that hallway. Memphis looked like she was in physical pain when she forced herself to look at me.

"You can have it," she said.

"What?" I asked.

"I'm not staying in his room," she said quickly. "And if he were here, wouldn't you be staying in there *with him?*"

Kyle chuckled. "Glad that answered that question. Had no fucking clue how to ask which one of you it was. Or if it was *both* of you. He never seemed like the kind of man who shared, but I don't know that any man in his right mind would turn that down either. Come on. There's an office and another bedroom on this floor. Two other bedrooms and one that he mostly just uses for storage upstairs."

Memphis opted to take the other bedroom on the first floor, and neither of us worked up the nerve to venture into Jersey's room or his office. We followed Kyle back to the kitchen when he was done showing us the house.

"There are a couple of cleaning ladies who come by every other week on Tuesdays," he said. "Do you want me to have them keep coming out, or are you two taking care of the place now?"

"I think we'll do it," Memphis said quickly. "As little traffic in and out of here as possible is best for now."

Kyle nodded. "I take care of the outside. He rents the fields to a farmer from a couple towns over, but they don't set foot on this part of the property, so they won't bother you. I've got a dog who stays out in the guesthouse with me. She has free run of the place so be nice to her. I'll get the garage open if you want to bring his car around back."

I followed him back out the door and went to the car while he motioned for me to follow the driveway around to the back of the house.

The man actually owned fucking farmland. *New Jersey*. Jersey had cornfields and barns.

What was this place?

I parked Persephone in the bay where Kyle had opened the overhead door of a detached three car garage. I got out to look at another Challenger. One that was nearly the opposite of the one that I'd become much too familiar with. Where Persephone was mostly black with hints of purple. The other was a deep purple with a black hood and black stripes down either side.

"Hades," Kyle said, stopping to stand next to me.

I laughed out loud. Jersey and his names.

Hades and Persephone

"It's the 1970 R/T with the 426 Hemi," Kyle added, proudly.

"I really don't know what *any* of that means, Mr. Groundskeeper."

"Really? How'd he ever trust you with this one then?"

"We didn't exactly have much of a choice," I admitted.

"You ladies in trouble?" He asked. "Still?"

"Yeah," I sighed. "I think we are."

"He still alive?"

"I think so. I *hope* so."

I couldn't stop the tear that escaped, but I wiped that little fucker away as quickly as I could.

"We've got kind of a lot to get figured out," I said, to try to mask the emotional whiplash that was coursing through me. "I imagine we'll be in and out quite a bit over the next few days."

"I'm not here to keep tabs on anybody," he said with a laugh. "I'll be here either way, keeping the outside nice like he wanted. I'm out in that house if you need something. There's an intercom in the kitchen that connects to my kitchen if you *really* need something. Haven't had to do much dirty work in recent years, but I reckon I still know how if the occasion really called for such a thing. If you ladies mean enough to him that he'd send you here for safety, I have to assume it's because he knew I'd do that too."

"You're willing to do all of this for him just because he lets you live here?"

This man looked at me like I might've been the least intelligent being he'd ever encountered.

"You don't really know him very well then, do you?"

"I really wish everyone would stop saying it that way," I said with a sigh and went around to the trunk to get the bags that managed to survive the last couple of weeks with us. "I met the man like two weeks ago. Against my will. And I still hate him just as much as I like him. So no, I don't know him. At all. And nobody seems to be interested in telling me anything about him."

He stared at me that time like I'd just busted out of custody from an institute for the criminally insane.

"Yeah," I added. "It's every bit as ridiculous as it sounds."

"I think I'd be more than willing to swap some of my stories with him for some of yours," he said and chuckled. "Yours sound like they're probably hilarious."

"They definitely don't feel very funny on this side of it."

"Here, let me carry some of those," he said, taking literally everything from my hands. "I think I'm going to like having you two around here."

CHAPTER SIX
jersey

The room that they'd moved me into at least came with the small convenience of a bucket. Though it took some convincing to make my own brain decide to actually use it. Seemed like it was really only convenient for whoever they might send in here to empty it, and something about making some other human get down on their hands and knees to scoop my shit back into that bucket sounded more appealing. It only took the logical side of me realizing that they'd just make me do it before I figured I was better off just going along with the bucket's intended purpose.

Unfortunately, that bucket was the *only* fucking thing that adorned this room. They'd taken the handcuffs from my ankles but left the ones around my wrists. They took my shoes, my belt, and the bag from my head. And that was that. It was me, a bucket, a set of handcuffs, my pants, and my shirt in a concrete box. All with a very unpleasant bullet still residing within my shoulder. If they knew what they were doing, it was only a matter of time before they took my clothes too, but I was under the impression that we'd be starting slowly. They would need me mentally present enough to be able to register and react to the kinds of things they planned on doing to me if they wanted to use my suffering to draw Trista and Memphis back out.

The beginning wouldn't be so bad. Regardless of their early tactics, as long as I could hold onto an image of either Trista or Memphis, I'd be able to keep it together. The only downside to that was that I'd had very limited contact with both of them. I only had a handful of moments where Trista truly smiled in my presence, even fewer when she'd laughed and looked genuinely happy. I saw Memphis a grand total of one time, and it was under wildly unpleasant circumstances.

The terrifying part was having to acknowledge that the moment those images disappeared, the thoughts of someone else would take their place. And those thoughts would send me into a tailspin that couldn't be controlled. Those thoughts unleashed the monster, and if that fucker got out again, I didn't imagine there'd be much of a chance at boxing it away another time. If I was being honest about it, that would probably be for the best once it got to that point. I'd made my peace with it that my death was coming at the hands of somebody in this building. Not having to be the one mentally present for that sounded easier.

Every time that door opened, I ended up with the most unpleasant, mad rush of adrenaline. No matter how often I told myself that I was trained for this shit or how many times I reminded myself that I'd already been through worse than anything these people could do to me, I was still nervous. It took me an extra second or two to figure out who they'd sent in here this time. I was looking at a younger version of Nate Evans, one who entered the room with his right arm in a sling. I laughed when I realized it was probably due to an injury from a gunshot; one that had been fired by me in a parking garage in Kentucky in a blind rage that I didn't even remember.

"New Jersey."

"Have we met?" I asked.

He smirked and I saw a flash of that same ruthless nature that crossed his daddy's face when the old man façade was peeled back.

"I suppose we haven't officially been introduced. I'm Bryce. I'll be ruining your life. Welcome to Hell."

"You're about six years too late to be conducting that train, my friend. Hell is actually my hometown. They just let me out to shoot an asshole or two every so often."

"I'm going to enjoy every fucking second of this," he said and offered me that deeply disturbed smile another time.

"In that case, could you maybe wear a cup or something while you torture me? If I'm going to have to be in pain, I'd prefer to be able to picture your sister's tight little cunt rather than have to stare at your raging hard-on the whole time."

He laughed at that and much to my displeasure, it sent goosebumps all over my skin.

"We'll get started soon, New Jersey."

CHAPTER SEVEN
trista

I stopped so quickly in the open doorway of Jersey's bedroom that Kyle bumped right into me. Memphis was sitting on the massive bed in the middle of the room, staring at something in her hands, crying so hard that her whole body was shaking.

"Uh, crying women are definitely not an area where I'm comfortable," he said quickly. He dropped all our shit right there in the hallway and turned back for the front door.

I was smacked in the face with a rush of cinnamon as soon as I crossed into the room. I even stopped a second time to look in every direction like the man might have suddenly just materialized in the room right behind me. I tried to make a mental note to remind myself to ask Kyle what the fuck he was having those cleaning ladies use in here to make the room smell like Jersey without him being here, but I had a hard time focusing on anything other than the sounds of Memphis crying the way that she was.

I went to the other side of the giant bed to climb up and sit right beside her. Crying women really weren't a strength of mine either, though. I took the framed photo from her hands and found myself crying right alongside her a second later. Jersey's wife really could have been a supermodel, and his daughter had his blue eyes. I wasn't sure if I was crying out of a weird and uncomfortable jealousy over this woman who'd known a version of that man who had died with them and I'd never get to meet, or if it was the deepest form of pain to see the little girl who'd been taken from him.

Faith.

Her name had been Faith. She had one of those perfectly round and full faces that only toddlers seemed to have. Jersey's blue eyes went beautifully with his wife's wavy blonde hair when they were combined in that small person. She had a tiny gap in the middle of her front teeth and looked like the kind of child who was perpetually smiling. She felt too perfect to have been something that came from Jersey. Well, she felt too perfect to have come from the Jersey who I knew. Maybe she was a miniature version of the man he used to be. Everything about that made the pain deep in my stomach so much worse.

"I don't think I can stay in this room," I said in between the pathetic sniffles.

"I don't think she was ever here," Memphis said, trying desperately to wipe the tears from her face. "He wouldn't have needed a place like this from the Marine days. His parents were from New Jersey. He ended up buying a house in the same neighborhood as them once he was married. I don't think they ever lived anywhere else."

"Even if that's the case, how does it fucking smell like him in here?" I sobbed.

"Thank God," she said. "I thought I was losing my mind already. I was only in his physical presence for a matter of minutes, and I felt like cinnamon was burned into my nostrils. I wondered if my mind just decided that this room was *supposed* to smell that way."

"He *always* smelled like that."

We both held our breath to try to be as quiet as possible when what sounded like jingling keys came from the hallway. Then a door closed a moment later and we could both hear light footsteps.

"Mr. Groundskeeper?" I asked.

"You can't just call him Kyle like a normal person?" Memphis whispered.

"I really can't," I said and even giggled. "That's a story for another time."

"What the fuck is that?" Memphis said, staring at the doorway.

We both laughed at the sight of a golden retriever popping its head through the door. It sniffed around for a second before it decided it was coming the rest of the way toward both of us, the tags on its collar jingling the whole way. The dog stopped and whined just beside the bed, next to Memphis. She sniffled another time and the dog whined again. It laid its head down on the edge of the bed to try to get as close as it could without actually being on the furniture.

"Oh my God," I said and got off the bed to go around to the other side. "He said he had a dog."

I knelt on the floor beside it and reached for its tags.

"Dandelion," I laughed. "Her name is Dandelion."

I turned the tag over to read the other side. "PTSD Service Dog. Protected under federal law. Do not separate from handler."

"He didn't know what to do with us, so he sent his dog in here?" Memphis asked laughing. "That's the cutest fucking thing I've ever been part of. God, him and Jersey might as well be the same guy."

She got off the bed to sit on the floor with us too. I wouldn't have expected just the presence of a dog to ease so much of the discomfort in my soul, but it definitely did.

"I know you think I know all these secrets about him, and that I'm just being a bitch by not telling you all about this guy you're in love with," Memphis said quietly and laid her head against the dog's. "But I never got to really spend time with him like you did."

"Like I did?" I asked and laughed like a lunatic. "Memphis, he spent like two days just stuffing me into the trunk of his car. We fought each other. And I don't mean we yelled at one another. Physically. We physically fought. Several times."

"And you still *feel* closer to him than anybody else, don't you?"

She asked. "Something in you connected to something in him. I don't want to make it weird. I really have no desire to be *with* him. I don't want you to think that. I just — I don't know. We spent so much time on the phone. All day, every day. Something in me always thought that, eventually, we'd get to be friends in real life too, but I only had *minutes* with him."

"I think you already are *real life friends*," I said. "He cares about you in a way that he's never cared about me."

"I think I could say the same about you," she laughed. "Maybe when I'm not prone to constant crying, you could tell me what he's like in person?"

"An asshole," I said, with zero thought beforehand. "He's an asshole."

We stayed sitting that way with the dog in silence for a long time, until it was nearly dark outside. I told Memphis that we'd brought in the few bags that she'd packed before Nate's people picked her up from her house. Then I warned her that I would plan to sleep in this room, but not to be surprised if I ended up on the floor next to her bed because this had been one disaster after another and being alone sounded daunting. When she disappeared down the hallway toward her own room, I took Dandelion back to the door. I'd seen the guesthouse somewhere out behind the detached garage, but I felt weird about just knocking on Kyle's door to return his service animal and thanking him for letting us love her.

I didn't have to do any of that anyway because he was sitting in a patio chair at the edge of a fire pit, watching the flames burn like he might find the answers to the world's most serious questions in them.

"You know, when you said you had a dog, I imagined like a Rottweiler or a Doberman," I said and sat in the empty chair next to him, with his dog between us. "You, a big scary former Marine man, have a goldie named Dandelion."

"And I call her Dandy," he said proudly.

"You have to be two of the weirdest guys I've ever met."

"You've really only known him for a couple weeks?" He asked. "Hard to imagine him sending you to his safe house."

"Did he tell you about his job?"

He shook his head. "Said he found work that could use his messed up talent and detached nature. He needed somebody to sit on this land and keep it nice. Not to talk to anyone around here about him."

"And that was a good enough explanation for you?" I freaked out a little when he glared at me over that question. "I am in absolutely no position to be a judgey bitch about your decisions, dude. I was genuinely asking."

"When it came from him, yeah. It was plenty explanation, *dude*."

Another old guy to figure out how to tolerate.

Fucking eye roll.

For as much as I wanted anybody in the fucking world to tell me about the confusing heap of a human who was Vance Anderson, I'd spent a lifetime not trusting anyone. Even knowing that Jersey had trusted this person with his real name and tasked him with keeping his dropout house prepared, I didn't know him. And if Jersey hadn't told him anything about his fucked up job, there was probably a reason for that too.

"I'm out here every night," he said with a chuckle after my silence was apparently noticeable. "Take your time getting used to me, honey. I'll need just as much to get used to the two of you being here."

"It was sweet of you to send Dandy in there."

CHAPTER EIGHT
trista

I still cried when I made it back to Jersey's room and had to go into it alone, but I opened the pink duffel bag that held his clothes and immediately changed into his sweats and his plain white T-shirt. I cocooned myself in that giant gray comforter right in the middle of his king sized bed and tried to imagine that he was the thing wrapped all the way around my body. I was also tired on a level that I didn't even realize was possible, and I didn't even remember actually closing my eyes to try to fall asleep.

The sun coming in around the edges of the curtains woke me up at some point the next day. I laid there in my bundle of warmth and tried to imagine what might need to happen next. Instead of coming up with anything useful, I ended up staring at the picture of Jersey's wife and daughter that sat on the nightstand next to the bed, wishing he'd been in the picture with them. About the time that I felt like I might cry, fucking again, I forced myself to just get up. The bedroom wasn't huge, but it was bigger than any space I would ever need. All six of the outfits that went everywhere I did in my backpack would easily fit in here with me. There was enough room for a giant padded bench that sat at the end of the bed, two overstuffed chairs in the corner with a small table between them, and two small bookshelves. I went toward them with every intention of being nosy but abandoned that endeavor just as quickly when I realized they were all photo albums. Someday I might work up the nerve to look at pictures of his life, but that sure as shit wouldn't be today. I hadn't thought about it before I went to the giant sets of windows on the far wall, but this room sat on a side of the house that I hadn't seen from the outside yet, and when I opened the curtains, I was staring at an immaculately kept in-ground pool. This place came with a new surprise every fucking time I turned around.

Frantic knocking on the bedroom door had me jumping half way across the damn room. Memphis didn't even wait for me to actually get to the door to open it myself before she came in to meet me right where I stood.

"Here," she said and handed a piece of paper to me. "This is what I'll still need. I was able to get quite a bit packed up before they took me. And he's got a solid start for internet connection and the ability to secure it for this place. But I still need everything on there. I tried to be as detailed as I could be because I wasn't sure how much you knew about these kinds of things. If you find the right store, any employee will know what all that is if you just give them the list. Just maybe don't offer any explanation about what any of it is for."

"Did you sleep at all?" I asked. Her hair was in a frizzy ball on top of her head, she was wearing the same clothes she had on yesterday, and she looked like she'd spent the night rage-crying.

"Yeah," she said. "Wait, no. I took over his office. Think he'll care?"

She looked like a child who was afraid that she was about to be scolded. I didn't usually find other women cute, but she was adorable.

"No, Memphis. I don't think he'll care."

"So, can you do it today?" She asked.

"You're not coming with me?"

"I don't like the world," she said.

"You're somehow under the impression that I do?"

"You might not like it, but you've for sure spent more time out there than I have."

"*Out there?*" I repeated and laughed. "There wasn't an apocalypse recently, you know that, right?"

"I have a lot still to do *here*, okay? Just get that stuff. Please."

"Is it expensive?"

"Use Jersey's card," she said.

"He won't be pissed that we're blowing through his money?"

"He won't even notice that amount, Trista."

"You guys make me sick."

"Oh, I didn't put it on the list, but stop somewhere and get me some nail polish too."

I looked down at my own fingernails. Every single one was jagged, broken, and caked underneath with dirt. I couldn't even remember the last time I'd painted them.

"It's just something I do when I need to stop and think," she added quickly. "I need something to do absentmindedly when I can't figure out problems."

I wasn't about to argue with her. The chances of getting Jersey back were pretty much nonexistent without her. So, what Memphis needed, she was going to get.

"You think Kyle would go with you?" She asked. "I feel like Jersey wouldn't want you to go anywhere alone."

"I think he'd be even more annoyed by me spending too much time with *Kyle*," I said and laughed at how hilarious I found myself. Memphis only looked annoyed. "I'm going to shower first, and then I guess I'll go explore Indiana."

"Okay, I'm going to get a phone setup for you, so don't leave until you have it," she said and disappeared from the room just as quickly as she'd blown in.

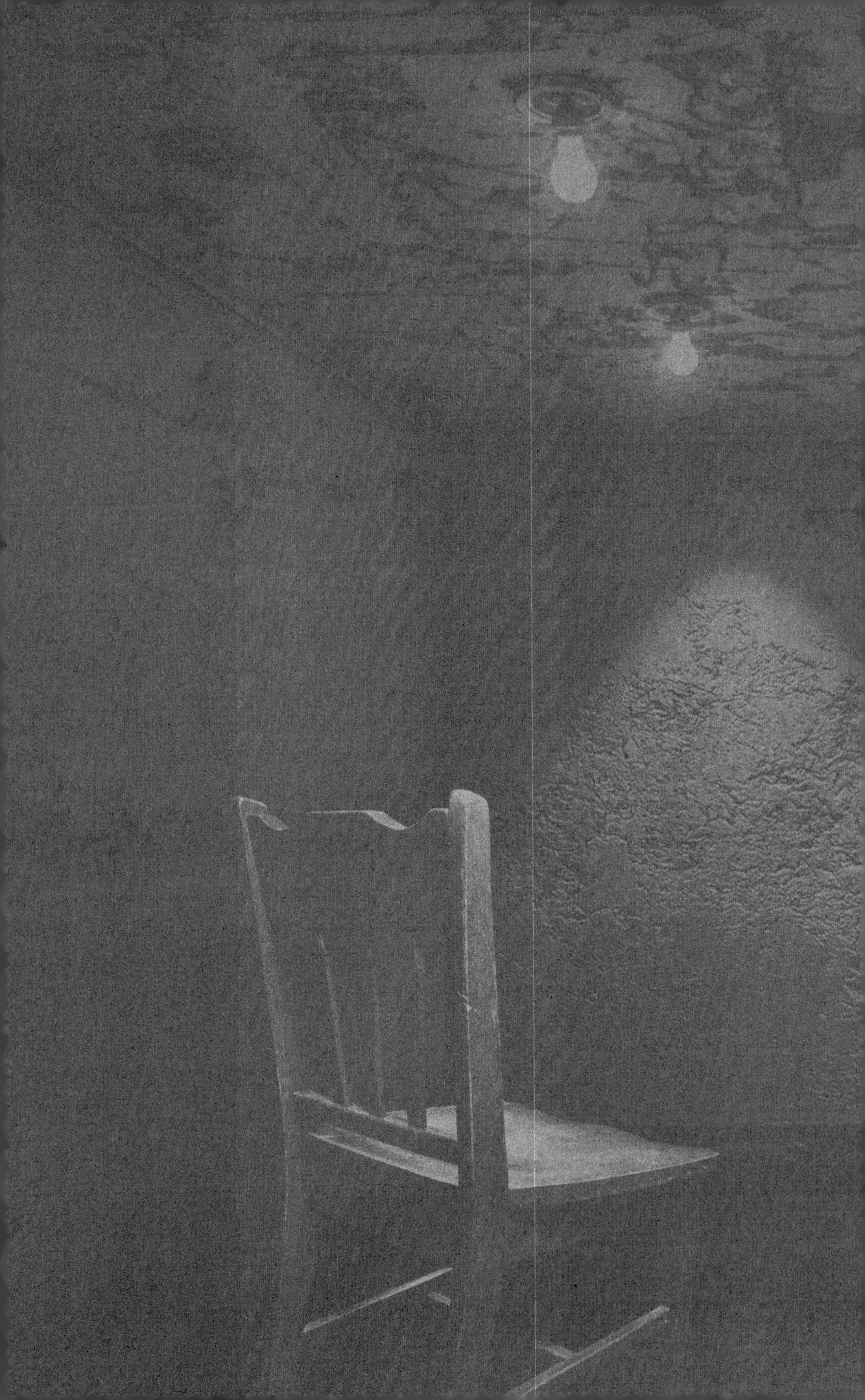

CHAPTER NINE

jersey

The game they were playing with me was already weighing on my nerves, and I was already pissed that I was letting them get to me that way. I had no way of knowing how much time passed since they'd brought me in here. The people who came and went from this room with scraps of food, sips of water, and a disgusting fucking bucket didn't do it on any set schedule for me to start keeping track. It felt like it had been long enough that they should've started fucking with me by now though. Not that I was looking forward to it, but having to just sit and wait on it was equally exhausting.

I think I would have been less shocked if an actual ogre had walked into that room the next time the door opened. Bryson came in first, but a small blonde woman followed right behind him. She carried a tripod and a camera, and she was entirely unable to so much as glance in my direction.

"Found your girls, New Jersey," he said and shrugged the bad shoulder out of the jacket that was draped over it.

"Then you found them because they *wanted* you to find them."

"If it makes you feel better to think of it that way, sure," he said and turned to watch the woman setup the tripod.

"How is it that you never caught her yourself?" I asked. "She retired all those other teams who were trying to bring her in alive. You were just trying to kill her. For like four years? And you couldn't make that happen? It only took Memphis a whopping half a day to find her."

He leaned back against the wall to smile at me.

"Why'd you do it?" He asked. "You two were about to be at the top of this business. Just bringing her in would've set you both up for life. You could've just chosen to retire with that payout."

I couldn't have answered that question if my life really did depend on it.

So, I stayed right where my happy ass was on that floor and just stared back at him.

"Her pussy couldn't really taste that good?" He added with that fucked up smile again.

But it could.

Because it did.

Ecstasy.

That memory was enough to ground me for the duration of whatever this little meeting was about to entail.

The little blonde nodded her head at Bryce when she was done setting up the camera directly across from me. She pushed a couple buttons on it before she stepped all the way back to the other corner of the room, still never looking my way.

"I'm going to need you to tell them that we're willing to offer two of you quick deaths if Trista is brought back to Philadelphia, back to Nate, alive," Bryce said.

"Which two?" I asked.

"You and Trista."

"What happens to Memphis?"

"We've got other plans for her," he smiled again when he said it, and rather than running cold, my blood turned to boiling lava. "Tell them," he said and nodded to the camera.

I looked right into that camera. There was no way it was a live feed. They'd never risk me saying anything worthwhile to either of those girls. "Stay where you are, Fancy Face. Right where you are. They have no idea how to find you."

Bryce was on top of me a second later, swinging the fist attached to his good arm over and over again until blood was pouring out of my mouth and the whole room looked fuzzy. He shook his hand and wiggled his fingers when he stepped back.

"Sorry. Did my face hurt your fist?" I asked and spat out a mouthful of blood in his direction.

"Ready to try again? We'll offer two of you quick deaths. Trista goes back to Nate. Otherwise, what happens to you only gets worse with every day that passes from this point."

"How does it feel?" I asked instead. "To be outsmarted by two girls? Knowing you have no chance at finding them yourselves if they don't want you to?"

He hit me hard enough that time that I was little convinced he cracked a tooth.

"You don't even know her," he said. "What do you get out of protecting her?"

"If the end result is my death either way, what does it hurt to give her the chance to survive?"

He wasn't happy about that response either.

But we played that game until he was mad enough to knock my ass out cold.

CHAPTER TEN
trista

I spent the last two days driving all over this bland state in search of the things on the list from Memphis. Any worker in any of these stores would know what she wanted if they saw the list, my ass. She intended to establish some kind of presence online, one that Nate's best would be able to find, but not the lower level tech crew so it didn't look obvious that she was just out for information. She wanted them to find this created space, that had no link to our location, so they'd be able to start sending whatever it was that they would demand from the two of us in regard to Jersey. I tried to tell her more than once that what they wanted was me. And that they wanted me back in Philly. They'd want me dropped right at Nate's front door. That was going to be the demand, but it probably wouldn't be in exchange for releasing Jersey. He'd been right. They'd never let any of us just walk away from this now, but Memphis was certain that having some form of communication opened with them would provide a path for her to find where they were keeping him. Then we could figure out a next step from there.

After telling her for the last two days that whatever it was that she so desperately needed from this list simply wasn't available in

Indiana, she said she'd call in a favor to another Judge from Nate's organization. No amount of pleading with her changed her mind either. It was a bad idea all the way to its core. Involving any of them was dangerous. I couldn't even begin to wrap my head around how she could trust any of them who were still tied to that crowd, but for every question I asked, she was quick to remind me that our options were limited. She'd arranged for me to pick up whatever was left of her list at some middle-of-nowhere truck stop in Northern Indiana since the person bringing it would be coming from Michigan. I wasn't supposed to be meeting with or talking to anyone. The person leaving *the package* was supposed to be able to beat me there by a long shot. It was supposed to be hidden in a false trash can somewhere on the lot, and it was supposed to be obvious which would be the correct one.

Shady business deals were nerve wracking though. I wasn't even a full hour into the drive North and I'd already convinced myself that somebody driving a blue Mercedes had recognized me when I stopped for gas and had been following me ever since. When that car was still behind me an hour later on the interstate, I gave in and called Memphis.

"Problem?" She asked by way of answering the phone.

"I think somebody is following me, but I'm also wildly paranoid now and I don't know if I'm just losing my grasp on reality a little more with every day that passes."

"So, is this like an *I need to look into something for you* kind of phone call? Or more of a *having an existential, quarter-life crisis* kind of phone call?" She asked.

"I don't even know how to answer that, because both? It feels like both."

"What can you tell me about who you think is following you?" She asked. I could actually hear the girl trying *not* to laugh at me.

"It's a blue Mercedes. Maybe someone at that gas station I stopped at recognized me," I said.

"You know how *little* that tells me?"

"I do."

"Would you be able to stop somewhere to see if they also stop? Put yourself in a position to get a license plate number?"

"And here I called you thinking you would have a way to get me *further away* from this person," I said and sighed.

She did laugh that time. "Just stop at the next gas station or restaurant, literally anywhere. Don't get out. Pull into a parking lot and sit there. See what they do."

"Okay, but what if they actually *do* something?" I asked. "I'm not Jersey. I don't just do this kind of shit for fun on the weekend."

"No matter what they do, you're sitting in a car that comes stock with over a thousand horsepower, Trista. It has an eight second quarter mile time. I can guarantee that you're in the faster vehicle. All you have to do is drive away if you feel like there's a problem. Just maybe don't put your foot all the way down if you don't know how to handle it because you'll roast the tires right off of it and end up in a ditch."

"What the fu —? Why do you even know that?" I asked.

She sighed. "I, unfortunately, have come to know everything that there is to know about that car. What do you think Jersey talks about when he gets bored?"

"Oh, God. I'm going to have to figure out how to listen to car talk *and* look interested in it, aren't I?"

"Welcome to the club, sister. I'll make us T-shirts," she said. "Now, find a place to stop. Stay on the phone with me."

There was a sign for some family-owned restaurant at the next exit from the interstate, so that's where I was headed. It was right off the next road, so I pulled into the lot and waited. I left the car in gear while my heart pounded loud enough to drown out any other noise. Memphis must have been able to hear the sharp intake of breath that happened without my permission when I watched the Mercedes pull into the opposite end of the lot and park where they could sit and stare at me through their windshield too.

"Okay," she said quickly. "I need you to slowly drive toward them. If that car moves at all when yours does, you leave. Don't stop again, don't even slow down. Back to the interstate and just go. If they just sit still and wait, drive all the way around it until you see a license plate number and read it out to me as you go by. Still don't stop, even if you miss a number or letter. Just tell me what you see as you see it."

I'd never been less certain of my ability to simply read numbers or letters than I was in that moment when I eased off the brake to start rolling forward. The Mercedes shifted into reverse and started to move backward the moment I applied the slightest pressure to the accelerator to advance toward them.

"Nope," I said and cut the wheel all the way to the right to head back for the road. "I'm out. They're definitely following me."

Memphis laughed again. "Just stay calm. You've still got another couple hours of just driving. We'll try to lose them, and if it doesn't work, I've got a couple other ideas we can look into when you get closer."

"Why are you laughing?" I demanded. "Why are you *calm*?"

"This is where I excel," she said, like it was quite literally the least exciting thing she'd ever done. "I'm safely on this side of the phone call. I make the decisions calmly and quickly for you so that you don't have to worry about making irrational ones based on your emotions since you're the one in the moment."

"Fuck," I said. "*You* were what made Jersey good at his job, weren't you?"

She didn't bother to answer. She didn't need my praise or my reassurance.

Memphis spent the next hour guiding me through a never-ending series of "turn here, and then here, and then there" instructions to get me off the interstate, all over several backroads, and then back to the interstate. But none of it worked. At some point in every side trip, the Mercedes popped back up.

"Alright," Memphis said impatiently now. "I'm going to mute this call because I need to talk to someone else real quick about the next steps. Scream bloody murder until you get my attention again if you *really* need something over the next few minutes. Otherwise, just stay on track and keep moving."

I tried to think about absolutely nothing for what had to be the longest six minutes of my life while Memphis was on the phone with somebody else. I put all my effort into just reminding myself to keep breathing. She needed whatever we were trying to retrieve. She would've told me to just turn around and call it quits, to just drive somewhere else until this Mercedes gave up if she didn't truly need whatever was being delivered for me to pick up.

"So," Memphis said through the speakers again and giggled nervously. "You're probably not going to like this."

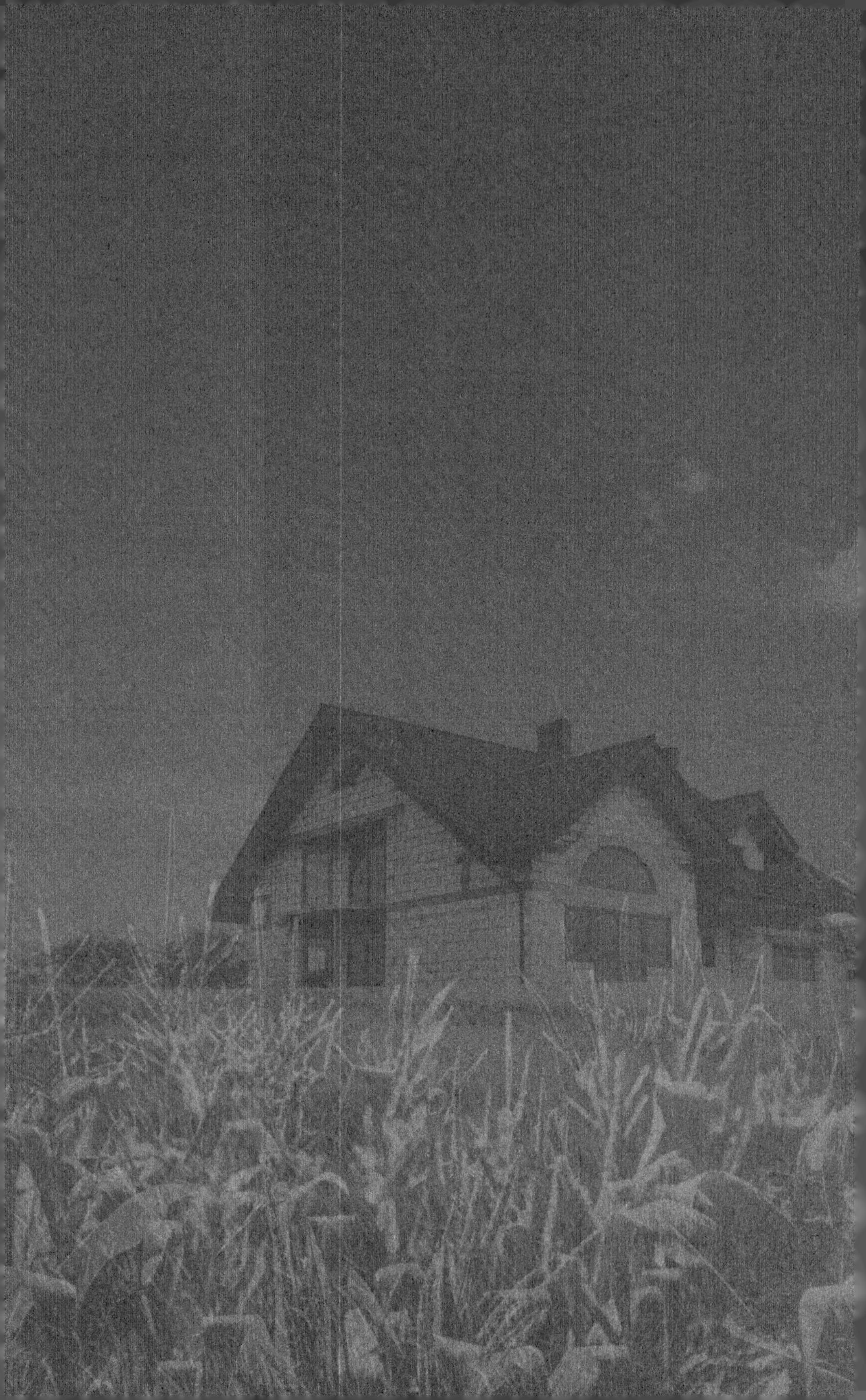

CHAPTER ELEVEN
trista

I did not like it, but I couldn't come up with anything better when Memphis asked if I had another solution to offer.

"His name is Utah," Memphis said. "Rather than dropping everything off and just leaving, he's going to wait for you there. Hand everything off to you. Then he'll stay there to run interference to give you a chance to get moving back this way until you're far enough ahead that this person won't be able to just catch up to you. And I'll get you on a different path back here that doesn't involve any part of that interstate."

"I cannot, for the life of me, understand why you think this is a good idea," I said. "You can't possibly trust this person to *not* shove me straight into the trunk of his car and run straight toward Philly."

"Well, my understanding is that he'll be in a truck so, you know, he won't have a trunk to stuff you in," Memphis said, like that was somehow supposed to ease my nerves about all of this. "And no, I actually don't know much at all about Utah. I know his Judge. I think we're onto something big just under the surface of Nate's organization and Indy wants to be on our side of it, rather than the President's."

"*Indy?*" I repeated.

"Yes," she said. "Indianapolis. Utah's Judge."

"And what am I supposed to do if this other Executioner simply isn't on the same page, Memphis?" I pressed. "What the fuck am I going to do if he just decides he'd rather have the money in exchange for my bounty?"

"He won't."

"You can't possibly believe that," I said.

"We are running out of time. They're going to start hurting Jersey because they haven't had any communication back from us," Memphis said. "If you want to help him, we just have to believe that Utah is coming because he wants to help us."

"I just want to go on the record as having said that I am not in agreement with any part of this plan," I said, even knowing full well that I was already prepared to just fucking risk it anyway if it meant getting Jersey back.

"I will add a note of your protest to the very official set of statements that I update every time we speak."

"You're nowhere near as funny as you seemed to be when you were doing this shit to Jersey," I said.

"Listen, I have no chance at being successful in this without you. Just like you don't without me. So, just go into it like you're every bit as nervous as you sound. Take Jersey's gun with you, leave the car running, be ready to fight your way back out."

"That's terribly discomforting. Thank you, Memphis."

I pulled into the parking lot of the truck stop where I was supposed to be meeting Utah and tried desperately to get my panic back under control. I tucked Jersey's gun into the front of my jeans and looked all the way around me. The Mercedes pulled in only a couple minutes later and parked two rows behind me.

"Who am I looking for, Memphis?" I asked quickly. "The Mercedes is already here."

I watched the driver's side door open and a very tall, thin man somehow unfold from the tiny car.

"He's getting out of the car, Memphis," I said much more impatiently. "I can't just sit here."

As I was saying the words, the most ridiculously large, bright fucking orange truck I'd ever seen pulled up right behind Persephone and parked perpendicular to the trunk, between me and the Mercedes man.

"You've got to be kidding me," I said mostly to myself, but very much out loud.

"Is it really neon orange?" Memphis asked with a laugh. "I kind of thought Indy was just fucking with me. That's why I didn't say anything."

"The fuck am I supposed to do here?" I asked.

"He'll tell you what to do," Memphis said. "Just, you know, don't get in his truck or let him force you anywhere."

"That's so not fucking helpful, Memphis," I said in so much panic because this new Executioner was climbing out of his mountain-sized truck and getting closer to interacting with me with every word Memphis and I spoke. He wasn't anything like I expected. I was used to Jersey's weird sense of professionalism with his suits and walking around like he was better than everybody. This guy looked like he was my age, and he was wearing basketball shorts with a sleeveless hoodie. He had dark hair that was cut short on the sides but was longer and spiked in every direction on the top with a short beard that was very neatly trimmed.

"Jesus," I definitely didn't mean to say out loud.

"What? What's wrong?" Memphis asked.

"He's got fucking biceps that are the size of my waist," I whispered as he got closer.

"Oh, for fuck's sake, woman. Please. Control your hormones and get out of the car."

I forced myself to open the door and stand. This motherfucker walked right up to me like we'd known each other for an eternity and were completely comfortable being only a few inches apart.

"Take this," he said and handed me what looked like a business card. "Go there now and wait for me. I'll keep him busy."

I said a grand total of zero words before he'd already turned back for his truck.

"Do it," Memphis said from the speakers in the car. "Do what he said. Go."

"The fuck?" I mumbled and dropped back into the car to get the hell out of there before I had to witness whatever was about to happen between these two men.

"What's the address that he gave you?" Memphis asked. I read it off to her and just started driving, without bothering to look back.

"Okay, so I'm going to call Indy. Utah gave you an address for nothing. It's just a field. Like empty, open farmland. And I don't think I want to let you play that game. I'm going to find somewhere public for you to go wait for him. Just keep driving and I'll send an address through to your GPS when I figure something out."

"How is this just your fucking day job?" I asked no one, because Memphis was already off the phone with me.

She had me sitting in a crowded hotel parking lot twenty minutes later, pacing around Persephone because I couldn't force myself to sit still for the life of me. I had every single window rolled down because Memphis was waiting to listen in on this interaction when Utah did show up.

"What are you doing?" She asked.

"What?"

"I track your phone," she said. "Are you just walking in circles?"

"Yes, Memphis. I am. Are you somehow *not* nervous?" I asked. "Don't bother answering. I really don't want the answer. And he's here."

"Just take what he's bringing and drive away," Memphis said.

"Then maybe you should've fucking come to do this yourself if you know what needs to be done," I whisper-shouted through the windows while I walked around to stand between Seph and this massive truck that was parking next to her.

It.
The car.
God.
What was happening to me?

I waited in uncomfortable silence while Utah got out and opened the back door of his truck to pull out a giant box. I leaned back into the car to hit the button to release the hatch. He didn't look even the least bit nervous while he placed the box in the trunk and closed the hatch. I just stared at him, awkwardly and still in total silence when he took a single step in my direction. Was I supposed to thank him? Shake his hand? Memphis said she called in a favor, but were these people her friends? Or was this just some weird arrangement of convenience, and they all actually disliked each other? Whatever it was, I got a look at his hands before he stuffed them into the pockets of his shorts. Both sets of knuckles were bright red and had blood on them, so I was certainly not shaking his hand.

"Yeah, I'm looking at her now," he said and paused for an uncomfortably long time. He shrugged the giant boulders that sat in the place of his shoulders, and this motherfucker looked up and down my entire body.

"She's not really what I expected, but yeah. I'd still say she's hot," he said.

"Excuse me?" I asked. Then this joker raised his hand in my direction, to tell me to be quiet like I was a toddler interrupting his phone call. And I nearly rolled my eyes right out of my skull when I realized he was on his stupid, little ear radio with Indy.

"What? No," he said and paused again to listen. "Because I said no. I'm not taking a picture of her. It's rude. Quit being weird."

"But it's less rude to stand here and have this conversation in front of me?" I asked. "The fuck is wrong with literally every person who works for this company?"

He ignored me completely.

"Well, yeah. I mean if I met her in a bar or something, I wouldn't turn her down. But for several million dollars, I think I would've just kept it in my pants," he said and paused again. I took a very noticeable step backward at that comment, wondering if I was about to have to run.

"Indy. I am not taking a picture of her. My God, man," he said and hung his head back to stare at the sky for a second. He sighed before he looked back to my eyes that time.

"Can I take a picture of you?" He asked.

"What? No. Fuck off."

"There. See. Now you've upset her," he said and paused to listen again. "Because it's fucking weird man. That's why. I asked. She said no. Drop it."

"Yeah, I'm leaving," I said and started to back away, because I was a little terrified about turning my back to this man.

"Oh, okay. That's one way to treat people after you've done exactly as they've asked. Moody little shit hung up on me," Utah said, walking the rest of the way toward me. "Sorry about that. Indy doesn't do a lot of face-to-face interaction. He's — amusing. So, Virginia was unconscious when I left him. Should give you a solid head start, but do you want me to follow you back just in case?"

"Virginia?" I asked. "He's another Executioner?"

"He is."

"Why would you do that? Won't they start coming after you now?" I asked.

"Oh, they have no idea who I am," he said. "I wouldn't have known who he was if his Judge hadn't been screaming his name from the speakers in his car."

"Yeah, if you're still working for them, I don't think it's a good idea to have you follow me anywhere," I said. "I have *several million dollars'* worth of skepticism about you."

His smile in response to that scared me even more.

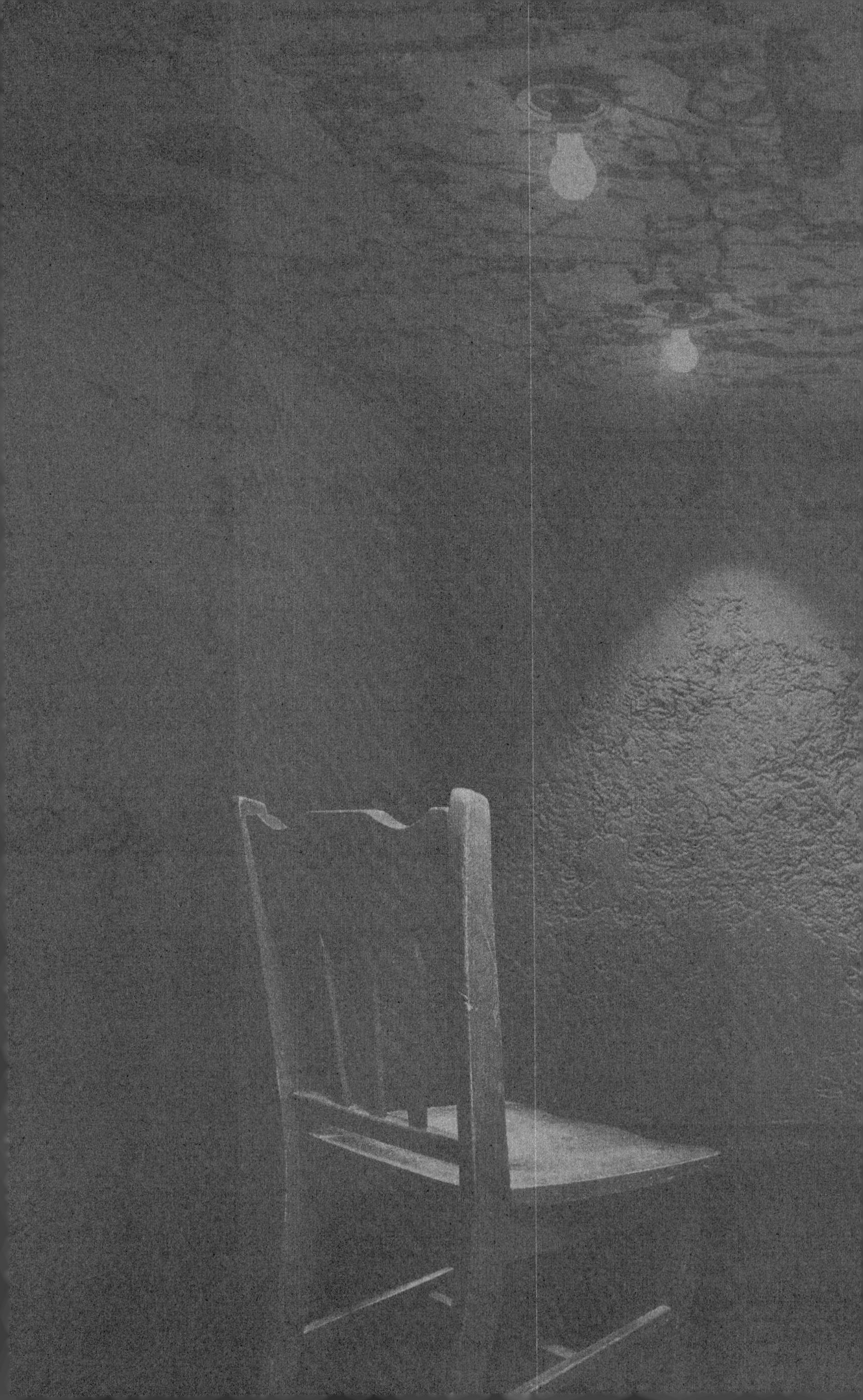

CHAPTER TWELVE

jersey

I spent most of my time just attempting to sleep to pass the days. They'd been giving me just enough water and just enough rotten food to make sure I wouldn't die. They brought someone in to make sure I wouldn't bleed to death from the shot to the shoulder, but they didn't bother to remove whatever bullet fragments were still embedded in my body so the pain from it never really subsided for more than a minute or two of sitting perfectly still. Even in the moments that I did manage to fall asleep, just breathing too deeply would send bolts of pain through my body to wake me right back up. That, combined with being trapped in the body of a thirty-seven-year-old man who was being forced to sleep on nothing more than concrete left me in a pretty perpetually shitty mood. Everything ached all the way into the fucking marrow of my old man bones.

Keeping my thoughts under control hadn't reached a difficult point yet. The real torture hadn't started though. I didn't believe they'd actually made contact with Memphis yet, so they had no use in torturing me. It wouldn't do them much good to risk killing me before they'd gotten any use out of me. The only thought so far that bothered me more than the others was having to acknowledge that if the girls had made it to Indiana like I'd hoped, it meant they both had access to the master bedroom in that house.

There was nothing I could do from here about the picture that sat next to my side of the bed. It wasn't something that I'd planned to keep from Triss forever, but having the chance to hear it from me first probably would've gone over better. I had no way of knowing if Memphis knew about those years of my life. She'd never mentioned any of it, but she'd also never mentioned knowing my real name before she screamed it when she was being abducted. Whether she'd heard about my previous life from Memphis or from Kyle by this point, I couldn't imagine it was an easy pill for Triss to have to swallow without me being there to answer her questions about the situation.

It surprised even me that the sound of the door opening felt like a relief. Drag my ass out of those thoughts before they could actually start this time around. The small woman who usually brought the camera and the tripod in had been replaced by the President himself for this visit with Bryson. They looked even more alike when they stood side-by-side with the same overly annoyed expression.

"We're going to discuss this like adults now, Mr. Jersey, because my patience is wearing thin," Nate said.

"Then you might want to excuse your baby boy from this conversation," I managed to choke out, despite having a mouth that was still filled with dried blood and a throat that hadn't had water in hours. Baby boy immediately stepped forward and clocked me right in the jaw another time for good measure.

"We're going to be honest with each other, because that's how men handle these problems," Nate said. "I'm tired of waiting. Tell me where Trista is."

"You can see that I'm not currently with her, right?"

Another punch from baby boy, to my nose this time.

"We're both broken men, Mr. Jersey. And it stems from a common pain."

"It's a little early to be playing that *you and I aren't so different* card, isn't it?"

"We both know how it feels to lose a child," he said. "And wouldn't you do whatever was necessary to be able to face the person who took your child away from you?"

"Yeah, I'm going to have to stop you there. Your shitball of a son got exactly what he deserved."

"That's a pretty awful thing for one father to say to another father."

"But a pretty accurate thing to say to an asshole."

"Then I might as well say it right back to you if talking to an asshole is the only requirement for it," he said.

I couldn't help but laugh. "That my four-year-old *deserved* to die? Sure. The difference there is that you and I both absolutely know that *that* isn't true. Just like we both know that your son raping and tormenting a girl who had no one to help her puts him squarely in the category of deserving it."

That brought all of Bryson's fury down on top of me another fucking time. To drive his point home, he wasn't even aiming for my face anymore. He dragged my ass out away from the wall to drop me to the concrete below him so he could stomp right down on the already wounded shoulder. For as much as I normally preferred to *not* show my torturer the kind of pain he was inflicting with every blow, I couldn't do fucking shit about the scream that came out of me after that. I about passed out that very second. The only thing that kept me conscious and coherent was realizing that if this asshole ever did get his hands on Trista, this was exactly what he intended to do to her. And to prevent that, I was more than willing to just endure this until my last breath.

"You can make this easier on yourself by telling me where to find her," Nate said. "Or even just by telling me how to contact Memphis."

My girls.

CHAPTER THIRTEEN

trista

I kept my eyes on every mirror in that car more than I actually paid attention to the road in front of me. It had to have been by the grace of something unholy that I made it back to Jersey's property. Memphis was on board with Utah following me back, but I was not. I was entirely prepared to bet on myself. I knew I could get far enough away before I had to worry about Virginia waking back up, and I absolutely drove like a psychopath to make that happen. Part of me was still also completely certain that Utah had followed me anyway. I didn't see him at any point on the drive back, but I still felt him; the same way I could feel Jersey when he was always right behind me.

Kyle came out from behind the garage when I pulled Persephone back inside and asked if I needed help. I opened the hatch for him, and he retrieved the box from it without any hesitation. I still had so many questions for him. The willingness to just coexist with the two of us while he cared for someone else's property, without even knowing what had happened to Jersey, felt so odd to me. But he was helpful and kind. He kept to himself pretty much all the time, unless he was coming by to ask if we needed anything. I opened the doors to the house for him so he could carry the box inside, and we found Memphis perched at the kitchen island staring at her laptop. She didn't so much as glance in our direction when we walked in through the door.

"Did you have Utah follow me back here anyway?" I asked.

"*Utah*?" Kyle asked and chuckled. "Jersey. Memphis. Utah. You ladies are mixed up in some weird stuff."

"We're going to need his help," Memphis said, still without looking at me. She pushed the laptop toward the empty space in front of the stool next to her and put her face in her hands. I forced myself to breathe before I sat beside her. I pushed the play button in the middle of the black screen and stood up to back away from it like it was on fire when a video of Bryson standing over Jersey, punching him repeatedly, started to play.

"Indy sent it to me," Memphis said. "It's from a few days ago. They've sent it out to all the Judges in case any of them are still in contact with me. In case any of them are able to locate us."

"There's no sound?" I asked, stepping back toward the computer and the island. "He looked like he was saying something to the camera."

"No sound."

"It wasn't meant for us to see?" I asked. "Didn't say where to meet them or how to go about exchanging us? Nothing?"

"They're not interested in an exchange. Nobody just goes free from this, Trista."

"Then what do they want?"

"Both of us. All of us," she said and laughed uncomfortably. "You and Jersey will get merciful deaths if we just go to them easily."

It was upsetting all on its own that that sounded like a pretty solid deal at this point in my life.

"And you?"

"I don't know," she said. "They just *want* me."

Kyle sat the box on the island and came around to stand next to me. Without bothering to ask, he reached around me to play the video again. He smirked after the part where there were back-to-back moments of Jersey very clearly saying something to illicit Bryce's fury.

"Never was any good at keeping his mouth shut," he said, and even managed to smile.

The truth in that statement was outrageous.

"Why did Indy send this to you?" I asked Memphis. "Does he know where we are?"

"No, not yet. He sent it because we're friends and he was trying to warn me that others would be out looking for us. The contract on us is massive now. But like I said, we're going to need help. I can do this part of it behind the scenes by myself now, but someone is going to have to do the physical retrieving. I can't imagine that's something you'll want to attempt alone."

"You think we're just going to bust into wherever they're keeping him, steal him, and stroll right back out?" I asked.

"We?" She asked motioning between herself and me. "No. You and I, absolutely not. But with Utah, maybe."

"How well do you know this person?" I asked.

"I don't," she said, like that should've been obvious. "None of us ever really *knew* anything about the others. That's how it worked. That's how it was organized. I just — do my own research when I need information."

"But we're going to just trust this person to not ruin our lives? Allow him here and hope for the best in the end?"

"Jersey took a chance on you," she said and slammed her laptop closed before she snatched it up under her arm and started to walk out. "We're *going* to take this chance for him."

Kyle chuckled again beside me. "Sun will be going down soon. I'll be out by the fire if you need to not be in here."

AN HOUR LATER, I was dragging my own patio chair out to Kyle's fire pit to sit with him and Dandy.

"I really do want him back," I said as I plopped down beside Kyle. "I just strongly dislike the idea of involving more people. Especially people I don't know."

"I didn't ask, honey."

"Right. Just feels like Memphis thinks I'm not willing to do whatever we have to do to get him back. I am. And I will. I feel — I don't know. Things. I feel *things* for that asshole that I really don't know how to explain."

He smirked, but still said nothing and picked up a stick to poke at the logs that made up his fire.

"You don't say much either, huh?" I asked.

"Never really had anyone out here with me to do much talking," he said and laughed. "Dandy doesn't say much back, and sometimes words just kind of ruin the calm that this place can bring, if you let it."

"Oh," I sighed. "Sorry. I can just go back in."

I stood to start back toward the house, intensely annoyed that he'd invited me out here just to call me annoying and essentially tell me to leave. He grabbed my wrist before I even made it a step away.

"I wasn't telling you to go anywhere," he said. "Sit back down. I just don't get visitors. Come on, tell me about him."

"I would think you know him better than I do?" I asked, sitting again.

"I doubt it. You bond in very different ways when your life depends on someone else's ability to use a weapon versus wanting to fuck them."

My mouth fell right the fuck open, before I laughed.

"Sorry. That was rude. Like I said, not many visitors out here."

"I really don't know much about him. He left me in the trunk of his car for like the first two days of knowing me," I said. "Crazy sexual tension aside, we didn't do much getting to know each other on that trip."

"What was the purpose of this trip? Why the trunk? I don't even know what he does these days."

"He's a bounty hunter for a psychopath," I said, imagining the kind of organization my stepfather would run. "They take contracts from people with way too much money to find other people who they think have wronged them in some way."

"Who thinks you wronged them?"

"My stepdad."

"And Van changed his mind about keeping the contract? Decided he'd rather have you?"

"I guess it was something like that."

I couldn't even begin to grasp why he hadn't asked what the bounty on me was for. He seemed so uninterested in the details of all of it.

"Will you tell me something about him?" I asked.

"Everything I know about him is probably a little messed up for normal people," he said and chuckled.

"I don't think I really count as *normal*."

He sighed and rubbed the top of Dandy's head before he spoke again.

"The kinds of things we had to do turn men into weird animals. It wasn't always terrible or bad. We did do a lot of good things overall, but it changed all of us in more ways than one. Van sort of did that in reverse at one point."

"What's that mean?"

"Usually when you say a Marine *has changed*, you're telling everybody that he's not really stable after he's back home from doing whatever he had to do."

"And he was so messed up from the start that he was already unstable going in, so he pretty much stayed the same?" I interrupted and giggled at myself. He didn't even react to my question.

"You get to know the men you serve with more on a cellular level than an emotional one. These guys who would annoy the shit out of you if you'd met them under other circumstances became the men you trusted more than anyone anywhere in the world because they're all you have. That city kid who showed up on the first day was the kind of punk I'd beat up on the weekend just to take his girl home for a night."

"I can't really imagine anyone successfully beating up Jersey *for fun*."

"He turned into somebody I'd do anything for. We all knew he had a family. A wife and a baby, that his wife wasn't okay. He didn't talk about that part of it much, but he talked about *them* nonstop when things would get scary. And one time, he came back for another deployment...different. Something in the core of who he was had shifted. I couldn't figure out what it was. We hadn't been out together in nearly a year at that point, so I thought maybe he just seemed different because it'd been so long. But one of the other guys who had kids nailed it down. Van's kid started talking. Really talking. Not that in-between stuff where every third or fourth mumble of gibberish is a real word. I guess she had this game where they would come up with nicknames for everything. And I mean fucking everything. She really got a kick out of it. Van brought that to all of us, like he couldn't turn it off. The people, our gear, our weapons, fucking nicknames everywhere. They weren't as child-friendly as I'm sure they were when he was home, but it gave him something else to hold onto when things got rocky. Motherfucker had all of us doing it. A whole band of assholes running through the desert or some city or awful jungle, calling our weapons the sexiest women's names we could come up with, giving each other the worst names we could think of."

I tried so fucking hard to swallow the sobs that wanted to escape me.

"He still does that," I choked out. "Calls me *Fancy Face*. Calls Memphis every name in the book because she won't let him use any particular one on a regular basis, so he just keeps trying. I just thought he was weird."

"*Fancy Face*," he repeated and laughed. He made a noise at

Dandy, and she moved to sit at my feet while I cried. "Your turn, honey. Tell me something."

"I wish I had stories like yours. Mine are...awful," I stopped to laugh, because they really were just terrible. "I guess if we're sticking with the name theme, I spent like nine hours trying to guess his real name. I only ever knew him as Jersey. I pulled out every douchebag name I could think of just to piss him off to see if I could get him to break. He never did tell me his actual name, but saying your name like I was auditioning for a porno sure got a rise out of him."

He stared at me like I'd lost my mind for a solid minute before he laughed. "I have a douchebag name?"

"Kyle is very much a douchebag name. You're not so bad, but the name isn't so good."

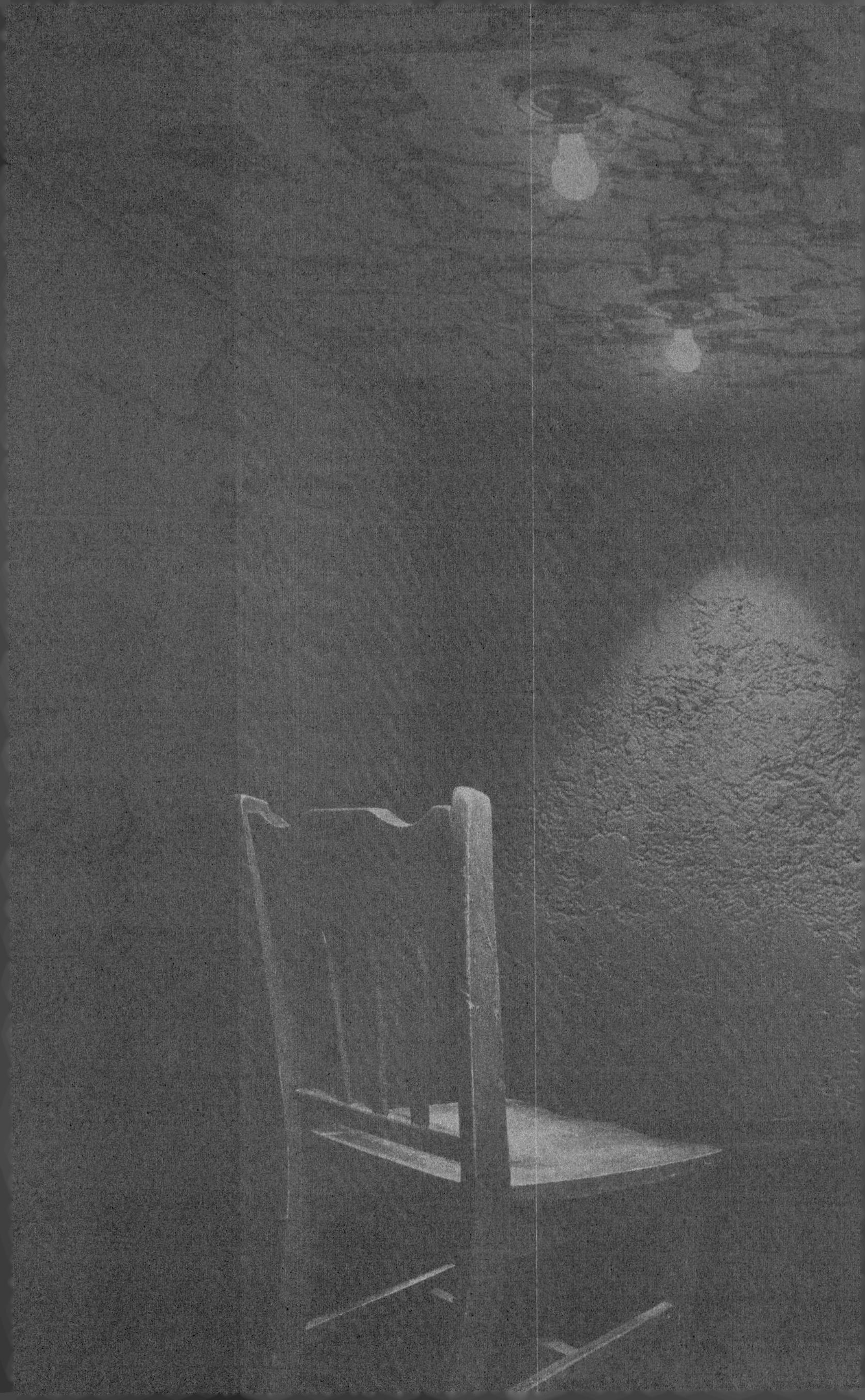

CHAPTER FOURTEEN

jersey

A swift fucking kick to the ribs woke me up from the unpleasant sleep I'd found myself in on the floor in the corner of that concrete box. Shit was getting bad for me quickly if the door opening and closing didn't even wake me up anymore. They'd managed to cut the water and food rationing back just enough for it to be devastating. I hadn't been here *that* long, but I was already badly injured before this started. And they added on extra beatings at every opportunity. Even in its fog, my brain knew that all of that in addition to shitty sleep, no nourishment, and no water resulted in a combination that went south fast. Even strong bodies deteriorated quickly under those conditions.

I watched a set of men carry in a massive wooden table and two chairs while the small blonde woman returned with her camera setup. Bryson stood over me the entire time with a box under his good arm, just watching me. He stayed that way until the other two men each grabbed me by an arm, completely ignoring the shrieking sound that came from me when the motion strained my shoulder again. They sat me in one of the chairs before one of them unlocked the handcuffs. That was when my eyes landed on the center of the table in front of me. There were shackles built *into* it, ready and waiting to bind me to this table.

"Is this about to be a sexy day?" I rasped out from the driest mouth I'd ever experienced. "Sorry, I haven't had much of a chance to clean up for it."

"That doesn't sound like such a bad idea. Bring someone in to let him make you his bitch," Bryce said walking around behind where I sat. "Let you find out what it feels like to be the one getting fucked for once."

I managed to laugh. "Bold of you to assume that it'd be my first time."

The gentleman who'd released me from the handcuffs got to work fastening my wrists to the table. Bryce rammed the tip of a knife into the table in between my hands while I was still being shackled and scared the other man enough to make him jump back away from the table.

"Then maybe I'll just cut your dick off now," he threatened. "I can't imagine you'll be needing it again."

I made a point to look back down at the knife. "You better have a chainsaw somewhere."

Rather than just trying to knock my teeth loose that time, this son of a bitch slapped me. Hard enough and solid enough to leave the entire side of my face stinging. I shook my head violently while they finished locking my hands flat against the table.

"Alright then," I said. "Now that I'm awake, let's do this. What's the goal today, boys? Excuse me, boys *and* girl."

The woman had already setup the camera and shifted to the corner the furthest away from where I was forced to sit, the corner where I usually tried to sleep. She made eye contact with me for the fastest split second before I watched her right hand come out of her pocket and that whole arm shift behind her body. I convinced my brain there and then not to look at her again for the duration of their stay with me in this room after that.

Bryson dropped heavily into the chair across from me and

slammed the biggest fucking rat trap that I'd ever seen down on the table between us.

"This is one of my favorite games," he said. "And it's got the easiest rules to follow, to remember."

He pulled the sling away from his body so he could use the limited mobility that he had in his bad arm. He reached into the box and pulled out three more of the massive traps.

He smiled. "Extras. Just in case you last longer than anticipated and one of them breaks."

He pulled the bar back on the trap that sat between us on the table to hook it into place, and then I watched him raise the fingers of my left hand just high enough to slide the wood of the trap underneath them. I couldn't lift my hand any higher with the way that it was shackled. The only option was lowering it, and that would set off the trap.

"I only have one question, New Jersey," he said. "I'll ask it. And you obviously have a choice. You can give me the answer. Or we can find out how many snaps it takes from a rat trap before your fingers are detached from your hand. We're going to record the whole thing. That way we can send it to your friends. If you're not interested in telling us where they are, they might be interested in coming to us after seeing what they're putting you through by hiding."

I locked my jaw right the fuck into place and slammed my hand down into that trap as hard as I could while I leaned forward into that table as far as I could to get closer to Bryson. Tears burned my eyes and fire flared from my fingers all the way to the bullet hole in my shoulder, but I held the stare that I'd locked onto that motherfucker.

"I'm not playing your game," I hissed. "You might as well just cut them off and get it over with."

He smiled and leaned back in his chair to get a good look at my hand. I hadn't managed to look down at it myself yet. I imagined that would make the pain unbearable, whether I had Trista's angry eyes pictured in my mind or not.

"Yeah, I was kind of hoping you'd put up a fight," he said. He sat there until I couldn't control the shaking that had taken over my whole arm. Then he calmly sat upright again to free my hand from the trap to set it again. I about bit through my lip when he raised my hand from the table again to slip the trap back underneath.

"New Jersey. Where is Trista?"

I couldn't prevent my eyes from shifting to that camera before I looked back at Bryce. "Fuck you."

He reached out with a single finger and flipped his end of the trap up so that it snapped closed on my fingers again when the release touched my palm. He didn't wait nearly as long that time before he was reaching to reset the fucking thing another time. I still hadn't looked, but I already couldn't breathe. I tried with every bit of willpower in my body not to even attempt to move any piece of my left hand.

"Trista. Where is she?"

"Phrasing it differently doesn't change the likelihood of me answering it."

He flipped the trap up into my hand another time. It cut through to bone that time. I was certain of it, without even having to look.

"Oh, yikes," Bryce said. "That one looked like it hurt. Got a little messy."

The shaky and unsteady noises that came from me that time when he released my fingers just to reset the trap bothered me. Trista's pissy face was starting to fade already. So I tried like fucking mad to imagine Memphis bossing her around every second of the day that I wasn't there to run interference between the two of them.

"Where is she?" He asked another time.

And another few seconds later, the blood from the snap splattered up to my face.

"This can stop just as soon as you tell me where they are, New Jersey," he said while he set the trap again.

The adrenaline that should've been pumping through me at full force to keep me going wasn't there. I was tired. So fucking tired. And everything hurt worse than it should have. It didn't matter where I looked around that room, the edges of my vision were blurring. Like a fog was moving in on us from the walls.

"You don't look so good, New Jersey. Still with me?" He asked while he moved the trap beneath my hand another time.

"Don't throw up, man," he added. "I won't stop just for somebody to clean it up. And then we'll have to sit here in that mess while we finish this. Where is Trista?"

I dropped my own hand into the trap again just because it hurt too much to hold it up any longer, and I fucking squealed like a pig that time.

"Getting a little unpleasant now?" He asked. "That smug face doesn't seem to be plastered in place anymore."

Trista faded. Memphis wasn't there.

And another voice snaked in. A tiny whisper from some ethereal place between my brain and my skull. Something that was always there, but somehow also never *really* there.

Van, do you ever think about us having a baby?

I shook my head as hard as I could and shot up out of that chair to try to fucking bust my way out of those shackles. At this point, it would probably hurt less to rip the whole fucking arm off anyway.

CHAPTER FIFTEEN
trista

"Hey, guys," Memphis said from behind where we sat around the fire.

"What's wrong?" I asked, standing immediately. Of all the days we'd already been at this house, I hadn't seen her outside of it even once.

"They sent something else," she said quietly. "I already called Indy. Utah is on his way here now. I set up a place online for them to think they've found us so they can communicate with me, and it's not good. It's going to get even worse real fast now."

I hurried toward Memphis, but stopped when I realized Kyle wasn't following me.

"You're not coming?" I asked him.

"He didn't want me to even know what his job was now. He never wanted me involved in this part of his life," he said and shook his head. "Regardless of what happens, he wanted me to stay here just to keep this place ready. That's what I'm going to do."

Part of me wanted to scream at him for not being willing to help us, and the other part of me could see plain as day that that was absolutely what Jersey would want. I turned back to Memphis to follow her to the house.

"Let me know if you have problems with the new person," he called back to us. "Intercom is always on."

"So, I think I'll wait until he gets here to go over everything with both of you at the same time," Memphis said.

"Have you already watched it?" I asked. "What they sent this time?"

"Yeah."

My stomach threatened to empty itself when I realized that she didn't intend to offer any other explanations or insight on what they sent.

"When will he be here?" I asked, following her into the kitchen. She'd emptied the giant box already and had things spread out all over the place.

"Just a few minutes now."

"So, you absolutely had him follow me back here earlier today."

Her lack of response to that was response enough. I rolled my eyes and looked through all the equipment that she'd laid out everywhere. She went back to the seat where she'd set up two laptops this time and went back to typing away. The moment there was a knock on the door, she pulled her phone out and called somebody.

"I'll get the door then?" I asked. She didn't even look at me. I couldn't even believe that I was in the presence of someone who was worse at doing people things than I was. I didn't have a fucking thing prepared to say to Utah when I opened that door either, so I just opened it and stepped off to the side to let him through. It dawned on me when he didn't bother to say anything either that none of these people were good at acting like humans. That's why they all ended up in this job. He moved away from me to wait for me to lead the way. He stopped cold in the doorway of the kitchen, and I looked back at him just in time to watch him choke on nothing momentarily while he stared at Memphis.

"Hey, Indy," Memphis said taking the phone from her ear to lay it on the countertop beside her computer. "He just walked in so we're all here."

"Utah," I said and nodded toward her. "Memphis."

He nodded at her, but I watched his Adam's apple bob up and down a couple times when he tried to swallow.

"I already sent the video feed to you, Indy," Memphis said. "I'm going to let these two watch it now. Stay on the line after. We've got a lot to discuss."

"You got it," Indy said through the speaker.

Utah and I both went to stand behind Memphis and watched her push play on the next video.

"They, uh — they sent it with audio this time," Memphis said quietly before she looked back at me. "Do you want to hear it?"

"Yeah," Utah said.

"I wasn't asking you," Memphis snapped at him.

"I want to hear it," I said.

"It's — rough."

She played the video without any further warning. My whole body involuntarily convulsed at the sight of Jersey slamming his own hand down into a rat trap. I'd jumped badly enough that I even felt a hand on my lower back like Utah was prepared to catch me if I was about to faint.

"Jesus fucking Christ," Indy whispered through the speaker. "Who is this guy?"

"My stepbrother," I said into my own hand, that I hadn't even realized I'd brought up to cover my mouth.

"No," Indy said. "We all know who *that* is. I meant New Jersey. Because my God. He's such an impressive smartass. Even under pressure."

"Down, Indy," Utah said. "His girl is standing here too."

"Ah. Is he *only* into girls?" Indy asked.

"This isn't the time, man," Utah snapped.

I felt his fingertips dig into my back ever so slightly when he said the words. He was — comforting me? At least, that's what he was intending to do, but it was just weird for someone who didn't want to be touched by another Executioner as long as my life went on.

I stood there and watched in horror until the moment that Jersey snapped, and his body thrashed up out of that chair like something otherworldly had taken over his movements. I jumped again when I was suddenly a little concerned that he was actually about to break his own arms to try to escape those restraints. Memphis sniffled about the same time that I started to just fucking sob while the video went on for entirely too long.

"Neither of you *need* to watch this," Utah said quietly. "Just turn it that way and *I'll* watch it."

Neither Memphis nor I said anything but we both shook our heads. Jersey was enduring this on behalf of both of us. I didn't really know Memphis well enough to think I could speak for her, but I absolutely felt like I needed to be part of this with him in any way that I could. Right through watching Bryson free Jersey's nearly limp wrists to have two other people toss him into the corner of what looked like a room that was nothing but concrete. And the camera zoomed in on them from where it was across the room to show Bryce take a hammer and some giant fucking nails right over to Jersey. The two other men held him by the arms while Bryce put one of Jersey's feet where he wanted it on the floor just to drive one of those big ass nails right through the top of his foot. I closed my eyes and hung my head when he moved to the other foot.

"Can't have you going anywhere," Bryson said to Jersey, who looked nearly lifeless by that point. His whole body looked like it was shivering, but his eyes weren't open anymore. And the moment that the other two men released his arms, he slumped to the side against the wall. Bryce came back to the camera to tell us that we could end this much faster for him if we just went to Nate's house. If we wanted to prevent this from getting worse for Jersey, all we had to do was say we were heading that way and they'd stop.

CHAPTER SIXTEEN
trista

Memphis closed that window on the screen as soon as the video ended. Utah pulled the stool beside Memphis out away from the island and gently pushed me toward it to get me to sit next to her. Then he just waited, with more patience than I imagined any man ever having, while Memphis and I tried to get our emotions back under control about what we'd just watched.

"Everybody still there?" Indy asked through Memphis' phone.

"Hush," Utah said instantly. He paced around to the other side of the island to lean back against the countertop on the far wall to just wait.

"What now?" I asked, looking straight at Utah for some unknown-to-me reason. He looked from me to Memphis and back to me again.

"If you want our help, I need to know what this is," he said.

"I don't understand," I said and shook my head.

"We've all heard The Retirement rumors. We've all got our own theories about what happened, about who you might be," he said. "What's the real story?"

I hesitated and looked at Memphis. She knew exactly what I was asking her.

"Everything," she said quietly. "Just tell them everything. We're going to *need* them."

Everybody stayed terribly silent while I told them about Jersey snatching me out of that motel in Washington all the way through meeting Utah earlier today.

"I'm not interested in that part so much as I am what came before all that," Utah said. "Who are you to the President? And don't just tell me you're his stepdaughter. That's not helpful."

"She had another stepbrother who did terrible things to her," Memphis spoke up quickly. "Things a young girl shouldn't just have to live with. When she couldn't take it anymore, she killed him, and she ran. You can't ask people for details when it comes to things like that. She broke down part of the President's weapon organization to cause enough of a distraction for her to get out. He's pissed. He wants her back. That torturous demon," she waved a hand at her laptop, "has been after her for years because he just wants to kill her himself."

Utah looked from Memphis back to me. We both noticed how upset she sounded about a story that wasn't hers. He chewed on his bottom lip for a second while he stared at me, like there was a moment of concern that maybe we were just fucking with him to get him to go along with what we needed. It was easy to imagine that everyone who worked in a business like theirs would be suspicious of every other human they ever encountered.

"Jersey asked me to find everything that I could about the President," Memphis said. "So, I did. But I didn't get the chance to tell him that I started by looking at his own life. Indy and I talked about this some already. It was the only way that I could convince him to send you to help us," she said and nodded to Utah. "I don't know what awful backgrounds you guys came from, but I know what happened to me to get me into this organization. And I know what happened to Jersey. I'm wildly uncomfortable telling his story to all of you, but if it means you'll help us get him out of there, so be it."

She stopped for a second to lean forward with her elbows on the countertop and laced her fingers together in front of her mouth. Utah stepped back up to his side of the island to put his hands on it and lean forward. He was studying every move she made, like some sixth sense would spring up to tell him if she was lying or putting on a show.

"I'm listening," he said, so gently that it almost made my heart hurt.

"I think the President played a significant role in getting all of us into his organization. And I don't mean he just sought us out because we were broken people who needed work. I mean, Jersey's wife, his daughter, and his parents were killed," Memphis said and paused. I stood from the stool in a heartbeat and started pacing around at the way that she'd worded that.

"The story that was told was that his wife, who already had a history mental health problems, finally snapped the last time that he was deployed and that she killed all of them before she killed herself. But when you look as hard as humanly possible into what happened, there's just no way that's how it went. I haven't found what I need to feel like I can prove that yet, but I will. I think the President sent someone to murder his family with the intent to send Jersey's life into a pit where he had nothing and no one, and he was in a prime position to accept a fucked up job with other fucked up people. Us."

How Utah didn't even react to her words blew my fucking mind, because I felt like somebody dropped a damned anchor directly on my chest. He glanced in my direction while I paced back and forth like a crazy person, trying to breathe and failing miserably. At some point, I'd started crying again? I think I almost pulled some of my own hair out. And it shouldn't have even been that surprising. Nate was a terrible human. The worst kind, even. I already knew that. He spawned small versions of himself and raised them into extra antichrists to do his bidding. It should've been blatantly obvious that he'd destroy lives just to manipulate people into his employment. He'd *end* lives to manipulate people into his employment. Not even a four-year-old little girl would be off limits to a man who had no soul. And no doubt Jersey had spent all this time being pissed at his wife for doing such a thing, pissed at himself for being gone while it happened. God, I still couldn't breathe.

"She have anxiety?" Utah asked Memphis and nodded toward me.

"I'd say she does right now," Memphis said.

He chuckled and chased me down to stand in front of me, but he was blurry. Like his body was somehow vibrating. He grabbed both my wrists and put my palms flat against his chest and then he moved his hands to hold onto my elbows. His mouth was moving, and he looked at me like he was expecting me to say something back to him, but I hadn't actually heard anything he said. Everything in my head sounded like the deafening white noise of rushing water. I could very easily imagine it was the sound of my blood coursing through my body with the fury of hurricane, because that's what it felt like was happening.

"What's your name?" He asked. I heard that one. But he knew my name?

"Tell me your name," he said again.

"Trista."

"There you are," he said.

Words that Jersey had said to me before too.

But Jersey had done it mid-crazy fucking.

Why the fuck couldn't I focus on anything?

"Can you look at me?" He asked. "Up here. My face. Can you look at me?"

He seemed to stop vibrating when my eyes found his.

"Can you feel my heart?" He asked. I shook my head and realized that my hands were still on his chest. That's why he was asking.

"Find it," he said. "Find my heartbeat, Trista."

My fingers instantly stiffened against him, like my nails could dig beneath the surface to the steady thumping underneath.

"There you go. Find it."

He waited another few seconds. "Feel it?"

I nodded when it was just suddenly apparent beneath my fingers. Pounding away like it was right under his skin rather than hidden away inside his ribs.

"Focus on it. Hard as you can. Until you can almost hear it, like it's the only thing in this room with you. Because you're standing right here in front of me. It's safe here. *You* are safe here. You can breathe. You can cry. You can scream. You can do anything you need to do because you're safe and you're right here."

My eyes dropped down to where my hands were digging into his chest in absolute disbelief, like I'd see something fucking magical happening right in front of me now that my lungs had decided to work again.

Was he a fucking witch?

Could men be witches?

He was probably just another regular demon.

"If you don't get it together soon, Trista, I'll have to start singing," he said. "And my rendition of *This Little Light of Mine* is mind-blowing, so I feel like I need to warn everybody here that it's on deck."

I was suddenly very aware of the sound of my own heart when I looked down between us to realize we were standing entirely too close. And I realized his hands were still holding firmly onto my elbows when he squeezed them gently again. I took my own hands back quickly and he let go of my arms the next second. He took a step backward immediately and waited until I looked back at his face again before he winked at me. At some point, Memphis had come around the island to stand right next to me too. And all I could wonder at that point was how long had we stood that way? Because I was instantly fucking exhausted like it was somehow the middle of the night already.

"The fuck was that?" Memphis asked Utah. "Are you a Trista whisperer?"

"*Trista Whisperer,*" he repeated and laughed. "I'll take that as an official title now. Panic attack. I grew up with a lot of kids who had issues with anxiety. I wanted to help them, so I learned how."

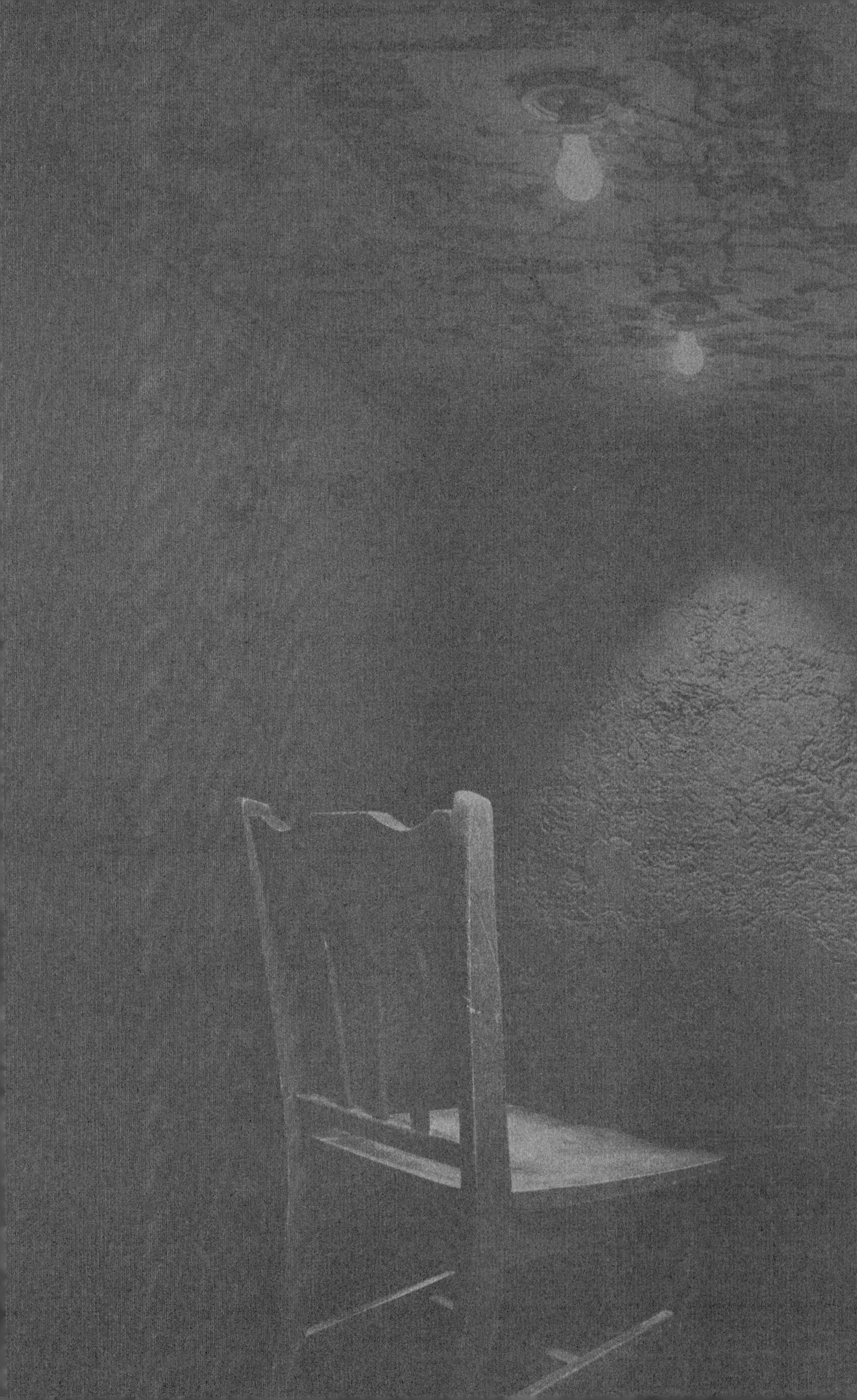

CHAPTER SEVENTEEN

jersey

It was a pill.

The small, blonde woman who worked the camera left it here. She'd stood in this corner, waited until I noticed her, and dropped a tiny, round pill for me to find once everyone else was gone. I only spent maybe four seconds wondering if I should swallow it; if it was something that would kill me. I decided even that would still be preferable to what was being done to me daily now. Swallowing it dry was less than pleasant. I felt it scratch and stick to my throat all the way down because every piece of me was terribly dehydrated. Even if the result was a painful death, it couldn't have been much more painful than a fucking rat trap slowly cracking its way down to the bones in my fingers and my hand. It couldn't have been worse than having nails driven through my feet hard enough that they'd broken into the concrete beneath. The amount of willpower that it took to get my feet free from the floor and then rip the nails out was astronomical, and it took every ounce of the energy that I had left.

It didn't take long before my breathing slowed, and a familiar slightly nauseous feeling accompanied by an instant drowsiness told me that my small blonde savior had left me a painkiller. It didn't take away all the pain. Whatever she'd brought me was fucking good, but there was *a lot* of pain and no chance that just one pill could erase it, even for a short time. All I wanted out of it was a solid round of sleep though, and it was looking like that wish would be granted. It left me wondering desperately who this woman was while I drifted into nothingness.

THE LEGS of that fucking table being dragged back across the floor into the room woke me up. I didn't feel any better. I'd slept right through the high from that painkiller and my body felt like it managed to age another twenty years in that timespan. Everything ached, my head was fuzzy, my mouth might as well have been made of fuzz, and I was in a piss poor mood.

"You ready for another round, New Jersey?" Bryson asked as he walked through the room. He came to kneel right in front of me and immediately picked up the two nails that I'd pulled out of my feet so I wouldn't be able to use them against anyone.

"Hope you're up to date on your shots," he said and laughed at how hilarious he found himself while he tossed the nails up and down a couple times in his good hand. I didn't figure it'd do much good to remind him that my body wouldn't last long enough for an infection to be the thing that killed me if he held this pace of torture with no treatment in between the sessions. My mind had an even worse chance at surviving by this point. Trista had been slowly fading. She'd started out so clearly. I could picture her anytime I wanted. Now, I had to close my eyes and concentrate if I wanted to see her, and concentrating on anything was taking a lot of effort. I hadn't had enough time with her for the memories of her to get me through this, and unfortunately there was another voice that was always ready and waiting to rush me at my lowest moments.

Van, do you ever think about us having a baby?

Another violent head shake to force her voice back out before I was hoisted from the floor and placed back in the chair at the table. I had to put actual effort into keeping my mind blank this time. Keeping her at bay was work now. I didn't even notice that Bryce had occupied the seat across from me at some point once my arms were fastened to the table again. I got another look at my mangled hand. I'd spent most of the time since they'd destroyed it asleep, but looking at it now that I was somewhat coherent was…rough.

"The girls have essentially created an online chatroom to make themselves available for communication," Bryson said and started laying instruments across the table in front of him. I didn't bother to look at them. I didn't need to add extra worry to what was being done here. He'd pick one and he'd use it, no matter which one caught my eye or my fear.

"But we still don't know where they actually are, New Jersey. Memphis really is the best at what she does. We've had everyone trying to break down the system that she has around it to trace it back to a home computer. Nobody has come up with anything at all."

He chattered on for another few minutes, or few seconds, about something. But I was seeing a tiny bundle wrapped in a Pooh Bear blanket and that was an image that I had no desire to fight off. I was defenseless against that one, no matter the circumstances around it.

"You still there, old man?" Bryson said and slammed his good hand down on top of my fucked up one. The pain scorching all the way up my left arm did bring my attention back to his face. I couldn't recall a single moment in my life when I'd been more pissed off about someone interrupting a memory. The image of a Winnie the Pooh blanket was quickly replaced with bloody, disturbing thoughts of beating Bryce's face until it was nothing more than pulp that slid through my fingers with each blow.

"Let's just get started," he said and swung an ancient fucking potato peeler from the tips of his fingers in between us. "I don't want you fading out before we've even had any fun this time."

"Cut the theatrics. Do what you're going to do and get the fuck back out."

"Awe. Drained all the attitude out of you already, did I? Which part did you in? Was it the nails? I imagine it was the nails," he said. "Anyway, you got a favorite tattoo in this mess?" He asked and waved the potato peeler over both forearms.

"I dislike them all equally."

"Yeah? One seems to stand out. Only one that's done in color," he said.

I put every bit of effort that I had left into not reacting to that bait at all. I couldn't stop whatever he decided to do about it either way.

"He was your daughter's favorite, right?"

But I couldn't have prevented reacting to that question if my life really did depend on it.

Because why the fuck would he know that?

Nate knew the shit that happened. We had talked about it when he hired me. But I couldn't pull up any memory of those conversations where we'd gone into personal details about Faith.

Faith.

Fuck.

Flashes of blonde hair and a tiny stuffed tiger flooded my brain.

Bryce scraped the potato peeler right down the top of my left forearm in one lone swipe to draw my focus back to him that time. The scream that came out of me would put any horror movie to shame.

"Why do you know about Tigger?" I asked through a desperate attempt to avoid crying.

The smile on his face was nearly enough to make me feral.

"Because I know everything about her, New Jersey. I know everything about Faith. And your fucked up wife, Liz."

Liz.

Van, do you ever think about us having a baby?

This was it. The moment I was about to crash and burn right out of control. Her face was right in front of me. The way that she looked at me the day that she told me she wanted to try for a baby; like I was the thing in the world that could always save her, that could always ground her, that could always keep her present. And here she was, to drag me back into the oblivion of the past. Because what she wanted from me was what I always wanted to be. My purpose in life was to become the man she thought she saw when she looked at me. But nothing about that day was a happy memory anymore. I was supposed to have a lifetime of cherishing that memory and the way that she looked at me. It was supposed to be the kind of thing that I could look back at with fondness when I was in a rocking chair on my front porch at eighty-years-old. Instead, when my wife's face came to mind with that look, it meant I was about to fade into some version of myself that I didn't know anymore; where the memories ruled and caused pain so deep that I ceased to exist because I couldn't survive them.

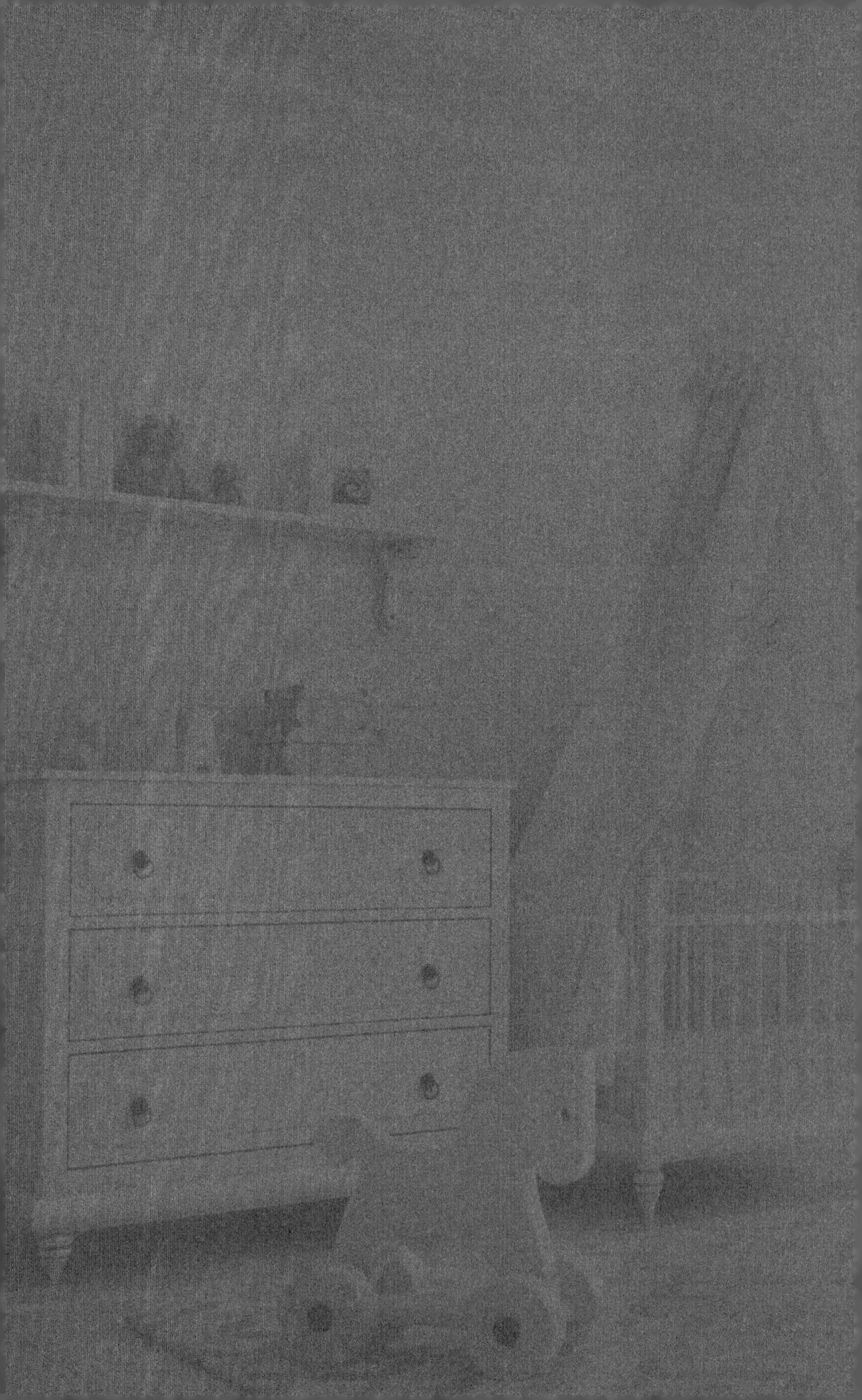

CHAPTER EIGHTEEN

jersey

THEN

Liz placed herself directly in my lap in the ridiculously overstuffed chair that she'd begged to have for nights like this in front of the fireplace in our living room.

"Van," she said and put both hands around my neck to get her fingers into my hair. "Do you ever think about us having a baby?"

In about seven seconds, maximum, she would feel the response from my dick underneath her.

We'd talked about children before we were married, and it was something we both wanted. I was on board for filling this house with as many kids as it would hold, but Liz settled pretty squarely on two. As she was the one who'd have to carry and birth them, I didn't feel like I had much room to build a case for my house-full. Nothing about it was a genuine deal breaker for me, not back then and not now. As long as *she* stayed in this house, I'd be a happy man. She'd always been a little rocky; a little unsteady when it came to emotions. She'd tried to hurt herself when she was younger, but it was only once. She said she was treated for it, and she'd never done it again, but the emotional scars were always there, just beneath the surface. Even I could see them. Sometimes she went through bouts of deep, deep lows where she cried all the time, over everything and nothing. I tried everything husbands were always told to do to help their wives out of those moments, but none of it ever worked. She didn't seem to see the flowers. She wasn't interested in getting dressed to go out for dinner. When I cooked for her, she sat across from me at the table and just pushed her food around her plate with her fork. She looked tired all the time, so I'd let her sleep when that's what she wanted to do. I'd run baths for her in a massively oversized tub that I'd had installed in our bathroom after I learned baths made her feel better. I'd wait beside the tub with a towel, so I was there when she was ready to get back out.

At some point, she'd just wake up one day better. She was back to herself. She would get dressed, she'd put on makeup, she'd go back to doing the grocery shopping and the cooking, the house ended up cleaned every few days, and she seemed happy again. It just came and went in waves that were inexplicable to me. Sometimes it was overwhelming and exhausting. Sometimes she was hard to love, but I couldn't fathom *not* loving her. Loving her even at her most difficult was still better than not having her.

I'd been ready for a baby from the moment that I married her. So, if she was ready for a baby, I was more than willing to do my part to make sure it happened. She knew babies were difficult and they sometimes strained marriages and relationships, but we both wanted children. If she believed she was finally in the mindset to move into that part of our lives, I was more than ready to do whatever she needed of me. And while I thought that just meant being present for sex when she said she wanted sex, nothing about that was true. Liz went through the effort of changing her diet, tracking cycles for the best days to try. I was suddenly told that some people believed certain positions led to creating a certain gender. Turned out there was even a right and a wrong kind of underwear for men to wear when they were trying to conceive a child, but I didn't even think twice about any of it. I was prepared to do anything she asked of me, even when she went so far as to tell me that using my own hands when she wasn't around was off limits because we needed *potency*. She was so excited, and it was beautifully contagious.

I wasn't keeping track the way that Liz had been, but it couldn't have taken more than a few months of some intensely mind-blowing orgasms before she was screaming from the bathroom. And my semi-fucked up head went somewhere sketchy anyway. I nearly broke the door down trying to get into that bathroom to her. She couldn't keep her hands from shaking when she held the pregnancy test out toward me, cradling it in her palms like the thing itself was a gift from the heavens. I'd never seen a single human who could look stunning when they cried, but Liz did. Usually, you think of puffy eyes, splotchy skin, and a snotty nose. Liz though, just the balls of her cheeks turned slightly pink. The color in her lips brightened. Her eyes looked bigger, deeper; like they were finally opening to let me see beyond them, to the otherwise unreachable things that went on inside her mind. She looked like she came to life when she cried.

"We're having a baby?" I asked, like a dumbass, while I took the test that answered that question for me from her trembling hands. She could only nod her head before the pools of tears spilled over and began their course down her pink-tinted cheeks.

"Are you happy?" I asked, because her emotions were a true rollercoaster. And just when I thought I had a handle on understanding them, those motherfuckers would pull an immediate one-eighty. A sob shook her whole body and she tried to say yes, but she mostly just choked on the word. Her arms were around my neck a second later and I scooped both arms around her waist to lift her right off the floor in that hug. She buried her face in between my neck and shoulder like she was trying to burrow inside me while I held us both there.

CHAPTER NINETEEN
trista

I woke up to what smelled like bacon and had never been more confused in my life. Kyle didn't come in to cook for us. Memphis didn't cook. I still got out of that bed like it could've been on fire for the smell of bacon though. I caught sight of myself in the full length mirror in the hallway and wondered if I should go back and put actual clothes on. I'd gotten used to sleeping in just the black button-down shirt of Jersey's that I'd taken and claimed as my own, but it covered everything well enough. And there was *bacon* somewhere in that house screaming my name.

Utah moving around Jersey's kitchen like he'd been in it for the last few months was more than my brain could process this early. He laughed when he spotted me, standing dumbfounded at the end of the hallway.

"Yeah, bacon gets everybody up," he said, and his eyes roamed up and down my entire body. "You're like a walking cliché."

"What?" I asked and also looked down at the front of my body like I was suddenly unaware of the way that I looked.

"Are you also spraying his cologne on your pillow before you go to sleep? Writing his name inside hearts in a notebook?" He asked and laughed at himself.

"I don't think I'd like you very well if you weren't also the source of the bacon."

"You feeling alright?" He asked and left me just as fucking confused as I was when I woke up.

"Uh, yeah?"

"Panic attacks are hard on people," he said, like I should be experiencing a hangover of some kind. He pushed a plate full of food across the island toward me.

"What is this?" I asked.

"Breakfast?"

But I looked at that plate the same way I would have if he'd shoved a live snake across the countertop at me.

"I didn't poison it," he said with a laugh. "Why would I let you try to dig my heart out of my chest to ground you during a panic attack if I just planned to kill you the next day?"

"I don't know. Jersey asked me on a date just to throw my ass into the trunk of his car when he picked me up for it."

"And *that's* the guy you're in love with?" He asked and laughed again.

"Be careful with that word," Memphis said from behind me. "They're both super skittish about it. Is that bacon?"

Utah choked on nothing for the second time in her presence before he cleared his throat and forced himself to look away from Memphis. I looked at her too. We hadn't been here all that long, but we were both comfortable with the fact that we were women. I slept in Jersey's shirt. She slept in volleyball shorts and a tiny white shirt that showed her belly button and usually her nipples through the thin fabric. I had those body parts too, so it didn't bother me to see them on her any more than it bothered her that she could probably see my ass cheeks from time to time. It had only been her and me in here. Kyle didn't just drop in unexpectedly. Utah was the only one struggling to handle it. And he cleared his throat a second time before he turned back toward the stove.

"Some kind of Indiana allergy going on over there, big guy?" I asked and took my bacon with me to walk right up behind him. "Or is it maybe something from Tennessee?" I asked just barely loud enough for him to hear it. The way that he glared at me was probably the cutest thing I'd ever seen a grown man do. I couldn't even remember what I'd found so frightening about him yesterday.

"Oh, I'm going to enjoy the shit out of this," I whispered to him and swiped another piece of bacon from the plate that he had beside the stove.

"I made you bacon," he whispered, like I was in the middle of betraying a lifelong friend just by realizing he had a crush.

"Yeah, and then made fun of my—," I stopped myself. My boyfriend? The love of my life? What the fuck was he? "Jersey," I finally added.

"*Your…Jersey,*" he repeated and laughed. "Awe. You're barely even a grownup, huh?"

"Oh, shut up. You don't look like you're any older than me."

"Twenty-six."

"Shit."

He laughed. "I'm going to start keeping score if you're going to make it this easy to win."

"Utah?" Memphis asked and froze the man mid-movement. I started to giggle and smacked my hand right over my mouth when he glared at me another time.

"Go ahead and keep score," I whispered and ran away from him to sit on the other side of the island beside Memphis. He did finally work up the nerve to turn to face us again, and I think my face would've been in physical pain if I'd smiled any wider. He didn't say anything, but he focused all his energy on Memphis.

"How good are you?" She asked.

"Good," he said, without even letting a full second go by.

"At what? What are we talking about?" I interrupted.

"What'd you have in mind?" He asked her, ignoring me completely.

"It's going to start moving at an unpleasant pace now that they know we're seeing what's happening to Jersey. They'll do awful things to him. Probably worse with every day that passes to try to force us to do something."

Imagining the kinds of things Bryson would do to him made my stomach twist. Not even bacon sounded good anymore.

"Our best bet will be finding a way to use Trista as bait. They need to believe we're giving her to them. They'll want it all done in Philadelphia. Try to make us go to them. I have no doubt that's where they're keeping Jersey, but I'm under the impression that they're filming these torture sessions in one place and taking the footage somewhere else to be uploaded. Tracing it back to an original location probably just isn't possible from my end. And they don't plan on trading with us. We have no leverage that would make them tell us where he is."

"You want to send them in one direction after her, while I go the other after him?" He asked.

"Are you that kind of good?" She asked.

He smirked at her challenge. "Indy told me a little about what you found on our organization, Memphis. Distracting them in one place with the possibility of retrieving Trista doesn't mean they'll leave New Jersey unguarded somewhere. Our President isn't an idiot. He might be an asshole. But he's not a stupid one. He'll have an endless number of people at his disposal to cover both directions."

"So, you're *not* that kind of good," she concluded, with a tone that I'd never heard come out of her. Like she'd decided that it was that way and spoken it into reality with her words alone. I watched his already broad shoulders expand even further while he breathed in deeply.

"I'm going to tell Indy to come here," he said after an uncomfortable few moments of tense silence. "He can help you. And once they figure out that we're helping you, he'll be in trouble too. I'd rather have all of you in one place if I'm going to have to keep all of you safe."

Had he just backed down from her challenge simply by changing the subject?

"Kyle probably won't like us adding more people," Memphis said and glanced at me. It was my turn to nearly choke on nothing that time just at hearing his name again. I'd never fucking get over it now.

"Seriously, what is it with his name?" Memphis asked. "Just tell me."

"Kyle?" Utah asked.

I nearly spit my coffee out.

"Trista," Memphis demanded.

"He's the groundskeeper here," I said to Utah. "I spent a lot of time trying to guess Jersey's real name. Picked a bunch of douchebag names to piss him off. Started moaning *Kyle* to make it worse. I obviously had no idea that he had an actual friend named Kyle. He, uh, didn't take it very well."

"And he what? Stuffed you back in the trunk?" Utah asked. "Like a real gentleman."

"Umm, no. He did — other things."

"Gross," Memphis said and picked up her whole plate to take it with her back down the hall to her room. "Call Indy. Let me know when he's here. I'm going to start tracing."

"You got it, boss," Utah said and watched her until she disappeared around the corner at the end of the hallway. He didn't move again until we heard her door close.

"That's cute. Jersey started calling her *boss lady*."

"*Bossy lady* feels more appropriate right now."

CHAPTER TWENTY
trista

I spent most of that day hiding in Jersey's garage while Kyle paced around nervously to watch every move that this body work person made around Persephone to inspect the damage from the bullets. Memphis was on edge and very clearly didn't have any interest in company today. I couldn't blame her. What we wanted to achieve was sitting squarely on her shoulders, and it felt pretty fucking impossible right now.

"You're probably making him uncomfortable," I said to Kyle when he made another nervous lap around the car.

"He should be uncomfortable," Kyle said. "You know what Van would do to all three of us if he screwed up?"

"I know what he'd do to me," I said. "But it's probably nothing like what he'd do to you two."

Kyle paused to look at me on his next lap after that statement.

"Do I even want to know?" He asked.

"I slashed all four tires when I tried to get away from him once," I said. "Left Jersey handcuffed to a bed. And ran."

I laughed when his jaw nearly unhinged as it fell open.

"How are you even alive?" He asked. "God, you must be the lay of a fucking lifetime."

"I think I just needed to be delivered alive if he wanted to get paid the full amount for me," I said, a little surprised at how much that upset me to say out loud. Kyle came to sit next to me.

"I think we probably both know that's not true," he said quietly. "And I don't even know you."

"But you know *him*," I said and nodded.

"Van has some — issues," he said.

"That's a nice way to word it."

"Some crazy PTSD stuff from what we had to do, something even worse from what happened with his family," he said. "But he's always had this thing about him. This caretaker, protector, whatever you might call it, *thing*. I think he's younger than me, and he still took it upon himself to take care of me."

"By letting you stay here?" I asked.

"No, I mean when we served," he said. I watched him swallow hard, and he started to squeeze his hands into fists just to release them and ball them up again. Dandy appeared out of absolutely nowhere to sit right at his feet and his left hand went straight to her head.

"We were in —," he paused and smiled. "Well, let's just say that we were in an unnamed, unfriendly city. We had this name for Van, because he did the nickname thing and he also had this weird as fuck anxiety reaction when things got intense. Somebody started calling him *Serk*, because he went berserk when he got overwhelmed. It was scary, but as long as it was aimed in the right direction, it kept us all alive more than once. He was in that messed up headspace and running between buildings under fire. He ran right over a grenade without ever seeing it. I shoved his ass as hard as I could and tried to kick it away. The blast seemed to miss him for the most part, but I was still close enough to catch it. I don't really remember it from my own point of view. A couple of guys told me about it afterward."

"This all sounds like *he* owes *you*," I interrupted. "Not the other way around."

"Yeah, it fucked me up good," he said and rolled up the left leg of his jeans to show me skin that had very clearly been burned and looked like it had been physically chewed on by an animal. He showed me similar marks that went all the way up the left side of his body, across his ribs.

"Van came right back for me," he said. "Something snapped him out of the *Serk zone*, the other guys called it. He went full-blown mom lifting a car off their baby mode instead, dug me out of the blast rubble, carried me to the next building. Forced his way inside, killed whoever was in there to make sure it was empty. Stayed there with me while the other guys carried on. We still had a job to do, and it still needed finishing. But I obviously wouldn't be any help in getting it done. They left most of the medical supplies with Van, wished him luck, and went on their way. No hard feelings about it because that's just how it went. Van should've gone with them. To this day, I don't really know how he got us out of there. The things he would've had to do..." his words trailed off right alongside his mind. I reached out and squeezed his right hand, because something in me told me that I needed to. I couldn't say any actual words. I had a pretty messed up life, but I'd never had to do or see the kinds of things that he'd experienced.

"I remember weird pieces of it," he said quietly. "Sometimes bits of it come back like a movie scene, but it plays out in my mind like a dream rather than something that actually happened. And I've never worked up the nerve to ask him what was real and what wasn't about those memories. It's cowardly, I know. I'm the reason that he would've had to do some of those fucked up things just to keep us alive and keep moving. I know it added to the shit that he already struggles with in his own head."

"I don't imagine he'd blame you for any of that," I said quietly.

"No," he agreed. "He wouldn't. Because he takes care of people when he cares for them. Regardless of what sacrifice that means making on his end. Turns out you can't ever get away from him once he's decided he cares about you," he said and laughed. "But he means well in his own fucked up way."

The most accurate way to describe Jersey that I'd ever heard.

"Bad time?" Utah asked from the side entry to the garage behind both of us. I panicked a little when I realized I was still squeezing Kyle's hand nearly as hard as I could, but his presence brought me a sense of comfort that no one else around here did, even if I couldn't prevent myself from giggling like a psycho every time someone said his name. He knew the Jersey who none of us knew. The one who existed before he became *Jersey*. Talking to him wasn't anything at all like talking to Jersey, but he was giving me the tiniest glimpses into what existed behind those icy blue eyes. I could feel like there was a piece of Jersey here between us when Kyle talked about him.

"Indy just got here," Utah said. "And Memphis has something else to show us."

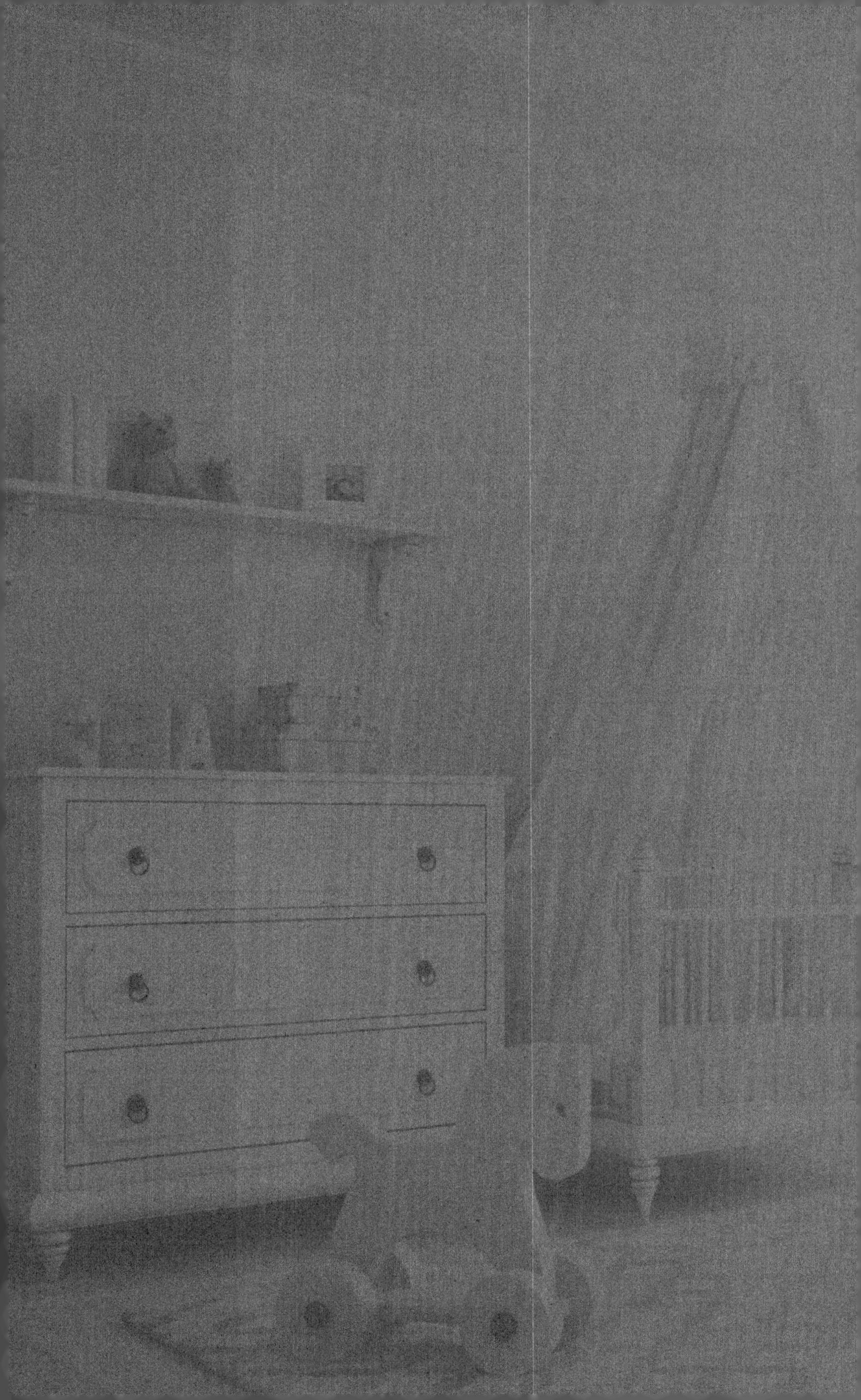

CHAPTER TWENTY-ONE

jersey

THEN

We'd only had the baby home for a few days. Faith Elizabeth. She was perfect in every way. Healthy and full of chubby, little baby rolls. Somehow, also the single most frightening thing I'd ever experienced in my life. And that was saying something coming from a man like me. We'd gone to the baby class, the one that was supposed to tell men how to behave during delivery. I knew where to put pressure on Liz's hips, how to rub her back, to let her try to break the bones in my hand when it was time to push. But for the life of me, I couldn't understand why there hadn't been a class dedicated entirely to surviving the first week with a new baby. I would've paid any amount of money just to have had someone tell me how the fuck I was supposed to drive the twenty minutes from the hospital back to the house with a brand new, totally defenseless human, who I created, strapped into the car seat behind me. There was absolutely no way that contraption could keep her alive if someone drove right into the side of my car. And then I'd have to kill everyone involved. What a shitty way to start parenthood that would be.

As far as what I was supposed to be doing once we did make it to the house — a twenty-minute drive that turned into an hour because nothing in this fucking world could force me to move that car over 20mph — where were the instructions that told me how to help my wife? Anything at all would've been appreciated. The nurses explained that Faith would need to eat at least every three hours, maybe even more often since Liz wanted to breastfeed exclusively and something about babies burning through breast milk faster than formula. They explained that her diapers were going to be horrendous for a few days but that it would get better; that she'd need changed very frequently in the beginning months. Sometimes it might take as little as holding her directly against my skin to calm her down, and sometimes she'd scream and cry for no apparent reason and there would be nothing we could do to stop it.

That was it.

That was the entirety of the fucking lesson.

Welcome to being a dad.

Good luck, keep her alive, bye.

We were okay for three whole days. Or maybe it had actually been closer to seven months. Fuck if I knew. Time was the most foreign concept I'd ever known in that first week. Liz said from the very beginning of her pregnancy that she always wanted to breastfeed. I never understood why, but she talked about it endlessly. The benefits for both of them, the bonding, that she'd be able to continue caring for our baby beyond keeping her inside. It mattered to Liz, so it mattered to me; even if I didn't fully understand why bottles and formula were the enemy in my wife's mind. But postpartum depression hit Liz like a fucking freight train.

At some point during the fourth night, Liz stopped getting out of bed when Faith would cry. I touched her arm, thinking maybe she was just exhausted enough to sleep right through the wailing. But she was wide awake. She shoved my hand off and rolled away. I did the only thing I could think of doing, as a male with perfectly sculpted but completely useless nipples. I changed Faith's diaper, took my shirt off, and paced the halls of our house holding her against me as tightly as I could without feeling like I was squishing her soft, little body. She fell back asleep in the middle of me telling her that Mommy just needed a break for a minute, and I'd never felt more successful in my life. I went back into her room to lay her into her crib – because I remembered the *safe sleep* speech like it had been driven into my brain with a hammer. She *had* to be by herself in a crib. Except she was awake and screaming at me again the moment my hands were off of her. Scared the fuck out of me so I picked her right back up and went to the doorway of our bedroom.

"Liz," I said quietly. "She's going to need to eat soon, honey."

She didn't move. She didn't say anything.

So, I went back to pacing around the house. Talking about everything and nothing.

This is a picture of your grandparents.

Do you hate the color of your bedroom? Because I do. Nobody likes yellow. Well, I guess Mama does, and we're not really allowed to argue with her.

Maybe we can convince her to change it to orange someday, huh? We'll say it's for Tigger rather than Pooh Bear. He's better anyway.

But she didn't fall back asleep this time. She continued to cry, and it only got louder with every hour that passed. I couldn't get Liz out of bed. Nothing I said or did got her up, no matter the noise that Faith made. Liz started crying too at some point, but she wouldn't even say anything.

My parents only lived ten minutes away. They managed to get me through the first week of being a baby without letting me starve to death. My mom would know what to do. I tucked Faith back into the car seat of my nightmares and put her back in the car to try to mentally prepare myself to drive again with her in the vehicle. Ten minutes. We could make that drive.

The sun was barely starting to come up and my parents liked

their sleep. There was no way they'd already just be awake this time of day. I probably should've called them first, but my frantic pounding on their front door along with the sounds of a screaming infant brought my mom to the door quickly enough. I told her what the night had been like and she just fucking left the house. Told me to keep rocking Faith, told me to hold her close and tight. That if I needed a minute, to give the baby to my dad, who also looked horrified by that idea. Then she was gone, in her car, driving away.

She was back in record time with a small grocery bag though. She had me hand Faith off to my dad and she showed me how to prepare a bottle with the formula she'd also bought. She showed me how to warm it since Faith was used to breast milk that was also warm. She told me over and over again that Faith wouldn't know what to do because she'd never used a bottle either, but that I could make it easier by holding it at a certain angle, by feeding her while I held her against me with my shirt off. She said that when Faith had her fill of the bottle, to hold her up on my shoulder and pat her back until she burped, to change her diaper again, and then she'd be back asleep in no time. I tried desperately to absorb everything that she was firing into my brain. But as soon as she had me set up in my dad's rocking chair next to their fireplace, baby tucked in close and both of us trying to learn how to use that bottle, my mom was headed back for the door. She had to have seen the absolute panic on my face when I asked where she was going because she actually laughed out loud at it.

"I'm going back to your house to be with your wife, Vance," she said, like it should've been obvious. "Sometimes people get so caught up in loving the new baby that they seem to forget the mother still needs love and care too. Especially the mothers who struggled emotionally before the baby."

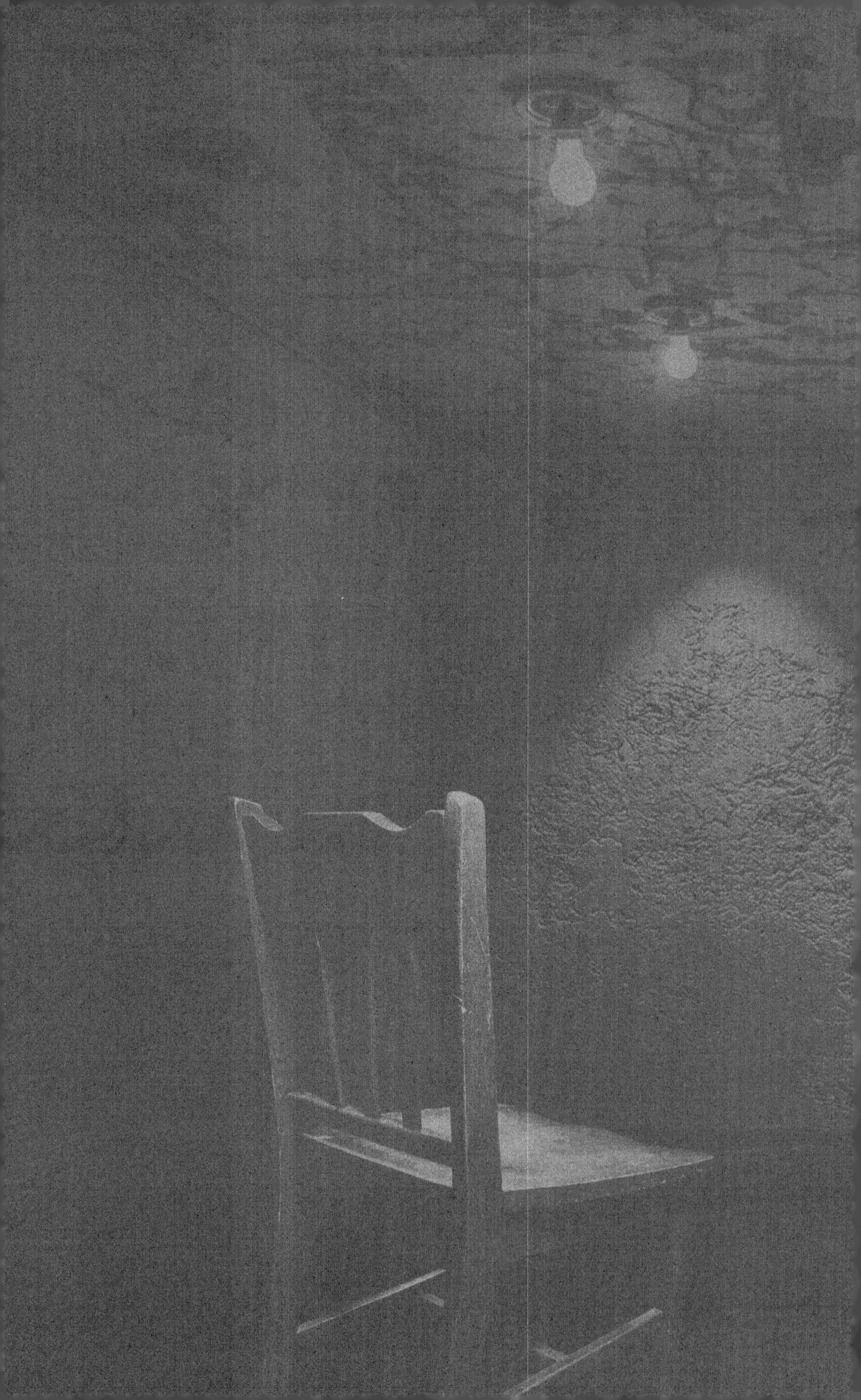

CHAPTER TWENTY-TWO

jersey

"Look alive, pretty boy."

Intense pin prickles in the hair on the back of my head told me someone was grabbing it, and then blinding white light in front of my eyes suggested someone had slammed my forehead against something solid. I tried to blink myself back into reality, but all I wanted to do was sleep. I was surprised to find that I could move my arms. I thought I'd been strapped back into the weird table handcuffs.

"Don't move," a new voice said firmly. My eyes still hadn't adjusted, so I just listened to that one.

"Can't have you dying already, New Jersey," Bryson said from somewhere nearby.

I tried to remember what put me into that spiral, what sent me back to Liz. Whatever it was, the top of the table felt cool against the side of my face and that took precedence for a few seconds while I let all my weight slump forward the rest of the way onto it. Then it hit me like Bryce's fist had been doing.

"How do you know about Tigger?" I asked again. I managed to

get my eyes open and focused well enough to realize someone was bandaging part of my left forearm.

Fucking potato peeler.

I heard Bryce laugh. He'd moved closer again.

"I remember when Dad hired you," he said. "You were supposed to become the best. You were supposed to be smart enough to be able to do whatever he told you to do, supposed to be able to survive anything. But your worst trait is how fucking stupid you become the moment you feel anything at all. He thought he gave you enough time to just get over it. But here you are, still making dumbass choices over pussy. Still not piecing together what actually happened to your own family. I tried to tell him that if you were even half as good as he thought you'd be, you'd figure it out and then it all would've been a waste. Turns out, he was right on that part. You were *only* smart enough to do the job you were told to do."

My brain hurt too much to try to sift through the insults and the nonsense to get down to what he was really telling me. Instead, I laid there with my eyes closed and hoped I'd just back fall asleep. I'd worry about thinking and logic later.

"He needs water," the voice right next to me said.

"No, he doesn't."

"He won't make it more than another day or two at this rate if you don't give his body what it needs to withstand this kind of torture. If you need him functioning for these recordings, he's going to need water, food, a minute in between to recover."

Still not piecing together what actually happened to your own family.

I rocketed out of that chair like I hadn't been tortured, starved, and dehydrated for who fucking knew how many days and whirled around to look for Bryson.

"See," that motherfucker said immediately. "He's perfectly fine."

"*What actually happened,*" I repeated.

"Liz was really pretty. Do you think she was depressed all the time because she really should've been with someone better than you from the start? Someone who knew how to keep her happy?"

Even through the rage intoxication, I could sort out that those words were weightless taunting. Anger-inducing all the same, but just words. And I wanted *real* answers.

"What happened?" I asked.

"You never stopped to consider how convenient it was that everyone who knew you was wiped off the face of the Earth in a single night just for someone to show up and offer you a job where you couldn't have an identity?"

"The implication being that Nate had them *killed*," I concluded. I did have a brain. And it worked. But I needed him to say the words. Something in me still hesitated about it.

No, I absolutely hadn't dug any deeper into their deaths myself. I couldn't. I wasn't even human anymore in the days after. Liz had never been stable. That was no secret. Everyone who knew her already knew that about her. She put up almost no fight when I suggested leaving Faith with my parents each time I was deployed because she also wanted our daughter to be cared for in the way that a helpless infant needed. It took an outrageous amount of love on her part to be able to acknowledge that she was not always the thing who would be best for her own child. And she crashed hard every time I had to leave. She knew that. I knew that. My parents knew that. The police were told that.

But everything about this could also have just been another layer to the torture game that we were playing. What better way to break a man apart than by making him realize that the thing he'd been devastated by for years didn't actually happen the way that he'd believed?

CHAPTER TWENTY-THREE
trista

The people inside Nate's organization got weirder by the day.

From the foul-mouthed, pushy asshole with the face I wanted to sit on every second of every day also being this deeply loyal and protective, unrecognizable father figure all the way to the new muscled truck man who started out terrifying and morphed into a soft-spoken kid with a crush before my very eyes, they were all just fucking strange.

I wouldn't have imagined Indy looking anything like the way he actually did either. He was sitting next to Memphis at the island in the kitchen by the time I'd followed Utah back into the house, but he stood to come toward us as soon as we'd walked into the room. Another unreasonably tall man to tolerate. Five-foot-five used to feel average, but Jersey was at least six-two. Utah and Indy were about the same height, but maybe just barely shorter than Jersey. I had the sudden urge to ask Memphis to stand up to really find out if I was that much taller than her. I felt like a giant around her anyway just because she was a damn rail compared to me.

Indy stuck his right hand out in my direction to shake mine and my eyes lingered for a second on the bright purple nail polish on his fingers. He wore wide black rimmed glasses that made his light blue eyes easier to see. And he had perfectly styled light brown hair that was so big and fluffy that it actually made him look a couple inches taller when I was closer to him.

"Yep, I can see why he'd just go blind to the millions being offered for you," Indy said and pulled my hand all the way to his face to kiss it.

"Indy," Utah said.

"What?"

"Regular people say things like *it's nice to meet you*," Utah said.

"It's alright," I interrupted. "I don't think there's any room left in this house for *regular* now."

"Hey, team of misfits, can we assemble?" Memphis asked.

Utah held his index finger up to wave a circle in the air between the three of us to tell us to get moving. Indy sat on one side of Memphis, and I sat on the other while Utah hovered around behind all three of us. Memphis made a point to make eye contact with me for several seconds before she looked back to the computer to play the next video. We all watched in silence that time while they set Jersey up at that table again, while Bryce asked about the tattoos, and picked up a potato peeler. Jersey looked worse than I ever could've imagined a man like him looking, but something about him shifted after the first couple swipes from Bryce's potato peeler down his arm. He wasn't reacting to the pain anymore. He wasn't reacting to anything. He was awake, but *he* wasn't there. We watched until there was blood everywhere, until Jersey's body gave in and slumped forward.

"They cut the sound out here," Memphis said. "I'm going to go back in a couple minutes to try to recover it, because Jersey takes part in the conversation actively once he's awake again. And he's super pissed about something that's said."

They brought in someone else who started to treat the wounds covering Jersey's body while he laid against the table without moving. I dropped my face down into my hands and forced myself to breathe, until I felt a hand squeeze my shoulder. I don't know why I expected it to be Memphis. She acted like physical contact actually burned her pasty white ghost skin, but I was surprised to find the hand on my shoulder attached to Utah.

"You don't have to watch," he said quietly. "We can do this part."

I only shook my head. His hand never moved. I went back to watching the screen. We watched through the part Memphis described, where Jersey burst to his feet suddenly and whipped around to look at Bryson with pure rage on his face again. The way Bryson continued to smile through their conversation made me feel sick. I'd seen that smile on more than one occasion. It was the same way that he looked at me years and years ago, when I first tried to tell the *family* what Dalton had been doing to me. Nate insisted that we make it a giant family discussion. A fucking spectacle for everyone to take part in, where they could take turns calling me a liar, calling me a whore, calling me anything they pleased because I dared to accuse one of his sons of such actions.

I hadn't even realized I was sobbing again until I watched Jersey lunge at Bryce. I couldn't imagine where the power or the strength came from. He was able to get Bryce to the floor underneath him before two other people rushed in to drag him off. The camera shifted suddenly when someone bumped into it as Bryce got back to his feet and went right back to mercilessly attacking Jersey. The brief look at a small blonde woman who was looking right at us with eyes just like mine before the camera was readjusted again sent me straight to my own feet, in a desperate attempt to escape the video, the laptop, this place. The stool toppled while I tried to get away and the sound echoed through the house like an explosion before I crashed right into Utah's open arms. They locked around the upper half of my body and squeezed until he was holding me so tight that my body was physically unable to shake because of it.

"Oh okay, but when *I* say she's hot, I'm being inappropriate. You just look for any chance to *Indy* me, but you get to do *this*," Indy said.

"Indy," Utah hissed.

"I think maybe it's your timing, my man," Memphis whispered to Indy.

"You don't have to take his side just because he's got arms like that, you know? He wouldn't be able to do a damn thing on his own. Absolutely useless if he isn't told exactly what to do."

Memphis chuckled a little. "Yeah, I've got one of those too."

"Can you two maybe shut up?" Utah asked. Snapped, really. "He's still alive, Trista." I felt his chin directly on the top of my head. I knew he was alive. I just watched him get pummeled and still manage to look back at the camera another time, but seeing my mother's face wasn't something I was prepared to deal with in addition to everything else today. I tried to push away from Utah and his arms tightened once more.

"You still don't have to stay in here," he whispered before he let go. I tried desperately to wipe the tears from my face before I turned back toward the others, and Utah just stood there and waited, like he was entirely prepared to go right back to squeezing me to death if I were to need it.

"I need to figure out where they're keeping him," Memphis spoke up first. "That's the holdup. Once we know, we can just take our chances on using *runner up Jersey* here and go for it," she said and waved her hand toward Utah.

"Ouch," he mumbled. "Right in the pride. Y'all can see him too, right? He's got to be a good fifteen years older than me. I can do whatever he can."

"Easy there, cowboy," Indy chuckled. "You can tone down the *y'alls*. We'll wait to measure dicks until he's at least back here where we can all watch, okay?"

"Jersey took the tracking device from you when we found you at that creepy house in the woods?" I suggested.

"It's not transmitting," Memphis said. "I look for it every day."

"Well," Indy interjected. "Let's see if we can *make* it transmit."

CHAPTER TWENTY-FOUR
trista

I couldn't understand a fucking word of the conversation that was taking place between Indy and Memphis while they were trying to figure out how to recover the deleted audio from that clip, or how they might trace any of it back to an original location. I stuck around long enough to listen to them discuss how Utah and I would make the trip to Philly to break into some place that Nate owned but rarely used, setup some kind of webcam to record a ton of footage of me just hanging out in this place, Memphis would put it out into the world of the internet to make it look like a live feed and send it off to Nate's people. Then Utah and I would use some form of black magic to break Jersey out of wherever they were keeping him.

I slipped out of the kitchen and out of the house while they continued talking though. I stood just outside the door and watched Kyle's fire burn for a minute, but I really wasn't sure that I wanted his company tonight either. Instead, I ended up lying on a lounge chair next to the pool just staring at the stars.

Kyle hadn't been wrong. There was no noise out here, no light, nothing at all to interrupt the quiet or the dark. It was probably amazing if you didn't have a lifetime of shitty memories behind you and nothing but anxiety about the future to plague every second of your time. I told myself earlier that I was done crying about this. It never solved anything. It just made everyone stare at you that much harder, until they noticed that you saw them and then they went out of their way to avoid looking at you. I didn't want to be *that* person in this weird collaboration. But I had to admit that it was painfully difficult to see my mother's face when I wasn't ready for it.

It still hurt. She'd done so little mothering in our short time together, and I really did let go of most of the anger over that years ago. The hurt over it still resurfaced every so often though. She was all I had left in the world when my dad passed away, and I would've thought she felt the same way about me. We should've been the thing the other counted on to get through it, but I was only six and I couldn't be the help that she needed.

She tried for a while, until one day I noticed that I had to start getting food out for myself when I was hungry. Hard bread and a single jar of peanut butter didn't last all that long though. I realized quickly after that that I was able to just stay awake all night in front of the TV in the living room if I wanted, but that left me wanting to sleep during the day and very much awake again the next night. I reversed that routine quickly when the TV stopped turning on and I had nothing to keep me company through the nights. The dirty clothes in the hamper in my closet flowed out into my room and eventually I had to start wearing some of those again because I didn't know how to do laundry. I remembered very clearly staring at the washer and dryer, but I wasn't even tall enough to reach the buttons to figure out which ones did what.

I don't remember deciding that I was going to stop going to school, but I noticed after a few days of my mother being gone all night and coming home to go right to bed herself as the sun came up that no one woke me up to get ready to actually go. I didn't know how to set an alarm clock. I didn't know how to fucking tell time. I was six. I very distinctly remember someone showing up at the house one day to explain to my mother that she'd come from my school and that I absolutely needed to go back to school. She asked about my health and our situation. She asked if my mother needed help with me. I heard my mom mention for the first time that she'd been seeing someone new and that he was going to start taking care of both of us; that I wouldn't be going back to that school anyway because I'd be starting at a new one soon. Those things weren't even lies. She moved us right into the same house where Satan lived and ruled.

"Doing alright out here?" Utah asked from fucking right behind me.

"Fuck, man."

He only smirked while he laid back in the lounge chair next to mine, like he was getting comfy and preparing to stay.

"What are you doing out here?"

He laughed that time. "My bad. Would you like me to just leave?"

How outrageously tempted I was to just say yes.

"It's hard to listen to them talk technology and electronics for that long," he said.

"I didn't imagine you'd be okay with leaving Memphis in there with someone who hits on quite literally everyone."

He glared at me. "He's been talking to her for years. If he had any real interest in her, I would've heard about it by now."

"When do we leave for Philly?" I asked, lying back to get comfortable again myself since he didn't seem like he planned to leave.

"Eleven-hour trip if we drive straight through. We should probably go as soon as we can."

"Jersey's car won't be done by tomorrow for us to leave that quickly."

He chuckled. "I'm more than capable of driving my own truck."

"Oh, I wasn't really worried about *you*," I explained. "Something about Jersey and that truck and you and all of it feels like it probably won't go over very well with *him*."

"He's going to have a problem with my truck?"

"He's going to have a problem with everything about you."

CHAPTER TWENTY-FIVE

jersey

They left me in a crumpled heap on the concrete again. Bryson had paid no mind to that doctor's several warnings that I was already too close to dying for him to continue with his assault, but I'd pissed him off to no end by managing to be this close to death and still getting a couple of solid hits in of my own. Their doctor tried to bandage and cover all the wounds from the last few torture sessions, but nothing had been done about the way that my entire body ached. A single bottle of water was left on the floor directly in the center of the room, but I couldn't make myself move to retrieve it just yet. Just like I couldn't make myself move to my regular corner to see if the angel of a camerawoman had left any gifts for me there. The kind of pain that my body was experiencing still didn't even come close to the kind of chaos that was happening in my brain and my heart.

I tried to say Trista's name out loud to pull my head away from the memories and the spiral that would take place any minute now if I tried to sift through the shit that Bryson had said. If I let myself start to wonder what had really happened to Liz and Faith or my parents, everything I'd ever felt about my wife from the last few years would be right at the surface again to devastate my very existence. That was a dangerous cliff to play right at the edge of while my physical existence was also being tested daily right now. But I couldn't get away from it. My entire face hurt, my mouth and my throat were too dry to actually speak. Trista's name wouldn't come out. I couldn't make my head focus on any specific moment that I'd spent with her. She'd faded too far, and I couldn't reach for her to force her to be the thing that pulled me back from this kind of turmoil.

Liz had been given too many of my years to be able to force her face, her voice, her choices out of my memories; where Trista only had the space of a few days. Too little time, too few moments to be able to cling to what I needed.

I had just enough energy to turn my head when I thought I heard something tap against the door across the room, but it didn't open. The light beneath it was being blocked by something though, so I hadn't just imagined it. Someone was out there. The doorknob jiggled for a second like someone was trying to open it. When it didn't give, the tapping happened a second time quickly before the shadow moved from underneath the door. They were gone.

I stared at the door for a long time, trying to will my brain to make my body move. The trip across the room would be worth it just because the bottle of water was directly in that path. Crawling took way too much effort, walking wasn't an option, and dragging my big ass with a shoulder that had taken a gunshot and an arm that had been eaten by a potato peeler was a laughable solution. I sat up and started scooting across the floor toward the water. I downed half the water before my brain told me it wouldn't be wise to drink it all at once, no matter how badly my mouth and my throat were demanding it. Then I worked up the nerve to scoot the rest of the way to the door. I wasn't even sure why. I couldn't begin to guess what my head thought I might find there just because somebody had knocked and left.

The fucking tracking device.

I'd stuffed it in my sock before I told the girls to run for it in Tennessee. Then these assholes fucking hogtied me and took everything but my pants. I picked it up to look at it closer, and stopped to wonder if this was some kind of game where I hadn't been told the rules. Were they waiting for me to turn it back on hoping that it would bring the girls here after me? Or was someone else trying to tell me that help was coming *for* me? That was a fucking gamble and a half either way.

It wasn't hard to imagine Memphis sitting glued to a chair in front of a computer screen every second of every day just waiting for a hint of this little device to register with her software. Who would she send here after me though? Because if Trista coming this way was the plan, I had no desire to turn the tracker back on. I was in no shape to be able to get both of us back out of this place. And for as much as she'd proven she was a teeny, tiny Rambo, she would never be able to get us out of here alive either with how many people this organization had just ready and waiting.

Trying to decide what to do with the fucking thing was at least enough to keep me from collapsing into another Liz spiral for the moment.

CHAPTER TWENTY-SIX

trista

"Not that I don't enjoy your weird company, Utah, but if we're really leaving tomorrow, I'm calling it a night."

"Can't imagine I'm any weirder than anybody else here," he said and chuckled. He stood from his lounge chair as I got up from mine to walk back into the house with me. Indy and Memphis hadn't moved at all. They were still sitting shoulder-to-shoulder at the island in the kitchen, both typing away on their own computers. I paused when I heard the door lock behind me and turned back to watch Utah pull on it a couple times like he needed to triple check that it wouldn't open.

"I guess we know who the group's daddy is," I said and couldn't help but laugh.

"Please call him that in front of Jersey," Memphis said quickly. "Like the very first chance that you get. Get it on camera and I will give you any dollar amount that you can come up with."

"He really is going to hate everything about you," I added looking at Utah again. "That's going to be the world's worst trip from Philly to get back here. And that's saying something because my first road trip with the man was a doozy."

Memphis laughed. "She kicked him in the dick to get away from him the first time. And that's not even close to the worst of it."

"He asked me out to dinner just to kidnap me," I countered. "He had that coming."

"I will be needing every single detail of all these stories," Indy said. "Right down to the dirty ones."

I found myself smiling. Genuinely smiling, and something that could only resemble happiness washed right over my entire body just by being in this house with this strange set of people.

"You have any idea how uncomfortable you make people when you say things like that?" Utah asked Indy.

"I think he's hilarious. You're the only one he's making uncomfortable, Daddy Utah," Memphis said and winked at Indy. Utah choked on nothing. Again.

"Awe," I said and slapped him on the shoulder. "Daddy Utah *is* terribly uncomfortable now. And I don't think it has anything to do with Indy."

"Sorry," Memphis added. "I'll stick with calling you Little Light. That one sit better?"

"Please don't start singing," Indy said instantly.

"Shut the fuck up. Do you really sing it?" I asked Utah. "Does he?" I asked Indy.

"Really?" Memphis asked. "I kind of thought that was a joke too?"

"Christ," Utah interrupted. "I'm going to bed. You assholes better not sit out here and talk about me when I'm not even here to defend myself."

"To be fair, you're really not defending yourself so well even while you're here, Little Light," Memphis said.

"You all suck," Utah said and headed for the hallway. I hurried right after him.

"Just tell her," I whispered.

"Tell her what?"

"That you think she's hot. What could you lose? We're leaving tomorrow. Why not go for it?"

"I'm not here for Memphis," he said and laughed.

"Since you brought it up, why are you here?" I asked.

He stopped right where he was to look back at me. It was the most unpleasant I'd ever seen his face look. Not that he looked angry, just like he'd pulled down some weird emotionless mask. The same kind that Jersey wore. I shook my head.

"Sorry, I wasn't trying to —."

"Good night, Trista," he interrupted. He turned around and disappeared around the corner, headed for the stairs.

"I wasn't trying to upset you," I whispered to the hallway.

My mind didn't stay on Utah much longer though. I was terrified of letting myself believe that I would really see Jersey again sometime in the next few days. There was still a chance that I'd never see him again. There was a damn good possibility that I wouldn't actually live any longer than the next few days myself.

I tried to keep that thought planted firmly in my brain to stay grounded in the reality of what this was. But those thoughts still never stood even a hint of a chance against the excitement that was building about *maybe* seeing Jersey again soon. I felt ridiculous about it. He was an absolute asshole and probably just a little bit of a psychopath. He was mean and he was confusing. He was somehow emotionless *and* had emotional bouts that were impossible to understand. Everything I did seemed to piss him off; just like everything he did made me want to slap him.

Even knowing all that, I made my way into the bathroom that was attached to his bedroom and caught myself still smiling in the mirror over one of the sinks of the double vanity. For a farmhouse that had probably been sitting in this exact spot since the beginning of time, everything inside it was beautifully updated. Half the space was taken up by a giant shower stall that was tiled from floor to ceiling, with two shower heads on either side of a rainfall head that took up all the space between them. An entire wall of glass enclosed it with a single door in the middle. As if this massive shower wasn't enough, there was a giant claw foot tub that sat just beside it.

It wasn't difficult to imagine the kinds of things Jersey would do to me in this shower if we made it back to this house together. Really, it was all I could think about while I stood under the rainfall. It only took a few seconds before my fingers were moving down my body with those thoughts. His breath would catch at the feeling of how wet I was even without the addition of the water, like it did every other time, like he couldn't believe *I* wanted *him*. How the man didn't seem to realize that he was a walking orgasm was baffling.

His hand would stay there, like mine was now, barely touching my clit until I could feel his heart beating out of control against my back while his other arm wrapped around my breasts to hold me there. His middle finger would start moving slowly, just enough to make me want to hurt him and enough to make me start to squirm against him to try to force the friction that my body desperately wanted. I'd call him an asshole for teasing me, tell him to just fuck me already, and he'd immediately smack my clit. He'd let go of me just to pull my hair until I was looking back at him over my shoulder.

If I hear any words that aren't Jersey *or* please *come from that mouth, I'll fuck it until you black out this time, Fancy Face.*

And I wouldn't be able to breathe. His words had that power when his voice sounded strangled and in pain because he wanted me as badly as I wanted him, but he got more enjoyment out of making me fight for it than he did out of just giving me what I wanted. He liked to torment me just as much as he liked to please me. That power to just rip all the air out of my lungs and all coherent thoughts from my brain seemed to come effortlessly to him. I wouldn't be able to taunt him once his hand started moving faster, once his fingers moved inside. I leaned forward until my nipples hardened against the cold glass, because his other hand would release my hair to move between my shoulder blades and push me forward this way.

"Please, J."

They were the only words that would be left available for me to use the closer that I got, the only ones in the entire fucking English language that I could remember. As soon as he heard them, his pace would change. He'd add his other hand so one could focus entirely on my clit while the fingers of his other kept their rhythm in and out until my legs started shaking.

Break for me. And shatter me with you.
And I would.
I did.
Just at my own fingertips.

My own useless fingertips that didn't make stars explode in front of my eyes, that didn't reach deep enough, that didn't keep going until I'd come so many times I nearly blacked out and couldn't hold my own body upright anymore even after I'd begged him to stop.

But Jersey would do it that way. Against the glass, against the wall, right on the tile floor. Anywhere and everywhere that he wanted.

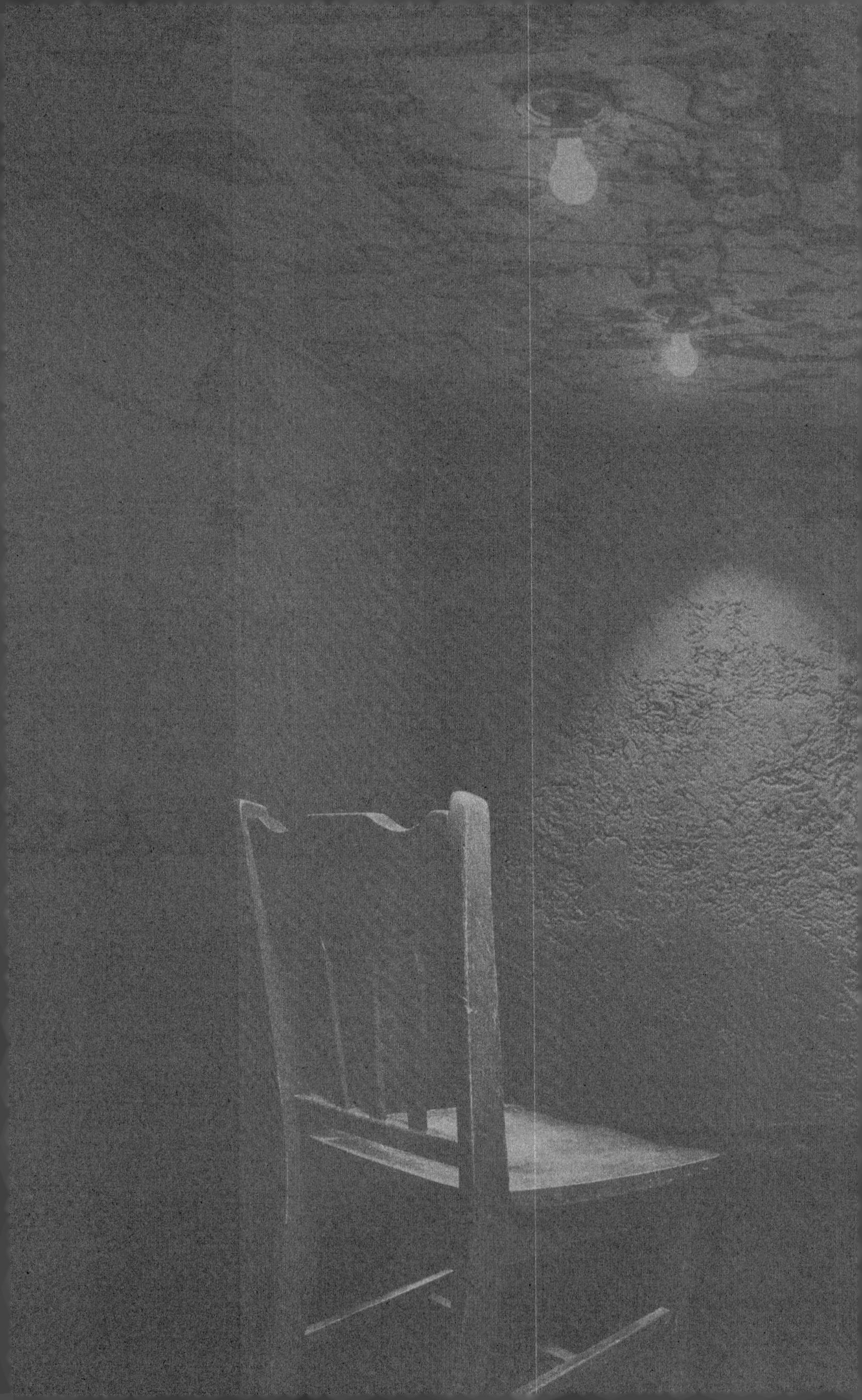

CHAPTER TWENTY-SEVEN

jersey

I turned the tracker on and just stared at the little red light while it blinked back at me for a few minutes, waiting for someone to break down the whole damn door and beat me until I wasn't breathing anymore because it had been a part of the game; a part that I'd failed. When that didn't happen, I felt like I might just dry heave myself to death at the thought of Memphis trying to come rescue me now that the device was transmitting. Turning it off wouldn't do any good now either. She'd still know that it had been turned on.

And now I had to figure out what I was supposed to do with the fucking thing to keep Bryson from finding it. He knew it had been taken from me when they first picked me up. Someone going through the effort of returning it to me would put that person in immense danger right alongside me if Bryson found out about it. Then they'd be in here relentlessly, searching for anything and everything that was being snuck in for me. They didn't come in and scour the room regularly as it was, and I sure as shit didn't want them to start. Shoving it up my ass would only work for so long. Sticking it in my ear risked the possibility of it being knocked back out with the next punch. I couldn't attach it to any of my clothing and trust that it would stay hidden. I swallowed it without giving myself much time to rethink it. That'd work longer than any other option at this point.

I'd managed to scoot my way around the entire perimeter of that room. When I didn't find any extra gifts left for me, I had to remind myself that I was a fucking prisoner and being tortured. I didn't get to be disappointed that the tiny comfort of sleeping for a few hours because of a secret pain pill had been withheld from me. Something as small as that wasn't going to wreck me.

The outrageous shit that people clung to when everything else had been taken from them was fucking depressing.

WHEN BRYSON BLEW through the door the next time ahead of his team of merry miscreants and their gear, he did it with the fury of a pissed off tornado. I didn't generally give in to feeling fear, but I was suddenly under the impression that he very much wanted to kill me on this particular visit. Dying would've been a pleasant release from the rest of what I'd been enduring, but it still wasn't something to which I was looking forward. I waited quietly while they set up our usual table, but I paid significantly more attention when the camerawoman carried in a laptop this time instead of the camera.

I watched them set it up on the table and place both chairs on the same side with the screen facing the chairs. The same two assholes from every other day came to drag me off the ground and drop me into one chair. I was suddenly faced with a rather horrifying image of myself in the corner of the screen. They'd set up a webcam for this. I didn't look much like me anymore. Even to me. I wasn't sure how many days we'd spent doing this. I didn't have a way to track time and I'd already lost count of how many times Bryson had been in this room, but I very much looked like a homeless person who'd been hit by a fucking car. The thought of my girls having to see me this way had me instantly hoping that today would be the day that Bryson just killed me, so they didn't have to see this anymore.

I hadn't even noticed that Bryson had taken the chair right beside me.

"Not so pretty anymore, are you?" He asked and laughed. "Can't imagine any gorgeous woman would want much to do with this version of you. Hope you had your fill already."

"Your infatuation with my love life is concerning."

"They don't even look anything like each other," he said.

"What?"

"Your wife and Trista."

There wasn't enough oxygen in the world.

"Your wife was stunning. That perfectly thin, little frame. Tall. Blonde. She had it all. That's what a woman is supposed to look like."

His minions fastened my wrists to the table another time while I fucking hyperventilated.

"That quiet, soft voice too," he said. "Until she was screaming for you, anyway. That kind of ruined it."

"You're going to want to kill me before you free my hands again."

Bryson smiled at that. "Set it up," he said and nodded to the little blonde woman. She was close enough for the first time for me to get a look at some frighteningly familiar black coffee-colored eyes. And I spent a few extra seconds in a confused daze rather than surviving the hellfire of rage that had consumed me a moment earlier.

Bryson waited for the screen to suggest that we were connected somewhere, and the video feed was transmitting live.

"Listen girls," he said and leaned closer to the computer. "This is the last time we're reaching out. The last time we'll give you the opportunity to end his life quickly. If I don't hear from one of you by the end of the day today, he'll be dead by this time tomorrow. I'm going to start now, but I'll make sure he lasts through tomorrow. I'll do whatever it takes to keep him alive, but in so much pain that he'll be begging me for his own death."

He paused to stand up and punch me in the jaw, then he stepped right up behind me to grab my jaw with his good hand to make sure I was looking right into the camera.

"I'll start skinning him. And I'll do it until I can see bone, Trista. Then I'll reach in and break those bones with my own hands."

He started squeezing my jaw until I could taste blood just from the inside of my cheeks against my teeth. This would probably be my last chance to speak.

"Don't you dare. You break for me and me alone, baby. Don't do it for them. Don't give in."

The punch to the back of my head after that felt like it damn near broke my neck.

But my heart stopped when I managed to catch just a single fucking glimpse of that computer screen before Bryson slammed it closed.

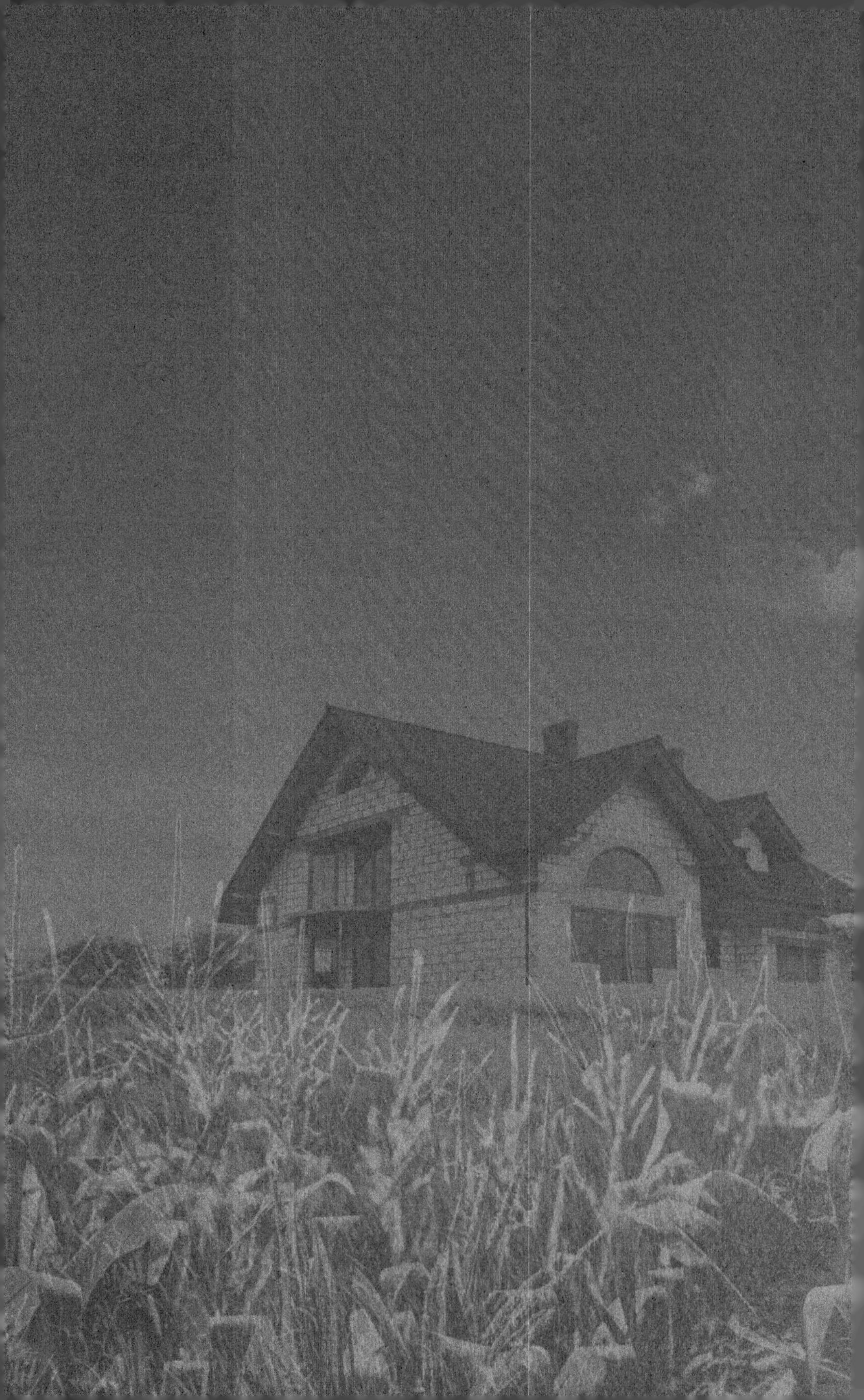

CHAPTER TWENTY-EIGHT

trista

Riding in the passenger's seat of Utah's truck wasn't anything at all like riding shotgun with Jersey. I wasn't overwhelmed with the need to annoy Utah until he snapped. I didn't feel like I needed to break the silence with senseless chatter just to pull a conversation out of him. I had no desire to force the truck into the ditch at the edge of the road to escape Utah's presence.

We hadn't spoken much since we'd left Jersey's house a few hours earlier, but it was really a pretty comfortable silence for it being with someone I didn't actually know. Where Jersey preferred the inside of his car in absolute silence, Utah blasted country music as loud as his ear drums could handle. Jersey *never* drove with the windows rolled down, because then dust would get inside. Utah hadn't even pulled out of the driveway before he had all four windows down. Jersey existed in the driver's seat like a statue, like he was as happy as he could be plastered in place in control of that car in silent respect of what it could do and what he could do. Utah was fidgety. He tapped his fingers along with the music. He shifted around in the seat, let his arm hang out the window and blow in the wind for a few minutes before he moved to the next position. The truck was rigged with gadgets inside just like Persephone had been, but that was the only similarity I'd been able to find to this point.

He laughed when the display on the dashboard flashed with a call from Indy. "And I thought we'd make it at least halfway there before they needed something."

He didn't even get a chance to speak when he pushed the button to answer the call.

"Pull over," Memphis said immediately. "Get the computer up and running. They're showing us a live video with Jersey."

I nearly ripped that laptop right off its mount trying to make it happen faster, while Utah was as cool as a cucumber pulling the truck off the road. The second that the screen came to life, Memphis had taken control of it and was moving open windows around until a crystal clear image of a very broken Jersey was the only thing that I could see. Bryson was in the middle of a speech about how this was our last chance to contact them before he'd start doing unspeakable things to kill Jersey slowly. I hadn't even noticed that my very shaky hand was trying to touch Jersey's face through the screen. He wasn't okay. Nothing about him looked right anymore. I was crying by the time Bryson was talking about skinning him, but something in Jersey's face focused so hard on the screen that I couldn't look away if I'd tried.

"Don't you dare. You break for me and me alone, baby. Don't do it for them. Don't give in."

The very audible sob that broke out of me was probably embarrassing.

"He can't hear you, Trista. But type something. Anything. It'll show up on their screen. Fast," Memphis was talking a mile a minute.

I sent him the only thing that I could think to say.

Survive for me, J. Please.

. . .

BRYCE HAD ALREADY PUNCHED him directly in the back of his head, but I wanted so desperately to believe that he was able to see it in that few seconds when he looked at the screen again before the connection was interrupted.

When Utah's grip tightened on my leg, I realized that I didn't even know when he'd put his hand there. The tiny sniffle that came through the speakers of the truck suggested that Memphis was probably crying now too.

"Indy?" Utah asked.

"I'm right here with her," Indy said.

Daddy Utah. Trista Whisperer. Little Light.

This weird as fuck man beside me.

He let go of my leg to close the laptop and push it back under the dash.

"We're going to get moving again," Utah said. "Apparently, we're running short on time now."

He reached for the button to end the call.

"Wait," Memphis choked. The noise that came out of Utah in response to her voice sounding that way even made my heart fucking hurt for him.

"It gets worse," she said and cleared her throat. "We've been looking into what happened to Jersey's family."

I leaned forward to put my face in my hands to try to prepare myself for whatever might be coming. Utah sighed and leaned his head back against the headrest to close his eyes.

"There's no way it happened the way that the police reports said it did," she said. "They didn't even investigate it like there could have been other motives, other people involved. Anyone who killed that many people with the same gun just to turn that gun on themselves, would've had a worthwhile amount of residue from the gun itself to show that it had gone that way. And it's common to inspect clothing for things like that. There's nothing that suggests they did any testing at all on Liz's clothes. Nothing that suggests her clothes were even kept for evidence."

"Get me the names of the detectives who handled it," Utah said.

"That's not why —," Memphis started to say.

"Indy," Utah interrupted.

"Sending it all to your computer now, hoss."

"Guys, that's not the point," Memphis tried again. "When you get to Jersey —. He already looked so —," she stopped again when her voice cracked.

"We won't say anything to him," Utah finished for her. "This one stays between all of us until everybody's back in that house. We'll figure it out then."

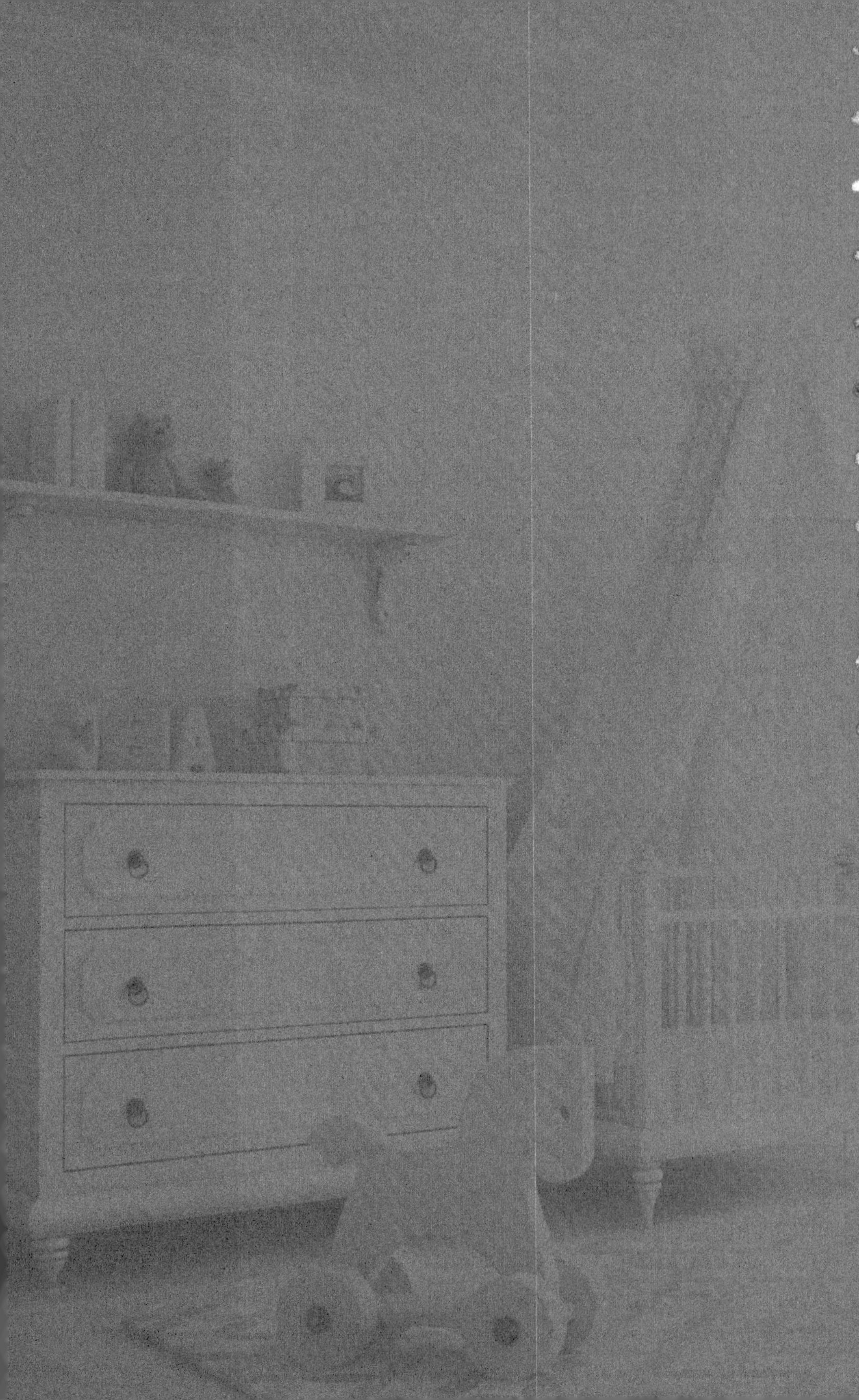

CHAPTER TWENTY-NINE
jersey

THEN

Liz was devastated from the moment that I'd suggested it. She didn't say a single word. She didn't burst into tears. She didn't yell or throw things. Any of those reactions would have been preferable to her just walking away, but she never behaved that way. I'd known her for years and to this day, I'd still never heard her yell. Even when we did get into serious fights, she never yelled. She never told me to leave or to find somewhere else to sleep. She didn't have it in her to act that way. She felt big and devastating emotions, but she felt them alone. She took them with her every time she walked away from a heated discussion.

This one hadn't even had the chance to get heated though. This one cut her straight to the heart and she opted not to participate in it at all from that moment. She went straight to the baby's room and disappeared inside. I wouldn't take the conversation in there because Faith was asleep, and those minutes when she did actually sleep were so fucking precious that they couldn't be interrupted. But

Liz hiding from that discussion didn't mean it was over. It was necessary, and she knew it too.

My next deployment was coming up and Liz hadn't been in the kind of headspace where she could care for herself and an infant from the moment Faith was born. She still spent more days being down than she did being even *just* okay. She'd given up trying to breastfeed because I was the one doing most of the feedings. I was the one doing most of the diaper changes, most of the rocking to sleep, most of the comforting. At this point, I was confident enough in my ability to swaddle so tightly that I could've wrapped a live badger in a baby blanket and not have to worry about it escaping.

I didn't mind carrying the weight while I was home. I really couldn't think of a more worthwhile way to spend my time than by being with my own baby as often as I could. I had no way to know how much time I'd really have with her. These kinds of deployments didn't come with time limits. I wasn't given a specific number of weeks or days to be overseas before I could return. We were given an assignment, and we came home when it was completed. Or we didn't come home. That thought was all the more painful. I could have a child in this world who might grow up never actually knowing me. Faith was way too young to be able to keep these memories of her time with me, but I would lock that shit up in the very depths of who I was to make sure I never forgot it.

LIZ CAME to sit on my lap on the couch later that night. She straddled me and put both arms around my neck to just lay her head against my shoulder, rather than actually look at me. We'd come to an understanding early in our marriage that I'd leave her alone when she really needed to be left alone, but she had to come back to me every time.

"I know you're right," she whispered into my neck. "I just hate that you're right."

"Spoken like a true wife. *My husband wasn't wrong like I wanted him to be*," I said and chuckled while I squeezed her whole body against mine. "Can we talk about it and figure it out? Or is this more of a *just hold me and shut up* kind of moment?"

"We need to figure it out. You won't be here much longer."

Her whole body shook when she said the words so I pushed her off my chest until I could hold her face in both my hands.

"My parents would *never* keep her from you, Liz. Never. I've already talked to them about it. They don't mind if *you* go stay with them too until I get back."

"I know they wouldn't," she said, and the tears broke loose. There were so many that my thumbs couldn't even keep up.

"Maybe we shouldn't have done this. Maybe I wasn't ready for a baby at all. Your parents shouldn't be responsible for this. You shouldn't be having to do so much of it alone," she collapsed forward on me again.

"I don't regret it. My parents aren't even the least bit sad that they'll get to keep their only grandchild in their own house," I said and squeezed her again. "Nobody is mad at you, honey. Nobody blames you."

"I'm so sorry, Van."

"I knew who you were when I married you, Liz," I said and laughed. "And I did it anyway because I love you. That was the case then. That's the case now. Just because it hurts sometimes doesn't undo that."

"I wish I wasn't this way."

I chuckled. "I just wish we'd get to sleep again. You think that'll ever happen?"

"No," she said instantly. "She'll be sixteen and trying to sneak back into the house after staying out too late with her boyfriend. We'll both still be sitting up, wide awake, right here. Waiting."

"*Boyfriend*. Dating. We'll start her firearm training in the morning."

"Can't hold her own head up, but sure," Liz said and laughed. "Firearm training."

She smiled at me when she rose up that time, and I felt more alive in that moment than I had in days.

CHAPTER THIRTY
trista

I spent a good portion of the drive entirely zoned out after seeing Jersey that way. If Utah had said anything at all in that timeframe, I didn't know about it. I cried for what felt like an eternity. I didn't snap back out of that trance until he stopped the truck for gas. Really, I hadn't actually noticed that we'd stopped for gas until my door was opening and it scared me enough that I nearly pissed myself.

"Come on," he said and held his hand out toward me.

"What?" I asked looking around.

"I'm going inside," he said. "And you're not staying out here alone."

"Right. *Daddy Utah.*"

He chuckled and shook his head when I did grab his hand for the fucking jump down from the cab of his truck.

"What are you planning to do with the names of those detectives?" I asked once I was walking beside him.

"Fuck if I know. Just figured whether it was me or New Jersey, somebody probably needs to do something about it."

"Why?"

He looked like a question had never confused him more in his life.

"Why would *you* do something about it?" I asked.

Utah sighed. "How old was his kid?"

I suddenly hated this conversation. "Four. She was four."

"Would you be able to *not* do something about that?" He asked. "Knowing what happened to a child?"

"But who is Jersey to you? I know why I'm here, Utah."

"Were you just programmed from the moment that you were assembled to believe all men are heartless monsters who hurt others just for the sake of inflicting pain?"

"All people, really," I said, trying desperately to ignore him essentially calling me a robot.

"What?"

"It wasn't really exclusive to *men* being heartless monsters."

"Well, once we get to Philadelphia, if we run into anyone who still needs reminded that you don't do that shit to children, I'll be right behind you to offer that reminder."

His words stopped me right there in the doorway while he held the door open for me.

"Everything about you is confusing," I said.

"Terrible humans getting what they deserve is confusing?" He asked and hooked his arm around my waist to push me the rest of the way through the door.

"I just don't understand what someone like you is doing in this *profession*," I said. "You don't seem —. You're —."

The fuck was I trying to say to him?

He wasn't anything like Jersey?

Because he had emotion and he cared about people?

But then what did that say about Jersey?

Or me, for that matter?

"*Someone like me*," he repeated and laughed. "You don't know anything about me."

"No but being able to have a job like that —."

"We don't all kidnap girls and drive across the country with them in the trunk of a car, Trista," he interrupted. "There's a reason Memphis reached out to us rather than anyone else."

"I can feel it coming that you're about to drop into stone cold silent mode about your past and what you do within this job and all, but for the record, I very much have questions about what that means," I said while he chuckled and walked away to do whatever he intended to do inside this gas station.

WE BOTH GREW MORE uncomfortable the closer we got to Philly. The easy silence was replaced with palpable tension in the cab of that truck.

"I think we need to stop and sleep before we actually get started on any of this," Utah suggested. "Long day of just driving and being upset, but the next couple of days are going to be even worse."

"Utah?"

"Hm?"

"If you don't really do what Jersey does," I said. "Are you going to be able to do whatever we're about to do? All the shitty jokes about you not being him aside. How are we going to do this if *this* isn't what you do?"

He smirked while he pulled the truck into the parking lot of a hotel.

"I don't do what Jersey does because I'm not a pompous bulldozing asshole who's every bit as flashy as he is good," he said. "They use me when anything needs done quietly, when there's a need for someone who has no interest in doing this for the bragging rights about what he's doing. New Jersey can be the company wrecking ball. I'm the finesse."

"You're going to sit here and tell me that you're the guy who specializes in *delicate*?" I asked.

He outright laughed that time. "I'm the guy who specializes in flawless, subtle performance. Some of us are called on to get people out just as much as the others are called to bring people in. Takes two very different kinds of human to be able to do those things."

He was out of the truck and taking both of our bags from the backseat by the time that I'd made it around to reach for mine. He just shook his head and slung it over his own shoulder to carry it toward the door.

"You want your own room?" He asked. "Or do you want to stay with me?"

My whole body physically paused, like English wasn't the language that I spoke best, right after sarcasm and sass. Alone was how I'd spent most of my life and should've been where I was most comfortable, but I hadn't actually been alone since Jersey came crashing into my world. Except the thought of being *this* close to Philly while alone was enough to feel like someone was slowly siphoning the air right out of my body. My head was already spinning out of control with how Memphis or Jersey might feel about me staying in the same room with this man too.

Fucking mess.

"I'm okay with being alone if you want your own room, Utah."

There. Make it his fucking problem. My God.

He cocked his head at me and smirked.

"Just because you've been alone all this time doesn't mean you *have* to stay that way," he said and laughed.

"What are you, a mind reader now too?"

"The Trista Whisperer, remember."

Jersey was going to hate *this man.*

CHAPTER THIRTY-ONE
trista

I answered the call from Memphis without even fully opening my eyes. I put it on speaker and just laid it on the pillow beside my head.

"I know where Jersey is," she said, without waiting for me to say anything. I heard Utah spring to life from the other bed at the sound of her voice. I raised my head up just enough to glance at the time on my phone and groaned at the sight of the three and the realization that it was still very much the middle of the night.

"How?" Utah asked.

"You're in the same room?" Indy asked.

"Focus," Utah said. "How'd you find him?"

"That tracking device that I handed off to him in Tennessee. It was offline for almost the entire duration of him having it. I just assumed they found it and took it. But it started transmitting again a little before they did the live broadcast. I hadn't checked the rest of the day because it hadn't been working anyway and that live shit was…distracting. But it's still transmitting now even."

"And you don't think they turned it back on just to see if it would draw you to them?" Utah asked.

"We responded to them earlier today," Indy said. "Told them the girls were going to start driving that way and to just give us an address to meet them, so they'd stop torturing New Jersey. Hopefully, anyway. If the tracker was intended to be a trap, I imagine they would've turned it off by now because they wouldn't think they'd need it. I think it's him somehow."

"Or someone helping him," Memphis added. "Either way, the address that they gave us doesn't match where the device is transmitting from."

Utah sighed hard and swung his legs over the side of his bed to sit up. I watched his silhouette in the darkness while he rubbed his hands over his face.

"What's the plan?" Indy asked.

Utah laughed. "Aren't you guys supposed to tell me what to do?"

"I don't know that I trust myself to think through this one objectively," Memphis said.

Utah sighed again at her admission and got out of the bed to start pacing around the little room.

"What if we were to let them think that Utah picked us up somewhere in between? He decided he wanted this bounty for himself, so he went for it?" I asked.

"What address did they give you?" Utah asked.

Memphis read it off to us and I gagged on her words.

"That's his house," I choked out. "That's just where Nate lives."

"I can't imagine he'd want just any Executioner knowing where he lives," Utah said. "The contract for you came with a different drop point. Indy could get in touch with them. Tell them we're taking you somewhere else in Philadelphia. That way we can keep to our original plan without the added risk of them wondering why the girls would disagree with just going to the President's house on their own."

"Doesn't really sound any crazier than any other idea we've had lately," I said and sat up myself to watch Utah keep pacing.

"Find everything you can about wherever that tracker is transmitting from, Indy," Utah said. "I want to know everything there is to know about the place before I ever set foot near it."

"You got it, hoss."

"Sorry, guys. Try to go back to sleep," Memphis said before she ended the call. Utah and I both chuckled. I watched him go for the laptop that he'd left out on the dresser across the room, so I flipped on the lamp that sat on the table between our beds.

"Do you think they'll just kill him once they hear that you're bringing us back?" I asked.

"No. You've spent too many years escaping right after being caught. They won't believe that I can do it either. They'll keep him alive to be able to use him against you until the President has you himself."

"Think it'll work?" I asked and tried to hug my own body to prevent the goosebumps from spreading too far.

"Are you asking me for comfort? Or the truth?"

"The truth," I lied.

"Fuck if I know," he said and chuckled at himself. "We are four people up against an entire criminal organization that's been operating successfully for decades."

"Okay. So, if I wanted comfort?" I asked and swallowed the sob that wanted to escape.

"I'll do everything I can to make sure it goes our way."

CHAPTER THIRTY-TWO
jersey

THEN

I still hadn't stopped smiling by the time I'd pulled the car back into the garage. Faith had no idea I was having Tigger tattooed on my arm when I left the house that morning. Her favorite game to play lately with my other tattoos was, "Daddy, wassat?" She wouldn't need anyone anywhere to explain this to her. He was the only one done in color, and while my skin was still very much bright red all around it and not even the least bit healed yet, she'd know exactly what it was. And that it was just for her.

Screaming from inside the house the moment that I killed the engine had me nearly blowing the car door off to get out and then attempting to rip the door to the house off its hinges to get inside. They weren't the kinds of screams that came when Faith was being chased or tickled. These came from fear, and they were also coming from my wife's mouth. I hated myself for the twelve seconds that I'd allowed myself to be purely fucking terrified that maybe I shouldn't have left Liz alone today, but she'd seemed better the last few days than she had been in months.

I toppled the little table that sat in the entryway from the garage to the house and I heard the plate and the lamp from it shatter when it all hit the floor, but I continued on my path through that house like a wrecking ball toward their screams. I found both girls in the kitchen. Faith was crying, huddled in one corner while Liz stood in the opposite corner holding a dustpan in one hand and a glass in the other. I couldn't see blood anywhere. Liz was shaking, but she wasn't crying. My eyes landed on the chair from our dining room table that was lying on its side in the middle of the kitchen floor.

"There was a spider," Liz said, and laughed. I watched her shoulders relax and she dropped her arms down to her sides like she could finally breathe again now that I was in the house. Faith stopped screaming once she'd looked up to see me standing there too. She sprinted across the room and clung to my leg like a leech.

"*A spider,*" I repeated. "You're both in here screaming *like that* because of a spider?"

"Up!" Faith screeched and pointed at the ceiling. Liz laughed again.

"It was on the ceiling. I had the flyswatter to just kill it, but Faith didn't want me to," Liz explained. "I thought I could just stand on the chair and nudge it into the glass then carry it outside to let it go. I just ended up knocking it off the ceiling, but then I didn't see where it went or where it landed. I about fell off the chair trying to get away from wherever it might've been. Then I ran for my life."

"*For your life,*" I repeated again. "From a spider, Liz."

"It was *huge*, Van," she said. "And I still haven't found it."

She looked at me like I'd lost my mind when I couldn't contain the laughter any longer.

"Come here, Liz," I said and motioned for her with my hand since the shaking toddler was still clinging to my leg. I laughed again when her eyes scanned the entire kitchen ceiling another time before she dared to leave the safety of her corner to slip under the protection of the arm that I was holding out toward her. I kissed the top of her head and breathed in the familiar coconut scent from her shampoo.

"Did you fall?" I asked. "You okay?"

"I'm okay," she said and finally laughed too. "I really didn't fall. I might hold a long jump record for the state of New Jersey now though."

"What about you, sweetheart?" I asked and shook the leg that Faith was still wrapped around. I waited until I was looking down into my own blue eyes set so perfectly in her little round face. "You alright?"

"No kill it," she whimpered and wiped her nose across my jeans.

"That's why you're crying? Because you don't want me to kill it?"

I watched the most beautiful thing I'd ever created bob her head up and down before I looked at my wife again.

"Hey, I tried to catch the nasty thing," she said. "You can see how well that worked out. It's your turn now, Dada."

I couldn't help but chuckle when Liz placed the glass directly in my palm before she backed away with her hands in the air. I pried my daughter off my leg so I could kneel in front of her to ask if I really had to catch the damn thing rather than just find it and kill it. When her eyes landed on the orange ink now on my forearm, all thoughts of that spider vanished completely.

"Tiggy, Dada!?" She squealed and started clapping her hands together. I was covered in tattoos, but the way that little girl lit up at the sight of this one had me considering going right back to my artist to have her cover every single one with my kiddo's favorite characters from her movies and books. I had to choke back some ridiculous emotions when Faith leaned down to kiss her beloved friend.

"Maybe we'll give it another try at talking your Mama into painting your room orange now, huh?" I asked and winked at her.

"There is absolutely no chance of that, Mr. Anderson," Liz scoffed.

CHAPTER THIRTY-THREE

trista

Neither of us had much success at sleeping after the call from Memphis. Utah spent the rest of the night staring at the computer screen in his lap while Indy sent him constant updates about the locations that we could use to say was Utah's drop point for me, information about where they believed Jersey was, and reading random, ridiculous text messages where Indy would ask Utah to ask me for my little insights into Jersey's personality. Apparently, Memphis was unwilling to offer any speculation on just how dominant Jersey was when it came to sex. It might've been wildly inappropriate, but it was also the only bit of relief that any of us had from the stress of the rest of the situation.

The moment that Utah sat his phone on the center console in his truck before we left the hotel parking lot, a text message popped up on the screen from a number that wasn't listed with a contact name. The way that he stared at the screen in confusion drew my eyes straight to it right after that. The smirk that took over his face once he picked it up held my attention, and then I watched while this dude, who had biceps the size of my entire waist, fucking blushed at the phone in his hand.

"Oh, my fucking God," I said and moved as fast as I could to get my own phone out. "That's Memphis, isn't it!?"

I couldn't get my fingers to work quickly enough to pull up her contact in my phone to see if I could remember the number that had flashed across his screen.

"It is," I said, still not actually knowing for sure. "I fucking know it's her. Why else would you blush? What'd she say? What's the message?"

He locked the screen on his phone and put it in his pocket rather than risk sitting it between us another time.

"It said, and I quote: mind your own business, you nosey little shit."

"And I thought we were friends," I said and held my hand over my heart like he'd just stabbed it. "Are you good with women? Or are you more like —?" I stopped myself before I could go there.

"Were you about to say *Jersey*? Please tell me that you were. This will instantly become the best day of my life if you were about to ask if I'm good with women or if I'm more like Jersey because he is *not* good with women."

"That's —. Okay, listen. Yeah, I was going to say Jersey —."

"I don't think I've ever actually been this happy," he interrupted.

"Stop it. Listen. That's not how I meant that."

"Oh, for sure, keep going. I can't wait to hear you try to talk yourself out of this."

"Utah!"

The way that he smiled at me suddenly had me hoping that all of us really would make it back to Jersey's house. The possibility of getting out of this situation alive, but without Jersey, left me with no real reason to keep trying to run. It all shifted in a matter of a few days and suddenly, everything about the future that I'd imagined hinged on Jersey. Then it shifted again when these other three people were dropped into my world. Bickering with this giant guy, who should've been ridiculously terrifying, just for fun was something I had just never done. I hadn't had friends since I was a child, but it felt like this was probably what friends did.

"Jersey is amazing with women," I said. "Just, you know, in a really messed up way that I imagine doesn't appeal to normal women."

"Is Memphis really a *normal* woman?" He asked.

"Awe."

"Okay. That's enough of that."

"I wish I knew more about her," I said. "I would tell you pretty much anything if I thought it would help, but I don't know her. Jersey's been working with her for like five years and he doesn't even know anything about her."

"Nobody knows anything about her. Indy's been a persistent little shit in trying to figure out who they both are. Hasn't gotten anywhere."

"Are all of you this crazy?" I asked.

"Probably."

WE SPENT that entire day in the creepiest of creepy abandoned fucking train graveyards, turning an empty shipping container into a makeshift prison cell that could record uninterrupted footage of me just hanging out in there for hours. It was the single most frustrating way to spend hours on end just to make sure there was enough of that recording to keep Nate's people believing it was happening in real time without any of it having to repeat.

Utah wasn't a fan of this part. That much was obvious. We only had this one day to get this done and I couldn't mess it up. I couldn't risk it not being believable because we didn't have an extra day anymore to spend time making it right. Utah asked several times before he closed that door if I was sure I was going to be okay, if I was claustrophobic, if I understood that he wasn't really leaving me there and he'd be right outside the door the entire time. He seemed more uncomfortable about it than I was at first.

I spent the first few hours pacing around, touching every surface in the container, looking in every corner. I counted the ridges along the walls. I did anything that I could do to make it look like I might've been looking for a way out. I was sure to flip my middle finger up at the little camera in the top corner of the container more than once in my fake searching.

I tried to imagine what would happen the first moment I saw Jersey again. I tried to imagine what the rest of our lives could be like if we survived this. It was difficult to picture dating Jersey, but that's what regular people did so I wondered if that's what we'd end up doing. Then I couldn't help but wonder where we'd be able to go for these make believe dates. His house in Indiana felt safe, but it wouldn't stay safe if we ventured out of it too often. Nate would never stop searching for any of us now. There would always be someone just waiting to see one of us. Our version of a normal life couldn't be what anyone anywhere else would consider normal.

It was a short hop from that thought to the self-loathing ones. The reason we'd all found ourselves in this position came back to me. I shot someone. I shot a twenty-year-old man right in the head. I couldn't do it to myself like I'd originally intended. I spent years being his victim. I spent extra years nearly fucking convinced that I actually was the problem. That somehow all those nights of Dalton showing up in my room had been only nightmares. Maybe I'd been delusional like they all called me. I was destructive in nature, and I was lashing out because I'd never gotten over my mother remarrying. I'd never gotten over losing my own dad. I had a brief moment of freedom. I had one whole semester of college to be away from it all, to convince myself that I never had to go back and that I could start over anywhere I wanted after that.

Except Nate and my mother were waiting right fucking there outside the building of my last class for the semester to pick me up and bring me back home for the break in between the semesters. He was paying for me to go there, so he was there to make sure his investment was worthwhile. He spent the drive back to his house asking about the kinds of things I would learn when it came to computer skills. He was suggesting that this degree, which was supposed to set me free, was actually about to trap me for the rest of my life in the form of employment for him.

I couldn't handle that.

And I couldn't handle Dalton in my room that very first fucking night back in the house. So, I ended it. Then I ran.

CHAPTER THIRTY-FOUR

trista

I was sitting in the far corner of that shipping container, squeezing my legs against my chest as hard as I could and crying into my knees when Utah opened the door. He sat next to me on the floor and just waited.

"We can go whenever you're ready, Trista."

"I swear I'm not usually like this. I know you don't believe that. I haven't been anything but an emotional mess since you showed up. But I really am stronger than this," I said, suddenly confused at how I'd ended up in this weird predicament of emotion. I spent so many years alone and never let myself crash down that path for this very reason. I couldn't even wrap my head around why I cared about what he might think of me.

I tried to glare right through him when he chuckled.

"You're one of *those*," he said and laid his head back against the wall.

"*One of those*?" I repeated.

"*Emotionless* and *strong* aren't synonymous," he said and stood back up. "Come on. Out of the box of sadness. Let's go."

He held his hand out to pull me off the floor.

"What's next, smarty pants?" I asked.

"I'm going to go save your wrecking ball boyfriend so we can all move on with our lives."

He waited all of about eleven minutes for me to get myself back under control once we were in that truck before he started talking about all the things that had transpired while I was having my shipping container breakdown. Indy and Memphis were ready and waiting to upload what would look like a live video to Nate's people so they could watch me pace around and flip off the camera and eventually cry myself into madness in a corner for as long as they wanted while Utah and I made our move on freeing Jersey.

Whoever Indy contacted hadn't been overly pleased that Utah took it upon himself to snatch me up for himself, but they didn't offer Indy any information about why it mattered that he'd intercepted me. Indy mentioned to them that Utah had another girl in his possession too and when Nate's people didn't immediately offer any money or instruction for her return, Indy opted to say that they'd leave the other girl behind because he hadn't been aware of a bounty for her. That saved us from having to figure out an explanation for why Memphis wasn't in the container with me.

Utah was both driving and speaking differently this time though. There was no playful undertone in his voice, no joking, no room for my sarcastic comments in return.

"Are we headed there now? For Jersey?" I asked. "Is that why scary Utah is back out to play right now?"

"We are," he said, and the leather on the wheel squeaked under the pressure of his grip while it tightened. "His tracking device started moving."

"Moving?"

"It barely moved from the moment that it turned on," he said. "Never shifted more than a few feet. In the last twenty minutes or so, it's been on the move. Whether that means he's decided to take things into his own hands or they're moving him, we've got to take our chance *now*."

I noticed for the first time that his usual basketball shorts and sleeveless shirts had been replaced by a long-sleeved black shirt that was tight enough on him to be a second layer of skin and black cargo pants, and my heart rate increased tenfold when I realized that he was prepared to hurt people very soon.

"It's transmitting from a warehouse near a dock that the President runs. My assumption is that it's full of people round the clock. Organized crime doesn't usually take dinner breaks or have nights off. They just swap out in shifts to make sure things keep moving. Whether it's a hub for drugs or firearms, it'll be busy. Getting in and back out as quietly as possible will be the only chance we have at being successful. If New Jersey is in there moving around on his own, he'll figure that out quickly too. Indy got me the original construction plans for the building. Some information about updates they've had done to the place in the time since our organization bought the place."

"Updates?" I asked, trying desperately to keep up with and remember everything that he was dropping on me all at once.

"Indy and Memphis are trying to work their way into the building's security system now. They've got cameras inside and out. With any luck, we'll be able to see inside the place before we ever actually try to go in, unlock doors for us, that kind of thing."

Adrenaline ripped its way through my bloodstream when he parked the truck in a public lot with the last bit of daylight and announced that we'd have to walk from here. He got out of the truck quickly and went around to the bed to lay the tailgate down and raise the cover. I made myself meet him at the back of the truck where he was placing things in two separate piles on the tailgate.

"Know how to use a gun?" He asked.

I nodded at him while he laid one on the pile closer to me, and then had another moment of panic when I realized that particular set of items was intended for me.

"Are you *good* with one?" He asked next.

"I don't want to use one, but I guess I'm effective enough if I have to be."

"Good enough for me."

He turned to face me after that and looked my entire body up and down.

"Can I fucking help you?" I snapped, like a lunatic. Thank God he laughed.

"Get over yourself, *Retirement*. You're hot, but you're mean as fuck, you sound like a dragon when you sleep, and I've got my sights set pretty squarely on someone else. Arms up."

I didn't even move in response to whatever the fuck he just said to me. He rolled his eyes and raised both my arms directly out to my sides himself before he dropped a vest over my head and started to fasten it together down my sides.

"Jesus, that's heavy," I whined.

"Can't imagine it'd do much good at stopping a bullet if it was flimsy."

Once he had the vest fastened around me to the point that I could barely breathe, he put the gun into a holster and looked at me again.

"Right handed?"

"Yeah."

He hooked the holster to the vest directly on top of my left breast, while I glared at him. He tugged on the holster a couple times to make sure it wasn't going to move before he looked at my face again. He released a heavy sigh when he picked up on the look that I was giving him.

"Will you stop that? That's where it fucking goes. I didn't design it."

He hooked several other items to the front of that vest before he draped a giant black jacket over my shoulders and then laughed at how it nearly reached my knees.

"Sorry," he said. "It's really all meant for me."

"Great. Jersey will just love that."

He ignored my comment and put another jacket on himself once he situated a belt and all his own shit around his waist.

"You don't have a vest?" I asked.

"You're wearing it."

"Utah."

"Don't make it weird. Come on, we're running out of time."

I jumped at what sounded like fireworks way off in the distance, and Utah slammed the cover of the truck bed back down before he locked the tailgate in place.

"What was that?" I asked.

"That means we're *out* of time," he said and started to run, motioning for me to keep up.

CHAPTER THIRTY-FIVE

jersey

"Wake up."

I turned my head away from the voice and groaned. "Fuck off. Just let me die in silence."

"Please. Get up. I can't move you. And if you're going to do this, it needs to be now."

My eyes ripped open at those words. The single lightbulb in this room somehow felt blinding in that moment.

So, add a fucking concussion to the list of ailments that I already had happening.

It took entirely too long for the woman in front of me to start to come into focus, and her nearly black eyes were all I could see clearly.

"Triss? How are you —?"

"No. Now, get up."

"What do you mean *no*?" I asked, before I realized she was blonde.

"I need you to focus. And I *need* you to get up. You don't have much time now. They're about to rotate workers. Somebody else picked Trista up. Nate will be going after her any minute now. This is your only chance. Fucking. Get. Up."

Somebody else picked Trista up.

I didn't even know how I got off the floor, but I did. How my body was able to stand upright on its own was beyond any reasonable understanding after the things that Bryson had done to me the last time. I should've already died by this point.

"I didn't have a way to sneak in a pair of shoes," she said. "But here."

I could only see out of one eye. The other was swollen shut as tight as could be, but I didn't need to be able to see it to recognize the feel of a firearm. I tried again to focus on this woman. Everything about her was familiar when she was this close. They were the same size, the same shape, they had the same round face that looked like it was never meant to smile. Her hair was blonde now, but the dark roots underneath gave her away too.

"Why?" I asked, thinking through the things Triss had told me about her mother.

"We don't have time for that," she said and shoved her hand into the pocket of her jeans. "Here."

I held my hand out when she reached for it. She dropped two more pills into my palm, and I didn't even hesitate to down those fuckers.

"Bryson will still be in this building," she whispered. "Out the door, to the right. There won't be anybody back here in the hallway right now. None of the offices have windows or doors. But there are several exits once you're in the open area on that side of the building. You'll just also run into people once you make it there."

"Come with me."

Her eyes filled with tears before she shook her head.

"I wasn't asking."

I forced my supremely fucked up hand to function just long enough to lock it around hers so I could pull her toward the door behind me. Much to my surprise, she didn't argue or even attempt to pull away. She never tried to kick me in the dick. So, she and Trista weren't all that alike aside from the appearance.

"Stay right behind me," I whispered while I cracked the door open to look into the hallway. She wasn't wrong, there was no movement out there. I made my way out and to the right with the gun raised as best as I could. I couldn't keep her hand in mine because my shoulder was too far fucked up and my hand was still in just as much pain. Everything everywhere hurt but that more primal part of me was in charge now to make my body just keep moving despite what my brain was demanding.

She squeezed my hips and stepped all the way against my back when we made it to the end of that hallway.

She even fucking felt like Trista.

"You need to make it to that hallway," she whispered and pointed around me to a different door. "There are other offices back there and an exit at the end."

The open area wasn't really just open space. There were sections of pallets stacked from floor to ceiling and entire stations of rows upon rows of tables. The only positive thing about this setup was that if someone spotted us on our way out, all we'd really have to do was dive into this maze of madness to find cover. Alternatively, the risk of not finding a safe way back out was just as real. The room was still full of people bustling around. No one was paying obvious attention in our direction, and I had just fucking had my fill of this place so I headed for the door that would open to that magical hallway of freedom.

We didn't make it more than a few steps before the shooting started.

There were too many people in the building to tell where it was coming from, so I pushed Trista's mother ahead of me and told her to run for the other hallway. We both made it behind the first stack of pallets, but the longer that we waited there, the more likely it would be for us to end up stuck there.

"Keep going," I said, forcing my body to accept that we were just going to have to fucking keep moving. "Now. Go."

She darted off again, but I couldn't move that quickly. Instead, I turned back to the room and raised the gun again to try to find the shooter while I walked backward. The familiar whine of a bullet buzzing right by my head suggested we were being shot at from somewhere to my right, which was the eye that I couldn't see out of anyway. I fired two rounds in that direction blindly while I walked, and it was enough to make the other shooter pause and retreat to hide momentarily. The commotion only resulted in more shooting from more directions, with the addition of everyone deciding to start yelling and screaming simultaneously. Some sprinted for cover, others sprinted for weapons, while everyone turned the volume way too high for my aching brain. I abandoned the possibility of defending us and put all my effort into just moving faster.

Trista's mother made it to the door first and held it open for me while I blew past her and into that hallway. I turned back to make sure she was in the hall with me, but she was already staring over my shoulder in a wide-eyed panic.

"Bryson! Don't!" She screamed. She rushed at me as quickly as she could to shove me against the wall as another shot was fired. She collapsed straight to the floor while I spun to raise my own weapon and the round that I fired back hit Bryson right in the center of his chest.

I knelt beside Trista's mother, while she bled from a bullet hole to her chest. She coughed out more blood when she tried to speak. She reached a very shaky hand up and I slipped my own mangled hand right into it. I nearly blacked out on the spot when she squeezed it. I'd spent my fair share of time in the presence of dying people, but this one felt different. The dying people I was around were usually dying because of me and weren't normally women. Let alone women I thought I hated but suddenly had very mixed feelings about.

"She deserved better," she choked out before her hand went limp.

She did.

That was no lie.

I'd never be able to carry another body out of here with me, so I laid her hand back across her chest and closed her eyes. I had to keep moving. Someone else had Trista. And I hadn't even made it out of the fucking building yet. Coughing from just a few feet away caught all my attention immediately. While I really was in a hurry to get out of that place, I was prepared to spare an extra minute using my decent hand to pound the remaining seconds of life out of Bryson Evans.

CHAPTER THIRTY-SIX

trista

I felt sick while I followed Utah *toward* the sounds of gunfire and men screaming. It hadn't taken anywhere near the amount of effort to get inside as I would've imagined. We watched people sprinting to get away from the building as we went toward it; like they didn't even notice we existed. I could hear Utah's voice. He was saying something to Indy through the radio in his ear, but I was wholly unable to focus on it. We made it to a small door at the back of the building after Utah used a knife to quietly kill two men who'd been between us and it. I heard the lock on the door release as we got closer, and my hand went right to the gun that was strapped against my own chest. Utah grabbed that hand to hold it right in place.

"That's the one, Indy. I heard it unlock. Cameras inside this door?" Utah asked.

He released my hand the next second while he listened to whatever Indy was saying, but he stopped to look at me before he opened the door. He tapped his finger against the gun.

"I don't care how loud it already is or what's happening in there," he said. "You don't use this unless it's going to save your own life. Got it?"

I nodded and he opened the door to lead me into the building. He had his gun up in both hands and moved down an empty hallway slowly. A woman burst around the corner in front of us. The moment that she spotted us, she screamed and raised both her hands. She was crying and screaming something in Spanish. She tried to press herself flat against the wall and kept both her hands up while she pushed her chin into her own chest as hard as she could.

"Afuera. Ahora," Utah said and nodded his head toward the door behind us. He kept the gun on her while she tried to slide by us without ever moving her body away from the wall. He waited until the door closed behind her and she was gone before he turned back in the other direction. The sound of that door slamming closed brought a man out of one of the doors that lined the hallway and Utah didn't even hesitate to shoot him. I watched him topple right into the hallway and a gun that I didn't even see on him slid across the floor. When we got closer to where the hallway turned, the corner from where the woman had come, Utah's arm swung out to hold me in place behind him. He was listening for something. I couldn't for the life of me guess what he was able to hear. I couldn't hear anything beyond the sound of my blood rushing through my own body like a fucking cyclone. Utah's hand returned to the gun in a split second to have it stabilized in both hands when another body stepped around that corner with a gun already aimed at him.

"Jersey!"

My hand flew out to grab the barrel of Utah's gun to try to force him to lower it. It didn't do any good. He didn't budge, and neither did Jersey or his weapon.

"J," I tried again. Neither man moved. He was in that crazy place in his head, the one where I usually slapped the shit out of him to pull him back out of it. But his face was so swollen, so broken in so many places that I couldn't bring myself to even try that. I shifted in between the men, in between their extended weapons to get closer to Jersey. I tried to keep my hands from shaking while I reached for his face with both hands. The one deep blue eye that was still open shifted down to me the moment that I touched him.

"He's with me, J," I said. "He's here to help get us home."

"Fancy Face."

He glanced back over his shoulder before he lowered the gun and stepped the rest of the way into me. His other arm wrapped around my shoulders to pull me against him, gently at first and then his fingers dug into my shoulder like he was trying to reach into my skin to make sure I was real.

"Back out the way we came, Trista," Utah said from behind me. "Now. Take him and get moving."

I had to pry myself away from his chest to slide under the arm that was around my shoulders to get him to walk beside me. I heard doors opening and slamming shut behind us as soon as we were moving back down the hall. I slowed for just a second to try to look behind us.

"Don't," Utah barked immediately. "Just go. I've got it."

I jumped at the sound of gunshots that were very nearby, but I finally had Jersey and Utah told me to just keep going, so I did.

"Pick up the pace!" Utah said from behind us with way more force than I'd ever heard in his voice.

"He's not exactly a toothpick," I grumbled back, like this was an appropriate time to argue with the man who was doing everything he could to keep us alive.

"Trista," he snapped back.

Jersey tried for a split second to glare over his shoulder at Utah just for the way that he'd said my name.

"The fuck is this guy?" Jersey asked.

"Right. Jersey, that's Utah. Utah, Jersey. Everybody good now?" I asked, still trying to drag him along faster.

"Utah?" He hissed and planted his feet to take his arm back. He swung around way faster than he should've been able to move for the state that he was in and raised the gun right back to Utah's face.

"You're the one who's trying to collect on her contract now?" Jersey asked.

"No," I said before Utah could even open his mouth and grabbed Jersey by the wrist again. "No, no, no. We don't have time to do this now. Memphis called him. He's *helping* us. Please. Let's go."

"Don't let him shoot me in the back," Utah said impatiently before he turned around to watch the end of the hallway again for anyone who was still coming after us.

"I swear we can talk about this all you want once we're out of this fucking building, J," I whined and started to pull his arm. He winced at whatever part of his body I was hurting, and I felt like the biggest asshole on the planet, but I pulled again because we needed to move. He caved after that one and lowered the gun again. I kept my hold on his hand that time and power-walked my way back toward the door.

That door swung open as I reached for it. Jersey managed to push me out of the way and against the wall to kill the two men who thought they were just going to walk right inside. He looked at the gun for a second after that and tossed it straight to the ground when he noticed the slide was all the way back. I immediately reached into the jacket that I was wearing to unfasten the gun that was holstered against my chest and handed it to Jersey. Even with only one eye to see out of currently, he'd be way more effective with the gun than I ever would.

"Go," Utah urged again. "They won't take a gunfight to the streets. We just need to get off this lot."

"You don't know Bryson," I said, suddenly very worried about Jersey having to walk all the way to where the truck was parked from here.

"Don't have to worry about him anymore," Jersey said. We made it nearly half way across the lot of the warehouse before there was more gunfire from behind us.

"Just keep moving," Utah said and swung back around to face whoever was shooting at us. Jersey tried to stop too.

"Nope," I said and continued pulling his hand. "You don't get to stop, J."

"He's going to need help," Jersey said.

"*We* need help. Keep walking," I argued.

An astounding level of deep and dull pain exploded from my right shoulder blade and blew me forward right out of Jersey's grasp, where my head promptly met the asphalt.

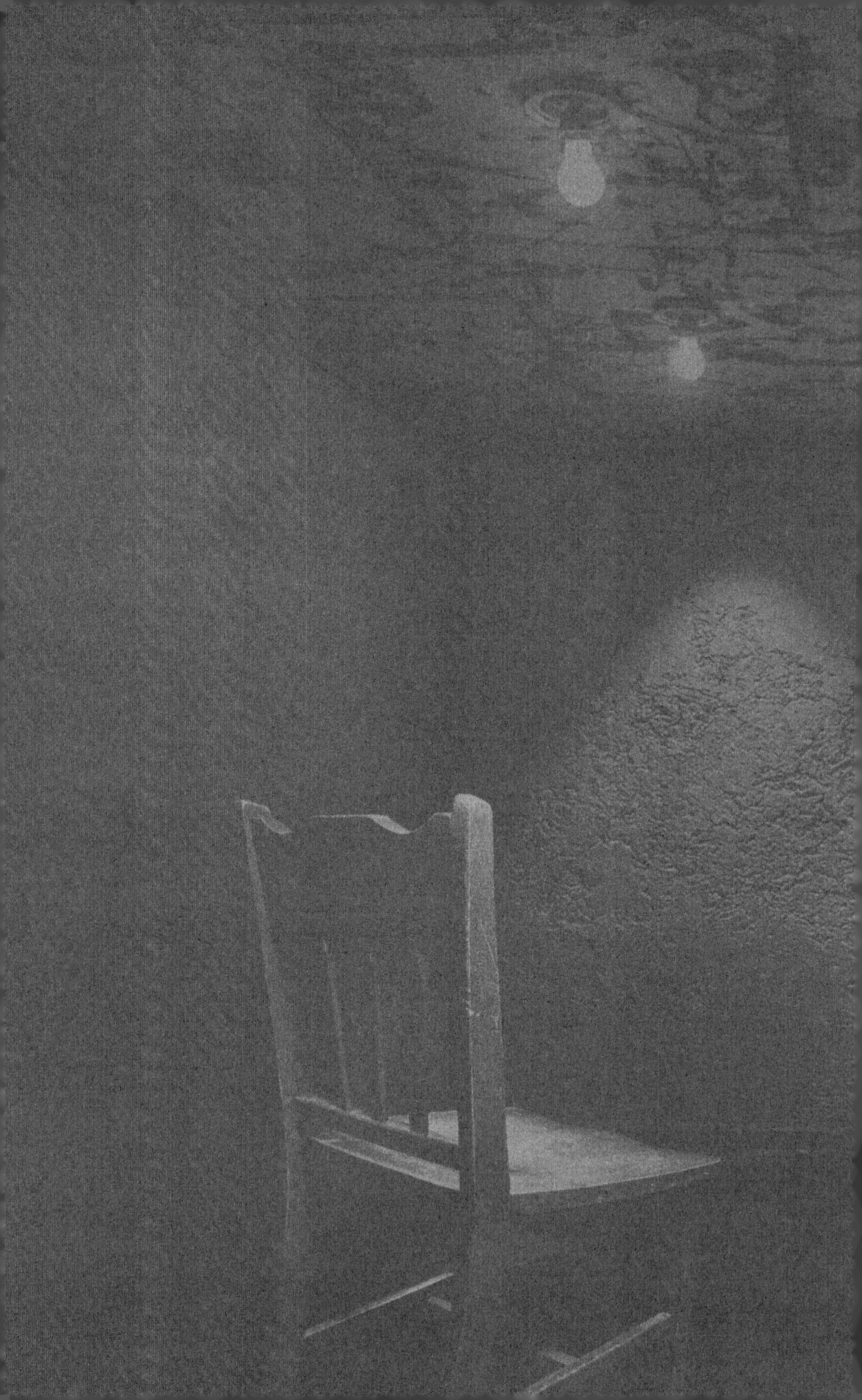

CHAPTER THIRTY-SEVEN

jersey

I collapsed to the pavement right there beside her to roll Trista to her back.

"She's got a vest on!" That other fucking punk shouted. I ripped her jacket open to see it for myself before I was able to breathe again. There was no blood anywhere that I could see, aside from the small trickle coming from the little gash on her forehead from where she hit the ground. I'd never be able to pick her up and carry her to wherever the fuck we were supposed to be going in my body's current condition. And that kid was obviously fucking useless at covering people while retreating. I went right back to where he was trying to pick off men as they came out of the building from which we'd escaped and grabbed his shoulder.

"Take her. Lead the way," I said and held my hand out toward him. "Give me the gun."

He only glared at me for a brief second before his brain seemed to grasp what needed to happen and he flipped the gun to place the grip in my hand. He hoisted Trista right up over his shoulder and started to run. At least he was able to do that much correctly. I paused to fire at another set of men who were trying to sneak their way between parked vehicles before I trailed behind Trista and that boy. I kept up as best I could while still having to stop and check behind us every few feet too. Our new friend slowed significantly once we were out of that parking lot to give me a chance to actually catch up to them. He didn't wait long though. As soon as I was within a few feet, he was walking again. I wouldn't normally think of myself as a bitch, but my body was very much trying to give out on this walk. Everything I had left went into making it this far.

"New Jersey!" That kid yelled. "She's coming back around."

That perked me up just slightly; just enough to pick up the pace again to catch up as he tried to lower Trista to her feet. My blood should have boiled at the sight of his hands on her hips while he tried to stabilize her. Instead, my blood felt like it was trying to stop flowing entirely. I dropped to my knees before I actually reached the two of them.

"Son of a bitch," that kid hissed. "I can't carry both of you *and* kill everybody else."

Lightweight.

"Come on," Trista said a second later. She was slipping her shoulders underneath my right arm to try to force me back to my feet. It took everything in my willpower to not scream while this punk shoved his body under my left arm. Every step he forced me to take that way was like touching my left arm to a live wire where all the electricity was directed straight to the metal shards of the bullet that were never removed from my shoulder.

Trista slipped out from under me when we got closer to a fucking pumpkin colored truck. I about threw up when she opened the back door.

"The fuck is that? Where's Seph?"

"Jersey, please. Just get in. We can't stop right now," she begged.

"Get in that Tonka toy? No, thank you. I'll walk."

"Back to *Indiana*? You have nail holes in your fucking feet. Get. In. The. Truck."

"Where's Seph, Triss?" I tried again.

"Alright, old man," the punk still under my arm said. "Sorry to be this way about it, but we've got to go."

CHAPTER THIRTY-EIGHT
trista

The absolute panic that coursed through me at the sight of Utah bending at the knees to just fucking pick Jersey right up off the ground and drape him over his shoulders was overwhelming. The movement put Jersey in so much pain that he didn't struggle. He didn't even say anything. The grimace that took over his entire face while Utah laid him across the backseat of the truck made my heart hurt for him. I sprinted around to the other side to get in the back with him. I lifted his head with the same care that I'd use to pick up an actual bomb to slide under him, so he was laying in my lap. Utah had us flying down the road in no time at all, but my focus was on the man sprawled across this seat. He didn't look anything like *my* Jersey right now. If he hadn't freaked out about the absence of his car while we were running for our lives, I would've been terrified that he might not actually be *my* Jersey under the surface anymore either. He tried to open the eye that wasn't swollen shut when I put my hand on the side of his face, but it was beyond obvious that whatever he was seeing, it wasn't me. My heart about stopped when I watched that eye roll back into his head.

"Utah?" I didn't even recognize my own voice. I didn't talk like that. I didn't sound like a terrified mouse who'd been granted the ability to speak. He glanced back at me for just a second before his eyes roamed up and down Jersey's body. He had Indy on the phone a second later.

"We need a doctor, Indy. A good one."

I didn't bother to listen to the rest of the conversation he had with Indy. I went back to staring at the motionless man in my lap.

"Keep your hand somewhere that you can feel his pulse, Trista," Utah said. "Tell me if it stops. We might still have to drive a while."

"*If it stops?*" I asked. "You're talking about his heart. If *his heart* stops."

He didn't bother to respond while I started to sob. I moved a very shaky hand down to Jersey's neck to find his heartbeat. I couldn't remember the last time that I actually prayed, but I was suddenly sitting here begging Persephone to be real because she would be the most likely creature to spare his life with the way that he worshipped her name.

"You can't die *now*, J. Even though it does kind of sound like something you'd do just because you're an asshole. Wait until I come save you so we can actually be together, die twelve seconds later so you don't have to live with me holding it over your head that I did save you."

"This has to be the weirdest fucking relationship I've ever witnessed," Utah chuckled from the front seat.

We spent what felt like an eternity driving. I was so terrified that I'd been placed in charge of being aware of Jersey's pulse that at some point, I started counting each heartbeat that I felt. Every time I even imagined there were too many moments in between beats, I started to panic. It was fucking awful. I couldn't begin to guess how long I actually spent in that vortex of terror before Utah stopped the truck. I still didn't dare to move my hand from Jersey's neck when Utah opened my door.

"You okay?" He asked, like this was the most normal thing we could be doing right now.

"No?" I snapped at him. "Are *you*?"

I could've scratched his eyeballs out with my fingernails when he smirked at that.

"Come on," he said and held his hand out toward me. "Hop down. I'll get him."

I stared back down at Jersey's face and couldn't even fucking convince myself to take my hand off his neck. Utah sighed and disappeared. He opened the door on the other side and moved the front passenger seat as far forward as it would go before he climbed right into the back with us.

"He's okay, Trista. He'll be fine," Utah said. He reached out to grab my hand and removed it from Jersey's neck for me, because I still couldn't do it myself. "Follow me, okay?"

He was talking to me like I was a child who wasn't paying attention, because I was functioning like a child who wasn't capable of paying attention. I jumped down out of the truck and ran around it to close all the doors before I followed Utah.

"What is this, Utah?" I whispered after I'd had the chance to look around. It looked like an abandoned mobile home community.

"This is the address that Indy gave me," he said and grunted while he carried that massive man across a sidewalk that was overgrown by bushes.

"I don't think there's anybody here," I whispered again.

"Then why are you whispering?" He asked and laughed.

"It's creepy here, you dick."

Headlights from behind us lit up the front of the mobile home that we were approaching.

"Get over here," Utah said. "Behind me."

I wasn't about to argue with that. I watched from around Utah's shoulder while a tall, slender man stood from the car to look at the three of us.

"He's not New Jersey, is he?" He asked.

"No," Utah said, in the calmest lie I'd ever heard. And that was saying something, coming from me.

"You sure?" He asked. "That'd make you Utah, and her—."

"Not us," Utah said again.

"I'm not armed," he said. The way that Utah chuckled at that made my whole body shiver.

"I don't intend to hurt you, Doc," Utah said. "Help him and we'll go. It's that simple."

"This one doesn't *feel* so simple," he said and closed the car door to come the rest of the way toward us. "But I'm not about to let a man just die if I can prevent it, and he doesn't look so great."

"You can let go of me," Utah whispered to me while Doc unlocked the door to the mobile home. I released my desperate grip on his arm and realized that my fingers actually ached from how hard I'd been squeezing him.

I was pleasantly surprised once we were inside, and all the lights had been turned on. It just looked like a tiny, traveling clinic inside. The place was completely spotless and organized, despite the unkempt appearance from the outside. It dawned on me that he probably used this space for that exact reason. He didn't want to conduct these dealings in his own home, and this certainly didn't look like the kind of place for a doctor to perform secret operations.

CHAPTER THIRTY-NINE
trista

I sat in one of the simple wooden chairs along the wall of what was probably meant to be a kitchen but had instead been transformed into a doctor's office. There was a single twin bed in the middle of the room, where Utah laid Jersey while Doc bustled about the space gathering things from cabinets and a closet in the back corner.

"Pull that cart over here to the bed, would you?" Doc asked Utah. "You comfortable with this kind of thing?"

"I can follow directions," Utah said.

That made one of us.

I could probably throw up on command right now. That would be the extent of the help I could offer.

"What's his name?" Doc asked.

"Jake," I said quietly from my safe space by the wall, thinking back to the name he'd handed out when anyone other than Memphis asked for it.

Doc took a tiny light from his pocket and used it to look into Jersey's eyes.

"Jake, huh?" He asked and chuckled. "Can you hear me at all, Jake?"

No response. No movement. No nothing.

"How long has he been unconscious?" Doc asked.

"Half hour," Utah said.

The fuck? The drive that felt like an absolute fucking eternity was thirty minutes?

I put my face in my hands and tried to stop listening.

I didn't move until I felt a hand on my knee, and I looked up to find Utah crouched in front of me.

"You alright?" He asked.

"Is he alright?"

Utah smiled and stood up, motioning for me to stand too. I didn't bother to ask why or argue. I was too tired to behave like my usual self, so I just did as he said. He took his jacket off me and started to unfasten the sides of the vest. He moved to stand behind me and lifted the vest over my head.

"Been shot before?" He asked.

I laughed. Because what a fucking question. "No. No, I have not."

He raised the back of my shirt up to my shoulders and my whole body flinched in response to his fingers touching my shoulder blade.

"Yeah," he laughed. "Doesn't look like it feels so great."

"Thanks. That helps."

He walked back around to stand in front of me and put his hands on either side of my head to tilt my chin down toward my chest.

"Got a bathroom in here?" Utah asked, looking over his shoulder to Doc.

"Down that hallway behind you. Second door on the left."

Utah nodded toward the hallway so that's where I went. The amount of dried blood on my face startled me enough that I tried to back myself right out of that bathroom once I caught sight of the mirror over the vanity.

"Nope," Utah said and laughed while he crowded me to get me to move forward again. "Head injuries always look worse than they really are."

I stood perfectly still while he used a wet paper towel to clean my face.

"He knows who we are," I whispered.

"I know," Utah said and titled my chin up to direct the top of my head toward the light in the bathroom. "I'll deal with it before we leave."

"You're going to kill him? He's helping. He's probably saving Jersey's life."

Utah stopped to look at my eyes then. "You're a confusing person, you know that?" He asked and smiled. "We'll just see what he does. We need him to look at your head first, regardless."

"I don't *want* you to kill him, Utah."

He laughed. "I will take that into consideration, Trista."

I couldn't begin to guess how long we waited while Doc worked on Jersey. I went from sitting in that uncomfortable wooden chair to pacing the full length of that mobile home, back to the chair, and then paced some more. I had no understanding of how Utah just stood there beside that bed, waiting to be told how he could help. They talked about stitches in one place and staples in another, then maybe he should glue some other part of his skin back together. He had no way to know if there were really broken bones anywhere without imaging equipment, but he spent an absurd amount of time pulling bullet fragments from Jersey's shoulder and closing that back up.

"Alright, team," Doc said. "I think I've done all I can do. I drugged him hard before I really got started so with any luck, he'll just stay asleep for a long time. I would keep him on this IV for another day or two if you're able. I can send some bags with you, if one of you knows how to change them out? I don't know that I've ever seen anybody *this* dehydrated *and* still alive."

"I can do it," Utah said. "Check her head before we leave."

"It stopped bleeding," I said quickly and went to stand next to Jersey instead. "I'm fine. Can we just leave?"

I watched Utah's face change into the intense and slightly frightening one that he kept hidden for moments that weren't usually friendly.

"So," Doc said, glancing between the two of us. "How are you going to play this, Utah?"

"Depends on the next words out of your mouth."

We both watched while Utah sucked all the oxygen from the room in the simple movement that it took for his thumb to unlatch the gun that sat holstered on his hip.

"I can't just *not* tell them," Doc said quietly.

"Wrong words," Utah said.

"What do you think they'll do to you if they realize that you knew who we were, that you helped us, *and* then just let us leave?" I interrupted quickly to stop Utah from drawing the gun.

"They know I can't ignore a dying man, regardless of who he is or what he's done," Doc said. "That's not how it works."

I looked back down at Jersey. So much of his body was covered in bandages now. "You really believe they'll care about your morals more than they'll care about you letting us leave? They'll want to know why you didn't call them as soon as you got here."

I watched Utah's hand lower away from the gun, and I closed my eyes to remind myself to breathe.

"I can give you any amount of money," I said quietly.

"Listen," Doc said. "I'm just going to leave. I don't want your money. I don't want anything from you that could tell anyone that I was ever here with you."

"Those are much smarter words," Utah said and chuckled.

"I'll come back later to clean up and lock the place," Doc said and hurried toward the door. "Just be gone by then, please."

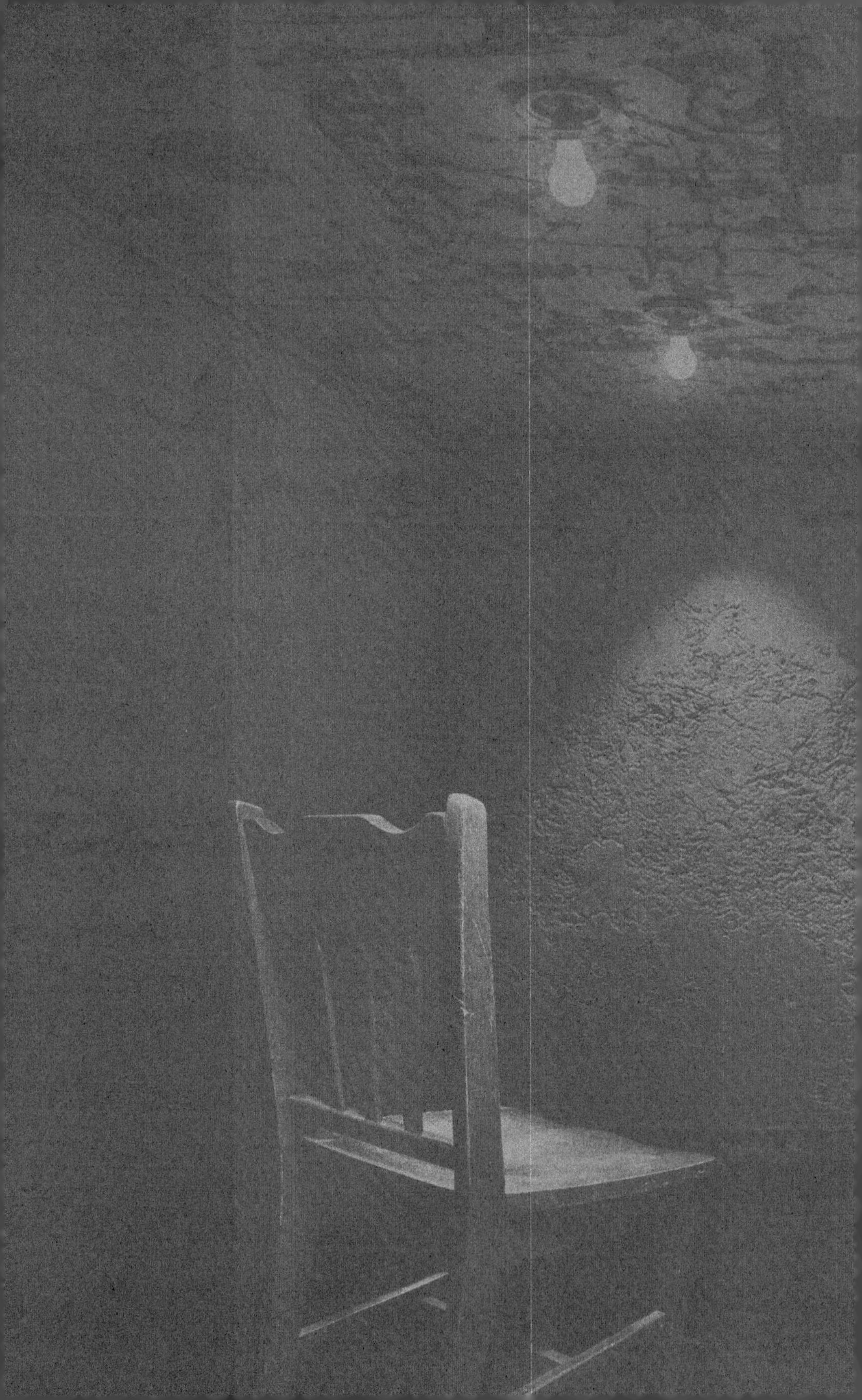

CHAPTER FORTY

jersey

"We're almost home, and she'll feel better if you're at least awake when she sees you again," I heard a quiet voice say from what sounded like miles away, but somehow also directly inside my skull. This was what normally happened when someone picked me up from the airport after a deployment overseas though. The second I was in a vehicle on safe ground, I crashed hard until someone woke me up to tell me that Faith was excited to see me, and I should be awake, so she'd see that I was excited to see her too.

"Liz?" I asked, bringing my hand up to cover the hand that was resting on the side of my neck.

The catch in her breathing forced my eyes open, but everything was blindingly bright and blurry for a few moments.

"No, J."

I shot upright at the sound of her voice. She wasn't the tall, thin, soft-spoken blonde who'd given me a child. She was the miniature, dark-haired siren who liked to pick fights just for the sake of what I did to her afterward. Sitting up suddenly felt like the worst decision

I'd ever made. I couldn't keep my eyes open, and I felt like I was spinning in circles.

"Just stay still for a minute, New Jersey," a fucking man's voice chimed in.

"Seriously, who the fuck is this kid, Triss?"

"That's Utah," she said quietly. "Memphis called him and Indy to help."

"What is that awful fucking noise?" I asked.

"Turn the radio off, Utah," Trista said.

"*Awful fucking noise?*" He repeated. "I'll turn it off just because his head's fucked up, but that is Bailey Zimmerman and I'll toss his ass in the bed for the rest of this drive if he's going to be insulting my music."

"Make him stop talking before I jump out of this fucking monstrosity of a vehicle, Triss."

"What did Ariel ever do to you?" Utah asked.

"Who the fuck is Ariel?" I asked.

"Like *The Little Mermaid*?" Trista asked and giggled.

"Bingo."

"Ariel," I couldn't help but fucking laugh when I repeated the name. "Flounder. It's Flounder. The annoying, too bright, bitch of a sidekick at best. It's not the mermaid. Seriously, Trista. Where is Persephone?"

"Jealousy isn't a good color on you, old man. Ariel could drive right over that sad little car of yours," Utah said.

"*Jealousy,*" I scoffed. "Says the boy with the worst case of *small man syndrome* I've ever seen in real life. The size of this truck won't do a damn thing to help the size of your dick, kiddo."

"Guys," Trista interrupted. "There's no fucking way this is really the first conversation that you're having. One of you is still half fucking dead," she said and glared at me. "And the other did everything he could *to help*. He got us out of there, Jersey."

"I was already on my way out before he showed up."

"Should've left you in that parking lot," Utah said.

Trista let out a heavy sigh and reached up between the front seats to squeeze his shoulder.

"Please," she all but whispered. He breathed in all the air in the cab of that truck before he nodded at her in the rear view mirror.

"What is this? Why are you touching him?" I asked, trying to set him ablaze with my eyeballs.

"Your car is at home. Your *groundskeeper* called someone to come work on the body. Fix the bullet holes and all that," she said and put her hand on my thigh.

"Memphis is there?"

"She is. Hasn't left since we first made it there."

I laid my head back against the seat to close my eyes and breathe now that there was beautiful silence in the cab of this stupid truck.

"She'll be excited to see you."

Everything in my heart screeched to a standstill at that unpleasant crossover between a previous life and this one. The memories of the time spent in that concrete box assaulted my mind all at once; of what it had taken to escape it. Every dull ache across my body flared to searing pain at the thought of Trista's mother.

"Triss."

I stopped myself the moment that my eyes were open again though. I didn't know anything about this punk in the front seat. Just because he'd helped didn't mean he could be trusted. Just because he was still here didn't mean he should be allowed to see her emotions. By the time I'd looked at Trista again, she'd already slid across the middle seat to be right next to me; staring at me with the same giant brown eyes that her mother had.

"Get this thing out of my arm," I said instead, looking down at the needle still sticking out of my right forearm. My entire left hand was wrapped in bandages, and I couldn't move any of those fingers to pull the needle out myself with the way that they had been wrapped.

"Leave it in until the bag is empty," Utah said.

A crazy chuckle came out of me before I even realized I did it.

"Remind me to kick this kid's ass when I have full use of my hands again, baby."

"I'll even let you restrain one of mine when you want to remind him of our date, Triss," he said from the front.

"Don't fucking call her that."

"Boys," Trista said and put her hand on my leg another time.

CHAPTER FORTY-ONE
trista

T hankfully, we were already almost back to Jersey's house in Indiana by the time he woke up, so I didn't have to play referee for that long. I removed the IV needle from his arm the moment that the bag was empty, and as soon as I reached to unhook the bag from where Utah had rigged it to hang from the handle just above the door, Jersey grabbed my wrist. He pulled me across him until I was nearly sitting in his lap before he let go of my arm to move that hand to the side of my face. His thumb brushed over the break in my skin on my head before his hand went back to my cheek.

"You're a dumbass, you know that?" He whispered. "You never should've come after me. You weren't *supposed* to come after me."

"You look disgusting, by the way. It's probably a good thing that we met before your face took this turn."

I wasn't even fucking standing and my knees still felt weak when he smiled. His hand shifted behind my neck, and he pulled me all the way into his chest. He moved his arm around my shoulders and held me squished against him. I couldn't recall a time in my life when I'd ever been so happy just to listen to someone's heartbeat. He held me there until Utah pulled the truck into his driveway, then he kissed the top of my head and released me. I watched his face come to life beautifully when he spotted Memphis already standing in the open doorway, just waiting.

She nearly tackled him right back into the truck the second that his feet touched the ground. I could hear her sobbing while I went around the back of the truck to see if I could help Utah with the bags. Then I felt like an asshole for a second for laughing at the way that Utah was frozen mid-movement while he stared at the sight of Jersey engulfing Memphis' tiny, shaking body. I smacked Utah in the ribs to get him moving again.

"Probably should've warned you about that," I whispered. "I didn't like it at first either, but trust me, *that* is not at all a problem for you and I. Outrageous brother-sister or daddy-daughter trauma bond thing. But not an issue for us. If anything, delivering him back here probably helped your case."

"Helped?"

We both stood quietly for a minute to watch Jersey let go of Memphis. He used the hand that was still available to wipe the tears from her cheeks. They were both smiling, talking quietly enough that we couldn't hear them. My heart seized up at the sight of him kissing her forehead before he turned to nod toward us and then he said something else to her. I watched Memphis look only at Utah after whatever Jersey said.

"Yeah," I laughed. "It definitely helped."

I went back to Jersey to slide underneath his arm to help him walk inside while Utah carried everything around all of us to get to the door to hold it open. Memphis flew around both of us to beat us to Utah. She had to jump to get her arms around his neck. Utah stood perfectly still like a dumbass for a few seconds with bags in both hands while she dangled from his body before his brain kicked in. He dropped everything and put his arms around her waist while she just continued to cry. She thanked him somewhere in the middle of all the sobbing and buried her face in his neck.

"Told you," I whispered to Utah while Jersey and I walked by them to get into the house. He chuckled but I definitely watched his arms tighten around her.

"Come on, Angel. Back inside," Utah said quietly against the side of her head.

I couldn't help but laugh when Jersey's head whipped back toward the other two while I kept pulling him into the house. Then he stopped dead in his tracks at the sight of Indy sitting at the kitchen island painting his fingernails.

"How many people did you move into my house?" He asked. "And why are they all children?"

"Don't worry. Your friend is still here too," I said. "You know, *Kyle*."

I giggled again as I said the name out loud.

"Don't start with me," he said and squeezed me harder with the arm that was still around my shoulders.

"That's Indy," I said. "Utah had him come stay here too when they decided to help us."

Indy jumped up to come around to our side of the kitchen.

"Man, they did a number on you. You don't look anything like you did when they sent that first video. Catfished the hell out of me. I'd shake your hand," he said and wiggled both sets of fingers in front of his face. "But they're still wet."

"My head hurts too much to even attempt to respond to that right now," Jersey said and kept his hold on me to make sure I walked toward the living room with him.

"I kind of moved into your room," I said quietly as we walked down the hallway. "I don't have to stay in there with you if it's weir—."

"Shut up, Fancy Face. I'm way more concerned about the other males you moved in here than about which room you picked."

"Memphis trusted them," I said while I helped him sit on the edge of his bed.

"Do *you* trust them?"

"I think so. I don't really understand why they're here or why they helped. I don't know what Memphis did to convince them to go against Nate."

Somehow, this didn't feel like the right time to tell him what Memphis had uncovered about the deaths of everyone in his family. I was entirely certain that such a revelation would go over better if Memphis was at least present when he learned about it, but my heart sank into my stomach when I watched him reach for the picture of his wife and daughter that sat next to the bed. He sighed and held it against his chest while he laid back on the bed and let his legs dangle over the edge.

"I didn't mean to keep it from you," he said quietly. "I wasn't trying to hide them. I never imagined you'd find out about them without me being the one to tell you. I didn't think —."

"You don't have to explain yourself to me, J. You're like a million years old. It makes sense that you would've had a life with other people before I was even born."

He chuckled. "Enjoy it while you can, baby. I heal quickly, and then I'll make sure everyone you've moved into this house can hear you scream your apology."

It probably shouldn't have been so comforting that he was still the exact same asshole I remembered, but it was. I stood there and smiled at his threat until someone knocked lightly on the door behind us.

"Hey, Jersey Boy," Memphis said quietly. "I told Kyle you were back. Asked him to come in and get you set up with another IV. I sent Utah out to get the supplies for that and to keep changing out all the bandages."

"*Utah*," he growled.

CHAPTER FORTY-TWO
trista

Jersey didn't do much more than sleep for nearly two weeks, and everybody in the house gave him a wide berth to do just that. While he started out in the bedroom with me, he wasn't there when I woke up the next morning. He'd moved to the couch in the living room at some point during that first night, and that's where he'd been ever since. I spent an outrageous amount of time trying to convince myself that he was just having to work through some things, or that maybe he was having a difficult time adjusting to being back in his own house. I tried not to believe that it had anything to do with me, but he did choose to leave the photo of his wife and daughter next to that side of the bed.

Kyle came into the house to check on him twice every single day, but they never really spoke. He changed bandages, provided medication, and gave Jersey updates on what he'd been doing around the property but there was no in-depth conversation. Memphis and I decided to hold off on discussing his family until he was in a better state physically, in case his mind was still in just as much turmoil. I put a significant amount of effort into convincing myself that it wasn't bothering me, but with every night that he spent on the couch and every day that passed without really being able to spend time near him, the weight got heavier.

The rest of us fell into a weird pattern. The thing that made it weird was that it was perfectly comfortable; to everyone, it seemed. Utah was up before the sun to make breakfast for all of us. The smell pulled us from our rooms, and we ate together in the kitchen while Jersey slept in the living room. Kyle would make a trip in to check on him. Memphis and Indy spent their days in front of their laptops. Utah disappeared in his truck for a portion of most days to run errands for the tech twins. And I just fucking waited for Jersey to come back to life. My patience for that seemed to be wearing down a little more each day, no matter how well I thought I was keeping it to myself.

"IF YOU SPEND one more day moping around this place, I'm going to start sending you out with Utah every day," Indy said from across the kitchen island.

"That'd probably bring Jersey to life faster than anything else," Memphis said.

"I'm not moping."

"You are," Utah said. "It's depressing as fuck."

"Then leave," I snapped.

"And take her with you. She's mean," Indy said and laughed.

"You guys all suck, you know that?"

"He just needs time, Trista," Memphis said.

"How much time?" I asked. "Because I think I'm losing my mind."

"Trista Whisperer, can you do something about this?" Indy asked and waved his hand in my direction.

"Oh, fuck off."

Utah laughed and pulled out the chair between himself and Indy before he motioned for me to sit between them.

"Come on," Memphis said. "Bitch it out so we can all move on."

I glanced into the living room on my way around the island to sit between the boys to make sure Jersey was still asleep on the couch.

"He hasn't even kissed me," I whispered, like Jersey might spring to life if I said the words too loudly.

"That's what you're upset about?" Indy asked and laughed.

"Guys, the man literally fucked me with no regard for protection the first time. Didn't even bother to ask about birth control or condoms," I said. "But he's been back here for like two weeks now and he hasn't even kissed me?"

"In his defense," Memphis said. "He already knew you had an IUD."

"What? Why do *you* know I have an IUD?"

"And how in any fucking realm is that *in his defense*?" Utah added.

"Those clinics you went to all the time on your cross country tour might have been free, but that doesn't mean they didn't keep records," Memphis said and laughed.

"*All the time*?" Indy repeated and laughed. "What exactly were you doing out there in the wild?"

"Why in God's name were you looking to find out if I was on birth control?" I asked.

"I wasn't," she said. "I was just trying to find you. Those clinics were really the only common places you visited from state to state. It was the easiest way to pick up on a trail. I pulled all their documents that were about you. Jersey is thorough so he went through everything that I found too."

"What a hilarious invasion of privacy," I mumbled. "How were all of you just okay with that job?"

"We're all bad people," Jersey said from the doorway behind us.

"It lives," Utah mumbled while my face turned bright red.

"Hey," Indy chimed in to Jersey. "Can you do me a favor?"

"Probably not," Jersey said and shifted toward the coffee pot on the other side of the kitchen.

"Can you just come over here and kiss this girl so we can get on with life around here?" Indy asked. Memphis spit her own coffee out on the countertop because she couldn't stifle the laugh, Indy slapped me on the shoulder, and Utah stood up to clear the area.

"Yep," Utah said. "That's where I draw that line. I'm out. See y'all later tonight."

"I thought we were friends," I whispered to Indy.

"We are. And you're welcome."

Jersey was standing across the island from me by the time I'd managed to look back in his direction, arms spread wide with his palms flat on the countertop on either side of him.

"Something you want to say to me, Fancy Face?"

"He actually calls you *Fancy Face*?" Indy squealed. "This is the greatest day of my life."

"Nothing at all," I said to Jersey, ignoring Indy entirely. He smiled and I about fell right off that fucking chair. His face was still noticeably bruised, but most of the swelling had gone down enough that he looked like himself again. And a slightly beat up version of this jackass was frustratingly attractive.

"Be out in Seph in ten minutes, Triss."

"Fuck. And he's a dom," Indy said.

"You *have* to stop talking," Memphis whispered.

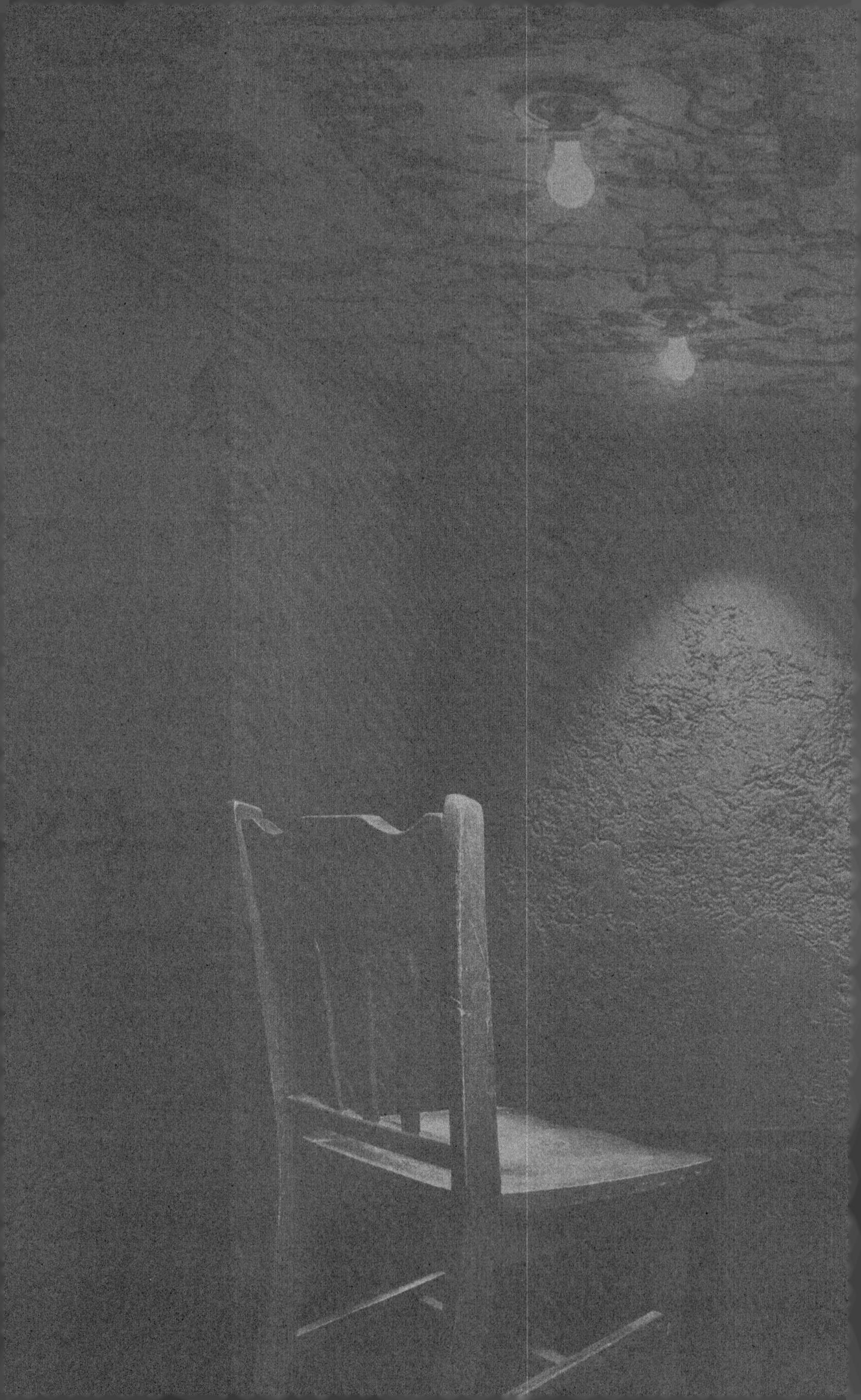

CHAPTER FORTY-THREE

jersey

She was waiting for me in the garage well before that ten minute mark even got close, but she stood in the corner with her arms wrapped around her own body.

"Why are you acting like you've never been alone with me before?" I asked and walked by her toward Seph. "Get in."

"Maybe because that's the longest sentence you've spoken to me in weeks?" She mumbled across the roof of Persephone before she opened the door to sit in the passenger's side. I tried to mentally prepare myself for the level of sass that was apparently ready to burst out of her any second once I was in the car beside her, but she fell right back into silence while I pulled out of the garage and turned around to get to the road. Somehow, this was even more uncomfortable than the first day that I allowed her to ride in that seat rather than in the trunk.

"What is it, Fancy Face?" I asked. "Why are you talking to the children of the corn about me instead of just talking to me?"

"Why Indiana?" She asked.

"That's what you want to ask me right now?"

"Yeah."

Stubborn little witch.

"It's quiet out here," I said. "I figured if I ever needed to come here for some reason, quiet would help."

"Does it? Does it help?"

The sigh came out of me before I could stop it. "Not yet, baby."

She shifted in her seat at that answer.

"Where are we going?" She asked.

"Nowhere," I laughed. "Did *you* want to go somewhere?"

"J."

I turned down one of the gravel access roads that cut through the fields around the edges of my property and had to fight to not laugh at how annoyed Trista was instantly by the fact that this car didn't move over five miles per hour once the wheels touched gravel. Eventually though, I parked in front of the massive pond at the back corner of my property. It was a natural spring that never dried up. It wasn't clear water and the land around it wasn't kept mowed, but it was even quieter here than it was everywhere else around the property. Something in me really was always convinced that the silence would help. If I just gave it the chance, maybe the silence could drown out everything that had ever fucking plagued the neverending, soul-crushing chain of events that kept shoving my ass back toward depression and the desire to kill it all with alcohol. Silence wouldn't help me in this particular situation though. Silence was making this one worse. I'd been married. I knew how it worked. Silence was the fucking worst when it came to someone you cared for deeply.

"Triss."

So much shit that I needed to tell her.

Zero way to know how she'd react to any of it.

"I know you get a weird high out of it when you scare me, but this isn't the fun kind of scaring me," she said quietly.

"Your mom was there," I said. "She's the only reason I made it out of that room. She snuck in that tracking device. She came to let me out of there when the others thought they were out searching for you. She's probably the only reason I'm alive. Even snuck in painkillers for me when she could."

"Of all the things I've tried to imagine you might say to me, none of them were even remotely close to *that*."

"She's dead, baby. Bryson killed her while she was trying to help me escape. Shot her. She was gone before I could do anything about it."

Her face was impossible to read. For some inexplicable reason, I was ready for instant sobs and even for her to take a swing at me. I thought maybe she'd lash out right at me in rage because I was the one within striking distance and delivering this news. Instead, she was perfectly expressionless. She shifted just enough to stare down at her hands in her lap rather than look at me any longer.

"And Bryce?" She asked.

"Dead."

"You did it?"

"Shot him," I said. "Didn't kill him instantly so I strangled him."

"Why would she help you?" She asked. She didn't even seem to realize I'd answered the question about her stepbrother. "She would've known who you were to me."

"She wasn't messed up on anything. And she was there just about every time they tortured me. She made a very obvious choice to continue helping me," I said, already trying to figure out if I was supposed to tell her about her mother's last words. Would it help to know that her mom regretted what she'd allowed to happen to her own daughter? Or would it make it worse for Trista to have to continue living without ever getting the opportunity to tackle the subject with her mom herself?

"Jersey —." She sucked her bottom lip in between her teeth to stop herself, so I reached across the console and forced my hand in between hers to hold onto one.

"I think I need to tell you something, too. But I was supposed to wait for Memphis to be around before I did it," she finally said.

"Why would you need to wait for Memphis?"

"I imagine there's some concern about you shifting into that out-of-control creature version of you when you hear it."

"I swear to God, if you're about to tell me that you're fucking that punk just because I've been unavailable, I *will* be that out-of-control creature faster than you can blink and not even Memphis could stop that."

She forced a smile for just a second before she added her other hand on top of mine to squeeze it.

"You're almost cute when you let the jealousy out," she said.

The overwhelming urge to rip her out of this car to fuck her just for recycling one of my own lines to use on me.

"Memphis found out some stuff about your family, J."

And suddenly, the overwhelming urge to vomit.

"She looked through everything nonstop. And I mean *everything*. She scoured those reports for days. The girl doesn't miss anything. She doesn't think your wife did it," she said, squeezing my hand even harder. "We all think it was probably Bryce."

I'd convinced myself that he was just fucking with me for the sake of torturing me in any manner possible when he talked about them. I should have taken my time killing him.

"I'm so sorry, Jersey."

"Don't be. Doesn't change anything now."

But now I had to figure out how to exist with the knowledge that I'd spent a portion of all this time *hating* my wife for the way that I thought it went; hating myself for not being there when I thought all she needed was my presence for her stability. What she really needed, what they all really needed, was for me to just not be a lunatic who was so good at being a murderous psychopath that some underworld organization would do anything to employ me. Or for me to have even just been physically present to protect them rather than half way around the world in some godforsaken jungle where my presence made no difference to anyone at all in the long run.

"She was pretty," Triss whispered.

"She was."

I could feel her eyes burning into me while my own dropped down to the Tigger tattoo on my arm. It was fucked up now. Bryson had done a disgusting number with that potato peeler, but there was nothing on this planet or any other that could undo my knowing what it was and who it was for.

"Your friend told me about the nicknames," she said. "It's cute."

"She called him *Tiggy*," I said and felt something deep inside me tighten into a knot. "That's where it started."

"It's even funnier now that I really believed you had a Tigger tattoo because you thought that highly of yourself to be one of a kind."

"I'm still one of a kind."

The way that she laughed loosened that knot just enough for me to keep breathing.

"I wish I could've seen the dada version of you," she said and squeezed my hand another time. "Even if that meant not getting the chance to know you the way that I do now. Sounds like he was probably good at it."

"It was what I did best. Right behind killing people for money like that was all that mattered in the world," I snapped and ripped my hand away from her.

I couldn't recall a single thing about the drive back to the house. I only heard the passenger door of Seph slam closed once we were in the driveway, and I was on my way back out to the road before Trista ever made it through the door of the house.

CHAPTER FORTY-FOUR

trista

I sent Utah a text message the moment that I was in the kitchen, demanding that he bring alcohol of any kind back with him. None of us had been comfortable bringing it into this house before, given Jersey's history; but drinking until I couldn't feel anything other than the buzz sounded like the best idea I'd had in a long time. I wouldn't leave anything left in the house to have to worry about Jersey getting his hands on it anyway. The sound of his car's exhaust rumbling back out of the driveway was enough to make tears sting the back of my eyes, but I blinked that shit away before I looked up to see that Memphis and Indy hadn't even moved from their places at the kitchen island. They were both staring at me uncomfortably, but my phone vibrated in my hand to take my attention away from them.

> UTAH
> That was fast. Prince Charming's charm wear off already?

"Guess that means there wasn't any kissing or making up, huh?" Indy asked.

"Where's he going?" Memphis asked.

"Why don't you just ask him," I snapped. "Or track him. Or fucking punch him."

I stomped my way by them like a pissed off teenager who was mad at her parents for giving her a curfew.

"I think maybe I'll call Daddy Utah," I heard Indy whisper before I slammed the door of Jersey's bedroom. The fucking bedroom where he had yet to return since coming home, regardless of all his shit being inside it with me. Trapping me in his memories, his smell, his style, his fucking everything. The outrageous urge to start ripping shit off the walls and smashing everything in the room was overrun by the terrible guilt that came with the sight of his wife and his daughter staring back at me from their place on the nightstand. All the years that he must've spent being mad at her for the worst moments of his life, just to find out that it wasn't her fault in any sense of the word. I should've just waited for Memphis to be around to break that to him.

I HAD no idea how long I sat on the floor, leaning back against the bed, with the picture of his wife and daughter in my lap, but I jumped when someone knocked on the door.

"What?" I hissed at the door.

Utah opened the door with a chuckle. "Normal people say things like *who is it* or *come in*."

He held up an entire fifth of Jack from where he stood in the doorway.

"Please, kind sir, do come in and bring your friend," I said in the nicest voice I possessed. "I'll try not to call you out on the fact that you brought *Tennessee* whiskey back here for me."

"And I'll try not to call you a smartass every time you open your mouth."

He walked in and dropped down to the floor right beside me before he sat the bottle between us.

"Thank you," I said and swiped that bottle from the floor as quickly as I could move to get started on it. Utah took the picture frame from my lap and looked at it for a second before he placed it face down on the bed behind us. The first pull from that bottle brought the tears right back to my eyes and lit a fire all the way down my throat until I started coughing.

"That's not anywhere near as smooth as I remember it being," I choked out.

"Probably because it's not even noon," Utah said and laughed.

"If you could take the judgement in your tone down just a hint the next time, that'd be swell."

"Didn't go very well?" He asked.

"He told me that my stepbrother killed my mom. I told him that the same stepbrother killed his entire family," I said and laughed like an absolute psychopath. "Nothing about that was ever going to *go very well*."

"That's a lot of devastation before noon," he said. "Bottoms up, girl." He stuck his finger under the bottle in my hand to lift it back toward my mouth.

"Are we too broken for each other?" I asked. "Does a relationship have any chance at all if both people have *this* much baggage?"

"*Relationship*," he repeated with a smirk. "Look at you with the personal growth. I've never heard you give this shit show any kind of label."

"Utah."

He smiled and reached out to squeeze my thigh. "I think you can decide to give the relationship priority over the baggage."

"What if *he* can't do that?"

"Can you love him through it anyway?"

I choked on the liquor again while he said those words, but it really didn't have much to do with the whiskey that time.

"Sorry," he said and laughed. "Can you pine after him from afar and keep your emotions buried as deep as humanly possible through it anyway? That better?"

"You're mean."

"I've just never understood the logic behind being afraid of the way that *you* feel," he laughed again. "The emotions are *yours*. That's not something to fear."

"Everything about that is actually terrifying. Do I really strike you as someone who was made for love?" I asked.

"Everyone was made for love."

"Okay," I laughed. "Chill with that, Shakespeare."

Why couldn't I just thank him like a normal person for saying exactly what I needed to hear?

I was a little worried that he could hear my thoughts when he chuckled again.

"Devastated people need other broken people to have a place where they don't feel so alone in their pain," he said.

"Misery loves company, or some shit?"

"Broken hearts need someone with duct tape."

"That might be the most Utah thing to have ever been Utah'd in the history of Utahs."

I WAS SUFFICIENTLY INTOXICATED by the time I heard Jersey's car pulling back into the driveway. I'd very much spent the entire day drinking. It was dark by then, but when he didn't come into the room, or even back into the house, I went out searching for him.

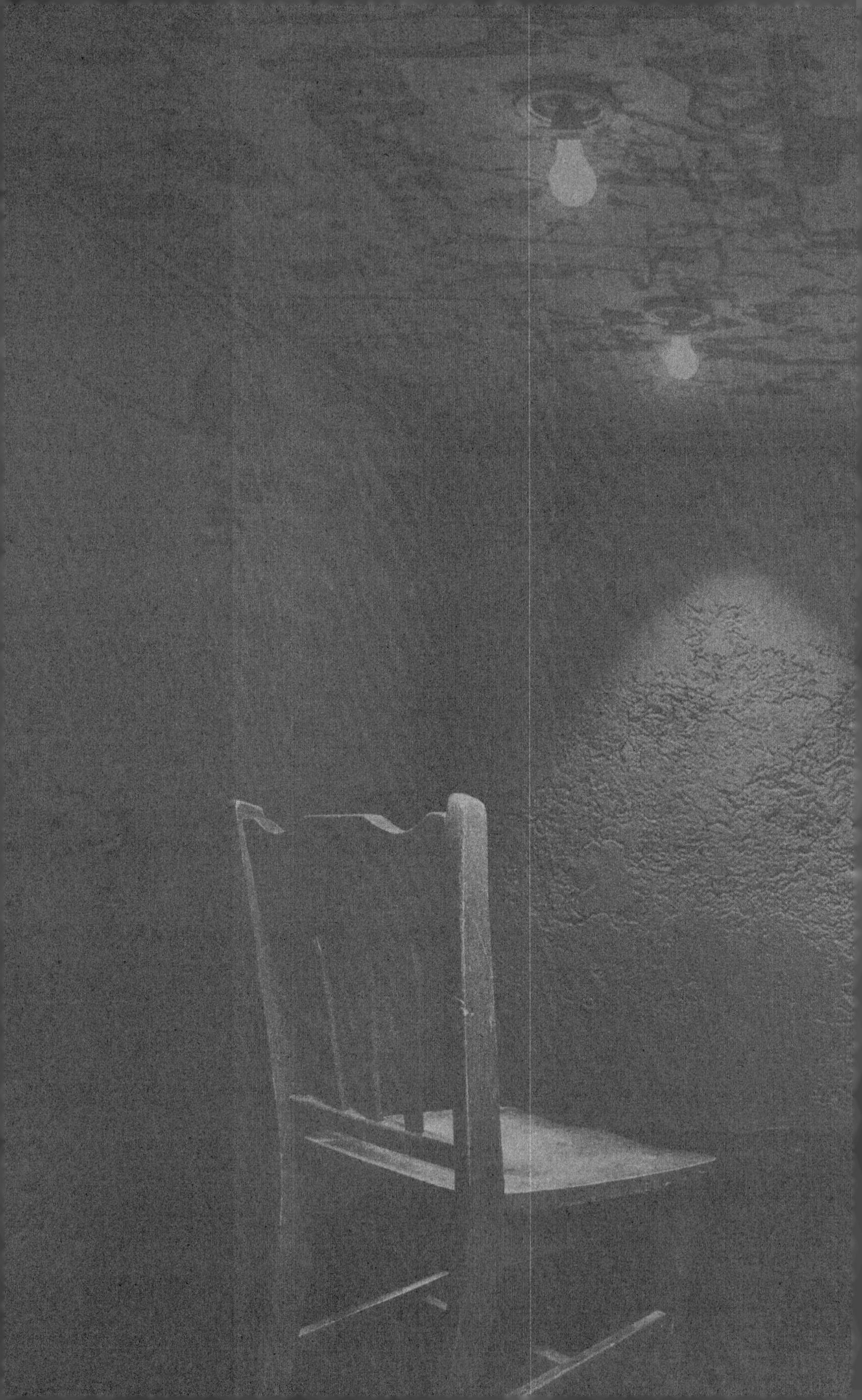

CHAPTER FORTY-FIVE

jersey

The glow from Kyle's fire drew me from the garage straight to the backyard. I pulled my own chair out there and planted myself next to him like it was something we'd been doing in perfectly comfortable silence for years. Dandy moved to sit directly on my feet as soon as my ass hit the chair.

"You should get one," Kyle said and nodded toward the dog. "They help more than I ever would've believed if I didn't experience it firsthand."

"No need," I said and laid my hand on the dog's head. "This one's already here."

"Can't go in your own house with all those kids in there?"

"Can't go in my own house with Trista in there."

"Really? She seemed awfully into you for you to have to hide from her."

"I'm not in control right now. I don't want to hurt her."

"You drinking again?"

"No."

"She's — incoming," Kyle whispered and got up to move his

chair a little further away from me to whistle for the dog. Trista knocked the air right out of me when she plopped down directly in my lap and turned to loop her arms around my neck.

"Something on your mind, Fancy Face?"

"You."

She leaned down the rest of the way to kiss me. Her fingers went into the hair at the base of my skull, and she dug her nails right into my scalp to hold me there like she was afraid I might get up and run for it if she wasn't holding my mouth against hers. It still wasn't something I should've been doing right then but kissing her never seemed to be something that I had much of a choice about doing. It just happened. And the familiar edge of the whiskey burn from her mouth was enough to send my tongue on a fucking mission deeper into her mouth. Her nails raked their way down the sides of my neck and to my chest while she pulled back.

"Where'd you get liquor?" I asked.

"Daddy Utah."

My whole body burst into flames.

"I'll kill everyone on this property if you ever use those two words side by side again, Triss."

"That's an absurd amount of jealousy coming from someone who won't even come near me on his own right now."

"We're a fucking mess, you and I, baby."

"You're so romantic," she snapped and put her hand on the side of my face to push me away so she could turn sideways a little more to scoot down and lay her head against my shoulder.

"But my heart beats again when you're around, and I don't think I hate it."

"How do you do that? Make me feel like I can't breathe?" She asked.

"Weird. When you're here, I feel like I can breathe deeper than I have in years."

She sat up again to look at me. She was usually better about disguising what she felt. There was always a filter over what happened beneath the surface, but not in this moment. It was intensely confused desire and the kind of pain that consumed every inch of her. I knew everything there was to know about those two mixed together. I put my hand on her cheek just to run my thumb across her lips and then dragged that hand down the front of her neck.

"Trust me, Triss, if I ever really want to control when you can and can't breathe, I will."

Her entire body tensing in reaction brought a smile to my face faster than anything had in a long time. Her hand went back into my hair to pull it until she'd tilted my head back and she kissed me again.

She was every bit as addicting as the whiskey that still lingered on her tongue.

She kept my bottom lip in between her teeth for a second when she pulled away that time.

"I'm going back inside, J."

She pulled my hair another time for good measure just to make the invitation as clear as possible before she climbed off my lap and walked back into the darkness toward the house.

Kyle immediately dragged his chair back around to my side of the fire. "I'm not great with women anymore, buddy, but I think she wanted you to go in there with her."

I laughed. "Yeah, she does."

"I don't *want* to call you an idiot for sitting out here with me instead but..."

I leaned forward to put my elbows on my knees and my face in my hands when I laughed that time.

"She told me a couple stories about your time together," he said. "About the handcuffs. She's cute. I wouldn't look at her and think she could pull a fast one on the likes of you like that, but that kitty's got some claws hidden away in there."

I sat upright to glare at him for a second before I laughed like a lunatic.

"I don't know about *kitty*," I said. "Maybe a mountain lion. Or a fucking wolverine. Something that has claws that *don't* retract at all."

CHAPTER FORTY-SIX
trista

I'd taken up spending my days next to the pool while Jersey did everything under the sun to avoid being around me. He'd spent another week sleeping on the couch in the living room, when he slept at all. Ever since I'd told him about Bryson and his family, he really did more wandering around the house aimlessly than anything else. Even in the middle of the night, I could hear him pacing up and down the hallway. I thought maybe he was working up the nerve to come into the bedroom the first couple of nights that it happened, and then I ended up a sobbing mess by the time the sun came up when he never actually made it through the door.

I WAS NEARLY asleep in my lounge chair while Utah was definitely asleep on the float in the water. The sound of very light footsteps had me cracking an eye open in the bright sunlight for just a second.

"Still no luck on the Jersey front?" Memphis asked, dropping into the lounge chair beside mine. The instant splashing around in the pool had a laugh bursting out of me in about half a second. Utah was about to drown just at the sound of her voice. She didn't even seem to notice his outrageous struggle while she pulled the oversized Volbeat T-shirt over her head and about sent the poor man into cardiac arrest. The bikini she had on was even smaller than the one I was wearing, but she was no bigger than a twig while I was curvy in just about every way. She was covered in tattoos that were every bit as black as her hair. Both ears had numerous piercings, she had two tiny hoops through her left nostril, and her belly button had a tiny revolver dangling from it.

"You'd better have a solid six layers of sunscreen on, my friend," I said. She truly had the palest skin I'd ever seen on a human. How she hadn't burst into flame like a vampire the moment that her shirt came off was mind-blowing.

"I seriously never would've guessed that Indiana could be this hot and have this much sunshine," she said and laid back in the chair.

"I'm not used to seeing you without Indy anymore. Everything okay?"

"Just needed a minute away from it," she said and closed her eyes. "He's been trying to dig into the backgrounds of some of the other Executioners to see what put them into the business. To see if we could find any leverage to sway some of the others to our side of it. We've had to do some messed up jobs with some messed up people, but this part — it's hard."

"*Our side of it*," I repeated. "It sounds like you're gearing up for war."

"That's how it feels, too."

"What brought you guys into Nate's business?" I asked and looked from Memphis to the man in the water, who still hadn't remembered how to breathe correctly. His gaze shifted from me to her for just a second before he moved to the edge of the pool to lift himself out of the water.

"And that's my cue to leave you girls to it," he said and went for the towel he'd laid on the chair next to me.

"You don't have to leave," Memphis said and laughed. "Nobody's going to make you answer."

"Something tells me you already have the answer anyway, Angel."

She didn't say anything, but she watched every step that he took back toward that house.

"Do you?" I asked.

She shook her head. "I haven't even tried to look into him or Indy. Were those *scars* on his back?"

"You'll sit here and notice imperfections in his skin but can't risk feeling too close to the pretty, muscly man who won't stop staring at you by looking into his background?" I asked and laughed.

"I don't think he's staring *at me*, Trista," she said and motioned down the front of her body. "Not when all that's going on right beside me." She waved her hand at me dismissively with that one, and I cackled at her.

"Why is that funny?" She asked.

"He thinks I'm a crazy person."

"You *are* a crazy person," she interjected quickly.

"Okay, well, I'll be ignoring that to preserve this friendship. He's got absolutely no interest in me, Memphis. He doesn't even know how to use his lungs when you're around, but your naïveté with the male population is adorable."

"Oh okay, queen of the opposite sex. Your love life is clearly going spectacularly. Please, teach me something about men."

"They all suck. That bit of knowledge I will offer freely," I said quickly. "That was a low blow, by the way. You dick."

"Maybe you could ask Indy for advice," she said and laughed. "He seems to be better with men *and* women than the two of us combined."

"Sex seemed like the only thing that we were effortlessly good at," I said. "And now it feels like he's never been less interested in it."

"I hope you can hear how intensely unhealthy that sounds at a baseline level, Trista."

"I do," I admitted. "But anything at all from him would feel better than what's happening now."

"Have you told him that?"

"I haven't told him anything. I swear he hides from me all day."

"Are you also kind of hiding from him though?" She asked and laughed. "You could go trap him if you *actually* wanted to talk to him, Trista. Talk. Not just fuck him."

"That sounds complicated."

"That's not complicated. *You* are making it complicated," she laughed again. "Fucking tell him you love him. Say the words and watch literally everything about this situation change."

"You and Utah with all these ideas," I said and rolled my eyes.

"Logic doesn't sit well with you, huh?"

"But what if there isn't really any room left in his heart for me now, Memphis?"

"What?"

"He's not mad at his wife anymore. He can't blame her for what happened now. What if he's just not capable of doing it all again?"

"Trista. Ask the man. He's an asshole, but he's really always been a pretty straightforward one."

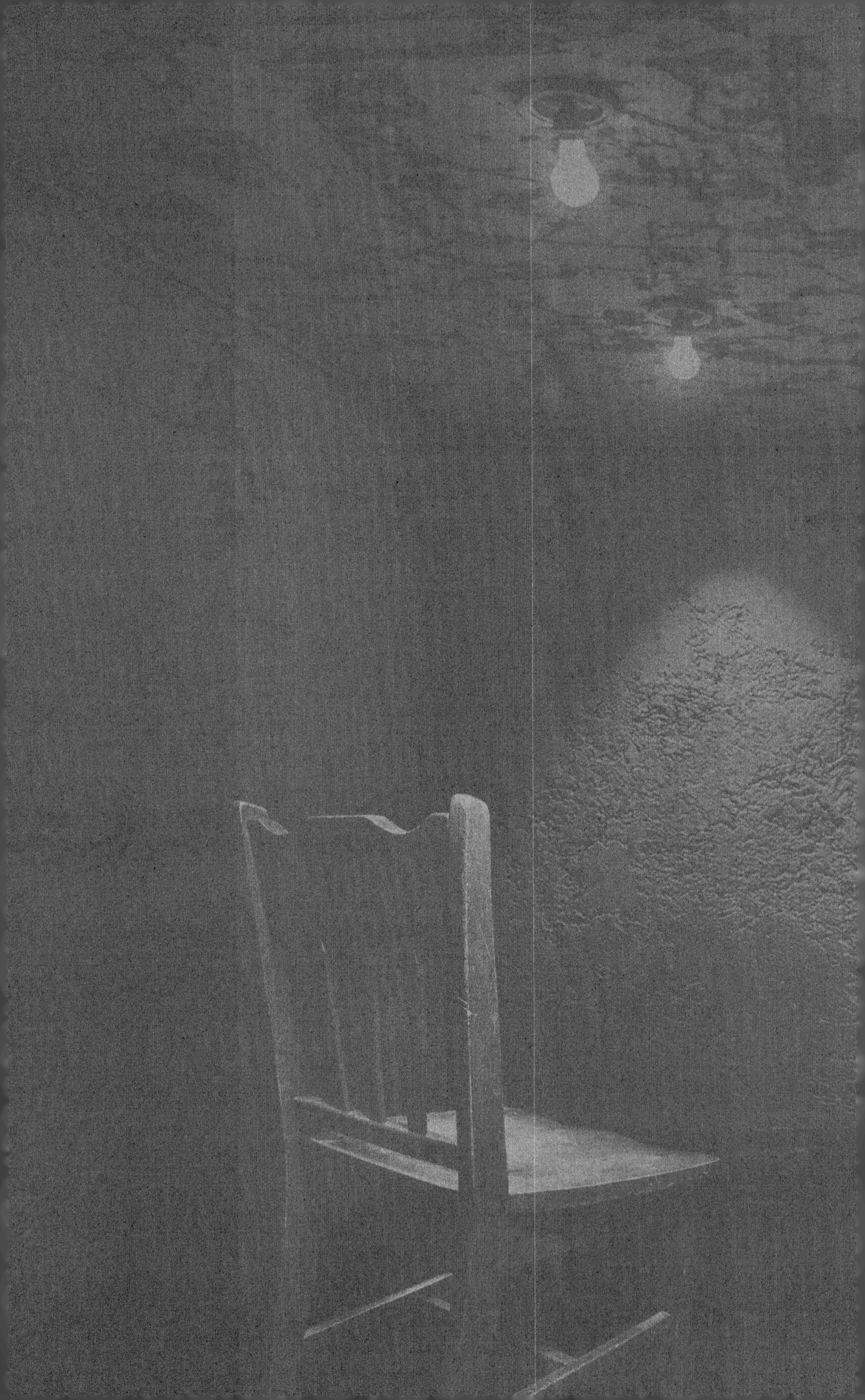

CHAPTER FORTY-SEVEN

jersey

She walked by me in the hallway like we were perfect strangers. She wasn't even looking at me when our eyes met. She looked right *through* me. She'd even turned sideways slightly to make sure no part of herself would touch any part of me. I stood there like a confused dumbass for a couple seconds trying to process it before I grabbed her by the wrist to stop her dead in her tracks.

"I don't fucking think so, little girl."

"Excuse me?"

She tried to jump away from me when I grabbed her face in both hands. I backed her into the wall until her head thumped against it.

"We've been through this, Fancy Face. You can't get away from me."

She all but melted at the words, and her hands came up to hold both my wrists. Every bit of the resistance in her body was gone by the time my mouth was against hers. My tongue barely even moved across the seam of her lips for her to grant me that access. She moaned right into my mouth when I forced the front of my body against hers as hard as I could, and her fingernails dug into my wrists. Her eyes were still closed when I pulled back, but I left my forehead against hers.

"Jersey," she whispered.

"You looked like you needed to be reminded who I am."

"You could come to bed and remind me."

"Triss, I don't think that's—."

"Please, J," she whimpered and closed her eyes again. "I can't take much more of this distance."

I meant what I'd told her. She did bring my heart back to life. She did make it easier to breathe when she was around.

But her words cracked my newly beating heart and halted the use of my lungs.

I put both arms around her and squeezed her until she probably couldn't breathe either. Her fingers were digging into my shoulder blades a second later like having me crush her against me still wasn't holding her tight enough.

"I don't know what you need from me right now, Jersey. I don't know how to do this. I haven't done any of this before," she mumbled into my chest. "But I'm here."

I felt her body shake when she tried to inhale the next time, and I let go of her quickly just to look down at her face.

"Are you crying?" I asked and forced my hands back to the sides of her face to lift it back up to mine. I shook my head at her. "Don't do that, Fancy Face. Not because of this. Because of me." I swept my thumbs under both her eyes and kissed her forehead.

"If you just tell me what you need from me —," she started to say, but my hand slapped right over her little mouth to interrupt that shit.

"Stop that. Now. I don't need anything *from you*, baby."

The tears were right back in her eyes, but I hadn't moved my hand from her mouth so she still couldn't speak.

"Understand?" I asked. "I don't want to hear that again, Triss. I'm not your problem to fix."

She nodded her head, so I released her face and kissed her again quickly.

"Come on," I said and squished her into me another time before I turned her back toward my room.

She at least stopped crying, but she hadn't said another word by the time I slid into my bed beside her. She rolled toward me the second I was beside her and tried to kiss me. I felt like an asshole for it, but I hadn't come back into this room with her for sex. Not because I didn't want her. I just had absolutely zero faith in my ability to stay in control of myself. I put my hand on the side of her face again and pushed my forehead against hers another time.

"Not tonight, baby."

I kissed her and promptly rolled her until she was facing away from me. I pulled her back into my body until there wasn't any space left between us and locked my arm around her waist like it could anchor her to me for the rest of my days. About the time that I thought I'd try to apologize to her for the nightmare of a roller-coaster she'd been on in her head over me, she was already snoring loud enough to put a lion's roar to shame. It didn't bother me so much tonight though.

I didn't even trust myself to fall asleep this close to her. Dreams, nightmares, and being unconscious in any sense held too many opportunities to wake up in some other unpredictable mindset. So, I'd just stay awake and hold her tonight. I wanted to touch every part of her again, to feel her around me, to do everything that made her squirm and writhe and scream that she hated me. I wanted her to be able to feel what I felt for her too, but that just wasn't worth the risk of what I might also do to her if I blacked out when the emotion flooded both of us.

Nothing about my headspace was stable. It hadn't been for weeks anyway, but now the knowledge that Memphis had significant proof about what had been done to my family, to my four-year-old, an innocent fucking child who wouldn't even tolerate me hurting a bug inside the house, *that* sent me spiraling in a bad direction. I blamed myself for it even when I believed my wife had pulled the trigger just because I hadn't been home to ground her, but now I blamed myself in having to acknowledge that my fucked up skill set was the reason they were all murdered. Someone set out to take their lives to be sure I'd plummet so deep into a pit of depression that I'd be more than willing to give up every tie I ever had to my identity in exchange for a job that would allow me to start over as someone different.

Every terrible thought that ever crossed my mind about Liz came rushing back to the front of my memories to send me on an uncontrollable guilt trip for ever believing she'd done it. And I hated to fucking admit it, but something in my brain was having a difficult time separating these women. Nothing about them was even remotely similar. They were separated by years, by death, pain, grief, personalities, behavior, appearance, the way they offered love in return, everything; and I still nearly called Trista by Liz's name more than once over the last week just because she was back in my head round the fucking clock right now. Something in me even started to wonder if it was because I never should've tried to love another woman. Was I even more of a monster than I originally realized because I was able to feel something for someone else when my wife had been taken from me the way that she had? After I fucking spent years blaming her for it, on top of that.

CHAPTER FORTY-EIGHT

trista

I should've just been happy that Jersey was at least staying in his room with me overnight, even if he didn't actually sleep or do more than just hold me until I was asleep. I'd spent the last three days waking up to his absence at some point throughout the night. He hadn't moved to the living room or to the couch though. He'd be standing at the window, just watching. Or looking through one of the photo albums from the bookshelf.

We still had a difficult time talking to one another, which wasn't anything new. We didn't communicate well, or nicely, from our initial encounter. Whether that bothered him as much as it did me was impossible to tell. He'd always been comfortable in silence before so maybe that was just how he lived in general. Either way, it left me still very much craving the explosive physical connection that neither of us had ever been able to deny successfully. I'd done everything I could think of over the last few days to entice him, and it was painfully obvious that he wanted it too, but the motherfucker just wouldn't let it happen.

I was gearing up to take another chance on it though when he followed me out to the pool today. He still couldn't get in the water because his body hadn't healed entirely yet from everything Bryson had done, but he was in the lounge chair right at the edge of the pool with every fucking inch of his annoyingly perfect broad shoulders on display. I made sure to wear the bikini that was really more of a thong than it was a bathing suit, and I left my hair down since he always seemed to enjoy pulling it. But he looked like he was fucking asleep while I thought I was putting on a show; getting in the water so slowly, tossing my hair back like those stupid models, wiping the water drops from my chest just to touch my own breasts like I was the one who enjoyed them. Everything inside me wanted to get right back out of that pool to rip the sunglasses off his face to find out if his eyes were even open, or if I was in here making a fool out of myself. I made my way to the edge of the pool where his chair was.

"Listen, I don't mean to sound like the nagging, insecure girlfriend, or even the overly pushy and horny boyfriend, because I get it that you're in a weird place right now and space matters. But if you don't touch me sometime soon, I might actually die."

He didn't move at all, but he laughed. "That sounds just a bit dramatic, Fancy Face."

"Jersey."

He chuckled again and adjusted the back of the lounge chair so that he could sit upright rather than recline. "Come here, baby."

He pulled me down onto his lap the second that I was within his reach, and I shifted until I was straddling him. Then I fucking laughed because the man might as well have had a piece of steel hidden under his swim trunks all this time.

"So, you *were* watching."

He smiled. "I mean if you're going to go out of your way to put on a demonstration like that, I feel like it would've been rude of me to *not* watch."

I moved his sunglasses from his eyes to sit them on top of his head.

Those perfectly blue eyes that I was still jealous over not having myself.

"You don't ever have to worry about me *not* wanting you, Triss. It's a pretty constant state of existence for me."

"Then what's been happening in here the last couple of weeks?" I asked and poked him right in the forehead. He smacked my hand away and laughed.

"You've seen what happens. You've been there for the blackouts. Sometimes, I feel something so deep that it rips open some other part of me and I have no control over whatever it is that gets out. Every so often, I can feel it coming and I can keep part of myself together, or sometimes someone else can intervene before it happens. But sometimes, I don't know it's coming, and I don't even know that it's happened until somebody is trying to shake my ass out of it after the fact. That part has been running loose lately, and I don't know if I can trust myself around you yet."

I felt like a lunatic that *that* made me smile, but it did. "Because you *feel something so deep* when it comes to me," I said. His entire body tensed underneath me. The muscles across his chest tightened and his fingertips dug into my thighs.

"I do. And for as much as I get a weird fucked up high out of hurting you with my dick, out of making you scream, there's a big difference between hurting you for pleasure, and *just* hurting you. If I did something awful to you just because I can't control this other thing right now..."

"We can find out if *I* can control it."

"That's not a smart game to play."

"I can't imagine adding one more bad decision to my life will really make that much of a difference," I said.

"You might feel differently about that if I killed you, baby."

The shift that happened in his eyes made me hesitate that time, and then I felt like an asshole when his fingers dug into my skin another time. Something in my face had changed to match his and he saw that too. I didn't want him to think that I believed he was this monster that he believed he was.

"For as much as I fucking love that you get off on the way I hurt you and the way I get off on your fear of me, I don't want to *really* hurt you. I don't ever plan to let you go either, though, so we'll have to figure it out eventually. I don't want to be just another man you feel like you have to escape from to find safety in someone else."

"I hear what you're trying to tell me. I really do. But I also still think I'm willing to risk it," I said and ran my hands from the top of his shorts all the way up to his chest. "This is *the* thing we do *really* well together, J. Otherwise, I'm just making you crazy and you're driving me out of my mind."

I moved my hands to the sides of his face and around the back of his neck into his hair.

"Triss."

It was supposed to be a warning, but the way my name sounded coming from him like that only made it worse. It was breathy, guttural, almost desperate. It was the same way he sounded every time he was buried deep inside me.

I leaned forward to whisper into his ear. "Don't make me call you *Kyle* again."

I didn't even get to sit upright all the way again before his hand was around my neck to pull me down to kiss me. For the first time in weeks, I felt like I could really breathe again. Like I was safe again. Somehow, I felt like I was home in the middle of this state where I'd never actually fucking lived and knew no one outside of the people on this property. I moaned into his mouth when his hips started to move up against me.

Friction.

Beautiful fucking friction.

Finally.

His hand went from holding me in place by my throat to the back of my neck and he untied the string of my bikini top before I could regain control of my brain to do anything about it. My hands immediately went up to my own breasts to cover myself.

"J," I whispered and smiled against his mouth between his kisses. "We should probably go inside."

"Why? I own the place out here just as much as I do in there."

"There are other people here, Jersey."

"Then they should probably consider leaving."

His free hand ventured further up my thigh until his thumb was resting against my clit, leaving just some hilariously thin fabric separating our skin.

"Jersey," I tried again. He moved my suit bottoms until his fingers found terribly sensitive skin and I sucked in a shaky breath at the slightest contact. My eyes closed and I leaned forward until my forehead was against his. I started to grind my hips against his hand before my brain reminded me yet again that we were just outside in plain sight. I sat up again, keeping my hands very much over my own nipples.

"Someone could see this," I insisted.

"Wouldn't bother me. Couple of them could use a good look at the way that I make you come for me," he said. "And me alone."

"The house is right there, you lunatic. It's like twenty feet," I said and nodded over his head toward the door.

"Oh no, baby. That's not how this works. You've been begging for this for days. And it's happening. Now."

He pushed a single finger inside me and used his other hand to grab one of my wrists. He pulled my whole body closer to him with it since I was still using my hands to cover myself. He just barely kissed me. Just enough to make me entirely prepared to beg for him to do it again.

"Move your hands, Fancy Face." He kissed his way from my jaw down my neck. "Let me see you."

I couldn't do anything but fucking moan at his words. He stopped breathing entirely when I finally moved to lace my fingers behind his neck.

"Fuck," he breathed out.

Everything happened in a blur after that. Neither of us were interested in taking our time or taking it slow. He was done using just his hands. I wanted to feel how badly he wanted me. The man who usually couldn't be forced to move any faster because he so thoroughly enjoyed torturing me with the anticipation was nearly feral trying to move as quickly as he could. I rose up just enough for him to get his shorts out of the way. He couldn't be bothered to even spend the extra half a second that it would've taken to untie the strings at my hips to remove my suit bottoms. He just moved them to the side and held them there while I tried to lower myself back down onto him. I hadn't exactly forgotten how big he was, but I definitely couldn't make myself just drop onto him to take him all in at once. He groaned and slammed his head back against the chair when his hands shifted to hold onto my hips.

"You've got about nine seconds to take every inch of me yourself. Make it happen or I'll do it for you, baby."

I couldn't begin to guess why I smiled at the threat. "Fuck you, J."

"Please do. You're down to six seconds before I take over."

It helped significantly when he shifted one hand from my hip so he could use his thumb on my clit. The sting from being stretched by the size of him faded out almost instantly. I had no idea how much time he actually gave me, but the growl that vibrated through his body when I had him fully inside brought my soul back to life.

Finally connected again.

I sat still on him for just a second, proud of myself for having done it. Like I deserved an award for it, even. Jersey chuckled and grabbed my face with both hands to pull me against him to kiss me again.

"I'll take it from here," he whispered and reached underneath the lounge chair so he could lay the back of it flat. He laid back under me and grabbed the back of my neck with one hand then wrapped the other around my lower back to pin me there on top of his body. My fingernails went straight for his ribs when he started thrusting. He didn't start slow. He didn't work up to a steady rhythm to let me get used to it. He was savage and needy. Desperate for depth, like burying himself in me as deep and as hard as he could might let him live through me rather than having to figure out how to do it in his own body anymore. I hadn't even realized I started squirming on top of him. I tried to raise my hips ever so slightly to make it more comfortable for myself and his arm moved instantly from my lower back so that his hand was across my ass to hold me even tighter to him. His middle finger rested on my asshole for just a second before he started applying pressure there and then his grip on the back of my neck tightened too.

"You couldn't possibly think I was going to let you get away from me right now," he hissed and somehow put even more pressure on every part of my body where he was touching. Nothing about that statement should've made me feel better, but it still did. This was the Jersey I remembered. The crazed possessiveness that wanted me and only me. I couldn't make my brain or my mouth work to respond to him in any form that would make sense. Instead, I just turned my face against him and bit into the thick, tattoo-covered muscle across the right side of his chest.

"If you're trying to get me to be gentle with you, that's for damn sure not the way to make it happen, baby."

He pushed me up and sat up so quickly himself that it nearly scared the shit out of me and made me think that we'd just unleashed that terrifying version of him that he was so afraid of me having to face. He shifted to swing both legs to the same side of the chair so he could stand up, still holding me entirely against him while he did it. Once he was upright, he lifted me up just enough to slide himself out of me. His sudden absence had me fucking whining while he lowered me until my feet were on the ground. He laughed and grabbed me by the jaw to kiss me.

"Don't worry. I'm not done with you," he said and spun me away from him. "I just want to see every piece of you again."

He stepped all the way against my back a second later and both his arms came up around me until his hands were on my breasts. One moved up from there to my neck while the other found its way into my suit bottoms to start circling my clit.

"Jersey," I gasped out and locked my hands around the wrist that was up by my neck to try to hold myself up while he quickened the pace with his fingers. He groaned right in my ear.

"Fucking missed the way that sounds when you say it."

He shifted the hand from my neck until that whole arm was across my breasts to hold me up when my knees buckled at the sudden orgasm that ripped through my body and my brain.

"I still want to hear you scream it, cry it. Beg," he whispered against the side of my head and slapped my clit with the hand that was still between my legs.

"Son of a —!" I tried to scream at him, but he interrupted me just as quickly.

"On your knees, Triss. On the chair. Now."

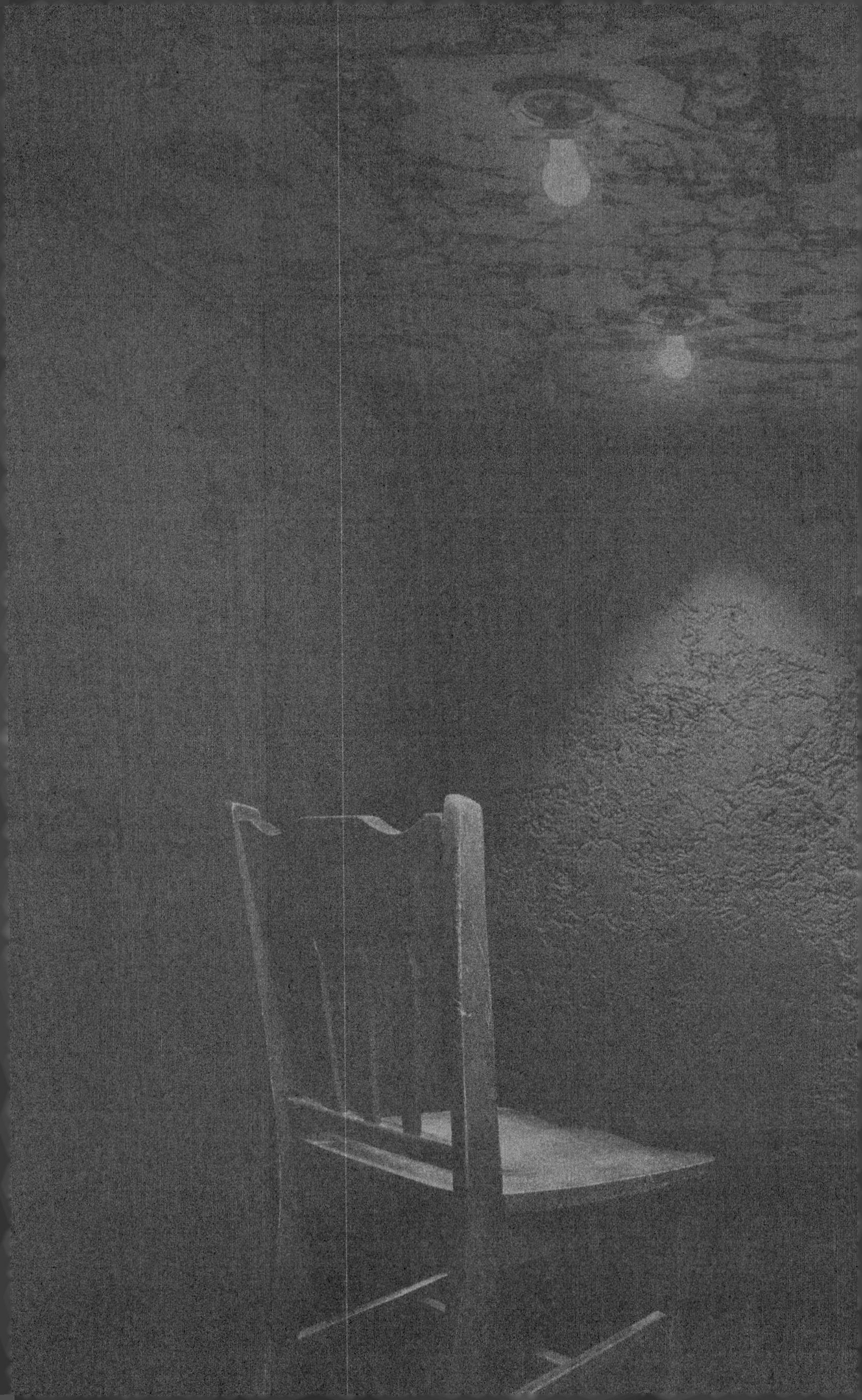

CHAPTER FORTY-NINE

jersey

She didn't even try to put up a fight, and I couldn't tell if I was disappointed by the lack of a struggle or even more turned on by her willingness to just fucking do as she was told for what was probably the first time in her entire life. Either way, I stood there stunned into silence for a second at the sight of the perfect arch in her back while she waited for me on all fours on that lounge chair. Then I watched goosebumps raise all across her skin when my hands grazed both her hips once I did step up behind her, straddling the whole fucking chair. I moved the bottoms of that ridiculously small swimsuit to the side to run my fingers from one hole to the other, and then up the full length of her spine.

I definitely also made a mental note to burn the whole fucking suit after this because there were way too many sets of eyeballs attached to bodies with other swinging dicks staying on this property now and none of them deserved to see as much of her as I did. That shaky sigh that she was so good at releasing to unravel every thread of patience I possessed had me slamming my way right back inside her while she screamed about it. I grabbed her by both biceps to raise her up off her hands until every muscle in her back was flexed while she tried to also hold herself in place against my thrusts without the use of her hands. I hooked one arm through her elbows to keep her arms trapped there behind her so she couldn't use them and held onto her hip with the other hand to keep us both steady.

"Fuck, Jersey. Fuuuck."

When every rock of my hips was rewarded with the most beautiful fucking combination of a whimper and a gasp, I let go of her arms to reach around and put my fingers on her clit. I grabbed a fistful of her hair in the other hand to pull it until the back of her head was against my chest and the bend in her spine was nearly unnatural.

"Open your eyes, Triss."

I took my fingers from her clit when she didn't.

"Please," she whispered not even a full second later.

"Look at me."

She still didn't open them, so I stopped moving my hips, too.

"No, Jersey. Please don't stop."

"Open your eyes," I demanded again. "When you break for me this time, Triss, it'll be the moment that you become mine. And only mine. For the rest of my days. Let me see it happen."

I smacked her clit, and she opened her eyes when she screamed. I loosened my hold in her hair just enough for her to be able to turn her head toward me until I could see her face. She reached both arms over her head to try to hold onto me when I started thrusting in and out again. She managed to dig the fingernails of her right hand into my right shoulder, but her left hand shook when she placed it gently in the place between my jaw and my neck.

"Take it," I growled against the side of her head while I picked up the pace on her clit. "Take everything I have, everything I am."

I could see the very moment that she realized I wasn't talking about my dick when actual tears pooled in those black coffee eyes.

"Take all of me, Triss."

I let go of her hair the moment that her entire body was shaking against mine. She collapsed forward on the chair to lay the upper half of her body down while she tried to squirm away from me, but I held her where she was by her hips to force myself as deep as I could get while she drained everything from me. I stayed that way until I could breathe again. Then I pulled back out of her and sat on the chair myself to pull her up to sit with her back against my chest. I watched in a state of pure mesmerization at the sight of her while her breasts rose and fell with every breath that she still couldn't catch. The sound of the back door from the house had me grabbing her towel from the chair beside us as quickly as I could move to throw it over Trista's entire body though.

"Go back inside, Pipsqueak. Daddy's busy," I yelled at Utah as he took one whole step out the door. He looked in our direction for just a split second before he'd raised a hand between us and his eyes.

"Jesus fucking —. Seriously, man? It's the middle of the day. In the open." He was still mumbling all the way back through the door.

"I told you someone would see," Trista said and laughed. She sat up and took the towel off herself to grab her bikini top. She held the tiny triangles against her breasts and swept all her hair over her right shoulder to wait for me to tie the strings again.

"And did you really just call yourself *Daddy* to Utah?" She laughed again. I grabbed her by all that hair that she'd just moved and pulled it until she was leaning back into me again.

"Careful. If you think you're going to laugh about it, I'll make you call me that too, baby."

I watched her eyes shift back and forth between mine, fully expecting her to have some sassy comment in return. I would've been more prepared for her to elbow me straight in the ribs than for what actually happened. She reached up to get her hand on the back of my head and pulled until I was close enough for her to kiss me. It was the softest moment we'd had since being reunited. Somehow, even more intense than every time I'd kissed her before this. I let go of her hair quickly and put both arms around her entire body instead. I squeezed her back against me until she was done kissing my mouth, then I kissed my way down her cheek and across her jaw until I could lay my head on her shoulder.

"I missed you," she whispered, like she'd been afraid to say the words out loud.

I smirked and rose up to kiss the side of her head. "Easy now. It almost sounds like you like me when you say things like that."

"I think I do. Sometimes."

"*Sometimes*," I repeated and laughed.

"Yeah. I mean let's not get carried away about it. I'm not going to lie and tell you that I haven't also hated you more than once in the last twelve hours alone."

"I love you too, baby," I said and kissed the side of her head another time. I forced myself not to laugh when she instantly sounded like she might hyperventilate. "Calm down, Triss. You can keep telling me that you hate me for as long as I'm alive and I'll still be just as happy to hear it every time."

She sat up again so she could look back at me over her shoulder and actually see me, like she needed to make sure I wasn't just fucking with her. I'd sit there and hold her questioning gaze until I was dead if that's what she needed to be able to believe that I meant every word. She didn't even move when the single tear escaped down her cheek. I shifted the rest of the way forward to wipe it from her skin with my thumb and put my arms around her again.

"Doing an awful lot of that lately, Fancy Face."

"I don't know why," she choked out. "I don't feel like I have any control over it anymore. I don't know when I started being fragile."

I scoffed. "Fragile like a bomb, maybe."

"Jersey —." She paused to look away from me, so I slipped my fingers under her chin to make her look right back at me. "Did you mean —? I don't think I've ever been in —. I don't know—."

"Are you planning to finish any of these sentences?" I finally interrupted.

"I really do hate you."

I laughed that time. "What are you trying to ask me, baby?"

"Did you mean it? Or was that just something that comes after sex for you?"

"Somehow, in like a fucking week, you clawed your way right inside me and latched on like a damn parasite. Now, there's more of you in my heart than there is of me. I can't even call it *my* heart anymore, Triss. It's yours now. You're the only one in there."

The tears fucking poured out of her after that. She gave up holding the little swimsuit top against herself and swung her legs over my left thigh to place the entire side of her body against the front of me where she could lay her head against my chest.

"Did I manage to make it worse?" I asked, confused by the sobs.

"I don't even know which of us is more fucked up anymore, J. That was the sweetest thing anyone has ever said to me," she said between all the crying.

"Then why are you —?"

"You called me a fucking parasite and it was *still* the sweetest thing anyone has ever said to me."

CHAPTER FIFTY

trista

I couldn't even believe that he just sat there patiently and held me until I got my shit back together long enough to stop myself from crying. It was an emotional blow for which I had not even been remotely prepared. I should've just told the man that I loved him too. I should've told him that I couldn't even remember the last time I'd heard someone say those words to me. Having to sit there and realize that it was probably back when my father was alive had me in uncontrollable sobs.

Even though I couldn't figure out how to tell him about the waves of emotions that were pulling me under, Jersey's arms stayed locked around me until I'd stopped shaking; like he could feel what was happening even without my words to explain it. I never thought I'd be the kind of woman who would cry after sex. I never imagined Jersey would be the kind of man who could keep his mouth shut about a woman who did cry after sex, but he didn't take the opportunity to make fun of me or even so much as laugh at me. That probably made me an even bigger asshole for not being able to tell him that I loved him too.

Once he'd tied my bikini top back into place and wrapped the towel around my body, he held my face in his hands just to kiss me another time. He was still an unstable disaster waiting to unleash chaos on someone. I was still an emotionally stunted mess who couldn't figure out how to express what I felt. In that moment though, I was finally able to feel like I didn't have to force any words out to try to fill the void that had been between us. For that brief walk back into his house, everything was simple and easy. I wanted him. He wanted me. We were both broken, and both okay with the other knowing it.

I could feel my face turn into a tomato to find all three of our housemates sitting together at the island when Jersey followed me into the kitchen.

"Listen, team," Indy said. "I don't want to make anyone terribly uncomfortable, but if you two just need someone to get things started between you again, I'm more than happy to volunteer to join you. I feel like maybe that would solve a lot of the tension that's just been hanging in the air around this house."

"You don't want to make anyone terribly uncomfortable and *that* is what comes out of your mouth?" Utah asked and laughed.

"Did he just invite himself to fuck both of us?" Jersey asked and looked at me.

"I don't think he was serious, J," I said, knowing full well that he was absolutely serious.

"I'm going to need every other human in this house with a dick to move the fuck back out by the end of the day," Jersey said.

"They don't need your help, Indy," Utah interjected, also realizing that Jersey's mood was about to head south quickly.

"They don't?" He asked. "Why do you know that?"

"Do we really have to discuss this right —?" Memphis tried to ask, only to be interrupted by Jersey.

"Baby boy caught the end of the show."

"You got to see it?" Indy screeched. "And you didn't think to say anything before this moment?"

"Why would I say any—?"

"Everything about this is disgusting," Memphis interrupted. "Nobody is moving out, Jersey Boy. Nate has contracts out for all of us now. They're posted absolutely everywhere. He's not even keeping it within his own organization this time. Dead or alive for Indy, Utah, and Jersey. Alive for Trista and me."

"What does he want with you?" Jersey asked Memphis.

"I don't know," she said quickly.

"Why are you lying?" Jersey pressed.

"Maybe a giant group session isn't the best time to do this," Utah said.

"I don't think I was talking to you," Jersey snapped. "I'm allowing your fucking Judge to continue breathing even after he suggested his own dick for *my* girl. I think you can sit there in fucking silence in exchange for that."

Memphis and I both shifted to stand in the path between the two men when Utah stood from his chair after Jersey's comment.

"You don't have to like one another, guys, but we're all stuck in this together for now," Memphis said from behind me. "Until we can figure out how to undo these contracts, we're all safer together."

I wasn't particularly concerned about Utah blasting his way through Memphis. I hadn't spent *that* much time around him, but there was absolutely zero chance of him shoving her out of the way just to get to the psycho in front of me. While said psycho in front of me presented a real risk of tossing me across the room just to get his hands on the person currently upsetting him. Jersey wasn't even looking at me. His eyes were locked directly over my head from the moment that Utah stood from that chair. I looked at the other two over my shoulder when I heard Memphis whisper again.

"Please, don't make it worse," she'd said. Utah's eyes dropped from Jersey in an instant when she placed her palm against his chest. He stared at her hand for a few seconds like he was worried that if he didn't keep an eye on it, it might pull off some inconceivable magic trick.

He sighed when he looked back at her face. "Come on, Indy. We've got things to do today."

"Do we?" Indy asked, looking around the room.

"We do now."

Jersey smirked and while I somehow both loved and hated that he was a cocky prick, the last thing that we needed was an actual face-off between the two titans in the house just then. I smacked him in the chest to force his attention back to me.

"Cut it out, J."

He smiled and put an arm all the way around my shoulders to pull me into him until he could lay his cheek down on the top of my head.

"Just because there's an audience here to save you now, that doesn't mean I won't put you in your place for it later when we're alone again, Fancy Face," he whispered.

"I know that whole moment was kind of my fault, but did it leave anybody else slightly aroused?" Indy asked Utah while they walked toward the door.

"*Kind of* your fault?" Utah repeated and held the door open for him. "It was *entirely* your fault, Indy. Go."

Jersey let go of me, and Memphis turned back to face us once the other two were gone.

"I know you're working through a lot right now, Jersey, but Utah is *not* your enemy," she snapped. "He didn't have to help, but he did anyway."

"Since you brought it up, why is he *helping*?" Jersey asked. "Why did either of them choose this side?"

This felt like it was about to be a terribly uncomfortable conversation. One that these two probably needed to have the chance to sort through alone.

"So," I said to no one, since they were both pretty well ignoring my presence by that point anyway. "I think I'm going to just — go anywhere else."

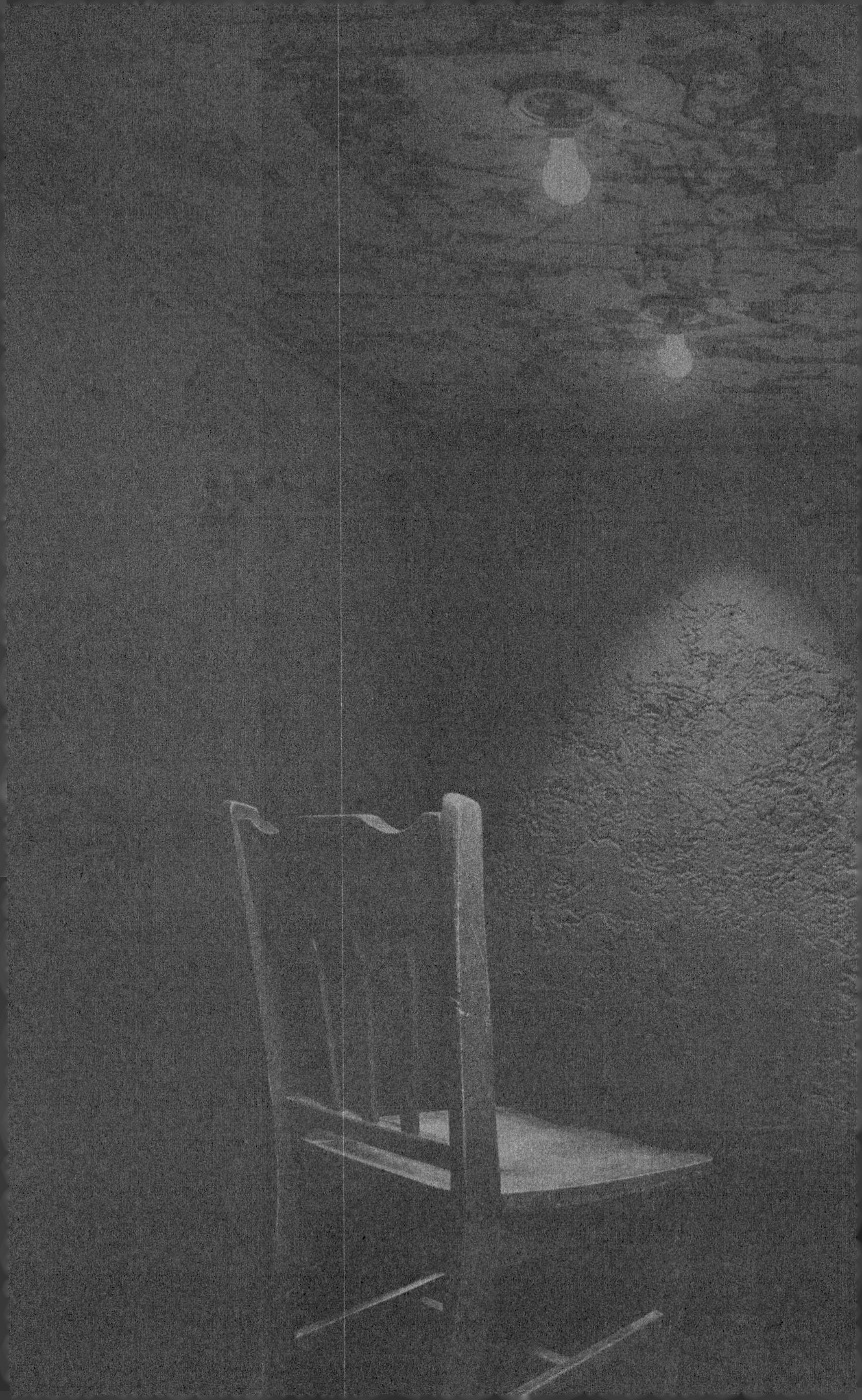

CHAPTER FIFTY-ONE

jersey

Memphis waited until Trista's footsteps weren't audible from the hallway anymore before she glared right back at me. I hadn't spent much time with or even around any of these people who'd moved into my house, and while Memphis stood here staring at me like she had every intention of smacking the shit out of me, I almost felt guilty about it. Of everyone here, I probably should've made a noticeable effort to at least be near her before this moment. She was the only thing that'd kept me tethered to this world for years.

"We *needed* help, Jersey," she hissed. "Trista and I never could've done that alone."

"That didn't answer my question, Memphis. Why are they here? What's in it for them? And how in the absolute fuck could you decide to trust anyone else in that organization after Texas and Chicago?"

Probably wasn't the way I should've been talking to the girl who'd tethered me to this world for years. I couldn't begin to guess what was wrong with me.

"Indy and Utah were in that organization, yes. But they did not do what you and I did," she said. "They handled different jobs. Indy was one of the first Judges who ever talked to me. He's different, Jersey. I know you don't believe that. I know you don't have any *reason* to believe that, especially now. But I'm asking you to believe *me*. Think about the things that've happened to you over the last six years, and all that you've learned about it in the last couple months. None of it happened the way that you thought it did. Now, imagine what those two might've had to experience to put them into this organization. It could be even worse than what you lived. And maybe that's why they're here."

It took all of about a quarter of a second before I felt like an absolute dumbass for not seeing it before.

I couldn't get across that kitchen nearly fast enough to crush her tiny body against me.

"I'm going to say this as clearly as I know how," I said against the top of her head. "Are you listening?"

She tried to nod her head, but she really couldn't move through how tightly I was holding her.

"I simply could not fucking care less about the life experiences of those boys, and I don't foresee that changing. I don't know them. I don't *want* to know them. But if *you* need to tell me what our President did to you and your world, I'm right here, honey. And we both know I'll kill everyone on this continent if that's what it'll take to make you feel better about it. Just say the word, boss lady."

Her body stiffened and I could hear her swallow. "I don't think it's that easy, Jersey."

She pushed out of my hold and turned away from me quickly to wipe both hands across her cheeks.

"It's absolutely that easy. Just tell me what to do. That's how it's always worked."

"I don't think it'd be wise to try to send you back out into the world for literally any reason just yet. You haven't exactly been stable at any point in the years that I've known you, and it's even worse right now."

"I'm fine, Memphis."

"That's cute. And not at all true."

"We're not talking about me right now," I insisted.

"We probably should," she said and laughed. "You're the only one who's been walking around this place looking for any reason to fight with anyone who breathes near you."

"I haven't done anything *to you*."

"But everybody else?"

"Trista —."

"Trista spent weeks crying anytime you left a room, Jersey."

"She cried today, too," I said quietly and couldn't stop myself from glancing down the hallway where she'd disappeared. The formerly emotionless, master manipulator spent weeks crying alone over me. Well, not even really alone. That motherfucking punk seemed to be ever-present these days. Who knew how much time they'd really spent together while I was hiding from all of them?

"Oh, my God," Memphis said. "I can actually see you getting pissy all over again right now. Just because she cries? Women have emotions, Jersey. You might want to come to terms with that."

"That's not —. No. I'm not mad that she has emotions. I was married to a woman who was nothing but emotion. Trust me, women and emotions are actually a strength of mine when I'm in the right mindset."

Memphis froze entirely at the mention of my wife.

"I'm really sorry that I looked into it so hard, Jersey," Memphis said quietly. "I'm sorry I didn't have the chance to be the one to tell you. I'm *so* sorry that it happened that way."

"It's got nothing to do with you, Memphis," I said and shook my head. "Bryson all but told me himself that he was the one who did it. I think I just chose to believe that it was part of the torture rather than to really believe what he was saying. Made it easier somehow."

"And now that you do know for sure?" She asked.

"Now," I said and chuckled. "Now, I really don't trust myself much."

"What's that mean?"

"I don't trust myself to not call Trista by the wrong name. I don't trust myself to not black out and hurt her just because she's the one who draws the emotion out of me. I don't trust myself to not hurt everyone else in this house just for being in this house when I always thought I'd be alone by the time I needed to be here."

"I'll tell the other two again to keep their distance," she said. "But they're not the problem, Jersey. You need to make your peace with Utah being around here. We're going to need him."

"We won't."

"You can't possibly be that cocky."

"And yet, I *am* that confident."

"You're a nightmare. That's what you are," she said and laughed. "Be better for Trista, Jersey. Get it figured out."

"You know, I don't think I ever would've expected to see the day when you ended up on *her* side."

"She's been through enough."

That was hard to argue with.

She'd handcuffed me to a bed, slashed the tires on my car, stole my money, still managed to walk right off with whatever was left of the heart I thought I didn't have anymore, and left me to disrupt every part of all our lives when I decided I was keeping her despite the repercussions of such a choice. I was staring down the hallway where she'd disappeared again with all those thoughts bouncing around in my skull.

"Just go be with her," Memphis said. "The other two are gone. It's not like you *need* to be doing anything else right now. She just needs your attention, Jersey. I got the feeling that she doesn't really know how to do relationships. She wouldn't know how to tell you what she needed even if you asked."

A few minutes later, I found myself staring at a perfectly naked, and nearly asleep, Trista in the giant bathtub in my bathroom.

CHAPTER FIFTY-TWO
trista

I heard the door to the bedroom, then the door to the bathroom, and I heard him stop breathing entirely once he was in here with me.

"You don't have to creep from the corner," I said and giggled. "I feel like maybe you've seen me without clothes before. A couple times, even."

He chuckled before he dragged the small wooden stool from the corner of the shower over to the side of the tub to sit beside it. He folded his arms on the edge of the tub and leaned forward to sit his chin on his arms.

"Figured you'd be out there with Memphis longer than that."

"She told me to come be with you. Apparently, neither of you want me around right now," he said and smiled.

"*Right now*," I repeated. "I think it's most of the time."

He smirked and his fingers dipped down into the water just enough to run up my arm toward my shoulder. I sat quietly for a moment to see what those fingers would end up doing.

"I'm sorry, Triss," he said so very, very quietly. "I'm having a hard time remembering the me that you know. Reminding myself that who I was isn't really who I am now. I know it's been weird for you because of that."

"The you that I know sure doesn't seem like the kind of man who'd sit here with me while I was in a bathtub just to apologize. Nothing about you ever really seemed like the apologizing kind of man."

He smirked while his fingers made their way to my collar bone and then up to my neck.

"My wife used to do the bath thing," he said. I tried instantly to sit upright and to cover myself at the same time just at the mention of her, like she was about to appear in this bathroom with us and catch me stealing her husband. He laughed and moved that hand until it was under my chin, where he could hold me by the jaw.

"She didn't do *the bath thing* in this house, Fancy Face. Calm down. I wasn't trying to make you uncomfortable. It's just — I don't know. I guess sitting beside a woman in a bathtub is just where I got used to talking about the hard shit that happens in relationships."

I stayed perfectly still, staring back at him while he held me where I was by my chin. He made it sound like it was perfectly normal to take a conversation about his wife and let it flow effortlessly into one about a different relationship, and I simply had no fucking idea how I was supposed to be reacting to such a thing. And I guess, maybe it was normal? I hadn't done this before. I hadn't been married and then had to figure out how to move on with another person. Hell, I hadn't even had an actual boyfriend from whom I had to move on

"Sit back down, baby. I'll stay here with you. We don't have to talk about Liz if it bothers you that much."

"I just don't know what I'm supposed to do, J," I said, sitting back in the tub again. "I know how it feels to have no one left. I know what it means to have human connection taken from you, but I didn't lose a spouse. Or a child."

"We're not competing for who's been hurt worse, Triss," he said and chuckled. "You don't need to know how it feels to lose a spouse. It feels just as fucking terrible as it does to lose your father."

"Do *you* want to talk about her?" I asked and tried to swallow an absurd amount of fear.

"Not particularly, but I don't want you to think you can't ask if you have questions about all of it. I never imagined you'd find out about them the way that you did."

"I don't want *you* to feel like you can't talk about them if you *need* to, J."

He smirked at that. "I made my peace with them being gone. I came to terms with it a long time ago. Now, I just have to figure out how to reconcile the way that I felt about her for the last half a fucking decade with the fact that she didn't actually pull the trigger."

His hand went back into the water to grip mine, and I just continued waiting quietly. Hoping desperately that he'd keep talking so I wouldn't have to figure out what I was supposed to say.

"Having to figure this out doesn't mean I'll stop wanting you, Triss. I don't want you to think that. I'm fucked up right now. I probably will be for a while. I don't even know what happens to me from minute to minute lately, and it's terrifying," he said and paused. "But I still want you, if you can figure out how to survive it with me. If you can survive me."

"If I survived the queen of Hell, I think I can survive you," I said and tried to smile. His hand tightened around mine in an instant and he sucked in a sharp breath like I'd slapped him right across the cheek just by mentioning his car. He stood up quickly to lean all the way across the tub to kiss me. Fucking hard. Not the soft and heartfelt kind that had been happening a lot lately. This one felt possessive and almost brutal, like he was about to try to prove a point.

"Fuck, J," I gasped out when he pulled back and looked down the front of my body.

"You've got two minutes to get your ass out of this tub and into my bed, Fancy Face."

His words ripped the ability to speak right out of me, so I just nodded at him while his thumb swept across my lips and down my cheek. He backed away to take my towel from the hook by the shower door and came right back to hold his hand out toward me. He pulled me to my feet as soon as he had my hand in his and he held the towel open while I turned my back to him so he could wrap it around me. He stepped all the way against me, and I felt his mouth on the sensitive skin just below my ear a second later. He seemed to be very much in a battle with himself over whether he wanted to use his tongue or his teeth on my neck, but his mouth moved right to my ear next.

"Two. Minutes."

How I didn't just collapse the moment that he left that bathroom was miraculous, but I'd never moved so quickly in my life to dry my body. I didn't even bother keeping the towel around me. It wouldn't stay that way much longer than me walking out of the bathroom anyway. Then I hated myself for a few seconds when I stopped to stare at my body in the mirror before I left. I'd really never been the self-conscious kind. I hadn't had actual boyfriends, so I'd never been cheated on. I hadn't experienced a boy, or a man for that matter, simply choosing someone else over me. But I hadn't been this man's first choice. Hell, I probably wasn't really his second, third, fourth, or even fifth choice. I was short with wide hips and a very round fucking ass. His wife was tall, thin, and perfectly feminine. I cursed like a sailor. I picked fights. I didn't keep any thought to myself, and I'd never even attempted to filter what came out of my mouth as a result. She was blonde with light skin. Everything about me looked dark and mean.

When Jersey opened the bathroom door again, I realized I'd spent my entire two minutes in a shady fucking place of self-doubt in my mind. This man stood there with his perfect jaw and thick shoulders, staring at me like he was about to consume every piece of me. He was nothing but infuriating confidence and absolute certainty. And he didn't spend even a single extra second before he was closing the distance between us. He bent down just enough to get his hands on the backs of my thighs and stood upright again to lift me off the ground until my legs were wrapped around his waist.

The way that he kissed me while he carried me toward the bed washed away every bit of the doubt that had overwhelmed me just a moment ago. He might as well have wiped my brain clean when he started lifting my body up and down like he was using me as the weight for his fucking bicep curls while my clit was being run across the ridges of his abs. There was not a single coherent thought left in my head after that. All of his weight crashed down on top of me a second later to take the air right out of my body along with my ability to think. He started thrusting his hips against me and I was never more annoyed that he hadn't used those two minutes that he'd given me to get his own jeans off. I was just as annoyed at myself that all it took to make me moan was feeling his trapped erection being pushed against my pubic bone. He smiled against my mouth, but there was no fucking way that I was going to open my eyes to have to endure seeing the smug look on his face over it. His face only recently healed. Smacking the shit out of him right now probably wouldn't go well.

"Who was taking care of this pussy while I was gone, Fancy Face?" He whispered in between kissing his way down my neck. He bit my neck when I didn't answer him immediately. "I asked you a question."

"Me," I managed to gasp out when his tongue swept across my nipple. I had a brief moment of panic when it dawned on me that he might've been asking if I'd actually fucked Indy or Utah while he was being tortured.

"Did you think about me?" He whispered in between the moans that he pulled from me with his lips on my breasts. "Was it me in your mind while you touched yourself?"

"Yes." The word came out without any thought. If I'd given myself the chance to think about it, I for sure would've told him *no* just to enjoy the reaction that it would get from him. He lifted himself back up to look at my face.

"Did it work?" He asked. "Can your hands do what mine can?"

Fucking with him was still my greatest joy in life.

"Even better," I lied. He stopped rocking his hips against me, stopped kissing me, stopped moving entirely. Then he lifted his whole body off me to just hover above me and smile.

"Show me."

The instant fucking panic and absolute regret.

I still hadn't ever touched myself for an audience, and I still didn't want to. The way that he continued to smile at me suggested that he knew that was exactly how I felt about it. My mind raced through the shit I'd said to him before when I wanted to piss him off just enough to make him do something.

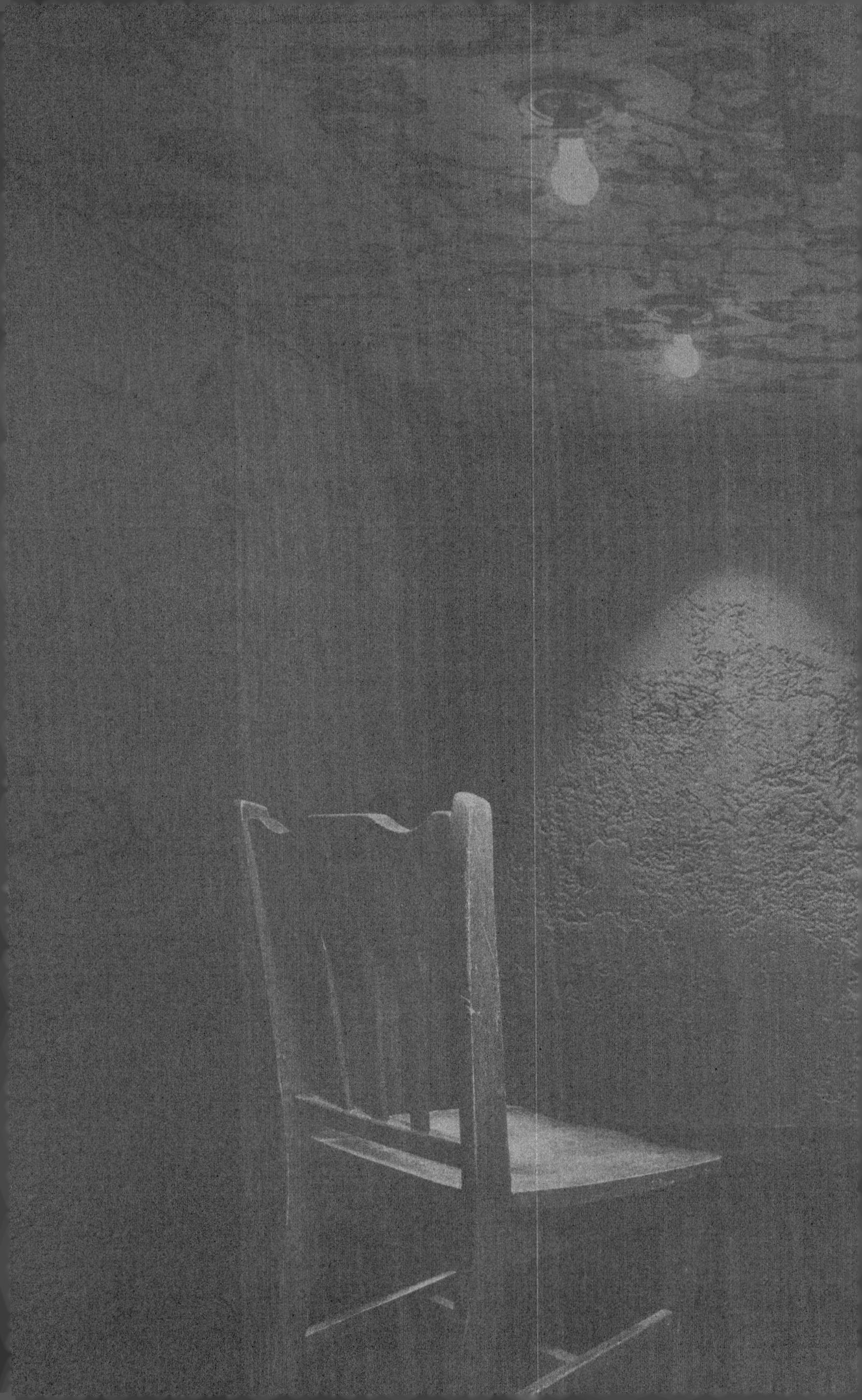

CHAPTER FIFTY-THREE

jersey

"Just fuck me, you egotistical shithead," she said and dug her fingernails into my back to try to pull me back down on top of her.

"Fuck yourself," I said and smiled again.

"J—."

"Go ahead. Teach me. If you're better than I am, show me what you need, Triss."

Neither of us moved, and she ended up adorably uncomfortable with every second that passed in the silence. I leaned back down to talk right into her ear, and she tried desperately to arch her back enough to get her breasts pressed against me.

"Do it your-fucking-self, Fancy Face," I whispered. "And then you can have what you really want. Touch yourself, and then you can have me. I'm not touching your clit again until you do," I said and raised up off of her again. "I'll fuck your mouth," I said and slid my fingers over her lips. "I'll fuck your tits." I moved that hand down between her breasts. "I'll fuck your ass. But I'm not giving you what you want until you do it yourself first, baby."

She was every bit as fucking stubborn as I was, and finding out if my willpower was strong enough to outlast hers was my favorite game. She locked her jaw into place and her eyes narrowed when she shifted just enough to drag her hand all the way down the center of her body. I was not at all prepared for that sight alone to have me nearly coming right in my jeans before she ever touched me, or even herself.

"What name should I be screaming?" She whispered. "Probably not Kyle, right?"

This little fucking menace.

I forced myself to chuckle.

"Pull that shit again and I'll have to kill *him*," I said. I went right back to her ear. "What name do you want me to make you scream when it's my turn? Which one fits? What am I to you?"

"Everything."

I rose up over her again until I could see her face, and there was a hint of panic in her eyes while they darted back and forth between mine; like she hadn't really meant to say the word. It just managed to slip out, and now she didn't know how to undo it.

"Yeah," she said after a silent few seconds. "Everything," she repeated like she was trying to reassure herself that she meant it. "You're everything I hate, and everything I — don't hate."

The way that I suddenly wanted to do everything to her at the exact same fucking time had me frozen in place, just staring at her.

"Sorry. Did I make it weird?" She asked. "We don't really do the *serious* thing. I ruined the moment, didn't I?"

I wondered if that was as close as I'd ever get to hearing her say she loved me.

Then I realized she was waiting for me to decide what was supposed to happen next between us.

I put my hand on the side of her face. "Baby?"

"Yeah?"

"If you don't fuck yourself *now*, I'm going to have to get mean."

"Prove it," she whispered, like she wanted desperately to challenge me, but she was still just a little afraid of actually doing it.

Everything about her was summed up perfectly in that one moment that lasted only a second or two. I couldn't help but smile at it, but I dropped my hand from her face down until it was collared around her neck. When she didn't even flinch, I started to squeeze. And as soon as I did, I could feel her hand moving in between us. I loosened my grip on her neck, but her other hand came up in an instant to hold onto my wrist to keep my hand in place. I smiled at her again.

"You could've just said *Jersey, I need help*," I whispered.

"We both know I could never say those words," she breathed out and arched her back to push up into me. I tightened my hold on her neck but I raised all the way off her so I could see what she was doing. I watched just her middle finger move in tiny, slow circles. Her eyes closed when she started to grind her hips against her own hand and her hold on my wrist tightened. I suddenly couldn't remember why I thought I wanted to play this game. I didn't possess the kind of self-control that this required. I'd nearly bit all the way through my own lip by the time her hand lowered and two of her fingers disappeared inside the tiny pussy that really wanted *my* fingers, *my* dick. She sighed when those fingers came back out completely soaked and went right back to her clit. And then I was fucking mad that she was that wet. I was even more annoyed that she'd let go of my wrist to move her fingers down to her nipple. She was doing everything I told her to do. She was about to get herself off without my involvement because I told her to fuck herself. And I was pissed off that she was able to do it? A tiny whimper came out of her when she pulled her bottom lip in between her teeth. I was fucking over it the second those brown eyes opened, and her back arched the moment that she'd focused on my face.

"Fuck this," I hissed.

She squealed when I smacked her hand away from her own body and shifted all the way down the front of her.

"Jersey —? What —?"

She probably had every right to be confused over me being shitty at her for doing exactly what I'd demanded that she do.

But that fucking whimper and every sigh that came out of her that way was supposed to belong to me. I sucked her clit into my mouth the second that my face was between her legs.

"Jesus fucking —. Jersey —," she panted and slammed both her hands into my hair. She raised her hips off the bed to push herself harder against my face, so I slid both my arms under her thighs and curled them around her to hold her in place. I watched her throw her head back on the bed and she was coming completely undone in a matter of seconds.

"Fuck, J."

Her hands fell out of my hair while she tried to catch her breath. I was off that bed in the blink of an eye to get my jeans off. She giggled and wrapped both arms around my neck as soon as I was back on top of her.

"Didn't like that my fingers do just fine on their own?" She asked and kissed the tip of my nose.

"*Just fine*," I repeated and laughed. I forced my hand down between our bodies to get the head of my dick inside her, and she tried to suck in all the air in the room. "Do your fingers feel anything like this?" I asked and couldn't help the groan that came out of me when I forced my dick the rest of the way into her. Her hands had abandoned my neck and shifted down between us where she could sink her nails into my chest.

"No," she finally breathed out when I slid back out and rammed in another time. "Please."

"Please what, Triss?" I asked without even so much as hesitating in the thrusts. I almost laughed thinking about what she might say given my constant demands for her only words to be my name or *please*.

"Fuck me, Jersey. I don't want to feel anything else. Fuck me until there's nothing left but you."

Son of an absolute bitch, if she hadn't frozen me right in place again. This weird fucking reminder that I was the thing that brought her to life just as much as she did for me, even if we were weird as shit when it came to trying to talk about anything other than sex. She was right. *This* was what we did best. *This* was where we connected. What happened between us definitely wasn't what any sane person would consider *lovemaking*, but I was able to fuck her into realizing she felt *something* for me, even if she wasn't able to come out and call it love yet. She was able to fuck me into feeling like I was still human enough to be what she needed out of this life.

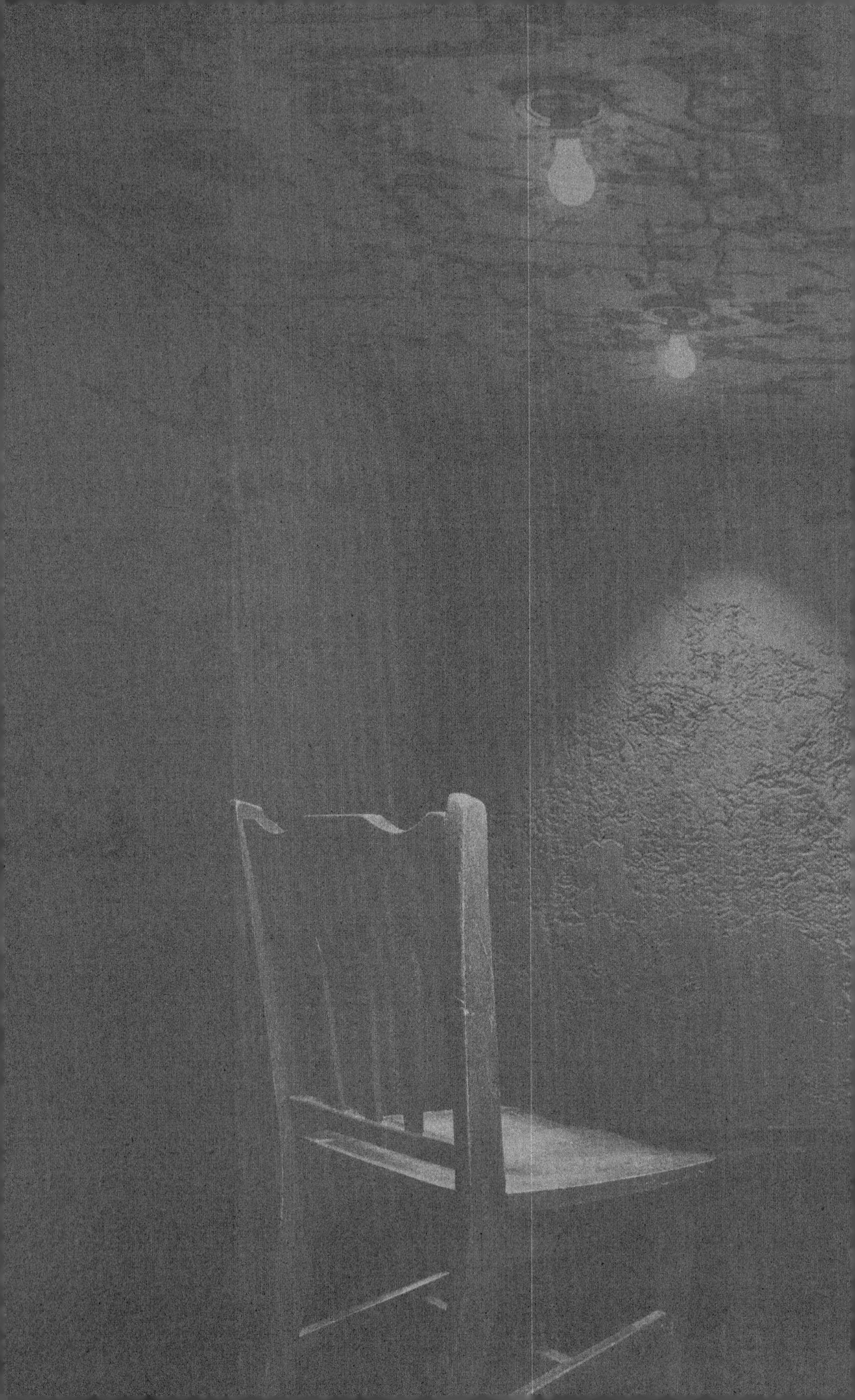

CHAPTER FIFTY-FOUR

jersey

I pretty successfully fucked her until there was nothing left but me. Everything about her might as well have melted away by the time I was finished. And even then, I really wasn't finished. I let her have a break in between each time, but we didn't leave that room the rest of the day. We both ended up in the shower before we actually attempted to sleep. Then getting to listen to her giggle the entire time that we swapped out the sheets on the bed so neither of us had to sleep in a puddle had me feeling some kind of way.

We hadn't sorted out any of the next steps that were necessary for either of us to move on with life. We hadn't talked about what still needed to be done about her stepdad's organization. We hadn't tried to breach the fact that neither of us even knew how to bring up those topics to the other but spending several hours attempting to rearrange the interior layout of her organs seemed to leave us both feeling better about everything anyway. Hiding behind sex until we were both drunk off each other let us push the rest of the issues off to another day.

Just when I thought she'd curl up right next to me and pass out, she threw the blanket off me and sat on me another time. My hands landed on her hips, because that was just where they lived now.

"We're not going to have a dry place to sleep tonight if we do this again," I reminded her. She started moving her hips to drag herself up and down the already growing length of my dick.

"We'll stay on your side then," she said and smiled. "This is the longest streak we've had of me not hating you. Don't ruin it."

"*Not hating* me," I repeated and chuckled. I put my hand on the side of her neck just to move my thumb back and forth across the ball of her cheek. I was comfortable with how I felt, but I wasn't about to continue saying it or pushing her to own how she felt if she didn't understand it herself yet.

"I haven't done this before, J," she said quietly.

"You've been in this exact position at least nineteen other times in the last six hours, Fancy Face."

She smacked my chest. "How do you know when something is real? When it's love?"

I about scared her right off me when I snapped my hand closed around her neck. I'd done this more than once in the last six hours too, but I squeezed way harder this time than I had any of the others. Both her hands ended up latched around that wrist when her cheeks started to turn pink and her eyes widened. But I did this so often now that she didn't actually try to escape. I didn't stand a chance at putting into words what she made me feel, so I really didn't expect her to be able to understand it at the level that I'd mean it if I offered her just words. Instead, I waited until she was squirming and becoming noticeably nervous before I released her throat, and she sucked in a giant breath.

"Do I make you feel like the rush that comes with that first gasp of air?" I asked.

She slowly nodded her head. "Yeah."

"That's how you know, baby."

I slipped my hand around the back of her neck to pull her mouth down to mine. She took her time with me after that, and I let her. I grabbed her hips one time, planning to roll her to take control of it myself but when she grabbed both my hands and held them against the mattress up by my head, I let her do that too.

Go figure.

I'd spent half the fucking day thinking about how we weren't the kind of couple who *made love* just for every move that she made in this moment to turn me into a liar. And I didn't have it in me to undo it. She was fucking powerful when she was fueled by emotion. Everything she did was so intentional, everywhere she touched set my skin on fire. Everything she did screamed the words that she still hadn't been able to force herself to say.

DISTANT SCREAMS PULLED me out of sleep, and then I realized that my body was being dragged across the floor. My brain reminded me that I was in that fucking concrete box and it was Bryson throwing me around while my daughter's cries about a spider haunted my unconscious moments from another lifetime. The full weight of his body was on mine the next second so I started to fight back. The sound of Memphis' voice broke through to my mind. She sounded like she was crying. She was screaming for me. Begging, even. It sparked something truly demonic inside me because if she was begging, it was because she was in trouble and desperately needed my help. The harder that I focused on what her voice was trying to say, the more I realized that she was begging me *to stop*. And I'd never been more confused by a single moment in my life.

When my vision cleared, fucking Utah came into focus first. Memphis was directly behind him. She had a white knuckled hold on his shoulder while she hid there with him between us.

"Don't hurt him, Utah," she whispered, and the second that our eyes locked, she disappeared. I was on my back, he was sitting directly on top of me, our arms were tangled around each other's but my eyes went back to searching for Memphis before I spent any more time being concerned about this kid. Memphis was in the corner of the bedroom. She was trying to pull Trista from the floor, where Triss was cowered with her hands over her face like she'd been crying.

I looked back at Utah, fully prepared to pummel this kid until he was nothing more than pulp so I could get to the girls across the room. I didn't end up having to say or do anything, when he and I had stared at each other for a long few seconds, he simply nodded his head before he released my arms and stood to get off my body. He even held his hand out to drag my ass up to my feet, just to add to my state of fucking confusion. I stared back at him once I was upright in front of him, but I tried to shake my head clear. I took a single step toward the girls, but Memphis was shaking her head at Utah, and he immediately swung an arm across my chest to keep me from moving. Memphis walked Trista out of the room with her arm around her shoulders while Trista continued to cry. She didn't look at me. Not even a glance in my direction. Out of an unpleasant habit, I looked down at my hands in panic. I didn't see any blood. They didn't hurt like I'd spent the last few minutes punching someone.

"What'd I do?" I asked that fucking punk, because he was the only one left in here. When he only shook his head, I immediately went for the door to find the girls. Utah grabbed my arm before I made it anywhere.

"Come on, man. Just give her the rest of the night," he said. "Let her be alone right now. She needs it. Looks like you need it."

"Did I hurt her?"

"She was screaming. And not like she was enjoying it, New Jersey. That's why we came in here. She was quiet by the time I actually got to you. Your hands were around her neck."

I looked down at my hands again, and nearly threw up everywhere.

"I didn't mean to —. I didn't even know —."

I couldn't even figure out what to say to this kid.

Fuck, I couldn't even figure out why he was still in this room with me.

"Can you tell her —?"

"She knows," he interrupted. "If even I know that you wouldn't *intentionally* hurt her, she knows it too."

I stopped trying to figure out why my lungs had shriveled up to nothing and looked at this kid instead, painfully confused by this weird moment of camaraderie with someone I'd spent the last few days despising.

"We've all got our shit, New Jersey. Just — just own it. Fuck it up before it fucks you up. You know? Don't let it ruin her life too. Figure it out for yourself so you're not the next thing that she has to recover from."

I couldn't even begin to imagine how I was supposed to respond to that.

CHAPTER FIFTY-FIVE
trista

All I wanted was to be alone, and that was the last thing that these people intended to allow. Memphis brought me back to her room and locked us in here. She pushed me down to sit on the edge of her bed, but she continued to pace around uncomfortably. I had no idea how long that went on before there was a knock on the door.

"No, Jersey Boy. Leave her alone for the night," Memphis called through the door.

"It's me, Angel."

She moved to the door so quickly that she was a tiny, little pale blur flying across the room. I started sobbing all over again when I heard Jersey's car start all the way from the fucking garage because the damn thing was so loud.

"You let him leave?" Memphis screeched. "Why? He shouldn't be alone right now either, Utah."

"I would've had to knock his ass out cold to keep him from doing something he wanted to do, Memphis."

"Then why didn't you?" She hissed. She went running around

him like she somehow believed she'd catch Jersey and talk him out of leaving. When Utah knelt in front of where I was sitting, I was suddenly very aware that I was just wrapped in the throw blanket that sat on the bench at the foot of Jersey's bed. I didn't even remember picking it up. I very distinctly remembered just falling asleep wearing nothing because neither of us had bothered with clothes for most of yesterday or through the night.

"Sorry," I said to him and tried to wrap the blanket a little tighter around me after realizing that that very much meant he and Memphis had a full look at both of us during what just happened in that room. He put his hand under my chin and pushed up until I was looking straight up at the ceiling.

"Can you breathe alright?" He asked. "Swallow?"

"It hurts," I admitted. It still kind of felt like a weight was just sitting on the front of my neck every time I tried to do either of those things. Utah sighed when Memphis stomped her frustrated little feet back into the room with us.

"He said he wouldn't come back here tonight," Utah told us both. "That way you could sleep and feel safe about it."

"I'm not going back in that room."

"I figured as much," he said and stood up. He pulled his shirt over his head and laid it across my knees. "Come on, ladies. Sleepover in the living room."

Utah herded Memphis out of her own room so I could at least put his shirt on, but she was still standing right outside the door when I opened it again.

"What happened?" She asked. "Were you talking about something? Fighting? Something else that I don't really want to think about?"

"Sleeping. I was sleeping, Memphis."

I went to the living room and dropped down onto the opposite end of the sectional from where Utah had setup camp. I rolled so my back was to the rest of the room and squished my face into the cushions to try to muffle my own sobbing since everyone was determined to sit here with me in my little box of emotional turmoil.

"Will you follow him?" Memphis asked. God fucking knew she wasn't talking to me so I didn't bother to move.

"He thinks way too highly of himself to hurt himself, Angel," Utah said quietly.

"Please, Utah?"

I felt the couch move while he stood up again before she'd ever even said his name.

"When he realizes I'm tailing him," Utah said. "I'm throwing you under the crazy bus hardcore."

I imagined she stepped all the way into him to hug him because I could hear him having to force his lungs to work and I could hear her muffled sniffles.

"I'm going out to Kyle's before I leave," Utah said. "I'll have him come in to check on you both after a bit."

"I'll send Jersey's location to your truck," Memphis said.

The couch moved again when Memphis sat right next to me on the edge of the cushion where I'd planted myself. I rolled part of the way toward her when she put her hand on my arm. She was the only female that I'd ever considered my friend, but we hadn't really become the kind of girlfriends who touched each other either.

Or maybe we had?

I was obviously the absolute fucking worst at navigating people.

"I know I'm probably supposed to tell you not to put up with that kind of behavior," Memphis said quietly. "Fuck that guy and you're better than this and don't let men mistreat you because we're strong women and all that."

"If that's what you're *supposed* to tell me, what are you actually going to tell me?"

"If you absolutely *need* to be away from him for a while, Triss, I'll help you," she said and sighed. "I really will. I don't think anyone would blame you. I can set you up to hide from him. For a little while, anyway. I don't think I could misdirect him for the rest of your life. Once he decides something – or someone – is his, there's really not much undoing that."

"Is that what you think I should do?" I asked, and wanted to cry all over again.

"I don't think I get to decide that for you."

"It's my fault anyway," I said and turned away from her again. "He told me more than once that he wasn't okay and that he didn't want to touch me because I make him emotional and that's when he gets worse."

"None of that makes it *your* fault, Trista. He was in a bad way before you were ever in the picture. He was just alone then. So it really didn't matter that so much brokenness existed inside a very lonely man. I don't think he even remembers how to be with other people."

"I don't want to leave, Memphis," I finally said and just started fucking crying again. "I've never had —. Everything I wanted pretty much depended on —."

"Trista," she said quietly and squeezed my arm again until I rolled back toward her.

"I haven't had a family since I was six. I didn't get to have friends. Now, I thought —. I don't know. I feel like I have you guys. But everything I thought I could have eventually, it all kind of centered around Jersey. He was the reason to keep running, to stay hidden while he was gone, to get him back here. I didn't bother making plans or even thinking about the future before him because it was *just* running. I wanted to think that if he was around, there could be more *with him*."

"He wouldn't hurt you consciously," she said, then she paused for a second and started laughing.

"This is funny now?" I choked out.

"It's insane. That's what it is. He wouldn't hurt you consciously *now*. Like he didn't also want to murder you a couple months ago over the tires on the car. Like he didn't toss you into the trunk every chance he got. Like he wasn't pissed off beyond measure just for having to let you ride in the seat beside him. I know you probably don't believe me when I say that he didn't mean to hurt you after you experienced all that. But I believe it. He didn't mean to hurt you. He was ready to just be tortured until he died to give us a chance to stay alive. I don't know what it feels like to be in love, but I can imagine it feels something like that."

"What would you do if it were you, Memphis?"

"I think —," she said and paused to sigh. "I think if you want to make this work, you probably need to realize that everything that's already happened was likely the easy part. Giving him the chance to repair himself, to figure out how to be better for you — getting through that will be the hard part. That's the kind of healing that takes years, Triss, and even once you think it's done it manages to resurface when you aren't ready for it. So, you can let the world crush you right along with it when it all comes crashing down on top of him. Or you can do what you asked of him, and you can survive it for him. *With* him. You can be the thing that gives him the strength to keep standing back up and to keep trying. If someone looked at me the way that he looks at you, I think I'd be ready to fuck up all his demons on his behalf."

"Everybody doing okay?" Kyle asked from the doorway to the kitchen. "That kid asked me to come in here."

"*That kid,*" Memphis repeated and laughed. "What is it with Utah and you old Marines?"

Kyle made a noise and Dandy trotted right across the room to sit next to the couch.

"You gals need me to stick around?" He asked, while he was already turning to try to leave.

"What happens to him?" I asked quickly. "Does it happen to you too? Do you have an uncontrollable urge to devastate the people around you sometimes just for the fuck of it?"

"Trista," Memphis snapped.

"Sorry," I mumbled. "I guess I'm not in a very *beat around the bush* kind of mood right now. I just want to understand, and he only knows how to speak once every three weeks."

Kyle sighed and came into the living room to sit on the end of the sectional that curved back around so that he could face us but still leave plenty of distance between himself and the sobbing girl who I'd become.

"I haven't hurt anybody in years," Kyle said. "But you can't hurt anybody if you don't keep anybody around."

"Is that why you stay here?" Memphis asked.

He looked down at his own hands and his dog moved right back to his side when his leg started to bounce up and down. He had no intention of answering Memphis.

"Are you happy?" I squeaked out between my attempts to strangle the sobs. "Living this way?"

He sighed again but he stayed quiet while he looked back at us.

I pulled the collar of Utah's shirt up over my nose to try to hide while I cried again. I knew the weight of feeling alone all the fucking time. I carried that shit everywhere I went for years. Something about having to imagine Jersey wandering alone around this world aimlessly for the rest of his life trying to digest what had actually happened to his family was more than I could handle.

"That's why he'd fucking do anything for you," I mumbled through the shirt to Memphis. "That's why he'd flip his shit and try to shoot some guy just for honking at him on the road when he was upset about you. That's why he'd just sit in a room and let someone beat him to death."

"He did what when somebody honked at him?" Memphis asked.

"Your weird relationship with him was always just over the phone before this," I said. "He could keep you and not have to feel so alone all the time, but you were always a safe enough distance away that he didn't have to worry about hurting you or scaring you away. Keeping me is what's complicated for him. All I do is piss him off."

I glared at Memphis when she chuckled at that.

"I think that's probably what he likes best about you," she said quickly.

"That he hates me? You're going to sit here and tell me that's what he likes *best* about me?"

Kyle fucking laughed that time.

"God, you do sound a lot like him," he said.

"You challenge him," Memphis said. "*You* are the reason for him to get it figured out. You're why he would want to be better."

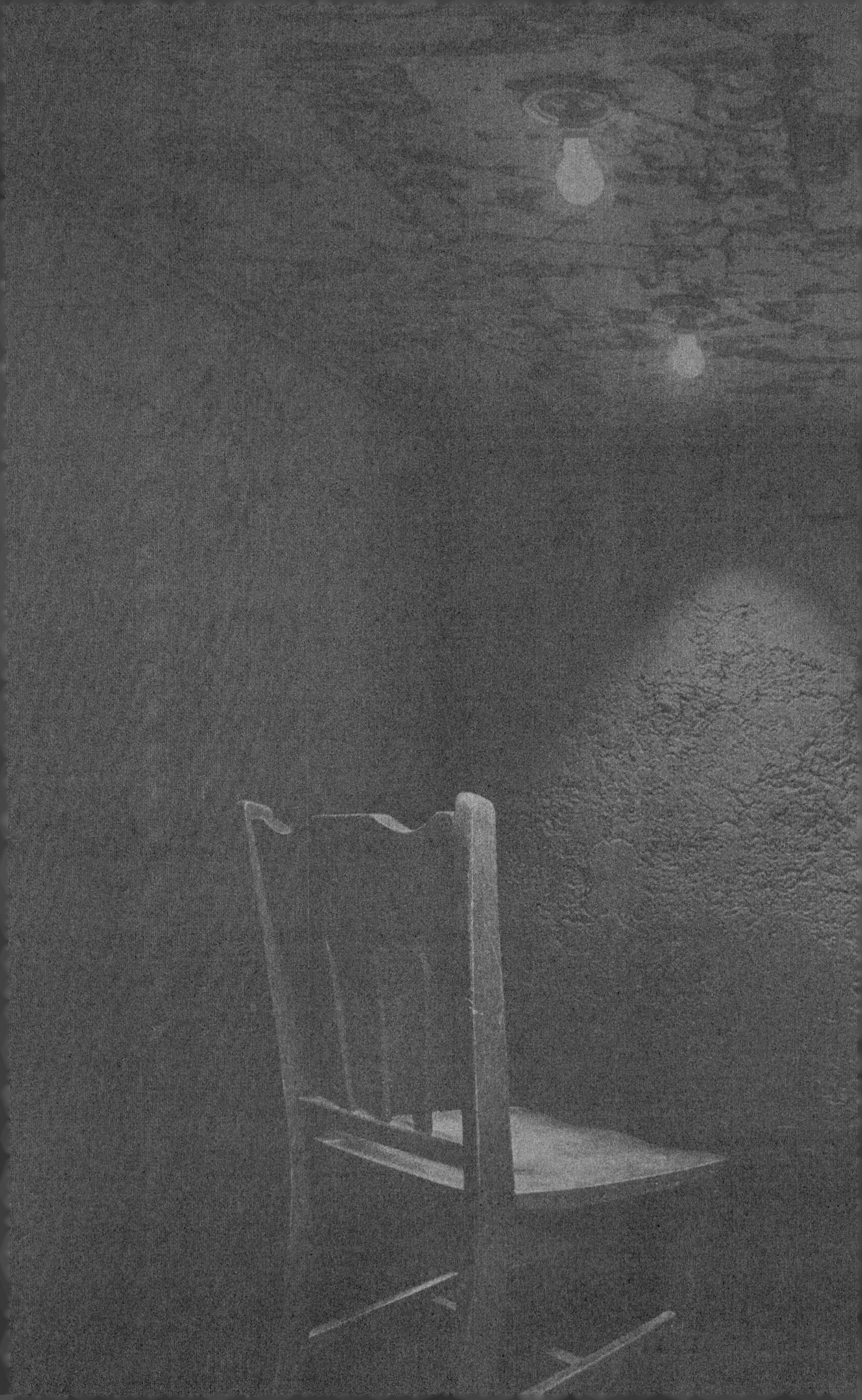

CHAPTER FIFTY-SIX

jersey

I had no idea how much time I spent just driving around in the dark. There was an endless maze of roads that separated the cornfields in this part of the state, and something outside of my own brain was deciding when and where I turned. How I ended up sitting in a liquor store parking lot was beyond my memory. How the fuck I ended up at a liquor store that was still open at this time of night was even more baffling. I had no recollection of hurting the only woman left on the planet who'd decided I was worth a damn, so it shouldn't have been surprising that something under the surface felt like it needed to numb that with alcohol before I really had to face it. I was in and out too much. My brain was trying to protect my conscious mind from experiencing what was really happening. I hadn't figured out how to go on living knowing what I knew now about my family. And somehow, I suddenly had to own that I really was capable of hurting Trista in the worst ways without ever meaning to.

My brain could block out giant chunks of time to keep me from having to confront those things, because I couldn't just plan out a healthy way to move past it. It could apparently guide me to a fucking liquor store, thinking that I would need to feel the familiar burn of alcohol to be able to survive the emotions that would be waiting for me right around the corner any minute now. But it couldn't fucking figure out how to force my body to just behave like a regular human. It couldn't figure out how to process what I thought about my wife in a way that would let me just fucking release her. It couldn't figure out how to see beyond what was behind me, so it wanted me to drown those memories and realizations until I couldn't feel anything at all.

The next thing I knew, I was staring down at a whiskey bottle while I stood next to Seph. It didn't look like I'd opened it yet, but I sure as shit needed to get rid of it before that happened without me realizing I was doing it.

"Don't do it, man," a voice said from somewhere beside me.

Motherfucking Utah in that stupid truck.

He was parked just a few feet away, and I hadn't even noticed that he was there until he spoke. I watched his arm drop down to reach for the handle inside the truck, so I launched myself in his direction to put a hand on that door and hold it closed.

"If you so much as set foot on this pavement, I will beat you to death right here and now, kid. You need to leave."

"I can't do that," he said.

"You must not be very smart."

He smirked. "The girls asked me to make sure you didn't do anything stupid, New Jersey. Trust me, I don't *want* to be here anymore than you want me here."

"If I didn't kill myself six years ago, I won't do it now either."

"Yeah? You remember driving here? Remember buying that?" He asked and nodded toward my hand.

"Leave," was all I could say before I allowed him to imply that I could kill myself without even knowing it. Although, I'd spent countless hours wondering why it hadn't ever gone exactly that way. I turned back toward Seph and heard that truck door open a motherfucking second later anyway.

"Do you think I'm joking when I tell you that I can't be around you right now either, slick? Or are you actually just that stupid that you don't know how to hear a genuine warning when it's being offered? I already want to kick the shit out of you on a regular day. If the fucking crazy me gets his hands on you, he won't stop until you're dead. And while I've got to tell you, that doesn't sound like such a bad thing to me, Liz would never forgive me for that."

I only made it another step away from him before I stopped and tried to force myself to breathe.

"Triss," I whispered, mostly to myself. "Triss would never forgive me."

"Jersey," Utah said quietly, and stepped directly in front of me. "You've got plenty of your own demons to fight right now, man. Don't add me to that list just because you're mad. I don't want to hurt an old man."

I chuckled at that.

And then I was pissed that I chuckled at that.

"Who are you mad at, man?" Utah asked.

"Right now? You."

He smirked again. "Who are you really mad at? Who do you see when *you* disappear? It's not me. I don't think it's Triss. Are you mad at your wife?"

"I'll use your face to break this bottle if you mention her again."

"It's just yourself then, isn't it? And that's why you don't know how to handle it," he said. "It's not Trista's fault. No part of this is. That's what you need to be thinking about right now. She isn't your wife. She never will be. And if you're thinking you'll find a way to turn Trista into some version of her to give yourself a chance to make up for what's happened, you probably need to let her go now so she can start letting go of whatever she thought this was. That's no way to expect her to live."

I pushed the bottle into his chest while I walked around him to Seph.

"Don't let me see you again tonight," I warned while I got into the car.

"Does this make us friends now?" He asked, and laughed.

"No."

CHAPTER FIFTY-SEVEN
trista

I didn't remember falling back asleep, but Persephone's exhaust was the thing that woke me up again the next morning. I was up off that couch like it was on fire and headed into the kitchen, assuming that was where Jersey would be in a few minutes. Memphis, Indy, and Utah were all sitting at the island together already, but nobody spoke while we all just waited for the door to open. Memphis chuckled when we all watched Jersey walk by the window, headed toward the front porch of the house.

"Should've seen that coming," she said. "He knows we're all in here."

I was headed for the door myself a second later.

"Triss, maybe you shouldn't —," Memphis started to say.

"I'll go," Utah interrupted.

I was outside and on my way to the front of the house before I'd realized that Utah was following me and that Memphis' concern was actually me being alone with Jersey again.

Jersey was leaning back against the porch railing with his arms crossed over his chest by the time I made it around the front of the house, very much just waiting for me. I felt like I might throw up everywhere when he looked my entire body up and down. I was still only wearing Utah's T-shirt. And to make that even worse, Utah popped up right behind me a second later. Jersey scoffed and hung his head back like it was taking everything in his power to just stay right where he was. I glanced back at Utah, and I felt better when he nodded at me. I went the rest of the way to Jersey while Utah jumped up to sit on the rail on the opposite end of the porch. Jersey was still glaring at Utah by the time that I was standing in front of him.

"I tried to tell you it was a bad idea," he said quietly once he finally did look back at me.

I was going to murder him.

"That's the first thing you're going to say to me?" I asked. "*I told you so, Fancy Face,*" I hissed at him. His whole body snapped upright at the tone that I'd used, and Utah jumped right back down off his perch on the railing.

"Don't you fucking *dare* come even a step closer, child," Jersey said and pointed at Utah. "She's fine."

I reached out and smacked his hand down. "*He* didn't do anything, J."

Jersey looked from where I'd smacked his hand back to my face, like he couldn't believe what I'd just done.

Which was fair, because I really couldn't believe it either.

"Feeling powerful now that you've got a body-bitch following you around, Triss?" He asked and glared back at Utah.

"This isn't about him."

"Trista," he started again, surprisingly softer that time. "I really did try to tell you. I already knew I couldn't be trusted with you. What I mean to say is —."

"What you mean to say is you're *sorry*, Jersey," I interrupted, completely baffled that such a thing hadn't somehow been the first thought he had. He sighed and put his fingers under my chin to raise it so he could look at my neck. He moved like lightning to get his arms around my shoulders and squeezed me against him.

"I *am* sorry," he whispered against my head. "*So* fucking sorry. I just don't know how to —. How am I supposed to explain it? You didn't live it. You weren't there. You wouldn't understand. How could you know what this is like?"

"I'd at least have a chance to understand if you'd just tell me how it feels," I said and tried desperately to swallow the sobs. He squeezed me even harder.

"*How it feels*," he repeated and chuckled. "It feels like having to feel everything all at the same time. Something that I thought I buried, something that I thought I left behind was just ripped right open. I spent so much time hating her. I spent so much time mad at her. Just to find out that it was more my fault than I'd ever even known. I always blamed myself for leaving, for keeping the job that made things difficult for her. But now —."

He stopped to try to swallow his own emotions then, so it was my turn to squeeze him. But I forced just enough space between us after that so that I could look up at his face.

"Keep going, J. Tell me."

"Now," he said and paused. "Now I have to find a way to face that they were all killed just because someone wanted my attention. I hated my wife for this. That she could do this to me. And now I have to spend all my life wondering what her last moments were really like. Did she know they were there because of me? Did she scream for me? Did she fight to stay alive? Did she have to watch Faith —?"

He couldn't even finish the last thought.

And I was glad that he couldn't.

I didn't want to hear it anymore than he wanted to say it.

Utah was gone by the time that Jersey let go of me after that, and Jersey couldn't help but smirk at the spot where Utah had been.

"Your body-bitch isn't a very good one," he said.

"Jersey."

"I'll stay somewhere else for a while, Triss," he said. "You guys can all stay here. Stay together. I'll come back when I get my head sorted out."

"What? No. You're not leaving. We *just* got you back."

"I would've killed you if he hadn't been there, Fancy Face. And I wouldn't have even known I'd done it."

He brought a hand up to my cheek and my heart broke all the way open to see tears in the man's eyes.

"I never understood why or how I managed to live through all that back then," he said quietly. "Some part of me understands it now. I'm still here because you were always going to need me. But that's kind of a double edged sword now too. I wouldn't survive it a second time, baby."

"Survive what?" I asked, a little afraid of the answer.

"You're what keeps me here, Triss. I'd never live through losing you too. I wouldn't even want to. I hate myself right now. I hate myself for the way that I felt about Liz for all these years. I hate myself for what I did to you. I hate myself for not knowing what the fuck I'm supposed to do about it now. But what I hate even more than all of that is that I'm so fucking terrified of how I'd have to feel about myself if I did something even worse to you. If *I* end up being the reason that I lose you too."

"We'll figure something out, J," I said and leaned into him again so he'd hug me another time. "Just please don't leave."

He chuckled while he squeezed me. "Before anybody does anything else, I'm going to need you to go burn the fucking shirt that you're wearing, baby."

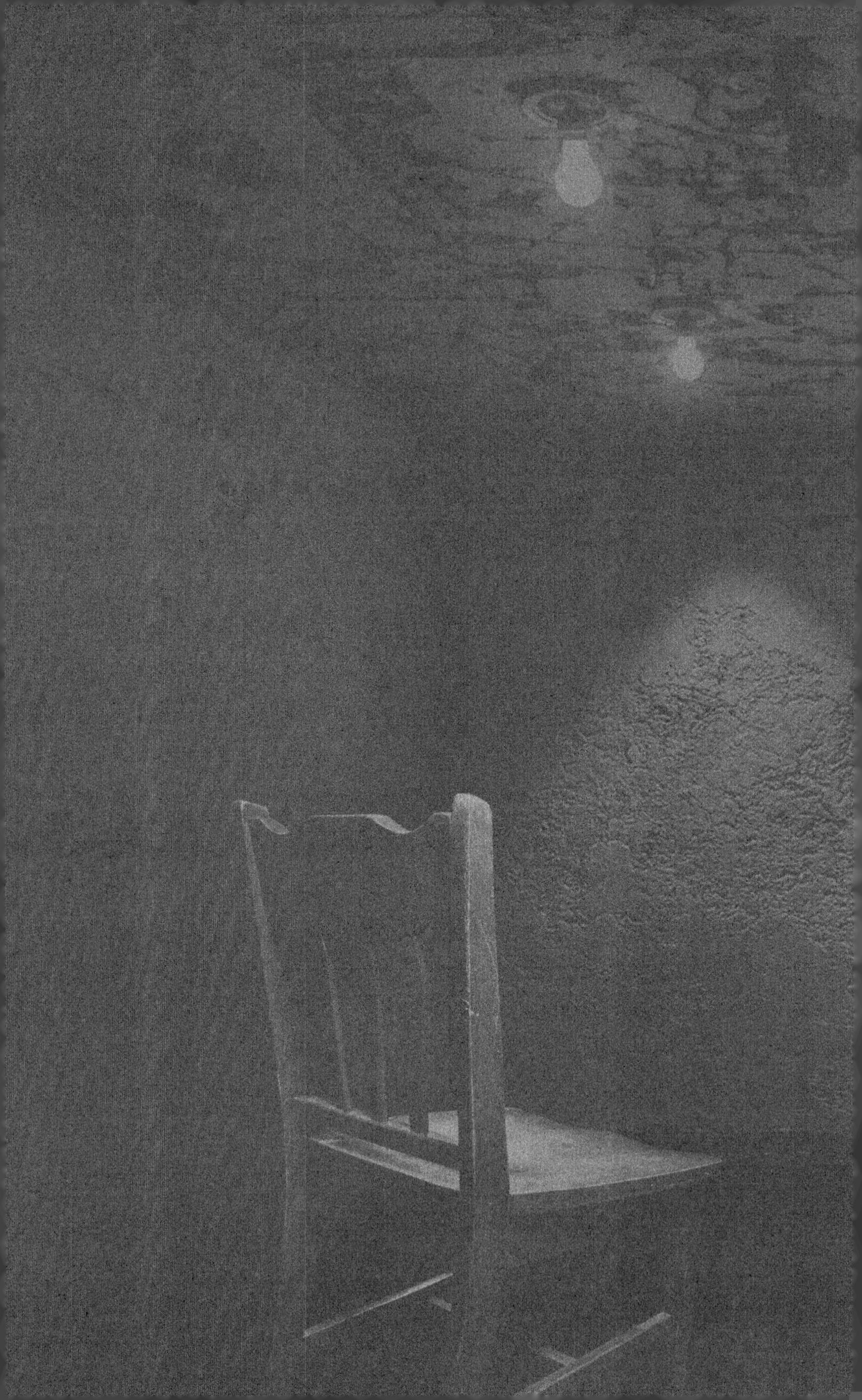

CHAPTER FIFTY-EIGHT

jersey

Trista spent the next few days doing everything in her power to keep me preoccupied. She was convinced that isolation wasn't the answer for either of us anymore and that we both needed to be leaning into the company of all these other fucking people around my house. And for some inexplicable reason, I hadn't been able to successfully refute any of her ideas. Everywhere that she went, I followed. Anything she asked me to do, I just did. Anywhere she wanted me to be, there I fucking was. She'd begged me not to leave. Cried. I didn't stand even the slightest fucking chance at walking away from her after that. She acted like I was somehow the thing that was holding her sanity together and that if I wasn't around, she'd just topple right into chaos.

For as much as I didn't like having to acknowledge it, she'd already managed to override every ounce of control that I thought I had left. I'd blacked out and tried to fucking kill her while she slept beside me, and rather than taking that as the most obvious fucking sign that she should've sprinted away from me as far as she could get, she was determined to hold me closer. She didn't spend even a second of her time acting like she believed I was a full-blown monster. She never stopped looking at me like I could walk on water if I just decided one day that I might try it. I spent days trying to prepare myself for her to recoil any time I reached for her, but she never even so much as flinched when my hands searched for her.

She was made of fucking stone.

She was also the bane of my existence, and the reason that I was sitting under the pool shelter next to Utah and his Judge, who simply never stopped fucking talking, while both girls were on floats in the water.

Trista might have been made of stone, she might've taken over every spare moment and thought I had, but she was well on her way to the punishment of a lifetime if she continued to wear the world's smallest bikini in front of this entire crew of males. Especially the male directly beside me, who'd apparently never learned how to *not* stare at a woman. I wouldn't have been surprised if he'd been sitting out here drooling this entire time.

"Put your eyeballs back in your head if you plan on keeping them, slick."

The punk laughed. "What?"

"I don't share, baby boy. Everything about that girl belongs to me."

"Yeah," he said and laughed again. "She's meaner than you are, dude. I don't want any part of Trista."

I couldn't even prevent myself from smirking at that.

She absolutely could be meaner than me when the situation called for it. Something about that was wildly impressive to me, and it really did make me believe that he probably wasn't actually interested in her. He'd never survive her.

Until I thought a little harder about what he'd said.

He didn't want any part of *Trista*.

But he absolutely had been sitting here beside me, staring at that pool like his life source was somewhere in the water.

I sat up as straight as I could in that chair to turn and glare at that punk.

"Oh, boy," Indy said in an instant. "You'd better put some distance between you, hoss."

Utah was up and out of his chair a heartbeat later to start backing away from where I was still sitting.

"You motherfucking, son of a —." I cut myself off to also stand. "Are you fucking her?" I screamed at Utah before I looked back to where Memphis was floating in the water. "Are you fucking him?"

"What?" Memphis asked, sliding off her float and into the water.

"Oh, God," Triss said and rushed from where she was in the pool toward the edge to try to get out as quickly as she could move.

"Listen, I know you're probably not particularly interested in hearing what I think right now but —," Utah started to say before I interrupted that shit.

"I will paint this entire fucking house with a cotton ball before I spend even a second of my life worrying about what you think, kiddo. What in the actual fuck is wrong with you?"

"Easy man, your age already puts you in heart attack territory. Your blood pressure is about to make it worse," Utah said and raised his hands.

"You shut the fuck up," I said to him without bothering to linger on his insults before I turned back to Memphis again while she was getting out of the pool. "Are you sleeping with him?"

"Jersey," Memphis said, moving to stand between us. "First, that's absolutely none of your business. Like in any way, shape, or form. And second, no."

"Then why the fuck are you trying?" I screamed right over her head at Utah.

"He hasn't actually tried anything?" Memphis asked, like something about this confused her.

"Why *wouldn't* he?" Trista asked and even fucking giggled. "She's gorgeous."

The way that Utah shrugged his fucking shoulders in agreement with Trista about sent me into a frenzy.

"No," I snapped. "She's not."

"Um, excuse me?" Memphis chimed in. "What?"

"That's not —. You're a fucking child. That's what I meant."

"I'm twenty-one?" She said and laughed.

"And he's only twenty-six," Trista added.

"Why do you even know that?" I snapped at her.

"And aren't you like *way* older than Triss?" Utah asked.

"If you open your mouth again, I'll knock every tooth out of your head, boy," I threatened. "And don't fucking call her that."

I watched him pull an imaginary zipper across his mouth before he smirked.

"I should've made popcorn for this," Indy added.

"Indy," Utah hissed.

"You stay away from her," I said and pointed at Utah another time.

"You don't get to decide that, J," Trista said quietly and wrapped her fingers around the hand that I was using to threaten that punk. She pulled my hand down and kept it firmly in hers.

"No?" I asked. "Then who the fuck does? Because it's for damn sure not him," I said and tried to point at Utah again, but she still wouldn't release that hand.

"Memphis decides," Utah said.

Memphis' whole body lit up like a red glow stick when every set of eyes around that pool landed on her after that. She couldn't have spoken in that moment if her entire life depended on it.

"I've been telling you from the start, man," Indy said quietly. "She's into the bad boy style."

Memphis glared at Indy that time.

"Just means she hasn't had a *real* man yet," Utah said and shrugged his shoulders.

"Fuck," Trista whispered and smiled. "That was smooth."

"My fucking God," I said impatiently.

"Alright," Trista said and squeezed my hand before she started pulling on my arm. "We're going back inside."

"I think —, I'll — come with you," Memphis said quietly after she'd looked back over her shoulder at Utah.

"Damn right, you will," I said and ripped my hand away from Trista to put it on Memphis' lower back to push her toward the house so both girls would be walking ahead of me. If he couldn't be trusted to keep his eyes to himself, he'd be stuck staring at my ass until we were all inside. Triss swooped in right beside her to link her arm through Memphis' while they walked.

CHAPTER FIFTY-NINE
trista

"I told you it wasn't me he's been watching," I whispered to Memphis.

"How long has this been going on?" Jersey asked from behind us.

"Nothing *has been going on*. Jesus," she said. "We've got way bigger things to worry about, guys."

"Do we?" Jersey asked. "This one feels like it's got my full attention."

"I don't want *this one* to have your full attention, Jersey Boy," Memphis said.

"Do you like him?" I asked her.

"No."

"Mmm, you answered that awfully fast," I said and laughed.

"We are *not* having this conversation," she said quietly and went for the hallway. It surprised me just as much as it did Memphis when Jersey simply sidestepped out of her way to allow her to escape. She even paused for an extra second to look at him like she fully expected him to reach out and grab her. He was smiling by the time that she was gone, and I'd never been more confused by a set of events in my entire life.

"Why'd you let her leave? I would've bet any amount of money that you were about to sit her down and have the sex talk with her right here at the kitchen table. Maybe slap a chastity belt on her. Go a hundred and ten percent psycho. True Jersey style, you know?"

Rather than actually answering me, that man came all the way across the room to trap me against the cabinets and grabbed my face with both his hands to kiss me. I had to lock my hands onto the edge of the countertop behind me to keep myself in place while his tongue left my brain without its usual firing capacity. Being able to feel his dick hardening between us was every bit as fucking distracting as his tongue. I was still standing there like a stunned, motionless fool when he'd taken his mouth back and stood staring right back down at me.

"So," I managed to say. "That was not at all how I imagined this going. You were so mad out —."

"I think we've got something to talk about, Triss."

He was smiling while he said it, but his tone was icy enough to send chills all across my skin.

"About Memphis?" I asked. "I don't think she's really that interested in U—."

"About you, baby," he interrupted. "Our room. Now."

He stepped back just enough for me to slip by him and I forced my legs to carry me away. I couldn't begin to guess why my stomach was tying itself into knots with every step I took, or why it got so much worse with each step of his that I could hear right behind me. I couldn't even come up with anything I'd done recently that would've genuinely pissed him off for me to feel like I was a fucking child about to get in trouble. And the smirk that sat across his stupid fucking face looked so amused that it made it even worse when I looked back at him over my shoulder. I stopped right inside the bedroom door just to remain close to an exit, and then I realized I was a dumbass. There was no realm where he was going to let me turn around and leave now just because I stayed close to the door. His hand on the small of my back a second later pushed me the rest of the way into the room anyway so he could close the door.

"I told you that Utah wasn't into m—."

Jersey's entire arm swung around my body to clap his hand over my mouth.

"I swear to God, Triss," he breathed against my neck. "I'll fuck his name right out of this mouth. You're *going* to learn that mine is the only one allowed on your tongue, and you're going to learn it now. On your knees, baby."

He let go of me and walked across the room to close the curtains. He smiled when he turned back to me to see that I was still standing right where he left me. I really hadn't intended to ignore his command, but my brain's messages definitely weren't reaching my legs. I almost didn't need my brain's involvement when he walked right back at me and didn't stop until my chin was pretty much in his chest while I stared straight up at him. I did everything in my power to stay perfectly still when his fingers started at the hairline at my temple and moved down to my cheek.

"I'm already going to hurt you, Fancy Face. Don't make it worse for yourself," he whispered. My eyes closed on their own when those fingers trailed down my neck. That still hurt. Hell, it was still bruised. But I plastered the rest of my body into place to make sure he couldn't see the hint of panic about his hands there again. Basic fucking instinct told me that he was still worth my fear, but something way deeper inside me was louder in reminding me that he'd allowed me to see just how broken his heart really was. If he were to see even a glimpse of my hesitation over what had happened, it'd ruin us both.

"Why?" I managed to ask when his hand ventured down between my breasts.

He smirked. "Get. On. Your. Knees."

I figured out how to follow through that time and was on the floor a second later, nearly afraid to even look up at him. He paced around behind me and I felt his fingertips graze my shoulders while he swept all my hair to one side. He untied the top string of my bikini and then the one around my back. I watched the little fabric triangles fall across my knees, until he grabbed some of my hair and pulled it so my neck was craned and forcing me to look up at where he stood behind me. He hadn't grabbed anywhere near enough of my hair. I could feel the strands breaking, could feel others being ripped from the roots. A hundred tiny pinpricks all at once had me reaching for his wrist.

"I've spent weeks wondering why I haven't killed that boy for looking at you," he said. "Weeks wondering why I haven't killed his Judge for running his fucking mouth. Wondering why I haven't even so much as made them leave this house to give myself the fucking peace and quiet."

His free hand went to my breast and his thumb brushed back and forth across my nipple for a few seconds before he pinched it between his fingers until I winced.

"You, baby," he said. "It's because of you."

He didn't just let go of my hair. He used it to push me away from him before he knelt beside me to untie the strings at both my hips. He forced his hand in between my thighs to shove them apart and then he dragged the full length of his hand from his fingertips to his palm across my clit and down to where I was already dripping for his touch.

"Fuck," he groaned against the side of my head when two of his fingers pushed into me. "This fucking pussy that's always screaming for my attention. Tell me, Fancy Face, how does your ass feel about me?"

I had no doubt that he could hear the sharp, panicked breath that I sucked in after that. Then the motherfucker withdrew his fingers just to slap my clit. I crumpled forward into his chest just for him to push me back. His hand went right back between my legs and he picked up the pace to drag the pads of his fingers back and forth across my clit until I was leaning into him again and I sank my teeth into the Marine tattoo across his chest. He froze right before that orgasm claimed me, and I considered biting right through the skin that was between my teeth. He stood and walked to the bed while he untied the drawstring through his swim trunks.

"Get over here," he said. I raised one whole fucking knee from the floor before his tone changed and scared me still again. "I didn't say you could stand. I said *get over here*."

I could feel my cheeks heat up at what he was suggesting, but the look on his face told me as clearly as fucking could be that he was serious.

"I won't tell you nicely again, baby."

Nicely.

What a fucking joke.

I leaned forward to also put my hands on the floor to start crawling across the carpet toward this man who'd already told me that he intended to hurt me for his enjoyment.

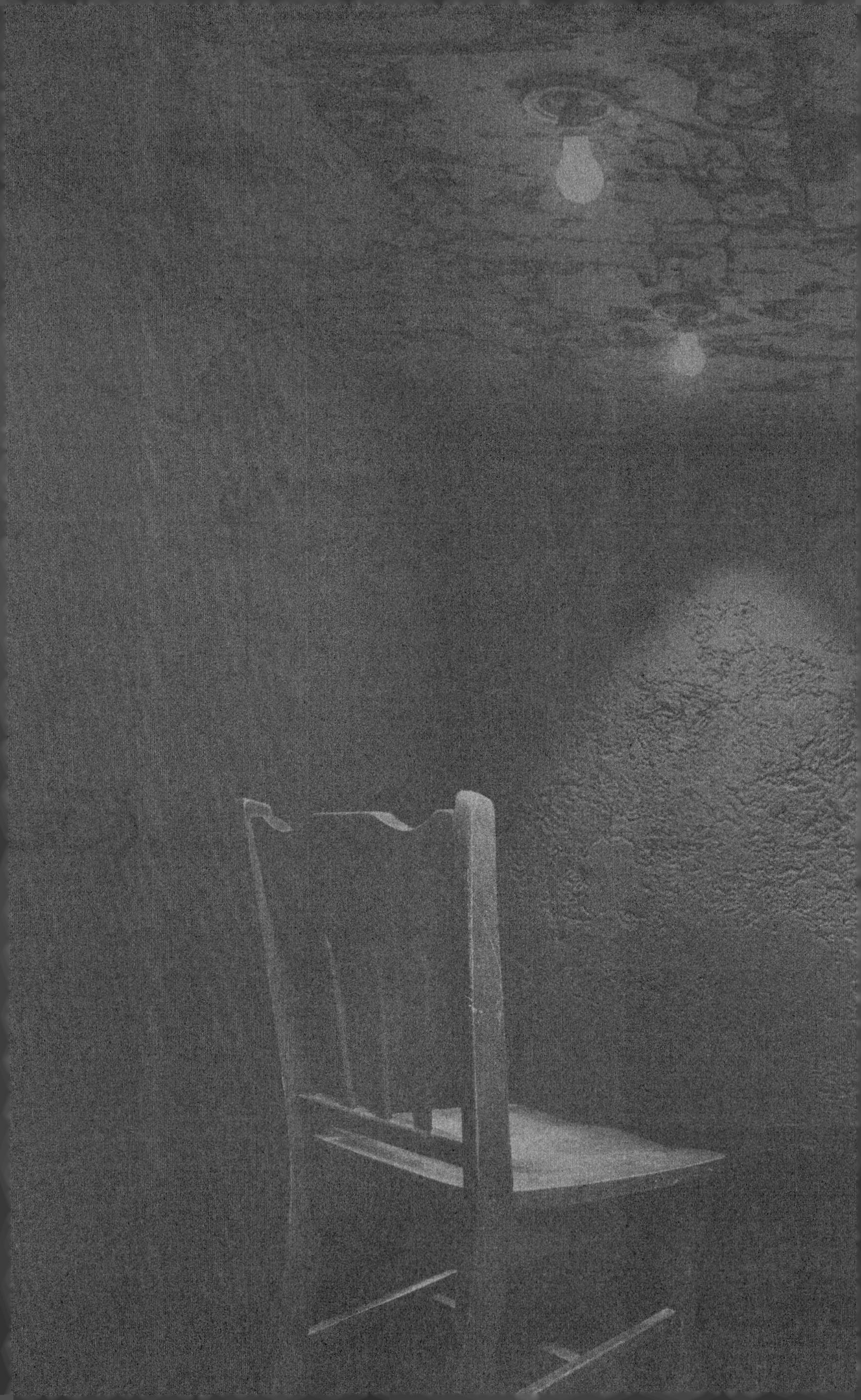

CHAPTER SIXTY

jersey

The sight of her crawling toward me on all fours was almost more than I could handle. For some reason, I expected her to put up a fight. I expected her to make it difficult. Watching her just fucking do it made me want to demand even more to see if I couldn't find her breaking point.

"Look at me, Fancy Face."

She paused for just a second to raise those black coffee eyes to my face, and I was suddenly concerned that I wasn't even going to win my own fucking game. I had to fucking convince myself to stay right where I was to wait for her to make it the rest of the way to me. She stopped at my feet to sit back on her own heels and look up at me. I ran my hand all the way up her throat to drag my thumb across her lips.

"Open."

I pushed my entire thumb into her mouth as soon as she did as I said, and I left it just sitting on her tongue.

"You're going to suck my dick until I say you can stop." She didn't even so much as blink. "You don't stop until I say. You can gag. Choke. Cry. You can beg. But you won't stop."

She closed her mouth just enough to bite my thumb, and I smiled at that tiny moment of defiance that crossed her face. I was impressed that all it took to get her hands tugging my shorts down was for me to nod toward them. She'd already had enough of my shit, and she didn't even bother to work up to it slowly. She pushed her head forward until my cock slammed into the back of her throat, and it only took her another second or two to readjust the angle, so I was sliding down it. I put my hand on the back of her head to hold her there once I was sure she couldn't breathe through it.

She was just as determined to be a stubborn asshole about this as I was. She kept her eyes on me even while her throat started to twitch around me, even while her eyes started to water, and she tried desperately to blink away the tears. I eased my hold on the back of her head so that she could withdraw enough to at least be able to breathe through her nose for a second, but I didn't give her much time before I started thrusting. She was less than amused that I was using my hand to pull her head against me just as much as I was pushing with my own hips, but she didn't try to stop me. She still didn't try to stop me even when I forced myself all the way down her throat another time and made her sit that way again. And just to fuck with me like the little witch that she was, she brought a hand up to start playing with my balls too. I wasn't ready for this to be over that quickly though. She ripped her head back once I removed my hand.

"That hurts, Jersey," she hissed and ran her hand up the column of her neck to massage it.

I laughed and grabbed her by both biceps to lift her right off the floor, completely forgetting that I was supposed to be forcing her to suck my cock until *I* said she could be finished. I piled up every pillow from that bed right at the edge and bent her over them. I ran my dick between her ass cheeks while I held her top half against the bed by her shoulder.

"And you're going to get off on it anyway, aren't you? The way that I hurt you?" I asked and stepped back to put my hands in between her legs to push them apart as far as her hips would allow. "You're going to thank me for every fucking inch even while I hurt you because this is how it feels to be mine." I forced my dick right into her pussy and didn't stop until I could see every muscle in her back strained against the weight of my body. I'd never been this deep before. So deep that it felt like there was a fucking barrier against the head of my dick with the angle the pillows had given me. I pulled out slowly.

"Wait, please. Just —," she tried to say.

"No," I interrupted and grabbed a handful of her hair to pull it. "You own every piece of me outside of this. You control everything about me every other second of every fucking day. You're in charge of my thoughts, you decide every move I make. But this," I said and thrusted back into her until my hips slammed into her ass. "When we're alone, Triss, this is where I fucking own you. And I'll make sure you remember that every time now." I pulled her hair so that I could see her face. "When it comes to this body, everything about you is mine. Mine to fuck. Mine to tease and torture. Mine to bend. And. Mine. To. Fucking. Break."

My heart about exploded right there on the spot when she held my stare and fucking nodded back at me.

Agreeing with me.

Giving in to me.

Giving *herself* to me.

My fucking queen.

My ecstasy.

I used my grip in her hair to push her head back down into the mattress and thrusted into her relentlessly while she shrieked with each one. I let go of her hair to grab her by the hips. I dragged her body from practically dangling off the edge of the bed until she was standing bent over in front of me with her elbows propping her upper half up on the bed. I reached under her to rub my fingers across her clit.

"Fuck, Jersey."

I fucked her right through the orgasm that had her legs shaking and her hands gripping the blanket on the bed until her knuckles were white. She raised up to watch me over her shoulder when I paused just long enough to pull a bottle of lube from the nightstand next to us. She surprised the hell out of me when she didn't say *no* or even attempt to tell me to stop. Instead, she fucking arched her back so the lube could pool at the top of her ass for a second while I tossed the bottle onto the bed. I spread it on two of my fingers and then across her while I started thrusting again. I reached under her to rub her clit again with my other hand.

"Breathe, baby," I reminded her when my other two fingers put pressure on her asshole to get the muscle relaxed. The smart thing probably would've involved asking if she'd done this before. Or if she actually wanted it. She'd just rolled with it every other time I'd played here with my fingers before though. And I was still pretty fucking worked up about the realization that she actually did hold all the motherfucking power in this relationship. She didn't even seem to notice it herself, and that made it so much fucking harder to swallow.

Even while I was entirely certain that this was going to hurt her, I wasn't going to go out of my way to make it worse. I took my time with my fingers, stretching, adding more lube, stretching some more. I didn't give her clit even a second of a break until she got off another time with my fingers knuckle deep in her ass too. I waited until I was right at the fucking edge and having to seriously distract myself to keep it together before I pulled my dick out of her pussy to press the tip against her asshole so she wouldn't have to survive it for that long. She sucked in a sharp breath when I rocked against her just hard enough to get the tip in.

"Touch yourself until I can take over again, Fancy Face."

For somebody who'd put up such a fight over me making her take care of herself the last time, she shifted so fucking fast to get her own hand between her legs now.

"Good fucking girl."

"J," she whimpered back at the words. "Deeper. Move, please. Keep moving."

"What?" Came out of me before I'd even realized it.

There was no fucking way I'd heard that correctly.

She raised up off the bed until her back was against my chest and she reached a hand around the back of my head to pull me down to kiss me over her shoulder.

"Fuck me like you mean it, Jersey."

Yep.

There was the girl I knew best.

"Get on the fucking bed, Trista."

She moved away from me to climb onto the bed. I grabbed the lube again to add an outrageous amount to my dick before I put my hand between her shoulder blades to push her down against the mattress. I pushed her legs apart until she was nearly lying flat on the bed in front of me, every inch of her perfectly displayed just for me. I added more lube to her before I was forcing the head of my dick past that intensely tight ring another time. She gasped when I didn't take anywhere the near amount of time making it happen again either.

"Deep breaths, Fancy Face," I said when I started barely thrusting against her. Her hand swung back to reach for any piece of me that she could find.

"Hips up, baby."

As soon as there was enough space between her and the bed, I held my weight off her with one hand next to her head and slid the other under body to get my fingers on her clit. She whimpered at the relief that the stimulation gave her while I continued to force my way deeper into her tight little ass.

"You were made for me," I said and leaned down to press my forehead against the side of her head. "Made to take me. Made to fight me. Made to fuck me."

"Jersey," she gasped. I slid my fingers down to push them into her and dragged my palm across her clit. Her entire body tightened in an instant. Her pussy gripped my fingers, her asshole nearly strangled my dick, and her soul managed to absorb every broken piece of mine.

"Take me with you," I said and thrusted my way right into that orgasm with her. I pulled out of her quickly to slip my arm under her body and roll her to her back. I kissed her until I felt like I needed to leave her mouth alone for a moment to give her a chance to breathe and I kissed my way down her neck instead, taking extra care to kiss every discolored, bruised part of her skin that still made me hate myself.

CHAPTER SIXTY-ONE
trista

The pushy, domineering lunatic from a moment ago seemed to disappear right before my very eyes, and within seconds he was replaced by this tender, overly affectionate man who couldn't stop touching me. I think he managed to kiss every inch of my skin before he made it back to my mouth. He kissed my forehead and lowered himself down to his elbows to just rest his body on mine. Everything he'd just done left me in such a weird fucking high that I was having a hard time focusing on his face.

"Are you okay?"

The instant change in him blew my mind so hard that I couldn't even figure out how to speak. I simply nodded at him after he kissed me another time. He smirked and his hand came up to my cheek to brush his thumb across it.

"Use your words, baby. You've been doing a lot of crying lately anyway, and I know it's been because of me. I don't know how to fix that yet, but if you need something from me right now, I need you to tell me," he paused just to stare through my eyeballs and into my soul. "Are you okay?" He asked another time.

"I'm alright, J. Little dizzy," I said and laughed. "I feel kind of drunk actually."

He watched my face for another few seconds, like he was waiting to see if I'd change my mind about my answer, then he kissed me again.

"That's what I figured," he said and kissed my head. "Don't go anywhere."

He climbed off me and off the bed to disappear into the bathroom. I tried to sit up, only to find that absolutely everything below my waist was already sore so I gave up and just flopped right back onto the bed. I think I was nearly asleep by the time I felt his arm slide under my shoulders.

"Come on, Fancy Face," he said and slipped the other arm under my knees. I still couldn't figure out a way to react when he carried me into he bathroom and lowered me into the bathtub while it was still filling. So, I just stared at him. He kissed my forehead again.

"I'll be right back."

And I just watched him walk out like he'd managed to fuck the ability to speak right out of me. I lowered myself into the water a little further and closed my eyes to try to remember some of the things he'd said. I couldn't recall a single moment of my time spent with the man where I felt like I was in control of him the way that he seemed to believe I was. And I damn sure never expected him to be the kind of man to consider himself under a woman's control. I found myself wondering yet again who he'd really been before he lost his wife if this softer version of him was still available under the surface of the control freak from time to time.

Jersey came back into the bathroom with two bottles of water and dragged that little stool right next to the bathtub again to sit them on it.

"Sit up, baby."

I didn't even hesitate to do what he said, and I was shocked another fucking time when he slid right into the tub behind me.

"What is this, Jersey?" I asked and laughed when he pulled me back into his body to lay his arms across me.

"Some people need to be reminded that they're loved after they've been used as a sex toy," he said and squeezed me a little harder. I wiggled around until I was comfortable under the weight of his arms before his words really sank their way into my brain.

Some people.

He hadn't said some *women* need to be reminded that they're loved.

Some *people.*

I swallowed every confusing emotion I'd ever felt in his presence and dug my fingernails into his forearm to hold on for dear life.

"I love you too, J."

I could feel him stop breathing for a few seconds before he seemed to remember the tough guy attitude that he preferred to present to the world.

"A smart woman wouldn't," he said and laughed.

"Luckily for you, asshole, I don't think anybody has ever accused me of being a smart woman."

"You're plenty intelligent, Fancy Face. Just maybe not in the common sense way that usually tells most people when to keep their mouth shut in the presence of dangerous men."

"Can I have the sweet Jersey back for just a couple more minutes?"

"There's no such man."

He sighed when I glared up at him over my shoulder.

"Fine," he said. "But don't tell anyone."

"Can I ask you something then? Before you shift back into shithead Jersey?"

His hand moved up my neck until it was under my jaw so he could tilt my face back toward him.

"I told you that you can be in charge everywhere else, Fancy Face. Everywhere and every time, except when we're alone. Do I need to remind you of that already?" He leaned down to kiss just the tip of my nose. "What do you want to ask me?"

"What kind of life do you think we get to have now?" I asked.

"What?" He asked and laughed.

"What are we supposed to do now? Do we just hide here forever? Keep Memphis and the others trapped here with us? Die in the cornfields someday? Are we common law married after you keep *me* here for however many years? Just — what happens next?"

Rather than continue to stare at me, he laid his head back on the edge of the tub to be able to look away from me.

"I don't know how I'm supposed to answer that yet," he said and chuckled.

"What do you *want* life to look like for us?" I asked instead.

"Baby, I can feel you leading up to something here, but I'm really not any good at this game. I can't see anything ahead right now when the past is blocking my view of everything. Why don't you tell me what it is that you're seeing and I'll figure out a way to make it happen, huh?"

"I never even thought I'd have a boyfriend. I don't know what we're supposed to be doing," I admitted. "*Boyfriend* sounds weird. Is that what I'm supposed to call you? Aren't you a little — I don't know — mature for that? Not in the sense that you act like a mature adult. More in the sense that you're nearly a hundred."

"I swear to God, Trista —."

"I want to go on dates, Jersey. I want to go to dinner. Do things regular people do. Be able to walk fucking anywhere without looking behind me every other step. I just want —."

"You want stability," he filled in for me. "Safety. I remember the conversation from our last date, Fancy Face."

"That did *not* count as a date, old man."

"Keep it up with the age jokes, baby. See where it gets you."

"Underneath you again?" I asked and smiled at him. "Oh no. Please. Not that. Sounds awful, you geriatric—."

"Hush."

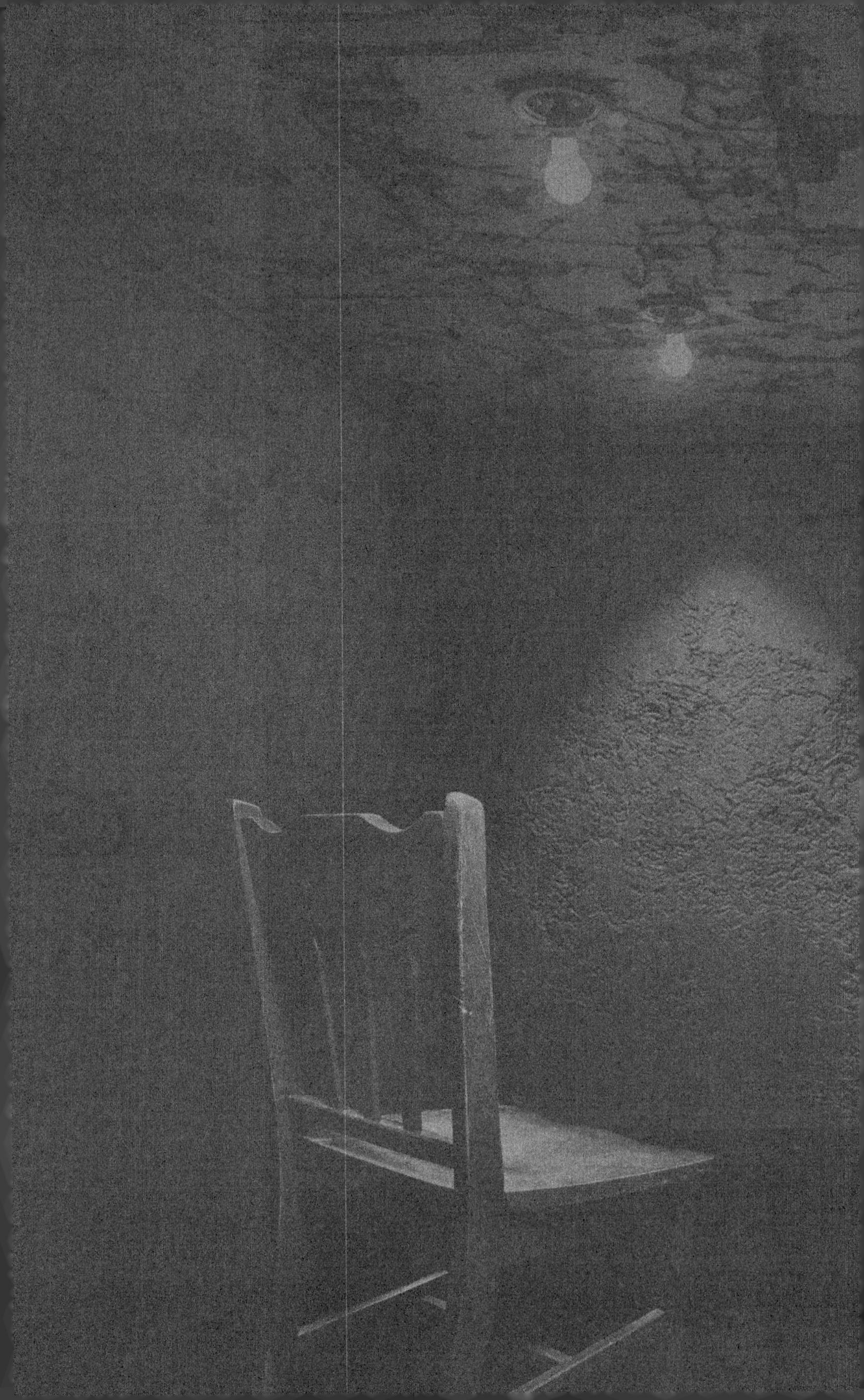

CHAPTER SIXTY-TWO
jersey

I was starting to believe I'd never sleep again. Truthfully, I wasn't even sure how Triss could still sleep at night knowing that I was next to her. I didn't even trust myself to sleep. How she trusted any version of me was baffling. She managed to look at me, to love me like she couldn't see the worst parts of me that lurked just beneath the surface of who I was. She knew those things were there. She'd seen firsthand what I was. Whether she chose to ignore it and act like it wasn't there, or just chose to see it openly and embrace the fucked up parts of me, I guess I might never know. What was purely certain about it was that she decided to love me anyway; broken pieces and all. And she was thinking about a future with me. She was seeing something beyond this house and this mess in which we'd all found ourselves, and now I needed to find a way to offer her whatever it was that she was seeing.

Roaming around our bedroom in the middle of the night to prevent myself from falling asleep didn't bring the answers I sought though. It usually ended up making things worse. Like it did tonight when I happened to stop at the window that overlooked the pool.

"That motherfucker," I hissed and whirled around for the door.

For not being anything close to a light sleeper, that brought Trista right to life.

"What?" She asked, dragging herself from the bed as quickly as she could move. "What's wrong?"

She caught me by the arm and rather than offering any explanation, I just pointed at the window. She hesitated, and then kept her hold on my arm to pull me with her when she went toward the window.

"Awe," she said. "They're cute."

I looked again myself to make sure we were looking at the same sight.

We fucking were.

Memphis was sitting at the edge of the pool with her feet in the water.

With that other fucking Executioner right beside her; his feet in the water too.

"They're what?" I asked, after staring for far too long to try to comprehend her words.

"Cute, Jersey. They're cute together."

"I'll be right back."

She grabbed me again before I'd even turned all the way around.

"Do *not* go out there."

"Why wouldn't I? You can see what's happening too, right?"

"Them sitting beside each other? Not even touching? Yeah, J. I see it. Can you believe the fucking nerve of that man to keep a respectful distance between their bodies?"

"That's not funny," I snapped.

"Well, it was a *little* funny."

"It can't be him."

"Why do you get to decide that?" She asked. "What's wrong with him, Jersey? He's not done anything but help since she called them."

"He's just —. He's so —."

"Not you?" She interrupted. "He's nothing like you? Do *you* want someone like yourself for Memphis, J? Or do you want someone better?"

"You think he's better than me?" I asked, like a jealous fucking toddler.

"For her, yes. Memphis doesn't need a pushy, dominating asshole who can't be told that he's wrong. That's what *I* need. She needs something...softer. Patient."

That left me oddly torn between wanting to walk out there to rip his body in half with my bare hands and being strangely satisfied that Triss considered him soft when compared to me. And once again, I was left having to swallow that I didn't even have an argument prepared to go against her.

The fuck did a man have to do around here to just be able to tell his woman to shut her trap and let him do what he wanted?

MEMPHIS and that other Judge were already sitting at the kitchen island when I made my way there the next morning. For as much as I wanted to ask her what she thought she'd gain from staying up all night and sitting by the pool with Utah, I still hadn't forced Trista's words out of my head. I was having a difficult enough time processing my own messed up world without adding my concerns about Memphis on top of it. I didn't like it. Not a fucking thing about it. But she was smarter than him, and I could always remind myself of that. That, and I couldn't very well stand here and scold her about that kid just to turn around and ask for her help about Triss.

"Fuck man, you look a little worse every day," Indy said as soon as I was standing across the island from them.

"Thanks. Why are you here again?"

"Jersey," Memphis sighed.

"*Jersey?*" I repeated. "I think you mean *Indy*. He started it."

"You can't be serious," Memphis said.

"Where's the other one?" I asked.

"Utah?" Memphis asked and laughed. "You mean *where's Utah?*"

"He's out," Indy added.

"How helpful of you. Can you go be wherever he is? For maybe a fucking a minute?" I asked him. I about came unglued when that boy smiled.

"What's on your mind, Jersey Boy?" Memphis asked. "You might as well just come out with it. Indy isn't going anywhere."

I stared down at my own hands on the countertop for a minute, trying to decide if this was really worth involving other people.

It was.

Because Trista was.

She'd been worth devastating the track that all of our lives had been on previously. So, she was worth finding a way to make her happy.

And I just didn't have the answer myself.

"Jersey?" Memphis tried again, noticeably softer that time.

"I don't know how to give Triss a better life than this," I rushed out to prevent myself from deciding against it.

Memphis looked from me to Indy, and back to me again.

"What?" Indy asked.

"She's been in fight or flight mode since she was a child. She deserves better than that now, because she deserved better than that then," I said, taking her mother's words to stab my own heart with them. "How do I give that to her?"

I watched Indy lean toward Memphis to whisper to her. "Is he asking for dating advice right now?"

I ignored him completely because I couldn't focus on anything other than the tears pooling in Memphis' eyes. She looked away from me just as quickly to shake her head and try to blink those tears away.

"I don't know anything about dating, Jersey," she said. "But if I'd spent my life running and hiding, I'd want to go somewhere that I didn't have to do either. If I didn't have to stay here for what comes next, I'd go anywhere else. Somewhere no one would ever notice me."

She grew more uncomfortable with every second that I spent just staring back at her. For as badly as I wanted to drill half a million questions right into her brain about how much she apparently related to Triss, everything in my own brain was telling me that doing such a thing with an audience present was not the right choice.

"We'd have to leave the country," I said quietly. "Somewhere no one would recognize either of us. Couldn't be on this continent, even."

"Might be good for *both* of you," Indy added. "Leave all the chaos and the trauma here."

"How soon can you be ready to go?" I asked Memphis.

She tried to smile. "I can't leave."

"Why?"

"Because we're not done here."

"Then I can't leave either if we're not done."

"You *can* be done, Jersey Boy. You can *choose* to be. You've already killed the man who took your family from you. Give your mind a chance to recover. Give Trista the chance to rest. We can do the next part."

"If we leave here, Memphis, there's no guarantee that we could ever get back into the States if you needed help."

Indy laughed that time. "If she needs you back here, we will get you back here."

"What's *the next part* for you then?" I asked.

Memphis glanced at Indy that time before she looked at me again. "We've been putting together this giant list of other Executioner/Judge teams. People who I think would probably be interested to know that their devastating life stories all have common roots that they maybe hadn't realized before because they were too close, and it was too raw. I think we need to find them. Tell them.

Dismantle the President's entire organization from within so he doesn't even have the ability to keep recruiting with these methods."

"And you don't think you'll need me for that?" I asked. "*You two* are going to deliver this kind of news to who knows how many sets of dangerous people?"

Memphis looked at Indy again, and the way that she hesitated about ripped my soul open.

"We've got Utah," Indy said and shrugged his shoulders. "We'll eventually have others once they're willing to see what we're trying to show them."

I ignored him completely once again just to watch Memphis.

"Besides," he went on anyway. "A loose cannon with a grudge and a blackout anxiety response probably won't really help our case when what we'll need is calm and quiet control to survive dealing with the other hotheaded Executioners."

CHAPTER SIXTY-THREE

trista

I most definitely felt like the monkey in the middle of the circus when everyone in that kitchen stopped talking, stopped breathing just because I walked into the room.

"You guys want me to leave again?" I asked.

Jersey smirked. "Come with me, Fancy Face."

Memphis got up to leave the room before I ever made it across the kitchen to Jersey, but he took my hand and continued to pull me toward the door anyway.

"Is she okay?" I asked.

"No. I'll sort that out later though."

He pulled me outside and looked around for a second before he picked a direction and just started to walk. He kept his hold on my hand. We probably made it a fucking quarter of a mile along the edge of one of his cornfields before I realized that we were just going on a walk together. It felt so absurd. So perfectly normal. And not at all like something Jersey would just do.

"How do you feel about beaches?" He asked.

"I don't mean to shock you with this revelation, J, but I didn't exactly have a lot of downtime to enjoy things like sightseeing over the last few years."

"Just answer the question, Miss Difficult."

"I guess as long as the sun was out and you weren't planning on feeding me to a bunch of sharks, I could be a beach person."

"Can't make any promises."

"About the sharks, or the sun?"

"Yep."

"You're an ass."

He stopped walking to step in front of me and face me. "Memphis suggested that we just leave. Go somewhere else. Somewhere you can be free again. Safe. Somewhere I can try to let go."

"Let go?" I asked.

"I can't give up any of the memories of my old life. Not even to make you happy. So, if that's what it'll take, I guess you'd better be ready to spend the rest of your days being pissed at me. But I was more than willing to give up every thought I'd ever had about a future for myself if it meant keeping you alive to give you the chance to live out whatever dream you had for yourself. Even if that dream was just finding stability."

I shook my head at him. "I don't expect you to just forget about her, J. I really don't. I don't *want* you to forget her or even stop loving her. I just — I don't know. I guess I need to know if there's a place inside you where I fit just as me?"

"I know you're not her, Fancy Face," he said and smiled. "I do. Every part of me knows it. And I don't want you to try to be her. It's not fair to either of you. You're absolutely nothing like one another. The only slight similarity between the two of you is this fucking insane blind willingness to love a madman. She was gentle in every way. She was softhearted, soft spoken. Nothing in me ever wanted to hurt her in any way. And you," he said and paused while I tried to breathe in all the oxygen in Indiana. "You're this abrasive, noisy, vulgar, little siren."

"I don't even fucking know why I expected you to make any

attempt to make me feel better about this," I said and ripped my hand from his to start backing away. He chuckled and grabbed my wrist before I made it anywhere. He pulled me right against the front of his body and wrapped an arm around my shoulders to hold me there.

"She was what I wanted then. I absolutely loved her. But she's gone, and so is the version of me who fell in love with her. I've been trying to live with only half of my heart since I lost them, and it's been fucking awful. I'll never just stop loving them. I'll never just forget them. But you're what I want now, baby. You're what I *need* now. I don't think there's anyone else in this world who could survive my kind of love now. And I *know* there's not anyone else in this world crazy enough to want it. To want *me*."

"You do that a lot," I practically fucking whispered because I couldn't breathe. "Call me crazy."

He smiled and I nearly had an aneurysm. "That's because you are."

"You want to just leave?" I asked, trying to figure out how to retreat out of the heavy fucking emotions that didn't seem to be crushing anybody but me.

"Do *you*?"

"Where would we go?"

"If you like beaches, I'll fucking buy you an island, Fancy Face. Rather have snow? You'll get a mountain. Tell me what *you* want, you'll have it."

"Did you just offer to *buy* me an island?" I asked and giggled. "That's the most Jersey thing I think you've ever said to me."

He put his other arm around me to squeeze me in a hug. "You're coming with me, then?"

"What about Memphis? The others?" I asked. "Are they allowed on this island of yours?"

He sighed and took me by the hand again to keep walking.

"I'm going to talk to Memphis again. She sounded pretty set on staying here to settle what we started with the President's organization. But if I can talk her out of it, I will."

"Just Memphis?" I asked and laughed again. It would've been physically impossible for him to roll his eyes any harder than he did.

"If their presence would help convince her to come with us, I'll consider it."

"And you're going to be okay leaving while it's unfinished?" I asked.

He sighed. "I don't think they want my help for this. I'd be more of a liability to what they're trying to do than I would be helpful."

I squeezed his hand. He was able to look at it objectively. From an analytical standpoint, a crazy, out-of-control, trigger-happy, former Marine with anger issues and an ego the size of Alaska probably wasn't the best choice to send in on the varsity team to break open a massive criminal organization. Being able to acknowledge that wouldn't make it any easier on him when it came time to leave Memphis here though, if she was truly determined to stay behind and see it through.

"So, where is this island?" I asked. "And I feel like it'd be wise, in terms of my own survival, to point out now that you're about to willingly trap yourself in the middle of an ocean with *just* me. *You* are choosing this. When you get tired of my mouth, I don't want to hear about it."

"We'll find a better way to keep your mouth busy, Fancy Face."

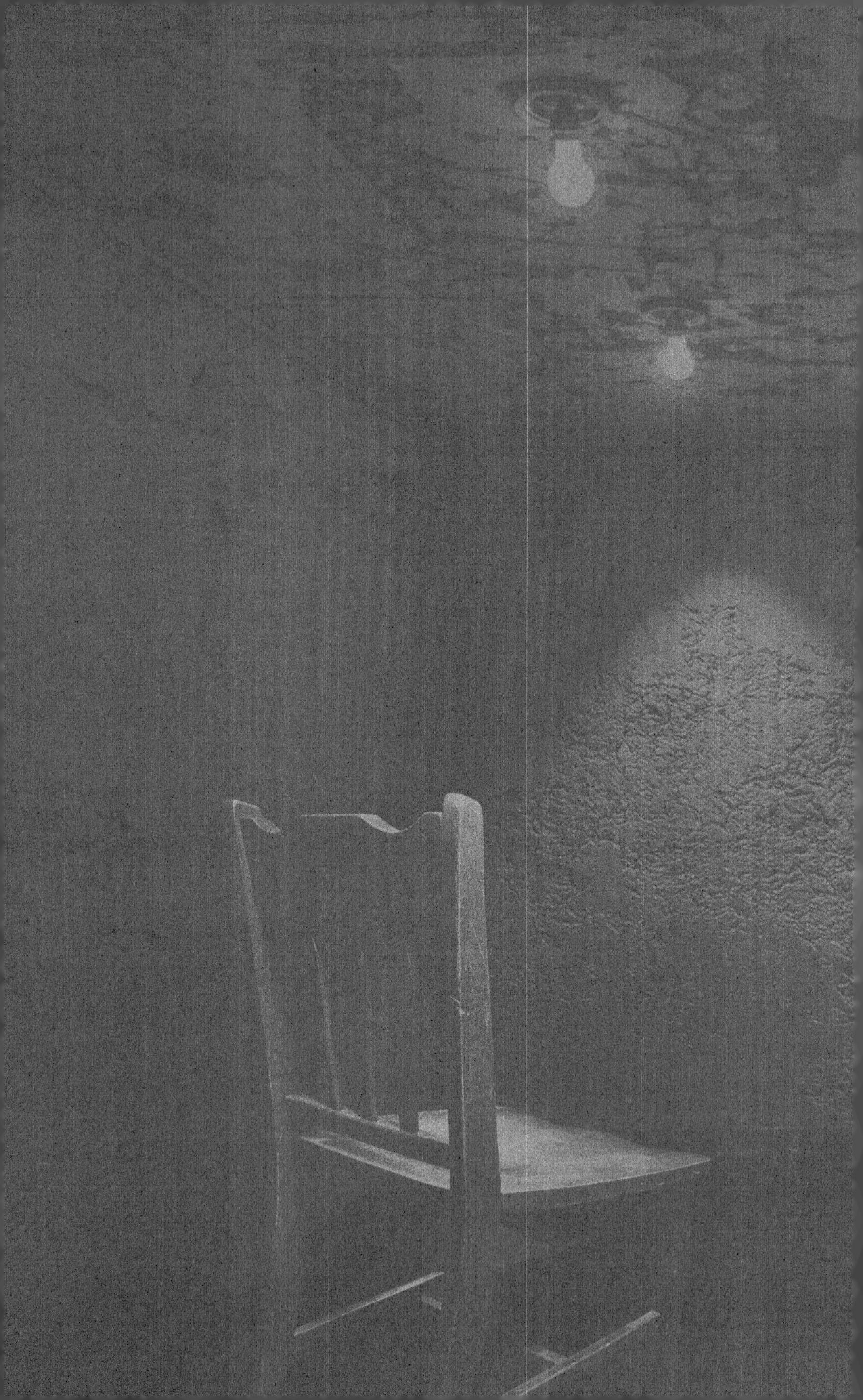

CHAPTER SIXTY-FOUR

jersey

She glared at me with the kind of fire that made me stop to consider whether she might actually bite my dick the next time I put it in her mouth just to remind me of that comment.

"Jersey," she said and stopped again to make sure she had my full attention. "Is this really what you want? Asshole jokes aside. There's a good chance that it'll just be me and you. We haven't exactly spent a ton of time alone just getting to know one another. And we both know I make you insane."

I tried not to see through to the fear underneath her concern, but there was no way around it. She was afraid. Being alone with me around here was still safe enough because there were other people who could help her if she was loud enough. The thought of being *truly* alone with me scared her. And it wasn't even remotely fair of me to try to convince her that she shouldn't feel that way.

"I know you're afraid of me right now. And I know why. You probably should be. Hell, you have every *right* to be."

"I'm not afraid of you," she said quickly, and then swallowed loud enough in her blatant lie that I could hear it. I couldn't even help but laugh at it.

"You don't have to lie to try to spare my feelings, baby. I know what I am. But if it makes you feel any better about it to know that we're on equal footing, I've never been more afraid of anyone, *of anything*, than I am of you right now. And that's saying something coming from me."

"What?"

"Whatever it is that draws me to you, it'll never let me go. And I'll never let you go because of it. I'm selfish enough to own that. Whether you're afraid of me or not, you're not going anywhere. Whether you want to be or not, you're mine. But what's even more fucking terrifying than that, Triss, is that *you* have *me*. I'm at your disposal now. Whatever you need, whatever you want. All you ever have to do now is say it, and I'll put my whole fucking life into making sure it happens. And you can use that power however you want."

"You're really just doing this *for me*," she said.

She hadn't *asked* it.

I watched the realization hit her like a hurricane. I'd never just leave Memphis here alone if this concerned only me. I'd never leave Memphis' safety in the hands of some other fucking Executioner. I'd never abandon Memphis in the middle of bringing this shit show to a conclusion. But if running away to hide for a minute was what Trista needed to feel safe, for the chance to be happy, I'd walk us both right off the edge of the Earth just so we'd land where no one could find us.

MEMPHIS HADN'T RETURNED to her usual post at the kitchen island by the time Trista and I made it back into the house.

"Where is she?" I asked the weird kid who'd moved in and apparently never planned to leave.

"Out by the pool," Indy said.

"You want me to come with you?" Triss asked.

I just shook my head. I wanted Memphis to be able to tell me whatever it was that she'd been keeping hidden all this time, and I didn't have much faith in that happening if there was an audience.

I almost couldn't force myself to sit beside her on the edge of the pool just because I couldn't stop picturing that punk sitting out here with her in the middle of the night. What the fuck would they have even been talking about? And why? I sat on the other side of where'd he'd been and took my shoes off too.

"You know that window behind us is my room," I said, because I couldn't help myself. Memphis glanced over her shoulder to look at the house before she laughed when she figured out what I was getting at.

"He's harmless, Jersey Boy."

But I could've lived my entire fucking life without having to see the way that she smiled after she'd said it.

"Well," she added quickly. "He's really not harmless, but he's nice to me."

I suddenly needed a refresher in those breathing techniques that my wife had been taught before going into labor with our daughter.

"Trista's on board with leaving," I said to change the subject. I watched Memphis suck her bottom lip in between her teeth.

"Are you out here to tell me goodbye then?" She asked.

"I'm out here because I still want you to come with us."

"I can't."

"Why, boss lady? This thing with the President can't be *that* important. That organization will still be here for you to rip apart later when we can all come back together after things have cooled off."

"Jersey —."

"You can even tell those other two jokers that they can come too, Memphis. I'm not fucking inviting them, but if you want to —."

"I have a sister here, Jersey," she whispered. "I can't leave."

The plethora of questions that flooded my brain all at once left me dazed and unable to ask even a single one of them.

"Then we'll take her too," I offered instead of questioning her to death.

She laughed, but she shook her head.

"It's really not that easy. We don't speak. I've been funding her life from a distance for years to make sure she's cared for and safe. But the family I left her with, I told them to try to convince her that she never actually had a sister. I figured she had a better chance at a normal life if I just disappeared and stayed away. By this point, she probably thinks I'm an imaginary friend that her brain created to help her through the bad days. Sometimes you're really not in control of the way that your mind reacts to trauma, you know?"

"Yeah," I chuckled. "I know a thing or two about that."

"You should go, Jersey Boy. Give yourself another chance to be happy. I never would've told you to go back into that building for Trista the first time if I didn't want you to be happy with her. I'll be okay here."

There was no changing her mind once she'd decided something. For as much as I wanted to keep pressing for information, everything inside me knew that she wouldn't give it. We'd always operated under a certain level of secrecy. The less we knew about the other, the safer everyone was. That had always been the case. Even if it did turn out that she actually knew every fucking detail that there was to know about me.

"Stay here as long as you want, Memphis. The house is yours for whatever you need. Kyle too, for that matter. I'll make sure he knows to keep an eye on everything for you. He's every bit as dangerous as I am when the situation calls for it."

She moved like lightning to wipe away a tear that escaped down her cheek, so I put an arm around her shoulders to squeeze her against my side.

"And if you're fucking convinced that those other two are necessary to achieve what you're planning, they can stay too," I said. "But *do not* let anybody near either of those cars, Memphis. Ever."

"Where do you want to go?" She asked and had to pause for the most painful sniffle I'd ever heard in my life. "Give me a few hours and I'll get everything taken care of for you."

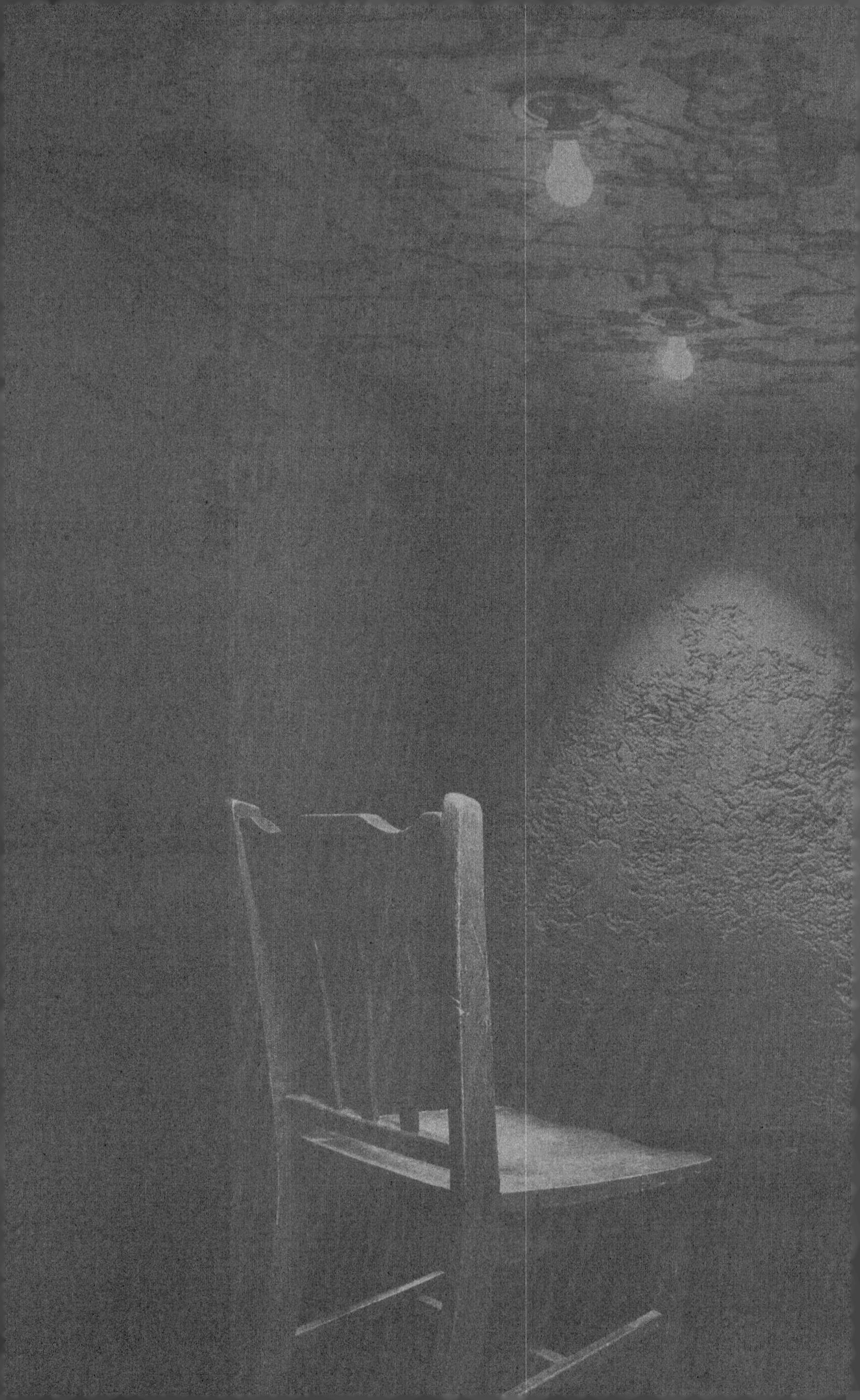

CHAPTER SIXTY-FIVE

jersey

I looked at the key fob for Persephone in the palm of my hand before I looked back at Memphis.

"We can take Seph to the airport if you bring her straight back here and put her right back in the garage," I said. "I'll need a picture of her back in her place as soon as it happens for proof."

"Why are you such a fucking crazy person?" Trista asked from the doorway.

"Yeah," Memphis said and pushed my own hand back against my stomach to close it around the key fob. "I don't know how to drive."

"You what?" I asked at the same time that Utah said, "For real?"

When she looked at him, rather than me, I couldn't do anything but imagine the satisfaction I'd get out of curb stomping that kid right into oblivion.

"I don't know how to drive?" She said, like she suddenly wasn't so sure about it.

"I can drive," Utah offered.

"Like hell you can."

He shook his head and smiled. "We can take Ariel."

"*Flounder*," I corrected. "Why don't you know how to drive?" I asked Memphis.

She shrugged. "I didn't have anyone around to teach me. And once I was old enough, I didn't have an identity anyway. I didn't really have a need to learn."

I laughed like a fucking madman when Memphis went to the front passenger's side of that truck. I might not be able to do shit about this once we were gone, but I sure as hell didn't have to just let it happen while I was still here. I put my hand on the door to hold it closed while Memphis stared at me like I really had lost my mind.

"Get up here, Triss."

She laughed too. "There's *no* way you're almost forty and still behaving like this," she said and smiled while I opened the door for her.

"That's because I'm not *almost forty*. I'm almost thirty-eight. Get in the pumpkin truck."

Memphis rolled her eyes at me, but she didn't argue while she climbed into the backseat and slid across for me to get in with her after I'd trapped Trista up front with Utah.

I couldn't focus on anything that Memphis tried to tell us on the drive to the airport though. She'd handed Triss and me a passport each, plane tickets, everything we'd need to prove the new identities she'd crafted for us. I'd spent the last day convincing myself that Memphis would be okay without me. She was smarter than anyone I'd ever known, and as long as she didn't go anywhere alone, she'd be fine. If she just did whatever she had to do from the safety of that house, there wasn't anything to worry about. For as much as I didn't care to admit it, or even think about it, Utah probably wasn't going anywhere either. And he might've been useless compared to me, but he was probably capable when compared to anyone else.

The silence that filled that truck when Utah stopped it to drop us off was crushing. Triss turned in her seat to look back at me like she thoroughly expected me to just tell Utah to take us back home. Memphis must've believed that was what was about to happen too because she opened her door quickly and jumped down to walk around to our side of the truck to wait for us on the sidewalk. Utah got out too and went to Memphis.

"You can still change your mind," Triss said quietly once we were alone.

"He's not going to stop coming after you, Fancy Face. And I'd have to lock you in that house all day every day to be able to guarantee you anything even similar to safety if we stay here."

I got out of the truck before I really did change my mind about the whole thing, but my heart just fucking hurt to see Memphis standing there trying to hug herself with tears in her eyes. She forced herself to smile at me once I was standing in front of her.

"Give yourself a chance to really be happy, Jersey Boy. Maybe use all that time on the plane learning how to smile. Triss can teach you what it's supposed to look like."

If this had been any other scenario, I would've started committing a homicide the very moment that Trista stood up on her toes to hug Utah when she said goodbye to him. But my eyes never even left Memphis.

"If I don't hear from you at least once every twenty-four hours, I'll be on my way back here, Memphis."

She smiled for real that time and it loosened whatever was trying to squeeze my heart until it burst. I looked down at the bundle of papers she'd handed me and flipped open the passport that was on top.

"Or," I choked out while I stared down at the photo Memphis had slipped in there, the one of her and her friends at that book fair. "If you ever decide that you just want me to come back to teach you to drive, I'll be on my way, sweetheart."

She gave up trying to hold back her own tears and crashed into the front of my body so I could hug her. I kissed the top of her head and had to squeeze my own eyes shut to keep from just fucking sobbing right there on the sidewalk.

"I'll see you again, Jersey Boy."

I couldn't tell if it was a statement or a question, but my response was the same either way.

"You will, boss lady."

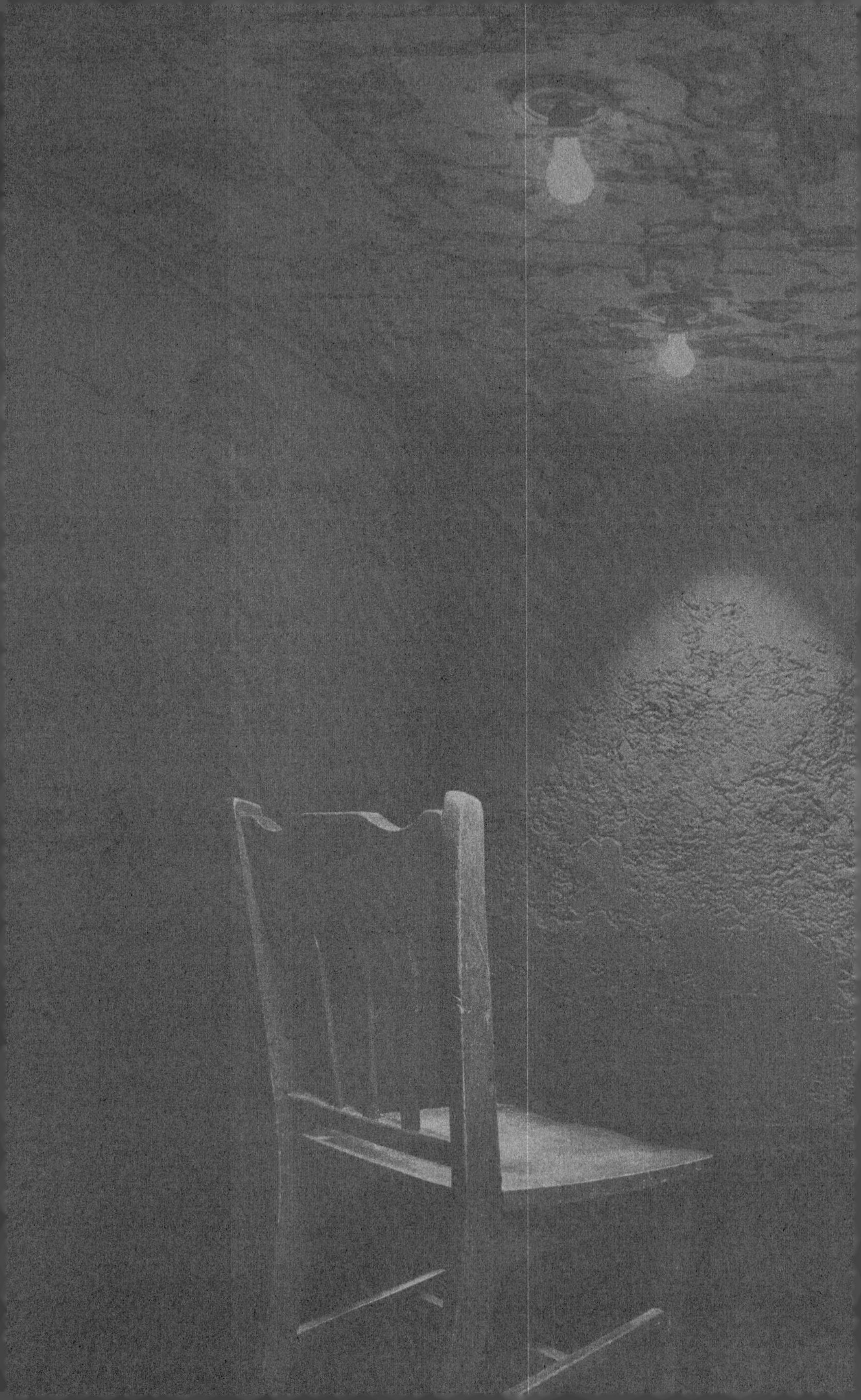

epilogue

TRISTA

He didn't turn into a brand new man overnight. We'd been here for months, and Jersey was still the very same asshole he'd been when he tossed me into that trunk the first time; but there was also very much a lighter side to him these days. The childish sarcasm and attitude seemed to be bone-fucking-deep personality traits that simply could not be removed from his existence.

But he laughed now.
And he smiled.
He did both a lot, actually.
He even pulled pranks when he got bored and decided that we needed to fight about something to liven things up again.

Memphis *never* failed to check-in with him within her allotted timeframe either. I think it meant just as much to her as it did to him. I didn't dare to tell him that I got text messages from her every so often too, because her messages to me were usually about Utah. She'd decided on the same time every single day that she'd text him though, and she kept to it religiously; almost as religiously as I could find Jersey pacing around with his phone in his hand in the few minutes leading up to that time every day. And when I say *religiously*, I mean Memphis missed her regular time by *three whole ass minutes* one day and the man had already called for a car to come pick him up and take him to the airport. We hadn't ever really talked about why *this* island had been the one that he chose, but there was never any doubt in my mind that it was almost entirely because it was outside of U.S. control *and* still only a four hour flight to Miami.

He didn't actually *buy* an island, either. He disliked people, but he knew I always felt better in populated areas where I could blend in and hide in plain sight if it became necessary. But he did buy land on this island. He had Memphis get her hands on a recreated version of whatever license this island required for foreigners to be able to purchase property here. Most of the people spoke English, there was an outrageous and constant flow of tourists in and out, and the ever-changing ocean of faces around us somehow really did ease my mind. Knowing that Jersey never actually *had* to go anywhere or be away from me was probably the real reason behind that. I had pretty sound reasoning that suggested I was already living with the most dangerous man on this island.

Within a week of being here, Jersey hired someone to come out and build a private dock that gave me a walkway straight to the ocean from the back door of the house. And the week after that he had one of those crazy little suspended huts on stilts built right off the edge of that dock and then furnished it like it was our own little honeymoon suite on the water. Needless to say, that was where I really lived. The temperature here never dropped below 70 degrees and the water of the Caribbean always looked perfectly blue. It was a strange little paradise to find myself in after spending years living out of a backpack with barely enough cash to survive and having to steal identities from other people. If anyone under the sun had tried to tell me I'd end up obsessively in love with the unhinged bounty hunter who'd locked me in the trunk of his car, zip tied my wrist to his, made me want to somehow simultaneously scream and stare at him in silent adoration, and fucked me within an inch of my life every single time, I'd ask for a hit of whatever drug they were taking, because it sounded like a fucking fantasy come true.

I laid on my chair on the dock, smiling to myself like a lunatic while I thought about the last year. I'd been kidnapped, stabbed, shot; and it was still the best year of my weird life, even with the amount of devastation that it included.

"Deep breath, baby," Jersey whispered from right beside me before I squealed and tried to squirm away from him because that meant he was here to tip the chair until I fell right out of it and into the fucking ocean.

And that was exactly what happened.

"You looked a little too peaceful," he said once I'd managed to get my head back above the water.

"I hate you."

He smiled while he stared at me for a minute before he leaned over the edge of the dock to hold a hand out toward me. I learned quickly that I'd never be able to pull him down into the water from this position. I'd tried on several occasions. It only resulted in him lifting me out of the ocean just to throw me right back in it for even trying to do the same to him. I usually settled for clinging to his body like a leech the second that my feet were on the dock in front of him just to make sure I could soak whatever he was wearing too.

We went out for dinner that night, just like we did most nights. Every time I ended up sitting across from him, I wanted to ask if he was attempting to make up for that first date that never actually happened and ended with me in the trunk of Persephone. But I was more than certain the response would be something sarcastic about how that was where I deserved to be just for strapping a knife to my thigh before that date, so I never did ask. Instead, I just enjoyed the sight of him smiling and I reached for one of the hands that I'd gotten so used to holding; hands that had the power to make the entire world spin, or to bring it grinding to a standstill depending on who they were touching.

JERSEY

I woke up entirely certain that flash hurricanes had become an issue overnight in the Caribbean with the way the wind must've been blowing. Then I remembered that I actually just slept next to a chainsaw each night. I didn't mind it. Anytime she woke me up this way, it was a guarantee that I was going to wake her up as well. She slept in that weird position that all females seemed to prefer. She faced away from me, half on her stomach and half on her side with one knee almost up to her fucking armpit. No complaints on my end about it. Easy access, since she still only slept in the black shirt that she'd taken from me all those months ago in that hotel room.

The bottle of lube that sat next to my side of the bed got a lot of use these days. I added it to myself before I made sure there was a little extra on my fingers and sent them exploring in between her legs. She never reacted immediately. The girl was the heaviest sleeper I'd ever encountered, and it made for a great fucking time. Her body understood what was happening before her brain ever did. She started squirming and sighing without ever waking up. Just the fucking sounds that she made were enough to have me rock hard in no time. I crawled over the top of her body until she was between my legs, and she started to stir when she felt the bed move around her. But she very much moved the wrong direction if she thought she was going to escape me. She ended up on her stomach under me, so I forced her legs apart and pushed my hips down against her until I was nearly halfway inside her. She tried to raise her upper body off the bed in an instant when she woke up.

"Nowhere for you to run, Fancy Face," I said and put a hand right between her shoulder blades to push her back down. "And even if you tried," I leaned down to whisper right into her ear. "There's nowhere in this world you could go that I wouldn't find you."

I rocked my hips in small movements until she had every inch. The little sigh that came out of her had me pulling all the way out just to ram back in as hard as I could until that sigh turned into a whimper.

"Fuck, Jersey, you could give me a second to wake —."

I interrupted her by covering her mouth. For as much as I used to enjoy using her neck, I didn't imagine she would ever be okay with it again.

"Do we have to have this conversation every time, baby?" I asked. "It's *Jersey* or *please*. Otherwise, shut your fucking mouth and take it until my cum is dripping back out of this pussy."

I released her mouth and pulled out of her to grab her by the hips so I could get her up on her knees. Then she surprised the hell out of me when she spun around to use every ounce of weight in her body to push me backward. I damn near fell off the bed. The chuckle that came out of me when she climbed on top of me sounded more deranged than it sounded like a laugh, but when my queen wanted to feel in charge, it was fun to let her think that way sometimes. I didn't put any effort into stopping her when she laced her fingers through mine to pin my hands to the bed under hers.

"You do this a lot, you know?" She asked. "*You* wake *me* up and then you act like *I* need to be punished for it."

"If you really want to play the blame game, I'm only awake because you snore like a fucking lumberjack, pretty girl."

"Fine. Then we'll call this payback for that time you let someone stab me."

"One. Time. One guy stabbed you one teeny, tiny fucking time. And then you punched me?" I said and laughed. "Was that not payback?"

"And then you told me that I hit like a cheerleader. So, no."

"I haven't fed you to any sharks yet, have I?"

She slapped her hand over my mouth that time while she wiggled her hips to try to get my dick at the right angle, and then she leaned down until her forehead was against mine.

"It's *Triss* or *please*, J."

It took everything in my willpower to stay where I was underneath her. All of the masculinity in my body was screaming at me to put her back where she belonged, but my dick was in charge, and he very much wanted her to do whatever the fuck she wanted with us. Just when I thought she was about to finally lower herself back onto me, this little witch started to crawl the rest of the way *up* my body.

"Playing games tonight are we, baby?" I said and chuckled while she placed her knees on either side of my head. "Bring it on, Fancy Face. Sit."

But she stopped right where she was.

"Those aren't the right words, J."

My queen.

My ecstasy.

She wanted to find out if I'd beg.

Like I wouldn't do fucking anything under the sun for her.

"Please, Triss."

I couldn't do anything but smile when I heard her sharp intake of breath over those two simple words. She stayed frozen right in place though.

"I'm still willing to play along, baby. But if you don't drop that pussy down here for me right fucking now, I'll take over again. We both know I can. We both know I will."

She listened that time and I was sucking on her clit a second later. I couldn't begin to guess why she thought this position would put her in control. She spent a few minutes grinding her hips against my face, but she never had any control over her own body when an orgasm was trying to crash its way through her. And the closer it got this time, the more she struggled to escape the stimulation. The moment that she was attempting to put some distance between her clit and my mouth, I wrapped both arms around her thighs to lock her into place.

"Jersey," she panted, and she grabbed as much of my hair as she could hold to try to rip it right out. She froze again and didn't make even an attempt to move once I had her clit between my teeth. She let go of my hair to stab into my scalp with her fingernails at that. Her whole body shuddered, and she nearly screamed the very moment when my tongue took over again. Once she stopped shaking, she put her hands beside my head on the bed to try to keep herself upright. I let go of her legs and she fucking jumped off me like a damn cat. I laughed when she rolled further away from me and right off the edge of the bed to get up and run for it.

We'd been at this for months now. Every so often she tried to find new ways to give herself a break in between orgasms. She'd tried physically running away, hiding, she'd tried picking fights, she'd tried refusing to give me access to her pussy. It never mattered which route she attempted; I got just as much enjoyment out of *never* giving her that break; but my favorite was always when she ran. Hunting Trista Hart seemed to be the thing that I was born to do.

I'D FINALLY STARTED SLEEPING AGAIN THOUGH. Not a lot, and not always well but it was better than it had been in months. And it was usually interrupted at some point by the tiny woman next to me trying to break the fucking sound barrier with her snoring. She'd been right though, all those months ago while she drunkenly rambled on about soulmates while we were in that state composed entirely of hillbillies. At this point, I'd take disrupted sleep every night for the rest of my life so long as it meant she'd be in that bed beside me.

I never would've imagined my ability to be content again hinged on this short, little bundle of mayhem and chaos coexisting with me.

She couldn't undo the things that had happened to my family, just like I couldn't change what had been done to her when she was younger. But for whatever reason, we could both breathe a little easier with the other around. The giant fucking cavern that existed directly in the middle of my heart was the perfect size to hold every broken piece of hers.

We definitely didn't fit together like those sappy puzzle metaphors that everybody talked about when it was time for wedding vows, but she'd been more than willing to let all my razor-sharp edges cut right into her until there was no telling where I ended, and she began. We weren't even puzzle pieces that had been forced into fitting together, because there was absolutely no chance of separating us again. We were broken glass that had been reglazed and fused together to create something new entirely.

a note to my heathen readers

This is where the story ends from the perspectives of Jersey Boy and Trista.

Happy now?
There was no mention of a thong.
No?
Still not good enough?
Of course not.
Because now you want Memphis and Utah, don't you?

I'm working on it.
GIVE ME A MINUTE.

acknowledgments

Lumberhubs: I'll love you hard enough for both of us. For always.

Also...thanks for tolerating the disaster show that this has so quickly become. I guess everyone everywhere else wants to fuck you now too. Sorrrrryyy. Ain't nobody out there who could love you as relentlessly as I do, baby cakes.

C: My superhuman all-in-one support system of a handholding hype woman who obsesses over all my side characters until they morph into main characters...thank you.

The OG Heathens: Thank you for allowing me to be exactly who I am in all this chaos. The questionable human behind the mask wouldn't be welcome just anywhere, but you all make me feel loved every time I bring the crazy your way.

God: Dude. Moms only vacation sometime soon? Please. I beg of you. These kids are killing me, and I miss you.

about the author

Ember Nicole resides in a small town in Indiana, having moved back into the same semi-haunted house where she grew up. While her husband and two children mean more to her than anything in the world and take up nearly all her days (and nights), weaving disastrously tangled webs of stories for her fictional friends remains her favorite off-mom/wife-duty way to pass the time.

She absolutely does not enjoy long walks on the beach because the thought of setting foot near water that can't be seen through is the most terrifying thing in the world. But coffee that's more sugar than anything else, a room filled with books, and a decent view of her rock-solid, lumberjack-looking husband are a few of her favorite things.

Her books aim for emotional upheaval. They all end with their own version of a happily-ever-after, but the journey to get to that point tends to involve broken people with disturbing pasts making poor choices in the heat of the moment because, more often than not, life is a hilariously messy disaster. If her characters haven't been dragged through the pits of hell on their way to happiness, they really haven't earned it.

She also has a dog. His name is Murphy and he's kind of a jerk.

Find her on Instagram: @embernicole.author

On Facebook: Ember Nicole's Bad Ashes

On TikTok: @embernicole.author

also by ember nicole

THE BROKEN BOUNTY SERIES

Break For Me (Book #1)

My Brother's Problem

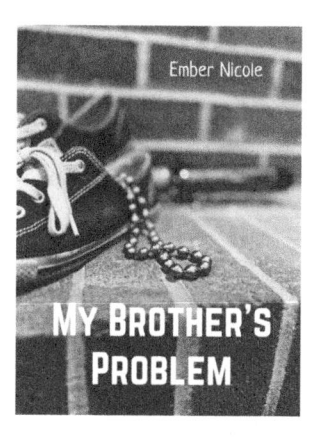

My Sister's Solution

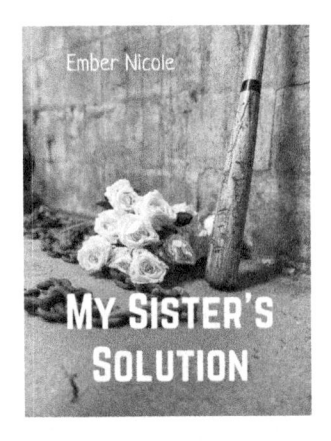

Made in the USA
Las Vegas, NV
23 April 2025